FLIGHT OF SOULS

FLIGHT OF SOULS

DAVID E. STUART

UNIVERSITY OF NEW MEXICO PRESS

ALBUQUERQUE

13   12   11   10   09   08   1   2   3   4   5   6

Library of Congress Cataloging-in-Publication Data

Stuart, David E.

Flight of souls / David E. Stuart.

   p. cm.

ISBN 978-0-8263-4262-1 (cloth : alk. paper)

1. Anthropologists—Fiction.

2. Mexico—Social conditions—20th century—Fiction.

3. United States. Central Intelligence Agency—Fiction.

I. Title.

   PS3619.T827F57 2008

   813'.6—dc22

             2007042755

Book design and type composition by Melissa Tandysh

Composed in 11.25/14.5 Minion Pro ▪ Display type is P22 Posada

Printed on 50# Nature's Natural

Frontispiece map by © Charlotte Cobb

For Ana Andzic-Tomlinson,
whom I carry in my heart,
and her parents, "Djana" and Branka,
who taught her how to love.

CONTENTS

Acknowledgments

First, I am grateful to Anne Egger for her hard work and good editorial advice, UNM Press and its team, especially Director Luther Wilson and Managing Editor Maya Allen-Gallegos, whose professionalism and skill make her a delight to work with. Thanks also to Sara Ritthaler, copyeditor Sarah Soliz, designer Melissa Tandysh, freelance mapmaker Charlotte Cobb, and Kathy Chilton for her cover photo.

I also want to thank Albuquerque's Kijrstin Bauer (now Minarsich), Danita Gomez, and Dawn Davis. They have reviewed so many of my manuscripts that projects never seem quite complete without them.

Finally, but certainly not least, I'd like to thank Mark and Jean Bernstein, owners of the Flying Star—this is the fifth book I've written entirely at their original coffeehouse on Central Avenue. The staff takes great care of me. Their names are listed below.

Dominic, Cynthia, Stacey, Erika S., Manuel, Rachael M., Lisa, Paul, Jadira, Alison, Eddy, Efraín, Nilka, Edwin, Aaron, Bill, Mazen, Ron, Kayla, Englan, Amanda, Steve-o, Janelle, Bill, Ashley, Rachel, Emily, Lisbeth, Alex, Amina, Alyssa, Adolfo, Javier, Pablo, Sal, Jonathon, Abe, Keith, Brian, Jeison, Valentina, Carlos, and managers Jesse, Rodger, Matt, Nicole, and Leo.

That's a lot of people to thank, but the Flying Star is, in my daily world, something akin to Paris's fabulous Les Deux Magots in Saint

Germain des Prés in the 1920s. True, F. Scott Fitzgerald, Alice B. Toklas, and Ernest Hemingway don't float through, but regional writers like Judith Van Gieson, Baker Morrow, and others stop or work here all the time. In fact, author/poet V. B. Price is sitting about thirty feet away as I write this. Whatever it is he's working on at this moment will likely show up in bookstores about the time that you, dear reader, are contemplating this . . . and don't forget to wave or say hello if you see me and my yellow pads at a table, writing away with my old-fashioned sailor pens, a gray fedora or tan panama on the table's edge. And, thanks for reading my tales.

David E. Stuart
Flying Star Café
Central Avenue–Route 66
Albuquerque, New Mexico
August 3, 2007

AUTHOR'S NOTE

This novel, set in Mexico, 1961–62, is a story of a world that no longer exists in the same form. Its places are used fictitiously. Its characters and events are fictional—with four exceptions.

John Paddock was real. Though used fictitiously in this story he really was an outstanding Mexican anthropologist/archaeologist. One of his real books is called *Ancient Oaxaca: Discoveries in Mexican Archaeology and History*. I recommend it. John is dead now, but he was an inspiration to me, so I've borrowed him to help me tell a story I think he might find interesting.

Second, Dr. Julia M. Baker was as real as Professor Paddock. She represents my first experience with a strong, powerful woman who did things her way. I've borrowed her, too . . . put words in her mouth that she might have spoken—but didn't—and actions that, though fictitious, were in character. Miss Rattray is real, too—an archaeologist who taught me a lot about ceramics.

Finally, there really was a Betty Anne, and fireflies did twinkle in her palms. Betty Anne, if by some remarkable chance you read this, please e-mail me at Anasaziamerica.com. I've been wondering where you are for nearly sixty years . . .

№ 1   FireFlies

A FRESH EVENING BREEZE rippled across my face and stars glittered brilliantly as I rose effortlessly from the town's oppressive late summer haze. Fireflies winked at me from below, rising to salute my passage.

Each night, when my soul took flight, I drifted through the darkness and everything around me became clear, calm, even hopeful. I was free. Whole.

I always noticed the two rust-red shingles my "dad" had used to patch our gray roof. They were my landing pad. A beacon to my personal runway. As long as I could see them, I knew I'd find my way home again.

But one night in August of my fourth year, perhaps motivated to escape the ominous veil of tension that seemed to separate me from others, I flew further than I ever had before . . .

At first it was wondrous. I discovered that Mr. Nesbitt's chimney was covered by an upturned bucket. A block away, little Linda Warren's house next to the Corner Store sported a TV antenna—the first I'd ever seen up close. From above, the chestnut trees had no trunks and cornfields were revealed as well-drilled regiments of walking sticks, which looked like they wore the peaked caps of French revolutionaries.

On a whim, I decided to leave Westchester and fly into the woods at the edge of town. I followed Matlack Street into dense groves of trees, with no streets, lights, or shingles to steer by, and a train rumbled below me, its whistle blowing. The whistle jolted me and I panicked, afraid I'd never find my way back.

I tried to steer with my arms but realized I didn't have any. I could see, feel, hear everything—but none of "me" was there. Terrified by the inexplicable, I shut out the vivid night and spun dizzily in an utter darkness—now unsoftened by fireflies and starlight.

Unable to breathe, I whirled upward, out of control, as a primal fear of death consumed me. At the moment of death I shrunk into a tiny point of light, then rocketed unexpectedly down through those two red shingles. Time itself flickered and I saw my body for an instant, lying on its tiny bed. I was surprised by how small and fragile I looked. A moment later I crashed into it with a jolt and awakened to find the sheets wet again. That meant another beating.

I didn't mind the pain so much as the sight of Him standing over me with His brass-buckled army belt. Usually I felt nothing. I'd long since learned to simply step away as the belt cut its relentless arcs through the air.

A few nights later, I was even able to fly away from the scene and visit Betty Anne who lived on the corner. She was nearly two years older and liked serving tea to the "little" kids. Betty Anne was gentle, smiled a lot, and often consoled me. She had warm blue eyes and delicate fingers. Her brow wrinkled when she spoke, her voice soft and tender.

"At least you have a father to beat you . . . I don't have anybody." Her parents had been killed in "the War." Something one didn't talk about when adults were around. Her grandmother fed her, clothed her . . . and worked her like a slave. But she smiled anyway. She wouldn't even put fireflies in a bottle—"It makes them lonely, JA. I don't want them to be sad." She was the first to call me "JA." I loved her.

My fragile twin brother, Eddy, appeared magically while Betty Anne passed us warm milk spiked with vanilla. His voice interrupted my reverie. "But, John, 'Dad' isn't beating you anymore . . . is he? He promised!" I started to answer, "It's OK, Ed . . ." "Who are you talking to, JA?" asked Betty Anne, looking concerned.

"Eddy."

"It's just the two of us, JA . . . Eddy's not here . . . are you worried about him?" I was worried.

Perhaps that's why I miscalculated and left Betty Anne's house a bit too soon. It was my fault. I should have been more careful. He was still beating me as I slipped quietly into my empty body. Stunned by the pain of the belt, I showed weakness and screamed, awakening Eddy, who slept with "Mom." The buckle cut deep into my face. Blood splattered onto the sheets. Riveted with fear, little Eddy appeared motionless at the door, crying. And that made Him even angrier.

"You little bastard!" he screamed, his face contorted in rage. "You've upset your brother!" Ever afterward I fainted at the sight of my own blood, and I never willingly slept at night again.

Still, I knew it was my own fault. I tried hard to break the cycle—sleep, fly, wet the bed, then awaken to the swish of His brass-buckled belt—but I seemed to have no control over it. The very next night I went flying again, even though, to stop the cycle, I prayed not to—three times. God, it seems, agreed with Him—"Bed wetters are disgusting." So I went flying, exhilarated by the moments of clarity. Addicted to the fleeting sense of power. Moved to joy—JOY—by those heady moments of freedom. At peace in the cool night air. Safe out in the starlight where fireflies and Betty Anne awaited me. Sometimes I didn't want to come back at all.

The only thing that pulled me back was Eddy—I had to take care of him. Then I'd crash through the shingles again—a failure, as always. I'd fallen asleep, failed to be vigilant, and God had not heard. The bed was wet. And, just as predictably, the belt was remorseless. If I was quiet, though, Eddy wouldn't wake up and become frightened.

Sometimes the flying was odd. If I drifted off to sleep when it was dark I'd suddenly fall through the bottom of my bed, arms flailing as I crashed through the floor into the damp, unlit basement below. Once there fiery, hot trains would chase me, puffing smoke and trying to burn me. They laid track as they went and took it up when they passed so that I could not guess where I'd be safe.

Eventually one of the bigger trains would catch me and run over my outstretched arms, cutting them off. Then I'd fly away into the night, leaving trains, pain, and my body all behind me. Free. Alive. Soul flying.

¤¤

They sent Betty Anne away that fall to a "school" somewhere. In spite of the consequences, I cried for her. So did Eddy. For me, crying meant a beating, but Eddy was "sick," so they made allowances for him. When my brother and I were four, we'd sing a song my "mom" made up to cheer us up when He was gone: "When I grow up to be as big as Betty Anne, then I can go to kindergarten . . ."

By the time we were actually in kindergarten there was no more singing. My "mom" had gone away. Only the veil of tension remained. My brother had asthma and often couldn't go to kindergarten with me. And there was the brass belt. It often kept me away from kindergarten, too. And Betty Anne was gone . . .

Eddy cried a lot. "John, why can't we go find our real mother and go back to our *own* family?" Finally, in desperation, I told him what I'd heard late one night when our foster mother had argued with Him.

"Dammit, Earl, don't beat up on the kids like that!"

"Why not? The big one's got an attitude—thinks he's tough. I intend to break his little ass until he learns 'Yes, sir' and 'No, sir.' How did we get such losers anyway—it's not worth the money the county pays us to keep their smelly asses."

"God! Haven't they suffered enough? A mother dead in childbirth. Their father go—"

"Shut up, bitch! Bring me another beer and shut the fuck up!"

So I told Eddy as gently as possible that we had no "real mom" to go back to. I stroked his wrists and rocked him as he cried himself to sleep. "Mom" left one afternoon a few days later, still nursing the black eye and cut lip He inflicted when she had tried to pull Him out of Eddy's bedroom, shrieking, "You're a sick animal!" I missed her.

With both Betty Anne and "Mom" gone, I had only fireflies. But even they died as the weather turned cold. That was when I first temporarily lost the ability to fly. Initially, I panicked. Betty Anne, the fireflies, and my night flights were all gone. I wet the bed, but oddly, for a week or two, the belt did not visit me at night. He'd been too drunk to notice.

My life was now empty, and I wasn't allowed blankets at night. I was cold and I actually missed the belt. So I was bad. I pooped right on His favorite chair. But He fooled me and locked me in the basement for a few days. I didn't mind the dark. Didn't mind being hungry, but I was exhausted from constantly trying to outrun the trains. Until then I'd feared the big ones the most—it had always been a big one that severed my arms. But the little ones were faster and could burn me more often.

The basement was peaceful, and I rather liked the dark after a few days. I found a corner near the old oil furnace where the concrete was comfortable, the trains couldn't lay track, and the furnace's door gave off a bright orange-blue glow through a square of thick, wavy mica.

Warm and safe in the glow of the furnace, I slept and began to fly again. Betty Anne gave me tea. I watched the weathervanes swing on rooftops. Once-dead grass and fireflies came magically to life in the cold fall nights. I was whole once more.

Some days later the basement door opened. Tucked into a crack behind the furnace, I hid from the light. That made Him angry. But "Mom" had returned and insisted on putting another pail of water on the basement steps. They fought and he stormed out. I cried again—she was good to me when He was away. She fed me, even talked to me. Then He came back . . . and she withdrew in fear.

He heard me cry out for her when she left the pan of water. Angry, He came down with the belt—savage, His face twisted in rage. That was the last time I cried.

For another few days in the basement I was warm and safe in the dark. All was still . . . even the trains. But I don't remember anything about coming out. Yet I must have. The next thing I remember was a hospital. I was in a big ward with about ten other kids. Stuck in a large, steel-piped crib. A bag of clear fluid dripping slowly into my leg.

Not long after, two men in blue uniforms came to the hospital with Eddy. One picked me up. "We're going for a ride in an elevator, little man. How's that sound?" Eddy was excited. "It will be fun, John." But it wasn't. Once out of the elevator, they took us both to an orphanage and left us. "Mom" visited us once, bringing Eddy his teddy bear . . . she said "good-bye" as she left. We never saw her again.

The next few years were jumbled. The orphanage was much harder on Eddy than it was on me. The other kids picked on him when I wasn't around. But it was OK for me—no one beat me and they fed us every day. I didn't like having other kids around us, but by the time we were six, I'd discovered that the staff would do nice things for us if we did well in school. I became Eddy's tutor as well as his protector. They even let us sleep on bunk beds in the same room.

Then one day a grim-lipped, middle-aged social worker came and explained that we'd become "socialized enough" to be sent into foster care again. Our new "family" lived in a grimy, run-down row house in South Philadelphia. There were four other kids. "Foster care" was apparently the family business.

Two of the other kids were older boys. They thought they ran the place. The biggest one, Big Jack, a classic bully, went after Eddy the first week. Jack was about twelve. I smoothed things over, trying to make it work. But Eddy was unhappy. He spent afternoons in school staring off into space—a sad, dreamy grin on his face. It was gray and rainy all that winter, and I got stuck with getting the two younger kids ready for school each morning while "Mom" and "Dad" slept off their nightly vodka.

In the spring, Big Jack beat up on Eddy again. Since Eddy didn't want to be there anyway, I taught Jack a lesson, breaking his fingers over backward so he couldn't make a fist. He was twice my size, but I got the job done. They sent us back to the orphanage. I was happy, but Eddy was not. He still wanted a "family."

When we were nearly eight, they sent us to another family. After a few months our newest mom said she was sorry. "I can't really take care of both of you." So we went back to the orphanage again. Then another social worker came . . . a new "home." This guy was just like Earl had been . . . a mean drunk who favored Eddy and kept us apart. His wife was a gaunt, nervous woman, so pale she looked as if she were already dead.

That's the house where I lost my ability to fly. One night, Eddy came to my room, bleeding from the butt. "He hurt me, John . . . why did he do that?" Eddy sobbed. Then he went silent for days. This time I was old enough to figure it out.

A week later I broke "Dad's" balls after he came to put Eddy in his own bed again. "Dad" went to the hospital. I went to reform school. Eddy followed a few weeks later after he swore he'd helped me hurt "Dad."

Reform school was a horrifying experience for poor Eddy. But less so for me, so I had lots of guilt over it. Eddy wasn't any safer. In fact, I had to watch him even more. All they'd done at the "special facility" in Queens was to gather the elite of the really dangerous teenage psychos from several East Coast cities and pack them into one gray-green monolith where predators outnumbered prey by about ten to one—an inverted food chain, as it were.

The statistics of everyday behavior were predictably dreary. Anal rape was the specialty of the Puerto Ricans. Stomping the weaker white boys and razoring off a finger, or a guy's balls, to energize their self-images, were art forms for the blacks . . . the Italian boys, especially the Sicilians, were into "honor" and the Polish . . . well, let's just say that between their over-the-top Catholicism, their inevitable guilt, and their psychotic tendencies, that they were the least predictable among all of us.

Me—I didn't belong. Though I felt little, I had a conscience of sorts. True, I couldn't count on it when in a pinch, but I had one. I wasn't going to go after a cell mate who merely looked at me the wrong way—cut 'im, cook 'im, and eat 'im like the head case known only as "Crazy Karpinsky" had done four cells away. That he'd eaten part of a Puerto Rican punk before the smell of sterno-cooked meat had drawn unwanted attention didn't improve racial relations one iota in our three-tiered cell block.

And if I didn't belong, Eddy sure as hell didn't, either. In protecting him from sodomy by our foster father of the moment, I'd inadvertently dragged him into a world where merely taking a three-minute shower in an open stall with only one guard on duty was an unacceptable risk. I accepted the responsibility and promised to protect him.

Protecting him kept me very busy for the first year till the general population learned that my conscience was a come-and-go thing where Eddy's safety was at issue. I never knew if I was "respected" as the Sicilians defined it, but I was feared. After a while only the newcomers messed with Eddy.

The hardest parts for him were the fear and isolation. His dreams of one day having a family died, leaving him depressed. He also craved respect—probably because he had been abused. So he hid in the infirmary, doing chores, in the two hours of free time after school each day. That's when I did my homework, having discovered that I could milk the system for safety, in the form of watchful teachers and an occasional candy bar for Eddy, by doing well in school.

The average IQ hovered around seventy-five to eighty according to Eddy, who made notes in infirmary files for the two overwhelmed nurses. By those standards, Eddy was a good student . . . and I was a freakin' genius. I suffered from the confinement—not on account of safety—but because I could not walk in worlds that I'd read about, not even ones I could see from our cell window. The skyline of Manhattan across the East River drove me nuts. "I'm going to live over there some-day," I'd tell Eddy as I watched the lights at night. He always nodded, "I'll pray that it happens for you, John."

The hardest moments of each day were when we'd line up in our cells waiting for them to lock the peepholed steel doors. As they'd move to each door, lock it, and move on to the next one, Eddy's panic would rise. I'd often have to wrap my arms around him and stroke his wrists to calm him down. Any fuss at door-locking time got one a night in the windowless steel cell they called the "Meat Locker." As a consequence, I came to both hate and fear the sounds of slamming doors because of what they did to Eddy.

I managed to keep us together by a combination of filing "failure to protect" complaints on Eddy's behalf—which energized the hoped-for "So *you* watch him, smart-ass" bureaucratic response—and mak-ing outstanding grades in school, mostly by reading everything in sight to escape the tedium of the long nights trapped across from magical, brightly lit Manhattan.

At age sixteen, and already a senior in the reformatory's high school, I scored a near-perfect 790 on the PSAT, the Scholastic Aptitude Test I'd been encouraged to take by my physics teacher. He explained to me, "The SAT is the gold standard for normal middle-class folks cream-ing to get their kids a shot at colleges like Princeton and NYU . . . even Columbia on the Upper West Side. This is big time stuff, John. Won't you try the exam again in six weeks or so . . . just to see how it goes?"

Eddy and I talked. He didn't want me to leave him, but neither of us really believed anything would come of it, so I crammed like a madman and took several sample exams in the physics lab. Then came the day when they took me across the bridge to Manhattan to take the exam.

I suspect I was the only one of the three or four hundred teenag-ers taking it in leg shackles, with an armed guard behind my rear-row wooden desk. I was amazed. Girls! Kids with good teeth. Colorful clothes . . . and no one shouted at them. Elated, I did my best.

A month later the scores came back. They pulled me out of class to tell me . . . I was the first kid in the history of New York's penal system to ace out the SAT—a perfect 800. In one day my status changed from "psycho" to "poster child" for a "well-run rehabilitation center for dis-advantaged youths."

While the college offers piled up, they trotted me out to conferences and interviews like a pet goat, just to validate the system. I understood precisely what was going on but went with it anyway . . . I wanted to see the Empire State Building from street level. I got one full day to do that before they arranged for a halfway house up in Connecticut so that I could attend Wesleyan. That was a lesson in the "not in my backyard" syndrome. No one in Queens wanted me anywhere near their kids over on Manhattan Island, but it was still a ticket out. I got an early furlough at sixteen and a half to go to college on a trial basis.

I loved it, living in a halfway house for the first year. I reinvented myself in college—wore jacket and ties, introduced myself as "JA," acted like Betty Anne would have wanted me to be, and pretended I'd had a normal past. A Scottish exchange student named Fiona took to calling me "Alex," once she discovered my last name was Alexander. She had a big smile, freckles, delicate fingers, and a gorgeous head of wavy, auburn hair.

I visited Eddy a lot at the reform school, taking buses over to Queens. Eddy actually did OK without me. He dreamed of being a doctor but didn't do well enough in school. So he'd become an assistant in the orphanage's infirmary and liked helping people. "It's a way to be respected, John," he'd grinned when I touted college.

Later he went into the army. He was stationed at Fort Sam Houston when I graduated from college several months before I turned twenty. Having aced a GRE Spanish-language exam, I was offered a year's study in Mexico by a foundation dedicated to "rehabilitating troubled youths." I qualified. Since the army had become Eddy's guardian, there was nothing to hold me in the States. I took the offer . . .

¤¤

№ 2 Veracruz

I LAY ON THE dark stone bench in the ancient fort of San Juan de Ullúa in Veracruz's harbor. The Mexicans still used it as a prison. It was day number ten. The tide was out, so the floor of the cell was nearly dry. The six Mexicans in the cell with me left me alone. They had taken turns beating me the first night, and as always, I had merely tiptoed away to that warm basement back in Westchester, leaving them to their work. Apparently that spoiled their fun. Finally, I even got my turn on the stone bench like the rest of them. Amateurs.

"Fuck 'em," I chuckled to myself. They'd shit themselves when I drifted back after each beating and casually asked, "Are you finished?" After the second beating, I momentarily recovered my ability to fly. I imagined one fleeting glimpse of Betty Anne's arms outstretched to encircle me . . . then clumsily fell to earth again.

Maybe all prisoners have flying dreams, I pondered. You know, the fly-out-of-these-prison-walls syndrome. But here I was, daydreaming about flying again all these years later. At first, I didn't even remember when I lost the capacity to sail out among the stars. I was too consumed by grieving for the loss of it.

The fat bastard they called "Chato" snarled at me. "*¡Oye, Hielo!* (Listen up, Ice!) It's my turn to sleep." I ignored him. He whined, "*No me chingues, por favor* (Don't fuck me over, please)."

I'd won, again. No need to press it. So I nodded, vacated the bench, and took his place along the thick stone wall opposite the tide vents. He lay down and farted loudly. The beans . . . or satisfaction . . . hard to tell which.

The water wasn't so bad when the tide rose, but the hungry crabs that came with it were a bitch. So were the eels. At least the scavengers ate our shit and cleaned up after us.

I was twenty and I'd already lived in Mexico for nearly eight months. My Spanish was finally getting up to speed and the study abroad scholarship had allowed me to escape the Commonwealth of Pennsylvania, which had remanded me to the special reform school for psychos in New York, but still held legal custody of me till I was twenty-one . . . the consequences of my paying a foster father back at age eight for sodomizing Eddy.

The new prison situation was a major irritant, but Mexico itself was great. It was bright and colorful. The food was good. Women smiled back when you checked them out, and I was free, unlike in the States. Freedom defined Mexico.

True, as I'd just discovered, one had no legal rights in Mexico. But as long as you weren't in jail you were free. Truth be told, my own fear wasn't that I'd rot in the fort for twenty years. It was that I'd be declared persona non grata by the Mexican government and shipped back to the States—where I had never been free.

In foster care, in orphanages, on the street, in reform school—a truant. None of that mattered. The States were a jail sentence. Hard time. Eddy and I had been warehoused and isolated since we were six months old . . . the equivalent of a permanent sentence in solitary. The problem with the States was that a citizen—that is, a social security number with a name and body attached to it—had rights. But your essence didn't get squat by way of consideration from society. If your soul was enslaved, or just gone missing, tough. If you were living in a daily hell, get a lawyer.

But in Mexico, a soul had rights. Freedom, love, passion, music, friends. There were Betty Annes and *copitli* (Nahuatl, "fireflies") all over the damn place. I'd learned long ago that your body didn't mean much . . . just tiptoe away if it got too unpleasant. But I yearned to feel things again, as I once had when I was with Betty Anne. No matter how often

I extolled the virtues of Mexico as a place, María Inés, my girlfriend of the moment, insisted that it was my *soul* I was searching for.

At first I thought she was nuts and, me still a virgin, I humored her, hoping to get laid. But this business in Fort San Juan de Ullúa made me wonder—maybe the flying *was* a soul thing. One night back when I was eight years old, my essence, I believed, compressed itself into an iridescent point of light, blew through a slate roof in Philadelphia, and just plain disappeared. I awoke afterward, my body still in one piece, but my soul was no longer in it. My essence must have either died or gone away . . . and I knew it, because I could no longer feel ordinary emotions.

I assumed the inability to fly, or to feel, was penance for having used a ball-peen hammer on "Dad's" balls while he was passed out on Eddy's bed.

For eleven years I'd tried to feel something, anything, find my essence and come back to life. I had even felt a momentary thrill in Mexico City when María Inés first kissed me. A point of light hung suspended over my head for one instant. Interrupting our embrace, I had reached up to grab it.

She had been wide eyed. "*¿Qué pasa, Juan?*" "*¡Mi alma . . . la ví!* (My soul . . . I saw it!)" I'd blurted out. I was embarrassed, but she didn't laugh at me. Hell, she didn't even react as if I were nuts. "I'll light candles for you, *corazón*," she'd said. For a moment, Betty Anne's spirit flickered in Inés's eyes as she smiled, caressing my cheek. She had made me feel, and she and Mexico were as one being. Now, in the Veracruz prison, it was all at risk.

※※

I'd gone to Veracruz for a vacation with three American guys I'd run into on campus at the University of the Americas, out on the Toluca highway, a few miles west of Mexico City. At the last minute, Peter Mennen (yes— *that* Mennen), a rich American guy several years older than most of us and a friend of mine, backed out. So, we'd had to economize.

The trip had started off in an ordinary enough way—rented Volkswagen bug. Cheap shared hotel room on the industrial waterfront. Beach, beer, and sun.

Beer came first. On the street I ordered the essentials for the group. "Where'd you learn so much Spanish?" asked the streetwise, shaggy-headed guy known to us only as "Roadmap." "Puerto Rican guys in New York," I answered, with no further details, of course. I had no past in Mexico. It was, to my surprise, a new start. No one, Mexican or expat, cared who you had been—only who you were at that moment.

We were under the arcade of the big Colonial Bar, downing beers and peeling the free shrimp that came on the side, when out of nowhere popped a stunning natural blonde who hit on Paul—the tall, gangly guy who always had money and claimed his dad was the U.S. ambassador to Ireland. Not likely, in my opinion. He rarely changed his clothes, shaved, or even combed his hair. He was about twenty. She, thirty.

The next thing we knew he was screwing her brains out on the beach each afternoon. She was German and her name was Ana. She spoke good English and was pretty direct. On the second afternoon, California Jerry, at twenty-eight, the oldest in our group, touched up his jet-black pompadour and asked Ana, "Why Paul, baby? I'm available, too."

Ana laughed, "I'm into tall guys with big penises . . . get the picture?" Jerry shrugged, took another pull on his Corona, and grinned right back at her, "'Long' as in long . . . or 'long' as in staying power?" Ana laughed. "Why don't I bring my girlfriend with me tomorrow afternoon . . . you can share her while I watch."

Blond, strung-out Brian Lee, the often-stoned fourth member of our group, damn near had a seizure. None of us minded the next afternoon when Ana introduced us to Kristal, another German who was stunning in her black bikini. She did the rest of the group for a lark . . . all except me. Ana and I watched . . . separately. Kristal eyed me expectantly, but after all those years in institutions, I wasn't into sharing. Besides, I was saving myself for María Inés. A group of local mackerel fisherman gathered and cheered the *ménage á quatre*. The women even paid for food and beers. "What's not to like?" grinned Paul after Ana and Kristal had gone home for the evening.

The answer to that question came just one day later. We had hit the beach down at Boca del Río right after lunch. The German girls' tentlike cabana was set up as usual. But when we got there we found an unexpected scene. Ana was nowhere in sight; her girlfriend, Kristal, was lying motionless in the cabana sporting her little black bikini but looking far paler than she had just one day earlier. The small caliber bullet hole above her left eyebrow didn't reassure us, either.

A thick black trickle of blood had dripped from Kristal's eyelid, pooling around her lifeless eyeball before running on down her cheek. It ended in an odd, flamboyant smear, as if she'd tried to wipe it away. "Jesus," whispered Jerry. "She must not have died right away. Creepy." Instinctively, I butted in, "How could she have wiped it if she were dead enough not to have blinked when it first dripped onto her eye?"

"Good point, JA—there's no blood on her hand . . . Jesus . . . what does this mean?"

The group's veteran, Roadmap, summed it up with uncanny clarity: "Offhand, I'd say we're about to get screwed again—but not quite as happily as yesterday." Roadmap was obviously a psychic. By the time we'd scrambled back to the Volkswagen, an entire truck-full of Garand-toting Federales were waiting for us. They liked to use their rifle butts.

Grungy Paul really did have a diplomatic passport . . . and walked. The bastard! Meanwhile, the rest of us got a leisurely tour of the fort's lower levels. The Federales first stripped us of everything except pants, undershirts, and socks, then separated us so we couldn't "conspire" . . . as if four gringos with perennial erections might fuck the Mexican government into an even deeper state of chaos.

Roadmap and Jerry had money, so they got above-ground cells. My twenty-six pesos, or perhaps my attitude, had destined me to economy-class basement accommodations.

Nothing made sense until Chato's questions on day two. "The guards say the bunch of you were banging the East German attaché's wife, Ana." That got my attention, but I played it cool. "Nope, only the tall one with the diplomatic passport was doing her . . . and since when is that a federal crime in Mexico?"

Fat, farting Chato went into fits of mirth. I didn't laugh with him. That must have been considered rude since his smelly enforcer—a heavily muscled, stone-cold freak named "Angel"—grabbed me from behind and damn near broke my arm trying to teach me manners.

Fortunately Chato had a better hold on reality than his five loyal catamites. "Let Ice go, Angel. He doesn't know the rest." "So what is the rest?" I asked, easing my arm back into a more natural position. He snickered again.

"Her husband was found murdered in his penthouse apartment at the Hotel Emporio." Chato snickered and expressively put his finger to his forehead . . . "One bullet between the eyes." "That's the way we found his wife's girlfriend on the beach," I told him. He frowned, "The guards told us it was a love triangle—the bunch of you screwing his wife, then killing them both when things went bad."

"Chato—the woman dead on the beach was not named 'Ana.' She was the younger blonde's friend." "Well, Hielo, life is mysterious, is it not?" he tittered . . . "You could be here a *long* time. Freedom is sweet, no?"

"My freedom is not the issue—I was never free in the States. But there is a woman in El Distrito I'd like to see again." "Ah, love," leered Chato.

"No, actually—it is a matter of spirit."

He stared at me intently, then turned to Angel, who was getting ready to take his four-hour turn on the stone bench. "It's the gringo's turn, Angel!" In Mexico even cons understood the difference between one's body and one's spirit, so we made an unlikely peace.

We ate from small dirt-crusted bowls of rice and beans once a day, standing up, of course. The bowl held perhaps five ounces of food. Anything else one had to pay for. Since they'd already taken everything I had, I settled for the rice and beans, asking the other prisoners for nothing.

The rhythm of the days was driven by the tides. At high tide the oil-streaked seawater was mid-thigh in depth. The meal came each evening when it was already hard to see. The only light came from an overhead grate—the "door" to our dungeon cell—and, at low tide, two squarish cross-barred stone ports—about fourteen inches on a side—that had been built into the fort in the 1500s when the conquistador Cortés was still alive. As best I could tell, there had been no improvements to the infrastructure since that time.

On the evening of the tenth day Angel and another prisoner cracked and started shrieking uncontrollably. I shut it out and had tea with Betty Anne. But the others became agitated and started yelling at the two. After a few hours, even the guards above us had had enough. They lowered a rope and hauled them away. His enforcer gone, Chato paced, hip deep in water, and wrung his hands continually.

On day fourteen the short dark-skinned one they called "Negro" gave his food to the others, broke his stoneware bowl, and cut his wrists with the jagged fragments. It took him a long time to saw his way to the veins. Everyone ignored his groans except me.

"Negro—are you certain? I will share my food with you tomorrow, if you are alive."

He stuttered, "Kind of you, H . . . H . . . Hielo. N . . . N . . . No need. I have no family and no money for a lawyer. I will start screaming soon. When that happens they drop the rope and take you to the tobacco farms in the Valle Nacional—you work till you die in the fields. I want to die here in Veracruz where I was born."

"Whisper your Christian name to me, Negro, and I will light candles for your soul."

" T . . . T . . . T . . . Truly?"

"I swear it." He leaned and whispered to me, even as his blood, staining the water an odd rust color, drew in a fresh horde of crabs. I snatched two of them from the water to eat raw once it was dark.

On day sixteen only two of us were left. Me . . . and a pudgy guy who had never spoken. It was near dusk, and we'd just gotten our bowls when the overhead grate popped open again and a rope came down. "The gringo," growled someone from above. I wrapped the rope around my waist and back up between my legs. The silent one finally spoke as I was pulled up, "Don't forget Negro's candles, Hielo . . . his soul."

"*Yo sé* (I know) . . ."

※

№ 3 So American

I EXPECTED AN INTERROGATION, or a hearing of some sort. Instead I was hustled, squinting, into the harsh sunlight at the front gate, where I inherited two MPs from the U.S. Embassy in Mexico City. They were in street clothes. My former jailers watched, laughing, from the fort's huge iron gate. Forty seconds after our introduction I had a split lip, a bloody nose, and sported a pair of handcuffs. Otherwise, the MPs were cordial.

The big one with the flattop and "Semper Fidelis" tattooed on the back of his right hand explained, "Give us any shit, you Commie faggot, and we'll gut you and dump you on the highway for the dogs to eat." "Nice to meet you, too," I retorted. His oversized, faceted class ring cut a neat half circle under my left eye. I decided to let it go . . . and mentally slipped away.

I think they beat me again before we got to the embassy, but I'm not sure—I had retreated to dreamland again . . . I was four and had walked to the corner to drink tea with Betty Anne and my twin, Eddy. The grass was full of blinking fireflies and the summer night was brilliant. We had Tasty Cakes for dessert. Betty Anne smiled . . . "I love you," I told her. She kissed my cheek . . .

The next thing I remember was the lights. Shadowy figures moved behind them and a smoker, middle aged judging from the hoarse rasp in his voice, was asking questions.

"Don't piss me off, son. I asked you if the Federales roughed you up like that."

"No, sir. It was two American MPs in civvies. One had a flattop and "Semper Fidelis" tattooed on the back of his right ha—" I was interrupted. "Shut up, you little faggot. They don't want to hear your faggot Commie bullshit!" I went away again. Betty Anne smiled . . . "More tea?" Eddy laughed and clapped his hands in anticipation. I nodded.

". . . Was that a yes?"

"Yes to what?"

"Jesus, Bill," someone muttered. "He's not even coherent. Who beat him up like that?"

"The fucking Federales, I think." I managed a "No . . . your MPs!" It got quiet and the lights went dark.

Sometime later I awoke on a cot—an IV in my arm, wounds dressed. "Is anyone here?" I mumbled. No answer. I checked out my situation. Swathed in bandages and strapped to a gurney with the leather Hassett restraints they used on head cases, I wasn't going anywhere soon. I drifted off again.

Just when I was dozing and dreaming of Betty Anne's smile, the lights came on. "Rise and shine, asshole," cackled a shadowy figure. "The MPs are gone. Why not just answer our questions this time?"

"No one asked me questions before, mister."

"Huh? They spent nearly a day working you over and all you'd say was, 'Ask Betty Anne'!"

"Are you sure? I don't remember." "We're sure, son," came the smooth "Jesus, Bill" voice again . . . "So who is Betty Anne?"

"A neighbor. Knew her when I was four. She was six . . . I liked her."

"Goddammit! . . . no more bullshit, son."

That's when a new voice popped in from behind the lights. "It's not bullshit, guys; the chart is as steady as a rock." "You got me on a polygraph?" I mumbled through puffed lips.

"*We* ask the questions, son . . . got that?" I nodded.

"So Betty Anne's nothing to do with this?" I shook my head no. "OK . . . tell us about Gerhardt."

"Who's Gerhardt?"

"Son . . . you are a pain in the ass."

What's new? I chuckled to myself.

"Mac . . . what's the chart on that?"

"Steady, General." GENERAL? "Who the fuck are you guys?" I asked. No response. They were busy rattling chart paper.

"OK, son. The German broad. Tell us about her."

"Which one?"

"What do you mean, 'which one'?"

"There were two. Light blonde named Ana, so she said. And her girlfriend, Kristal."

"Did we know there were two women involved, Mac?" whispered the general, a bit too loud. "Uh, uh," came the reply. The general turned to me again. "Ana, the dead one on the beach."

"It was the other one, Kristal, who was dead in the cabana. Bullet hole over her left brow. Small caliber. She had darker blond hair and was older than Ana."

"Bill—check it out!"

"Right, sir!"

"What did either woman tell you, son?"

"Basically, nothing . . . just sexy chatter. They wanted to get laid. Paul, the tall one with the diplomatic passport, accommodated her. We watched some. She got off on it . . ." Paper rustled again. Someone had coughed at the mention of Paul's passport.

"So you never met the husband?" I shook my head again. "Never knew she had one," I whispered, trying to moisten my swollen lips.

"Never heard the name Gerhardt?" "No," I mumbled. "Are we done?" sighed a bored and frustrated general.

"Yes, General. Dry as a bone."

"We're outta here, then." "Can I go now?" I asked.

"No," someone answered, "they will get you ready for the next 'interview.'" I wandered back to Betty Anne's. Dozens of fireflies descended into her cupped palms and rested, safe in her gentle embrace. They winked at her before drifting away into the night. Her face glowed with pale green light, as if she were one of them. I reached out to touch her face, but someone shouted . . .

"Move that hand from the wall again and I'll break every freaking bone in it!"

"You've got to keep a close eye on that skinny Commie faggot, Barry. He's a sneaky piece of shit." Lucky me; Semper Fi was back.

To my surprise, Roadmap was next to me. "Hey, man . . . I thought we'd lost you altogether. You got a concussion or something?" I nodded. "Pricks," he whispered. Semper Fi shut him up.

They had reassembled me, California Jerry, and Roadmap and lined us up against the wall, fingers out, supporting our leaning bodies hours on end, the lights behind us. I laughed, "Hey, it's a reunion!" Someone hit me from behind. We'd already been leaning there for hours before I finally stopped playing with Betty Anne and came back to the present.

They shoved photos at us. I was in several taken in front of the Russian Embassy in Mexico City. So was Roadmap. They asked who our "contacts" were. But not one of us had realized that a building about three hundred thousand people walked past each day was the Russian Embassy.

I offered a suggestion: "The least the Russians could have done is hang a huge red hammer and sickle out there so us lost Americans have a clue." They weren't amused. I heard "faggot" snarled a few times before I passed out again. These pricks were even more tedious than old Earl had once been.

Four days later they took our passports, cut off the numbers, handed them back to us, and threw us unceremoniously into the street. Three weeks of my life—snatched by America's official pickpockets—had been lost. It was as if America just couldn't let its own disappear in peace. Bastards.

As Roadmap and I pieced it together in the aftermath, we'd first passed through the hands of the Federales, who made the original arrest and delivered the original beatings, then into the hands of the Veracruz State Police, who managed the fort. Then the American MPs who delivered more beatings. The U.S. Defense Intelligence Agency and General No-Name followed, then the CIA, who beat me and Roadmap again.

Finally, the embassy's "cultural attachés" cut up our passports and, aided by Semper Fi, threw us out a side door and into the street with a warm "You're free—now get the fuck out of here! If we see you again or hear of any complaints filed . . . any bullshit like that . . . then you are all dead faggots."

California Jerry decided to go back to California. I returned to my sleeping room on Campos Eliseos but was intercepted by the house's owner, Dr. Julia McVickar Baker, who immediately put me in her private clinic for a couple of days. She also phoned the embassy. "Keep your people away from my 'boys.' If your MPs come over here there will be serious consequences."

Dr. Baker was a legend. Already in her sixties or seventies—none of us knew—she'd been Pancho Villa's physician when his División del Norte had taken Mexico City in the winter of 1917. A huge blow-up photo of her in the carriage with him graced one wall of her glass-roofed patio dining room: there she sat, a tall, gorgeous twenty-something revolutionary, black leather medical bag on her lap . . . an interesting counterpoint to the twin ammo bandoliers that crossed underneath her still-firm breasts. Julia Baker was possibly the most powerful female English speaker in Mexico.

After absorbing some decent food, I exited Dr. Baker's clinic and went to see María Inés. I didn't get far. As I changed clothes at the house on Campos Eliseos, I was again intercepted, this time by a well-suited gent from the Russian Embassy.

He spoke good English, was polite, and gave me a card with a phone number on it. "Call if you need asylum or travel money, Mr. Alexander. We regret your recent, ah . . . difficulties." He fingered the brim of his hat, studied my war wounds for a moment, then nodded and disappeared down the outside staircase.

Well, JA, I told myself, *Why not? Officialdom in the United States has been a massive problem for Eddy and me since childhood—and no sign of a letup yet.*

Gina Lollabrigida waved at him from the roof terrace of her house next door, where she often sunned, seminude. I tucked his card away in my wallet, just in case.

Later, I saw the same Russian at a concert given at the Academy San Marcos, but he showed no sign of recognition, so I responded in kind. Pete Seeger was playing there . . . a stronghold of alleged Commies in Mexico City. Throughout the concert I had the odd sensation that I could hear the subtle clicks of tiny Minox cameras coming from all directions. Perhaps it was more than mere imagination. But María Inés loved the music. "So different, corazón." I imagined her cupping her hands for the monarch butterflies that sometimes fluttered in the city's gardens.

"I need advice . . . I promised to light candles for a guy who died in the fort at Veracruz." Her eyes widened and her delicate hands trembled. "Where is the best place to do that, Inés?" She trembled again.

Inés was petite, dark skinned, and had huge black eyes that matched the lustrous cascade of hair that flowed down to her waist. Her full lips quivered.

"Ay . . . the things you must have seen! And here I thought you had lost interest in me." She paused, smiled wistfully, then asked the necessary questions. "Was he Catholic?" I nodded. "Light skinned, or dark?"

"Dark, like you—I knew him only as 'Negro.'"

"Then you must go to the Basilica de Guadalupe . . . on the edge of the city. She protects the *morenos* (dark ones), just as she protects me."

The next day the two of us took the bus marked "Basilica." The square encircling the church was huge and crowded. Dozens of buses pulled alongside the outer plaza, disgorging hordes of poncho-wearing, dark-skinned Indians and poor mestizos. Mothers nursed their babies swaddled in the colorful *rebozos* (shawls) that marked tribal and district identities.

Food and religious charms were hawked by venders staffing dozens of pushcarts and stalls, and a line of crawling supplicants snaked their painful way on bended knees toward the basilica against a hill at the rear of the plaza. "Do we do that?" I asked Inés.

"It depends, corazón . . . was Negro a good man?" Such a question about a prisoner would never have been asked in the States, so it took me a moment to answer. "I doubt it."

She nodded, looking sad, her eyes veiled in that special, sorrowful, Madonna-like way. "Then you must go on your knees if you are to save his soul."

"But I'm not a practicing Catholic. What do I do? What do I say?"

"I will whisper all in your ear."

It was a long, slow crawl. It hurt and I felt stupid, so I started to stand up after about twenty yards, but Inés gently pushed me down and whispered in my ear, "It's for a man's *soul*, corazón." My knees were a mess by the time it was my turn to beseech the Virgin to spare Negro's soul. Inés whispered my lines and I repeated after her, rendering several flamboyant lies on Negro's behalf. If there really was a Virgin listening, I was going to fry, I feared. But Inés seemed cheerful.

As we exited the church, the sky opened up and rain drowned the bright scene. "It is a sign," sighed Inés. "Your prayer has been heard. The Virgin will embrace Negro's soul." Christ, I loved this country . . . Federales and all.

"Where to now, corazón?"

"To the phone booth downtown, *princesa*. I bought time to talk to my twin brother. He's working at a hospital in Texas."

"Eduardo?"

"I still call him 'Eddy.' The big brother thing, *¿sabes?*"

"How can a twin be the *hermano mayor* (older brother), corazón?"

"That's the way I view it, I suppose."

"Here's our bus, corazón. I'll get off near the Hipódromo. My father becomes upset when I'm away too long. He does not care for you . . ."

"Why? We aren't sleeping together."

"Gringos. He doesn't like gringos . . . says they have no feelings, no souls." It didn't occur to her what she'd just said, so I swallowed hard and tried to squeeze it out of my mind, but couldn't. "Did you light the candles for me, Inés?"

She smiled her Betty Anne smile. "But of course! Your soul is with you—you simply can't feel it just now . . . they beat you so! I didn't know your government was as corrupt and vicious as ours." María Inés never made stupid calls. In fact, as best as I could tell, there were no stupid people in Mexico. A fair number of uneducated ones, but not stupid. Everyone I'd met was either a philosopher, a mystic, or both . . . some of the cops were exceptions.

As the bus turned toward the wide avenue called Mariano Escobedo, Inés kissed me and rhythmically stroked the soft skin of my inner forearm, just as I'd once done for Eddy when he cried. Psychic, I tell you.

"When will I see you again, corazón?"

"Not sure, princesa. I'm behind in my class work at Las Americas. And I have a field assignment overdue."

"Does that mean you will go away again?"

"I'm not sure yet. This business in Veracruz messed up the first weeks of this term." Inés smiled back at me . . . looking like a dark, Indian Madonna. "Do not forget to take your soul with you this time, corazón," smiled Inés, again brushing my face with her fingertips. The bus jerked to a stop just as I was about to tell her I loved her. But I was thinking of Betty Anne, so it was just as well that I didn't.

Back at the University of the Americas I tried to set things right with my professors. I had a week of mad catch-up, compensating for nearly a month AWOL. My scholarship fields were Spanish and anthropology, and I'd also become fascinated by both archaeology and folklore. Mestizo and Indian Mexico were rich with feeling. That appealed to me. I took some classes at the Americas and others at the huge, colorful National University where Juan O'Gorman's amazing muraled library graced the campus as well as T-shirts, postcards, and coffee mugs.

I loved the color, chaos, and up-your-nose attitude at the National. They were on strike every other week. Not Semper Fi's kind of scene—the place was loaded with leftist *"mariposas"* (butterflies)—in Semper Fi's parlance, "Commie faggots." Busloads of them. But the profs were elegant—vests, ties, their black European book bags flapping over their shoulders—and the women, especially the dark ones with big eyes, were gorgeous.

Mexico—a country that I imagined to be full of dark-eyed Madonnas who made eyes, made love, made babies, made tortillas, lit candles for their men, and cupped their hands to catch passing butterflies. Afternoon breezes and starlight followed them everywhere. And why not? Everyone I'd met felt passionately about everything, had a soul, and knew precisely where it was at any given moment.

After negotiating the terms of academic penance, I took a series of *pesero* cabs back to Campos Eliseos. The aging pesero taxis crowded the main thoroughfare, competing with the city's buses. The drivers would stick a hand out of their window and hold up the number of fingers for places available. Fixed fee—one peso (eight U.S. cents). There were only two rules—you have to socialize, and "Don't slam the taxi doors on the way out." Twenty-four cents and thirty-five minutes later I climbed the outside stairs at Campos Eliseos 81.

Roadmap and Peter Mennen were waiting for me. Roadmap was excited. "Got the rest of the story, man . . . it's over the top!"

"OK—so tell me . . . and where are the others?"

Mennen butted in. "Paul is in Ireland with Daddy! Brian Lee Highfield disappeared—probably back to the States. Jerry M. went back to California. He's got a wife and kids there."

"No shit? And where the hell were you, Peter? This wasn't fun . . ."

Roadmap interrupted me, "Why don't you butt out, Peter. Let me tell him!" Pissed off, Mennen, accustomed to being the center of attention, stomped off in a huff. Roadmap shrugged and waited till Mennen slammed the front gate behind him . . .

"Now the story, man . . . that chick, Ana, is in Cuba. Left Veracruz on a Russian freighter bound for Matanzas while we were still in the fort. She's a 'friend' of Castro's, they say . . ." I interrupted, "Who the hell is 'they,' Roadmap?"

"CIA. They fucked up and shot her girlfriend after they did her old man."

"But it was the CIA who interviewed us, Roadmap!"

He shrugged. "Among others . . . it's run-of-the-mill spook stuff, JA. Ana got away. She actually saw the Federales take us. Best she could do was let the Russians know we were taking the fall. I had a visit from a well-dressed Russki who gave me a phone number . . . do you need it, JA?"

"No. He came to visit me, too. Offered 'help.'"

"Yeah . . . and I'm going to Cuba—courtesy of the Russian government."

"No shit? By way of Veracruz again?"

"No. I'm off to Progresso, Yucatán. I got train tickets. But no more Veracruz. I don't need those people . . . they bug."

"When are you going?"

"Tonight. Wanna go with me?"

"Can't, Roadmap. Gonna finish this master's degree and see how it goes with Inés. I like Mexico . . ."

OK—but be careful till I get back this spring, JA. This country is jumping with spooks. Craziest bastards I've ever met . . . and they've bought lots of Federales with their white-envelope dollars. Don't get your ass kicked again . . . and stay out of San Marcos. Semper Fi hangs out in the alley across the street on concert nights . . . and he hates your guts."

"Yeah. All I heard for four days was 'Commie faggot.'"

"I know. I never met a guy more hysterically in the closet—he's yearning for 'man milk' and can't deal with it." Roadmap appraised me for a moment. "Don't forget the stuff I've taught you, JA. You can't just be tough when they beat you. You got to be like a fox and elude the mothers. OK?" I nodded. Roadmap turned and vanished down the stairs.

Later I walked down to an awninged restaurant across the street from the tennis club where Campos Eliseos dead-ended. The Embers specialized in hamburgers, uncommon in Mexico, and diplomats, not as uncommon.

I ordered a Coke and a charburger with avocado and white goat cheese, then lit a cigarette while I waited for my order. A few puffs later a smooth, deep voice floated out of the crowd. English. Easy to sort. I walked over toward the source and took in the scene . . .

It was General No-Name from the embassy nightmare, regaling several diplomatic types, including two really good-looking women. General No-Name was about fifty with graying hair, a pinstriped business suit, Nunn Bush wingtips, and a country club tan. Tennis court body. Pale blue eyes. Empty. No soul . . . and none in sight. Probably didn't even miss it—he was the kind of guy who'd quietly left it on the chair next to him when he cashed his first paycheck . . . or ordered his first beating. Hard to tell which.

I must have lingered too long while I checked him out. He looked up, irritated. "What are you staring at? Do I know you?"

"Yes, General, I'm one of the American college guys your boys beat the shit out of in the embassy basement the other day. Perhaps you don't recognize me without blood smearing my face." He went pale. So did the younger of the two women. No-Name stared.

I went on. "I want my passport replaced . . . it's no good without the numbers. You know where to find me when it's ready." Well, it was ballsy, but I was still pissed off. It gave him time to regain composure. Cackling, his voice dripped with sarcasm.

"Is that all, *boy*?" I smiled back, stretching a couple of stitches in my cheek. "Actually, an apology for the beatings would be nice, but, lacking that, how about keeping that freak off the street." "And just who would that freak be, *boy*?" he leered.

"The one with 'Semper Fidelis' tattooed on his hand—he's a bad ad for the United States . . . and probably as queer as a three-dollar bill."

"You'd better watch yourself, son. You're out of line. You won't like it if I decide to take you seriously . . ."

"In that case I won't tell you where Ana Gerhardt is right now. See you around, General."

At the mention of Ana Gerhardt's name, the restaurant went dead quiet. Guess Roadmap was right. Mexico City was spook central.

I ate my burger in peace. But three different guys casually followed me out. So I grabbed a pesero. Automatic shake-off. Roadmap had taught me that one, too. Freedom and no tail . . .

Back at Campos Eliseos I worked on assignments through the night. I had a big sleeping room off of Julia Baker's private theater. Glassed patio, red tile floor, a view of Chapultepec Park . . . and an elaborate dressing table. On weekends my quarters were a dressing room for the actors who came to put on plays. I was usually out of town, so it didn't matter.

The next afternoon I worked on the narrow upstairs balcony while the maid, Chavela, cleaned the dressing room. Gina Lollabrigida saw me from her roof patio and stood up, dressed only in her bikini bottoms. "Honey, you'd better be careful. They are watching you."

"And who are 'they?'"

"The Americans. Soldiers in street clothes. One in the park and one in the alley behind the house."

"Did you see them?"

"I saw one behind us when my driver brought me home from lunch. But a friend at an embassy keeps me informed."

"The gentleman who visited me?"

"Yes. He's a diplomat. Not a Russian KGB agent. Very cultured. They aren't all like you Americans imagine them."

"I don't 'imagine' like most Americans. I don't even fit in there. I like it here. I don't care what they do as long as I can stay here."

"I see. Well, you have such a nice face. It can only tolerate so many, uh, 'misunderstandings.' ¿Comprendes?"

"¡Sí, comprendo, gracias! (I understand, thank you!)" No telling how many languages she spoke, but from the gallery at Dr. Baker's I'd heard her speak Spanish, French, and English in addition to her native Italian. Bet Russian was on her list, too. She must have noticed me gaping at her boobs, as she smiled coyly and casually lay down again.

Late that evening I took a stack of handwritten drafts to a gorgeous, starving Argentine art student named Marianna Capo di Monte, who lived four long blocks away. She made a little money typing on the side.

"I'm hungry, Alex. Can you give me an 'advance,' or better yet take me to the Punto Blanco for a sandwich and coffee?"

"You've never asked me to take you out before. What's up, Mari?"

"You look sooo cute with those stitches! And you look older." "You've got to be kidding," I laughed.

"Not kidding. There's talk in the street . . . they didn't break you at the embassy!"

"Who said?"

"The waiters are all talking about the Embers today. You dumped on an embassy big shot, they say."

Marianna was a tall, elegant, light-skinned knockout with hazel eyes, long, slender fingers, and a sultry smile. A tease. She was, so she said, twenty-five. An exotic older woman who had once modeled in Milan and consumed men like Kleenex. I wanted to be consumed, too, but never got anything from her except clean copy. Still I teased: "How about I feed you, fuck you, and pay you—in any order you prefer?" She grinned and pushed out her boobs. "Feed me first, Alex. Then pay me . . ."

We walked down the Reforma to the Punto Blanco—an upscale coffee shop in the Zona Rosa where I'd had my very first cappuccino. Brightly lit and art deco in style, the big front windows gave a corner view of the Reforma. Mexico's literati floated in and out nightly—Carlos Fuentes, INAH's Ignacio Bernal, a young woman named Elena Poniatowska; even Octavio Paz dropped in between diplomatic assignments.

The coffee was very expensive—twelve pesos (almost one U.S. dollar). But you could stay all night and float in a sea of lively, multilingual chatter. Watch Fuentes scribble away in his notebooks. Garibay sometimes translated Aztec poetry there in the afternoons. Paz worked his notebooks now and again.

History, books, poetry, and plays were all born there . . . and there was no veil of tension. People coached my emerging Spanish. They talked to me about history, folktales, and mythology. It was worth a buck any night that I had the money.

I held the door for Marianna and half the men in the place turned to stare. As dressed, we were both about 5'10". She weighed about 125 and wore a mid-thigh skirt, strapped "come fuck me" heels, and a brightly colored shawl that she never let hide her perky boobs. The other half of the male audience was too suave to stare, so merely stopped breathing till she passed.

I ordered us two sandwiches. Ham and white cheese. They came neatly quartered and speared by olives on long toothpicks with Mexican potato salad—the fresh green peas and diced carrots in it were a nice counterpoint to the usual Stateside version. Two minutes later a tall, dignified-looking Latino guy came to the table. "Well, Marianna, I didn't know you knew the town's most interesting foreign student! Introduce me, darling."

They did the European cheek-brush bit. I stood; Marianna was coy. "He's mine, Pablo."

"Please, Marianna, talk . . . I am contemplating a 'social note' in tomorrow's paper . . ."

"Well, just this once . . . Juan Alejandro, permit me to introduce you to Señor Pablo Mato Virreyes—social editor of the *Excélsior*." I extended my hand.

He smiled. "Quite the political activist, I hear."

"Actually not, sir. I'm just a student here . . . glorying in Mexico."

"How refreshing . . . not trying to change us, then?"

"No, sir. Trying to absorb it . . . just as it is."

He turned to Marianna. "I'd heard he was unique. But one never knows . . ." He turned back to me. "Forgive the aside. I love flirting with Marianna, *joven*."

"You have excellent taste, Señor Virreyes. I do the same, but . . . well." He sighed . . . "Oh, I know." Then laughed, "At odds with your government, I hear."

"I find them irritating—and an embarrassment." He laughed again, just as a flashbulb popped. Then he was off. Moments later, two glasses of wine appeared magically to accompany our sandwiches. I raised one eyebrow at Marianna. The waiter bowed and explained. "Compliments of *El Excélsior*."

Virreyes waved breezily from another table. Marianna was elated. "Thank you, darling, you played it perfectly." "Huh?" I gaped. She arched her back provocatively and laughed, mouth open and inviting, then picked up her sandwich. I watched her eat.

After dinner I suggested dessert. She smiled coyly. "Now, pay me! One hundred pesos." I pulled out my last big note and handed it to her, leaned back, and started to light a smoke. But before I could light it she leaned over and blew out the old-fashioned "Guerrero" match. "Ready?"

"Ready for what?"

"You said I could pick the order . . . now it's time to fuck me." She said it just loud enough that a group of men at the next table suffered a brief Mexican version of "The Vapors."

"Jeez, Marianna. Not so loud." Lips parted, she threw her head back and laughed again.

"Let's go—I want to lick your stitches."

Thirty minutes later while she licked, I asked, "So how did you know I was thinking about the stitches?"

"Didn't. I like kink . . . and you have a pretty face."

"How do you define 'kink'?" She demonstrated. I made odd, involuntary noises. In turn, she made several equally odd requests . . .

She tasted like a sun-warmed flower full of rich, musty nectar. I sighed at the sensation. She moaned . . . and a profound wave of pent-up emotions welled up from somewhere inside me. It was instantly addictive . . . the night sky was brilliant. Fireflies swirled around us. When she began to caress me, I panicked. Frightened at both the closeness and the loss of control, I shuddered and soared away.

I fell to earth again, called back by a new voice. It took me a moment to get out of the fantasy. "So, what do you think, Alex . . . better than regular sex?"

"Uh, don't know, Mari—never had any to compare it with." She stopped cold, blinking. "*That* good?"

"Don't know. First sex I ever had."

"Oh, my God . . . a joke, right?"

"No, Mari—you're the first." Instantly, her demeanor transformed from blasé temptress to Catholic and concerned . . . "Oh, honey? The Veracruz jail, the CIA, the beatings . . . and *I* am your first?"

"Yep."

"Oh, I shouldn't have been such a smart-ass, Alex. I'd no idea . . . I'm sorry . . . oh, God, you must think I'm a freak!"

"No. But I'd like it if you showed me the *normal* way. Then I could compare." She wasn't that tough to convince. And "normal" made me think of summer breezes. Mari even fixed me breakfast the next morning, chattering the whole time.

"Your eyes glittered like a cat's—emerald green—each time you came. Adorable. Hell, Alex, I could even get used to old-fashioned sex again." She grinned at me. "Lord—your eyes are glittering now . . . don't look at me like that." I blushed. She teased, "OK . . . *don't* stop looking at me like that! It felt 'nice' with you, Alex."

"Thanks, Mari. Last night when my eyes glittered, I saw a bright light—like a star." She looked confused. I changed the subject. "Do you have any tea?"

"Sure . . . and why are you still staring at me like that?"

"I want to remember you wearing only the apron, slippers, and that big smile."

"Darling, I'm no man's 'memory.' 'Nightmare' might be more like it." I believed her—but it didn't worry me. My whole life had revolved around nightmares. They were normal, comfortable, and familiar. She ended my reverie:

"Go get us a copy of *Excélsior* at the *kiosko* on the corner. I'll have the tea ready when you get back . . ." Still staring at her firm ass, I backed out, closing the door behind me. Once down on the street I stopped, looked up, arms raised to the heavens, and shouted, "Yes!" to no one in particular. Surprised at my own exuberance, I looked around, embarrassed. I was right next to a bus stop. One guy in a business suit grinned and gave me a thumbs-up when I looked up. Ah, Mexico!

I grabbed a copy of the paper and headed back to Mari's. She thumbed through it frantically, squealing when she spotted it.

"It's right here on page six, darling . . . oh, *madre de* . . . what a great photo!" She handed it to me. The charming caption read: "The stunning Argentine model Marianna Capo di Monte chats with her escort, *estadounidense* John Alexander, and *Excélsior*'s Pablo Virreyes at the Punto Blanco in the Zona Rosa last night. . . . Topic—eccentricities of the U.S. government."

Well, at least Marianna was pleased. "They spelled my name right!" Me—I was somewhat less pleased. I could almost feel Semper Fi's vise-like grip on my shoulder again . . . and I'd had time to realize that I'd not even thought about Inés when Marianna had offered herself to me. That bothered me.

Except for Eddy, I'd spent most of my life avoiding painful attachments. I'd been surprised at first by my intense attraction to Inés . . .

and to the relatively peaceful times I'd spent with her. She calmed me. I thought I might "love" her. But I'd forgotten all about her in the face of Marianna's charms . . . worse yet, I really liked Marianna—she was more like me. Edgy. Emotionally cautious and much less touchy-feely.

When I asked her why she was into kink, she confided that she'd grown up in a convent. That had been hard to imagine till she also admitted casually that the padres took turns abusing her while the sisters were at vespers. She wanted to tell me more but shrugged and changed the topic, repeating, "I liked the *Excélsior* article. Perhaps I'll get some modeling jobs again." When she said it, she became dreamy eyed. Almost wistful.

Her look reminded me of Eddy, so as the elation at my first experience with sex faded away I felt empty again . . .

⁊⁊

On Thursday afternoon I turned in four papers at the Americas and took the bus to see María Inés. It had been three days since I lost my virginity, at least in the sexual sense of the word, and I'd showered twice.

She took one look at me, then sniffed at my shoulder as I hugged her. "Oh, corazón, it makes me so sad that you have been with another woman."

How the hell does she know this? I wondered while trying to figure out what to say next. She guessed my thoughts, too. "And don't make it worse by lying to me, corazón."

"OK, I'm sorry . . ."

"You're not, corazón. You know you are not." Nonplussed, I shrugged.

"It made me feel alive, Inés. I saw the light again."

"That wasn't your soul, corazón—it was your *nagual*—your animal spirit." She paused . . . "Still, it was *she* who brought you close to the spirit world. I should have tried harder to help you rejoin your soul." She looked at me again, silent for a moment, then said softly, "Well, at least she was a whore of sorts . . . it could be worse." She studied my face for a reaction as she said it.

"Are you psychic, Inés?"

"No, corazón. If I'd known your need was so great, I'd have given myself to you."

"I don't believe that—you are a good girl."

She sighed. "Yes, a good girl . . . but one whose father reads *Excélsior*. Even he whistled and commented that my *novio* has good taste in mistresses."

"He didn't!"

"Oh, yes, corazón. I was crying and my mother became angry with him. She said, 'Papá, at least be angry on your daughter's behalf—for the love of God!' Papá leered at her, 'If God loved me, *gorda*, I'd have been the one in bed with her.' It was ugly. They forgot all about my pain and had a big fight."

"I am sorry, Inés." As I wiped a tear from her cheek, she smiled shyly. "It is not easy being a good girl, corazón. I wanted you to myself."

"It's not all that easy being me, either."

"I know, corazón, I know . . . that is why I care for you. It is who you are that compels me to love you . . . we must find your soul, corazón. Only then can we be together." Before I left she forgave me Marianna, a sad, faraway look in her eyes . . .

Her look also reminded me of Eddy. That's when the first twinges of serious guilt worked their way through me.

☙☙

№ 4 SHOWTIME

BACK AT MY OLD digs on Campos Eliseos I slept late, cleaned my room, then dragged out my tapes, field logs, and portable Hermes typewriter, which skipped . . . dammit! Time to get it fixed . . . and time to get a "field project" planned. My master's depended on it.

One of my professors, John Paddock, was excavating a site called Lambityeco down in Oaxaca, but I couldn't decide between that and ethnology among isolated Nahuatl-speaking communities. I'd aced a beginning course in the Aztec language of Nahuatl and was fascinated by their rich literature and philosophy.

On Sunday I took the bus out to Colonia Hipódromo and visited María Inés. Her brow furrowed at the first hug. "You still smell of her, corazón . . ." *How the hell is that possible?* I wondered, having showered another two times, gotten a haircut, shaved, and changed clothes.

Stressed out and guilty about her instantaneous observation, the Voice hammered away on me. *Don't be a sap! This one's never going to screw you. She was bred to be a Madonna, idiot.*

That Voice had haunted me since Eddy had been raped as a child by our foster father. I'd never been able to identify who the Voice was. It visited only when I was panicked and fragmenting. I lit a smoke, breathed deeply, and tried to blot out both the Voice . . . and my guilt.

The pause resolved nothing. "*Pues . . . no me has contestado, corazón*

(You didn't answer, love)." She'd said it in a slow, resigned monotone. "Well . . . ?" "Well, *what*?" I shot back. "You didn't ask me a question!"

"Is it the same one, corazón?" Jesus—she sounded so resigned, as if telling her would be of no consequence. Totally irritated, I blurted out, "You won't sleep with me . . . so I have an occasional affair." The look of pain and sorrow she threw at me was copied straight from a long-suffering saint's statue standing next to a high altar. Feeling shitty, I clarified, "Well, *twice*, Inés. I have strayed exactly twice. In fact, that is all the sex I've had in my whole pathetic life."

"Do you confide this to test my love . . . my ability to withstand pain, corazón?"

"Huh? You *demanded* an answer."

"A gentleman would lie, corazón. Besides, once we were married I'd have done my duty, like any good wife." *Duty? . . . I don't want duty!* I screamed in my head. She smiled, a sad-sweet "now that I've torn you up, I'll forgive you" look. So I worked up the nerve to say it . . . "I don't want 'duty,' Inés—I want passion. It brings my soul close to me . . . I need it."

Perhaps she said, "I thought you were different . . ." but I was already out the door. I stood on the curb, momentarily overwhelmed by loneliness. I didn't really want a Madonna . . . I wanted a raunchy, in-your-face, big-eyed girl who had secrets . . . not someone who ached for my soul. *Can you fuck your soul back into your body?* I asked myself as I headed to Marianna's with marked-over text from the Hermes.

I knocked at her door. Pablo Mato Virreyes, newspaperman, opened it with a grin. "Ah . . . the hot, young Alex . . . or so she says . . . ah, pity . . . she's been waiting for you and will likely send me away now that you are back."

"Another social column, recently, don Pablo?" I asked. He liked the "don" bit—a lot. Pablo laughed—smooth and unself-conscious. "Ah, she has good taste, young Alex . . . you are so cool, blasé . . . detached. And—free journalist's bonus—a certain U.S. marine with a singular tattoo has been everywhere looking for you. He hates you."

"Thanks! He's sick. A closet queer."

"Ah, so he actually wants from you what I can't get from Marianna? Good! It must be quite an inner conflict for him."

"By the way, don Pablo—for the record—a journalist's tip: I don't like to share." He grinned and shrugged. "Is that Alex, darling?" Marianna chirped from behind the door.

"Yes, my dear. I'll pack up and return home, tail between my legs . . . so to speak. Give me thirty minutes, Alex?"

"Sure, tell her I'll be at the *cafetería* across the street . . . and thanks for the tip on Semper Fi."

"Semper Fi?"

"Yes—short for the Latin 'Semper Fidelis'—'always faithful' . . . a marine thing." He still didn't get it. I pointed to the back of my hand. "The *tatuaje* (tattoo)." Finally he processed it. "Ahh. 'Semper Fi' . . . perhaps we should photograph him for the paper."

"You'd make an enemy for life." "How exciting!" he crooned as he shook my hand before closing the door.

⁂

Marianna came to the café about twenty minutes later. I watched her walk gracefully across the street. Her daring *mini-falda* showing off her spectacular legs. Her blond hair framing her pearly face made her look rather like an albino sunflower. High heels clicked on the restaurant's hard tile as she glided to me . . . and, as always, every man in the place followed her with hungry eyes.

"Don't be angry about Pablo, Alex." I hadn't expected that . . . it didn't fit with her endearing flair for casual decadence. She saw the surprise. "I don't need to ask forgiveness, do I?" I shook my head.

I played the game. "And, Pablo?" Her laugh was spontaneous—rich and throaty. "Come fuck me . . . I've been waiting." Nearby, one well-dressed guy in his thirties squirmed, trying not to lose it in his pants, I assumed.

"I'm not into 'seconds,' Marianna." She sighed, staring at me intently, "When I was with you I felt like my old self—like the girl I once was, before . . ." "The convent?" I asked. She looked away for a moment as if staring into an unknown place, "I *need* that healthy feeling again." "Eat first?" I asked. She leaned to me, a warm, sweet look fading from her face as she wrinkled in thought, "I can't, uh, 'love,' you know. Do you understand that, Alex?"

"Regretfully . . . yes. It's my problem, too. But I try . . . at least some-times." Her mouth wrinkled and her chin quivered. "I know. Oh, how

I know!" We ate spaghetti, the day's special, and spoke no more until we were back at her place, where she poured me a short tequila to keep me company while she retired to do whatever women do when they disappear for ten minutes.

Marianna Capo di Monte, model, woman of the world, sexually distorted by those who were supposed to protect her . . . and John Alexander, a kid no one wanted; both tried to beckon their souls amidst their bittersweet substitute for "love," twisted and anguished. Who knows where she went as spasms of pleasure transported her and her dilated pupils fixed on a quiet corner of the shabby apartment . . . but I saw fireflies, Betty Anne, and little Eddy. Sometimes you've just got to take what you can get . . .

She fixed *chilaquiles* in the morning. I nuzzled her bare ass as she stood at the stove, giggling like a schoolgirl. It didn't even sound like her as I knew her. She'd apparently gotten a little something out of it, too.

¤¤

№ 5 SEMPER FI

I LEFT THE PACK of manuscripts with Marianna and headed back to Campos Eliseos 81 where, according to Chavela, Dr. Baker wanted a word with me.

Julia Baker's infirmary and private quarters were in the front of the house, below her huge private theater—which fronted a narrow tongue of Chapultepec Park. Dressed as elegantly as ever, Dr. Baker motioned for me to sit on the settee opposite her while Chavela poured tea.

I tried to act respectable but was nervous. Dr. Baker was tall, regal, and every bit the model of a powerful female I'd had absolutely no experience with. Everything about her fascinated me—her clothes, the face job, her young tuxedo-clad escorts to the opera, her messy quarrels with a spoiled boy toy named Diego who was half her age.

But it was her directness that baffled me the most. I wasn't used to it. The only female figures I'd known had been either the weak, frightened, and morally bankrupt wives of my various foster fathers or the deep-in-the-closet dominatrix types who ineffectively acted out normalcy as reform-school house mothers and orphanage headmistresses. I simply had no precedent for a woman who was both feminine and in control.

Dr. Baker was to the point. "JA, we have been visited recently by several 'security' attachés from the American Embassy . . . it's still about that sordid affair turned ugly in Veracruz." I nodded, and waited for the rest.

"JA, I *don't* like those types around my house. Neither does Miss Lollabrigida next door." "And . . . ?" I interjected.

"So tell me what you know. Then I'll decide whether or not we can still accommodate you here."

It took about thirty minutes to give her the rundown. She watched me over the top of her teacup, elegant seventy-year-old legs crossed seductively as if she were thirty. As she took in the sexual details she even looked thirty. And thought like a thirty-year-old . . . "Lucky woman! The group sex sounds, uh, interesting . . . no matter. Were you 'sharing' her with the others?"

"No. I have a girlfriend here."

"What? The *morena* who comes to the gate now and again, always fingering her cross as she stares down at the sidewalk? She'll never bed you unless you marry her—and then only once a year . . . how charming of you to save yourself for her!" Dr. Baker's laugh was harsh, nasal, and surprisingly unrefined.

When her amusement passed she went back to business. "I've asked the ambassador to keep his men away. If they come back again . . . you go. He promised . . . but his promise is only good *if* you aren't involved in anything *new*. You are warned." "Guilty or not?" I asked.

"Yes—this isn't the States, JA. Guilt and innocence are immaterial—meaningless, abstract concepts. Mexico is about appearances." She stood.

"Please get dressed for dinner. Jacket and tie. Dr. Salk is dining with us tonight."

"Jonas? The polio guy?"

"No, his brother Benjamín—the brighter of the two. Dinner is in one hour. Let Chavela know if you need to borrow a suit jacket."

Her dinners nearly always made me nervous—you don't learn how to spoon soup and use fish forks in "Chef Boyardee" orphanages and foster homes . . . and you get only a spoon to eat with in reform school. But the conversation focused on tropical disease epidemiology: endemic pockets of "carriers" in isolated Indian and black communities—and what happens in modern Mexico when such folks come to the city to work. Or make pilgrimages to the Basilica of Guadalupe, for that matter.

I asked questions. Dr. Salk actually paid attention to me. Amazing . . . in the Distrito Federal you could rot in jail without due process one day and talk to people like Salk and Octavio Paz the next.

After dinner, the doctors repaired to Dr. Baker's tearoom for brandy and smokes. I climbed the stairs to my balcony room and changed into Wrangler jeans, jacket, and engineer's boots, then headed to the Punto Blanco about eight blocks away.

As I turned the corner at Campos Eliseos and Boulevard Mariano Escobedo, Semper Fi leaped out of the shadows to confront me. "Well, well, it's the little Commie faggot out for a stroll. I thought we'd lost you to some iguana country out in the boondocks."

"I like evening strolls—" That was as far as I got. When I came to I assumed I was in the basement of the American Embassy again, strapped to a cot . . . a small jar of ether and a gauze pad placed suggestively on a nearby table. The lights, as before, were blinding. Nothing moved. So I turned my head to sleep again.

"No you don't, troublemaker!" The general's voice hung in the air, dusty and repulsive like the scent of an uncleaned stable. "You just had to screw with me, didn't you, *Yankee boy*?" he crooned. I tiptoed away, catching one faraway glance of Betty Anne as I launched myself into a breezy summer night.

The next time I came to, I was in a ward at the ABC (American-British Cowdray) Hospital near Mariano Escobedo, and Dr. Baker was standing over me. "JA, my chauffeur saw them grab you and drug you. He had just dropped off Dr. Oliverieros and Dr. Salk at the Hotel María Isabel when he passed by you. It took me two days to get the ambassador to believe him and order your release."

"My hands hurt, Dr. Baker . . . why are they bandaged?"

"I know. You won't like what they did to you."

"What was that?"

"You lost several fingernails, JA. They tortured you. Why?"

"I don't know. It was the freak who stopped me."

"Who is he?"

"The marine I told you about . . . the one with 'Semper Fidelis' tattooed on the back of his right hand."

"Did you get that, Rafael?" Dr. Baker said over her shoulder. Rafael was just out of my view to the right. "Who's Rafael?" I asked.

"The secretary of *gobernación*—the president's minister of the interior."

"Am I in trouble with the Mexican government?" Dr. Baker turned, raised her eyebrows.

"Rafael?"

"No, joven. But your government's embassy seems to be out of hand. You are the second foreign student to be taken and tortured by them this week alone."

"Is the other from the Americas, too?"

"No. She's an Argentinean art student and says she knows you."

"Not Marianna!"

"Yes, she and Sr. Pablo Virreyes are in the next ward. Shall we bring her?" I nodded.

They pushed her in, still in a wheelchair. Her feet were bandaged heavily. I stared. "No toenails," said Dr. Baker. And her face . . . Marianna wasn't pretty anymore.

They had cut her from each corner of her beautiful mouth, in long curving arcs up to her lower eyelids, slicing through nerve and muscle. About two hundred stitches held her face together. She was grotesquely swollen, her eyes blackened, and she couldn't talk.

"Can you nod your head, miss?" asked Minister Rafael. She nodded slowly, looking directly at me, tears running down her cheeks. "Who?" I asked. She tried to say something but couldn't manage more than a funny sound.

"Bring her closer," I asked. I didn't realize it till she leaned to me—her face ruined and nothing left to distract me—all that was left intact were her soft, pleading eyes.

I reached out to touch her, my bandaged hand clumsy and throbbing. She cradled my hand in hers, clasping it gently against what was left of her cheek. "Who?" I repeated.

"General," she whispered, hoarse from the gauze and rubber drain sticking out at the base of her throat. "Did he do the cutting?" She shook her head no—pointing to a place behind her, then touched the back of her right hand.

"Semper Fi from behind?" She nodded. "Did the general watch?" She nodded, more animated. "Did they rape you, miss?" asked Rafael. She nodded.

Pablo Virreyes, silent till now, blurted out. "They've *ruined* her! I know people who would kill them for a price!" His voice was high pitched, ending in a hysterical rasp. Marianna turned away when he'd emphasized the word *ruined*.

The minister of the interior was cold with Virreyes. "Settle down, Pablo. You'd be more useful if you photographed her pointing out the general, then published it. It's childish to start a back-street war with the U.S. Embassy over a lover you can't acknowledge publicly." *Lover? Son of a bitch!* I sighed to myself. Then the guilt at her being hurt on my account kicked in. *Marianna is good for me—other lovers or not. At least I feel something with her . . .*

So I butted in. "She's not ruined—just hurt." Her eyes were sublime as she turned back toward me. Fireflies winked in the soft summer night. The musty and sweet scents of freshly mowed grass and bruised strawberries intoxicated me.

The two men left to talk. Julia Baker was kind. "Shall we leave you two together for a while?" I nodded. She turned to Marianna before leaving. "Don't worry, child. They can do miracles with plastic surgery these days. I know an excellent surgeon in Rome. We'll see to that in due course." "Really, Dr. Baker?" I asked on Marianna's behalf.

"Yes, JA, you have my word on it . . . and we'll need to talk when you are home again."

Julia Baker shut the door on the way out. Marianna took my hand again, snuggling it ever so gently. I fell asleep. When I awakened, she was gone. She'd tucked a note on my pillow: *Alex. Why did you get me into this? M.*

We talked the next day. Actually, I talked, and she nodded. "I don't know what these guys want. I never imagined they'd bother you since it all happened in Veracruz . . . can you forgive me?" I think she said, "Maybe," and shrugged, but her eyes said yes. I went with the eyes.

I was discharged two days later. Pablo Virreyes returned to talk. "I can arrange a lunch at the Embers after both of you are out of the hospital and have had several days to recover. Can you get Marianna to cooperate? . . . She's not speaking to me now."

"Yeah—*ruined* was a crappy word choice, don Pablo . . . you want the photos that gobernación suggested, I assume?" He nodded. I went on,

"Then you'd better come up with a decent plan, don Pablo—one with lots of hired muscle. If Marianna gets hurt again it's on you."

"I'll take care of it!"

At Campos Eliseos, Julia Baker was kind, but firm. "You can't stay here beyond another week or so. I'll help you find another place. I don't need the trouble that comes from renegades in the embassy."

"I understand."

"Well, actually, JA—*I* don't. You seem too calm about it. Not outraged enough. I don't think you've told me everything."

"I don't know anything else." She shook her head in disgust. I let it go. I'd had this conversation with "normal" folks too many times in the States to bother with it again. In the worlds Mari and I had come from, weird was normal . . . and no one ever had a good "reason" for the nasty stuff they did. Explaining this to the fortunate inhabitants of a world based on "reason" was an exercise in futility. Finally, Dr. Baker spoke again. "When does the young woman get discharged?" she asked.

"Two days more."

"She'll need someone, JA . . . at least for a while."

⁂

Marianna came home three days later. Back to her little second-story apartment near the western terminus of Campos Eliseos. I put her in bed, fixed soup broth for her, and we talked.

"Do you not find me disgusting, Alex?" she mumbled through the rows of stitches.

"No, your eyes are even lovelier than before, and anyway, you suffered because of me. I'm so sorry."

She took my hand again, planting a clumsy kiss on it, her lips still swollen and purple. "Could I stay with you here for a week or two—I'm being evicted." She nodded. "But I don't want to, uh . . ."

"No sex, Marianna." Poor thing, the schoolgirl she'd attempted to recapture was gone again—a sweet dream savagely expunged by a sicko with a knife. Now she was simply sweet-scared and very unsure of herself. Her alluring femininity must have compensated for many other things gone wrong, "before *IT* happened in the convent," as she'd said. She'd somehow known she didn't have to explain *IT* to me.

Maybe that's why we were together. Now she had yet another "after" to deal with.

I cleaned out my room at Dr. Baker's that night and hauled my stuff up to Marianna's in a taxi. Dr. Baker gave me her business card as I left. "For the young lady. The surgeon in Rome. Good-bye, JA." That night I slept on Marianna's sofa. I fixed her breakfast while she showered.

Later I fixed her lunch while she showered again. It was the same thing at dinner. My cooking was clumsy—the bandaged hands didn't help— and just plain bad. But she ate my burned omelets without complaint.

That night I slept with her, cradled in her arms, a votive candle flickering by her statue of Saint Francis. He looked down on us and sighed . . . just two damaged kids haunted by images of private, unspoken horrors that had no logic behind them. I answered Saint Francis silently. *I envy all those who have no clue.* He seemed to smile, as if he'd heard me.

❧

№6 GENERAL MACLAMORE BIRDSONG

THE NEXT EVENING WE met don Pablo at the Embers. We were an exotic sight—Marianna was dressed head to toe in black, and her purple and yellow bruises had an angry, determined quality about them. It was the first long dress I'd ever seen her wear. The bandaged toes sticking out of her heeled, open-toe sandals and her puffy stitches completed the effect—making her look like a Halloween prank gone terribly wrong.

Me—I looked less ethereal and much more like a tallish gringo who'd been thoroughly stomped by, well, an embassy guard. Don Pablo, in contrast, looked smooth and urbane, if not a bit nervous. He couldn't look Marianna in the eye. But that didn't stop him from checking out her ass as I seated her.

The waiter gaped at us, and Virreyes became irritable. "I hope this Birdsong character shows up." He fidgeted.

"Who?" we both asked in the same breath. He consulted a small card, then repeated, "The general . . . Maclamore Birdsong." The name seemed made up, so I asked to see it. Sure enough, it read "Brigadier General Maclamore Birdsong IV." "Where'd you get the business card?" I asked.

"From a friend at Los Piños."

Los Piños was Mexico's White House. "I'm impressed," I said. We ordered. Both Marianna and I settled for soup—the easiest thing to eat in public. Virreyes went with a thick, juicy steak. "Decent, but no Delmonico's," he noted.

The evening ended uneventfully—no general in sight. Marianna and I were willing to let it go—she was very self-conscious and withdrawn. Men ogled her from behind, then turned away once they got a view of her lavishly sutured face.

The rich Mexican matrons at nearby tables, probably assuming fair-haired Marianna was of gringo origins like me, made remarkable comments, which they assumed Marianna could not understand. One cow mooed, "She might have been pretty once . . . but why is *he* willing to be seen *in public* with her? Didn't he have some ravishing model in here with him a few weeks ago?" A tear trickled down Marianna's cheek and she hung her head.

"Maybe it's his wife," commented the man with her.

The cow retorted: "Then he needs a mistress—I can't imagine him being able to, uh, look her in the face, in bed." The Mexican version of a bag-over-her-head retort was inevitable. More tears ran down Marianna's cheeks. Don Pablo appeared uncomfortable, if not embarrassed. We left at 10:15 PM. Our mission had been a washout.

We returned two nights later but lingered on a rear patio. I smoked while don Pablo drank and Marianna shivered at the thought of being ridiculed again—or even looked at. But the strategy she'd suggested to corner Birdsong—if he showed—worked.

About 9:15 PM the general arrived at the front door with a small entourage. They waited in the embassy's Lincoln town car while an aide checked out the interior. The coast was clear so they entered as I watched from the rear patio. Don Pablo wanted to go in right away. I insisted not. "Let's stick to Mari's plan—give them time to get settled . . . and where are your cameramen, anyway?"

"Inside, eating. Three of them . . . and let me handle the conversation with Birdsong." Marianna shivered, nodded in assent, and crossed her arms. "I'm frightened," she mumbled. Don Pablo reassured her.

"Don't worry. I've put a lot of thought into this. All you have to do is point at him and nod, then we can go. The paper will help with protection issues and some money for the story."

"Will you have to show my face in the paper?" she asked.

"Yes," he answered softly, touching her shoulder gently for the first time since she'd been cut.

I got jealous so leaned forward and caressed her stitches with my still-bandaged fingers. "You're beautiful, Marianna—nothing has really changed." Someone whistled to us from the restaurant's service door. "¡El espetáculo! 'Showtime,' as you say in the States," grinned don Pablo.

We followed him inside. In one corner sat the general, holding court. A nicely dressed twentyish American chick sat next to him, making eyes. She reeked of old money. Perhaps it was the three-carat emerald on one middle finger, or perhaps it was the understated honey-blond hair pulled into a tight French roll. Either way she was young enough to be his granddaughter.

As we filed over to the general's table, don Pablo made a couple of hand signals. Two immense guys stood and moved to our flanks. I nudged Virreyes. "It's OK, they are our *pistoleros*—very experienced."

Nearly everyone in the restaurant watched our exotic entourage casually close the distance to the American big shot's table. We eyed Birdsong's little assemblage. He faced another aging diplomat and two big guys with bulging jackets who should have spotted us sooner.

A second American girl's back was to us. She chattered on, unaware. The straight, lanky hair, slightly horsy face, "oh-so-bright" conversation, and no boobs had marked her for life. She was a walking billboard for Smith College. Finally, Pablo coughed.

Birdsong looked up, astonished to see us. His date was smart enough to sense the tension. But "Smith College" was clueless. She turned to see who it was, pouted at the interruption, and shot us a complaint in nasal English. "*I'm* talking. Do you *mind*?" She oozed petulance, but don Pablo was unscathed.

"Actually, I do, *child*," crooned Pablo in impeccable, unaccented English. "General Birdsong and I have business." One of Birdsong's thick-necks reached into his jacket. But he fumbled the move, and before he could draw his gun, a big nickel-plated Colt government .45 auto materialized over my shoulder. From behind me, the huge pistolero holding it giggled.

Birdsong's helpless security man looked down its barrel, astonished that the Mexican bodyguard had the advantage. Birdsong gaped and flushed. Don Pablo grinned. "I think you folks call this . . . what was that phrase? . . . ah, yes, a 'Mexican standoff.'"

Scattered snickers erupted from the restaurant's clientele as Virreyes got down to business. "Marianna—please point to the man who held you while one of his goons cut your face." Birdsong's face was as red as a scarlet tanager's wing. Marianna shook but actually made eye contact with the general. Her voice low and raspy with rage, she pointed at him, "That is the degenerate who laughed and licked the blood from my face as I was cut from behind. He raped me as I bled."

An outraged male voice boomed from a nearby table, "¡*Pinche gringo cabrón!*" drowning out a chorus of background "Ooohs!" Birdsong's face contorted in rage. "And you weren't even tight, you pathetic bitch," he hissed through clenched teeth. He reminded me of Earl again. Smith College goggled at Birdsong, then went ballistic. "You bastard!" she shrieked and tried to slap him. The general's other bodyguard broke her swing. She squealed in pain. Birdsong's date was obviously over.

Big Speed Graphics materialized like magic, their flashbulbs popping like New Year's Eve fireworks. Birdsong rose, pulling his own pistol. Don Pablo stepped forward, undaunted, palms outspread in supplication. Birdsong grinned and paused, thinking he'd regained the advantage. That's when Virreyes sucker punched him. "Philistine," he snarled as Birdsong went down. The audience stood and clapped.

We left quickly, the paper's two bodyguards still with us. As we stepped into the street don Pablo apologized to Marianna. "I'm so sorry I couldn't bear to look at your face after . . . forgive me my shallowness, darling."

Still shaking, Marianna took his hand and nodded. "Thank you, Pablo." He took a deep breath and crooned, "Well, that's done. And you, young Mr. Alexander? Why are you so calm?" "Oh, I don't react a lot to this sort of stuff," I shrugged. Don Pablo studied me for a moment, his eyebrows arched appraisingly. "Well, then, let's get the two of you off to 'vacation' with an escort, courtesy of the newspaper. Two weeks should do." Marianna nodded absently, then retreated within herself again.

By midnight we were on a bus headed north to the provincial city of Pachuca, in Hidalgo state, one pistolero, named Benjamín, along for comfort. Marianna slept, saying little when she was awake. In Pachuca, we took another bus to Guanajuato, capital of the state known by the same name. *Excélsior* put us up in an elegant, renovated seventeenth-century convent next to the lovely triangular Plaza de la Unión. We had a balcony room. Benjamín was somewhere down below.

The next morning we lingered over a late brunch at a restaurant called El Retiro, just past the far side of the plaza. The food was spectacular and there wasn't another gringo in sight. Marianna seemed more animated and had only taken two showers since our arrival.

The swelling in her face had eased somewhat and she initiated the conversation, still unable to enunciate clearly, "Thanks for all the sympathy, Alex. You've been so kind." I think I turned red. She smiled, crookedly, still not able to control her facial expressions, "It did me good to point at Birdsong and get it out."

"I hope so, Mari. You were very brave! I was impressed."

"Really, Alex?"

"Yes! No one there will ever forget it. I didn't know it was *that* sick. Are you OK?"

She shook her head. "Not really . . . he's crazy, Alex. He really did lick my face as I screamed. It fueled his sick sexuality." That got my attention. I flashed back to the scene in Veracruz when we'd first found the dead, wide-eyed Kristal with that unexplainable smear of blackening, fly-blown blood on her cheek. Mari tapped me. "Weren't you listening, Alex?" I refocused on Mari, who went on. "At least the little tart who was with him looked shocked . . . do you think your government will continue to come after us?"

"I don't know, Mari. Until I came to Mexico, I thought we were a . . . civilized nation."

"Oh, Alex, you are *so* worldly in some ways, yet so naive in others—you 'Americans' have been spoiled by good government. You've come to expect it of every administration."

I laughed—uneasily.

Afterward we stopped to sit in the plaza. The dense, leafy trees and bright flowers were gorgeous, the benches clean, and the plaza itself spotless. Grandmoms and nannies pushed toddlers in strollers. Old men played chess and street vendors hawked tacos, *exquisitos* (hot dogs), and shaved ices. While Mari relaxed, I mentally reworked the scene in Veracruz. It all added up to Birdsong. I didn't like the addition, so repressed it and focused on our surroundings.

Young lovers nuzzled one another on the grass and an architectural history class unfolded in an open space forty feet away. The young professor, circled by a dozen graduate students, "professed" right there. Passersby stopped to listen.

The State University of Guanajuato was but three blocks away, nestled in the very heart of one of the most beautiful red tile–roofed colonial cities in the Americas.

Guanajuato, founded in the 1500s, bloomed from the late 1600s to the late 1800s, fueled by the fabulous wealth of silver extracted from La Valenciana mine, just several miles from the city's center. The counts of Valenciana had been rich and powerful and invested heavily in art, architecture, and opera. Guanajuato's remarkable cast-iron and glass city market had been personally designed and built by Eiffel, of Eiffel Tower fame.

So the university had followed the succession of counts' leads, specializing in art, music, architecture, and Cervantes. In the evenings roving bands of students strolled the hilly cobblestone streets, stopping in the small plazas to act out Cervantes plays . . . and serenade pretty girls. "I wish they'd serenade us," grieved Marianna as we stood on the balcony to our room one evening, tears cascading down her cheeks. She winced as the salty tears soaked through the sutures to the still-raw tissue hidden beneath.

But Guanajuato also brought us some peace. Its gentle contrasts to fast-paced Mexico City were wondrous . . . and healing. On the second day, the hotel's maids lined up and applauded Marianna as we came through the door. The doorman explained, extending a copy of *Excélsior*, "We thought you had been in an auto accident. We'd no idea you were a hero!" Marianna broke into tears. One of the girls embraced her. "So brave, you are . . . an American general . . ."

There was a full-page spread. The photos were spectacular. Marianna pointing at Birdsong. The very illegal butt of his Colt just showing. His security men looking furtive. Bet the two preppy girls' families weren't all that thrilled, either—both their daughters' faces had become part of diplomatic history, not included in the upper-class East Coast aristocrats' rulebook of, "A woman should be in the newspaper only three times—for her birth, her wedding, and her obituary." One caption read, "Our lovely Argentine ingenue Marianna Capo di Monte points out the so-called Norteamericano general M. A. Birdsong to Sr. Pablo Mato Virreyes, one of *Excélsior*'s senior editors."

"I love the 'so-called' part," I told Mari. She grinned, ever so subtly. Another caption read, "That is the 'degenerate' who violated me and licked blood from my cheeks as his accomplice cut my face."

Yet another, a shot of the American Embassy, simply read, "The *embajador estadounidense* has no comment on the incident at the Embers Restaurant on Avenida Mariano Escobedo, witnessed by dozens." I got another thirty seconds of fame and a far more poignant caption than I deserved: "The young man at left is John Alexander, North American student and uncompromisingly loyal companion of Miss Capo di Monte. His hands are bandaged from torture inflicted in the same recent embassy incident."

That evening don Pablo called. Marianna motioned me to the phone—holding the receiver so we could share the conversation. "Hey, you two—good news—the general has been recalled to the States, along with the two embassy *changos* (apes) in the photo. We are doing a follow-up story tomorrow. The public response has been spectacular. This afternoon a group of students from the Autónoma blocked the front of the American Embassy, and newspaper sales are spectacular!"

"What about us?" I asked.

"Oh, I'd say an extended vacation is in order. But we want to move you in the next several days. Security . . . where do you want to go?"

"Paris," mumbled Marianna. Pablo didn't understand her, so I shouted, "She said, 'Paris'!" Pablo laughed. "We can't afford that, darling. Besides, we can't protect you in Paris." Marianna glanced toward me and shrugged. "Waiting for a suggestion?" I asked. She nodded.

"How about Mitla, south of Oaxaca City—we could stay at the Hacienda La Sorpresa. It would be hard for those guys to drift into town unnoticed . . . and I can do my fieldwork from there."

"What does our charming Marianna say to that?" asked Pablo. Mari was already nodding animatedly and trying to mumble through the corners of her mouth.

"It's 'Yes,' don Pablo."

"OK. Who do we talk to?"

"Julia Baker. She's a trustee at the Americas . . . and the school owns the hacienda's museum and guest rooms."

"Done! I've known Julia forever. I'll be back in touch tomorrow . . . you kids have fun."

The phone went dead. I cradled Mari's head on my lap as she lay on the bed, fingering her rosary and staring at the Saint Francis she'd brought with her. Once she was asleep I went out to the balcony to smoke, unsettled by the visions of army ranger Eddy, who had been visiting me again in the nights.

The next afternoon we headed south to Oaxaca via Puebla, to the east of Mexico City. No point in running into old friends, like Semper Fi, in a Mexico City bus station.

Marianna didn't even ask for the window seat, as she had several weeks before on the trip north to Guanajuato. In fact, she no longer bothered to hide her face. The accolades from the hotel staff in Guanajuato had set her on a new course.

"I know my face is an oddity, Alex. But now when people stare, I can tell myself I am a heroine. Before, my looks made life too easy in some ways. I used them to get what I wanted from men . . . and now I don't even want those men around."

"And me, Marianna?"

"You're different. In some ways, you are still a boy. Besides, you've stuck with me at my ugliest . . . and you haven't even asked once about sex. Thank you." I looked away. She frowned, but said nothing for several minutes.

"Alex, will any man ever want me after . . . him? This?"

"Yes, Mari. I'm still aroused by you . . . perhaps even more than before. When I first met you I liked your cold, maverick streak. And you are beautiful . . ."

She stopped me mid-sentence, her finger to my lips. "God bless you! You said I *am* beautiful!"

"You *are*. And you smile now . . . that makes me happy." She laughed.

"My stitches are drawing the corners of my mouth up, silly!"

"Yeah, well, I lusted over you before. Now I could actually fall in love with you. Maybe it's already happened."

"Do you even know what love is, Alex?"

"No . . . but I feel warm inside when you smile. Is that close enough for now?"

She leaned to me and brushed my cheek gently with her swollen lips, then unexpectedly snaked a hand to my crotch to test for testosterone fever. Satisfied, she disengaged, leaned back, and stared. "Hmmn. You aren't faking, are you . . . you could like me this way?" I nodded. She shook her head wistfully, "I assumed your kindness, like Pablo's, was simple guilt—after all, Birdsong was *your* enemy, not mine."

"Well, I think guilt has been a factor. At first it was scary to see you cut up like that. But I like you much better now."

"Ruined looks and all?"

I smiled and shrugged. She finally let it go. How do you tell a woman that you were attracted to her because she seemed so like you—damaged, unfeeling, detached, edgy—then she gave you hope once she was wounded . . . just because her smile suddenly seemed *real* and her eyes much softer.

Mari snuggled against my shoulder and relaxed. I thought she'd gone to sleep when she surprised me and spoke again. "Can you wait awhile for sex, Alex . . ."

"If you smile a lot, I can wait." She sighed and went to sleep.

As we stood to exit when the bus stopped in Puebla, an older woman who'd been sitting behind us leaned to Marianna and spoke to her briefly, patting her good-bye. As we stepped into the station my curiosity got the best of me. "What was that about, Mari?"

"She said not to let you get away."

"Jesus! Is our business a public soap opera?"

"Yes," she giggled, "and don't curse like that." I looked surprised. She shrugged, "It's sacrilegious, Alex . . . don't tempt fate." I reacted inside, *Oh, no, not a conversion. "Conversions" scare me.* But I took a breath and thought before I responded . . .

"OK. You're right, Mari." She started to say something else, but Benjamín stepped up out of nowhere—we'd not even seen him on the bus. "You have a new bodyguard, Samuel Moya; he'll introduce himself in Oaxaca. It's been an honor." With that he strode away, never looking back.

We bought tortas, sodas, and cigarettes for the trip. Marianna seemed effervescent for the first time since she'd been maimed. "You seem so upbeat," I commented.

"Yes, Alex. There is a silver lining in all this. I am sure of it. I think I'm to get a new start on life."

The bus was cramped and hot. The journey required stops at the small cities of Tehuacán and Huajuapan de León before descending into the valley of Oaxaca. We reached Oaxaca City at nightfall, still wondering where, or when, we'd meet this Samuel Moya. We needn't have worried. He'd turned out to be the tidily dressed "businessman" two rows behind us. His cheap black leather "sample case," compact frame, and Indian-like face were his camouflage.

"I'm Samuel Moya. I know you are surprised, but a big, light-skinned *guardaespalda* (bodyguard) in Oaxaca just wouldn't work. Besides, my mother is Zapoteca—this is home country." We shook hands and I tried out my one line of Zapotec, "*Zusiguundá didxazá la?*" "Yes," he replied, "I do speak Zapotec . . . it was my grandmother's only language. But I didn't know any white guys, except a few *adventistas* (Seventh-day Adventist missionaries), spoke it."

"I was just showing off. I only speak a little . . . but much more Nahuatl." He laughed. "Well, it will be an interesting assignment . . . U.S. agents have been everywhere in El Distrito looking for you."

"Are we going straight to Mitla?"

"No questions yet . . . please . . . boss's orders. I'll hail us a cab." Up we went to the picturesque Hotel Victoria overlooking the valley of Oaxaca. Once there, Marianna stopped to gaze down on a twinkling Oaxaca City. It glittered in the sunset's fading iridescent light. The hotel's palms rustled in the fresh evening breeze and the last glow of sunset faded into a cascade of peach, electric blue, and swirls of pink that lit up the southern Sierra Madre to the southwest.

"It smells different here," sighed Marianna. "The light is different, too. Can we look for charcoals tomorrow, Alex? I'll need paper, as well. I'd like to sketch. It's the art community here that made me say yes to your suggestion of Oaxaca."

Samuel was about to answer when a smooth, oily voice from behind us said, "Big art colony here. Make a list, darling, and we'll take care of it in the morning." "Oh, Pablo. Thank you for being here," Marianna said softly.

"I wouldn't miss this for anything, darling. How often does *Excélsior* have the opportunity to both participate in international intrigue and sell obscene quantities of extras?"

Pablo ushered us into a private dining room off one side of the elegant lobby. Big iced pineapple juices arrived like magic. Pablo explained, "We'll enjoy a juice here while Samuel and another assistant check into your room and take your bags up. The rooms are rented in *Excélsior*'s name. Anything you need for the next several days will be billed to us . . . arrangements are still being made at La Sorpresa in Mitla." "I'd like to freshen up before dinner, Pablo," groaned Marianna.

"Of course, darling, no more than five minutes . . . my assistant will bring the key." A few minutes later an adorably cute slip of a twenty-something, dark-haired female assistant drifted in with our keys. Marianna took one look at her, threw her head back, and laughed as best she could.

The poor thing froze on the spot. "Did I do something wrong, Miss Capo di Monte?"

"No, not at all. In fact, everything is perfectly right!" Young Thing still looked confused. An urbane and delightfully shameless Pablo Virreyes smoothed the waters. "She approves of you, Elena . . . and she's *very* picky." Marianna laughed again . . . a cleansing, hearty tone rising from her gut.

"Oooh, I must stop . . . my face hurts," she cackled. Young Thing bolted away like a startled doe. Pablo grinned. "OK—you can stop laughing now, Mari. She's not my mistress—at least, not yet." Mari dumped on him, "Oh, you are such a bad liar, Pablo." He shrugged, palms up. Mari shook her head in disgust.

"Well, let's get cleaned up—back in thirty minutes, Pablo," I butted in.

Upstairs, Mari and I walked along the gallery to our room, the sounds of glasses clinking, dinner, and laughter floating up from the open lobby below. Our room was large. Floor-to-ceiling French doors opened onto a second-story balcony overlooking the city.

Once inside, Marianna surprised me by embracing me from behind, her face buried in my shoulder blades. "I'm going to have a new life, Alex . . . share it with me?" I went rock hard. "Don't answer now . . . I'll ask again in several months."

When she let go, I turned to her. Her eyes were soft and gentle, the little girl smile so familiar. "Do Tasty Cakes come with the offer?" I asked in English. She shrugged, "I didn't get that. Why English all of a sudden?"

"I was remembering the first person who ever loved me." "Another woman?" she pouted.

"No. She was six. I was four—"

"You were four . . . she *six*? Love?"

"Yep, love. Her name was Betty Anne. She made tea for me and Eddy. Gave us Tasty Cakes for dessert. I loved her. Your smile is just like hers."

"But I can't seem like a six-year-old. I'm a woman of the world."

"OK, but the little girl inside of that woman is someone I'd like to know better." She stared, blinking, her hazel eyes moistening.

"You're the first man who ever cared about what was inside . . . and you're too young for me . . . just my luck."

"Then we're even, Mari—you're the first woman I ever slept with . . . and you are too old for me, *ni modo* (whatcha gonna do?)."

"Let's go down and eat. I'm starved, Alex. We can sort out the improbabilities later." She gave me a squeeze and led the way.

At dinner Pablo summarized the situation. "The Mexican government, thanks to pressure from the paper and Julia Baker, formally declared Birdsong, the two guards, and the marine you call 'Semper Fi' persona non grata.

"The U.S. ambassador is pissed at everyone—his own renegades, the CIA, some other agency they won't really identify, our government, the newspaper, and you, Alex."

"Why me, don Pablo?"

"He asserts that you are some kind of Communist. Claims that you've altered your name and that there is no way in hell you will ever get your passport back. Any truth in his suspicions?"

"Yes. I was born 'Johann Strauss Alexander.' My father, who I never knew, was born in Germany. My mother was a Scotswoman. My parents were both dead by the time my brother and I were a few months old. Since there were no other kin in America, we were sent to an orphanage near Philadelphia—our names were Americanized when the Commonwealth of Pennsylvania took custody. Legally I became 'John Alexander' and that's the only name I ever knew."

Pablo was quiet for a moment. "Sorry . . . I didn't know."

"Neither did I, Alex," put in Marianna.

"And the 'Communist' thing, Alex?"

"*¡Mierda!* I'm not politically active at all. But someone took photos of several of us from the Americas passing the Russian Embassy. I didn't even know what the building was. So when the business in Veracruz happened some idiot added up two and two to equal eight." Pablo nodded.

"No one who casually passes through the Distrito Federal would know what that building is. They took down the flag and hammer and sickle some years ago. Out of sight, out of mind—as they say in the States."

"So, what do I do without a passport?"

"We'll work on it. The U.S. ambassador doesn't have the final say on that. If that doesn't work out, the paper could sponsor your request for permanent resident immigrant status here in Mexico. Does that interest you?"

"Yeah! I like it here. But why would the paper do that?"

"Ah, young Alex, we have so few examples of individuals who've told the United States to 'take a flying fuck' as you say back home. It's an inspiration to our readers. Even the president of Mexico is following this saga." "You're kidding," said Marianna.

"No, darling . . . the two of you are like Robin Hood here in Mexico— a folkloric tonic for the many frustrations with our northern neighbor." "You sure know a lot about Stateside slang and culture," I butted in. He answered in English.

"Of course I do, young Alex. I'm an alum of Choate, then Harvard. I spent my formative years on 'the other side.' Actually, I liked the social freedom in the States quite a lot. I liked the emerging, nearly genuine meritocracy even better . . . but remained addicted to the advantages I inherited here in Mexico. Had I stayed in the States I'd still have been a struggling journalist driving a fifteen-year-old auto and doing my own laundry . . . and no Stateside wife would ever have put up with my wanderings. So, here I am."

"Well, at least you have the distinction of being the only editor in Mexico to have slugged an American general," Marianna cackled.

"Yes, my dear . . . and good for one hell of a promotion, too! So, *Excélsior* will continue to help you . . . oh, as long as the copy sells . . . I'm being honest, kids." "While we're being honest, don Pablo . . . we're broke," I lied.

"All provided for . . . you are to each draw twenty-five hundred pesos a month for the next three months . . . all interviews and news exclusive to *Excélsior*. We own your public lives for the next three months. Elena—do you have those papers with you?" She nodded, her hands shaking in front of Marianna. Pablo continued, "Good . . . sign these. Your cash is to be delivered in the morning."

We signed and toasted while an *Excélsior* photographer burned more bulbs. "What will these photo captions say?" asked Elena.

"Oh, something like, 'Sr. Pablo Virreyes, *Excélsior*'s distinguished senior editor, dines at an undisclosed location with the luminous Marianna Capo di Monte and unrepentant John Alexander, while they recover from the injuries that the American Embassy denies inflicting on them . . . a prize of one thousand pesos to any reader in the republic who can identify the location.'"

"You are incorrigible, Pablo," hooted Marianna. "But I'm no longer luminous, I fear."

"Yes you are, darling—your inner glow is working its way to the surface."

"God! That's what Alex just told me upstairs!" Pablo looked at me . . .

"Really? Alex—I can't believe you are interested in the 'inner' woman?" "Pablo—don't discourage him!" chided Marianna. Don Pablo put his palms up in surrender.

After dinner, Pablo bade farewell and the two of us went upstairs to the hotel's front balcony. A cold Bohemia with lime and a smoke accompanied me while Marianna stood, hanging over the rail. Contemplating her new life, I assumed. I didn't expect it when she turned to face me.

"Why didn't I know about your childhood, Alex?"

"Not something I talk about, Mari. There's a lot I don't want to remember."

"So that's how you learned to ignore the pain, the beatings . . . just leave the scene . . . ?" I nodded.

She was silent for a while. I hoped that would end it . . . but it didn't. Still leaning against the railing and staring at me, she spoke in a tone I'd never heard before. It almost sounded like awe, or reverence. "I wasn't able to fly away when they . . . the padres . . . uh—"

"I'm sorry, Mari."

"I know . . . I relived some of it when the general . . . you see, they held me down when I was a girl, too. Pairs of them. Two priests at once.

Over and over . . ." "I'm sorry," I repeated lamely, thinking of Eddy and his sad helplessness back when we were in Philadelphia.

"I know you are, Alex . . . can you show me how to do it . . . to fly away? Is that what your 'soul' thing is about?"

"Yes . . . I don't know if I can show you. But why would you want to? It's scary."

"To be invulnerable, Alex . . . I'd give almost anything. At times you are beyond reach. Safe. I want to go wherever that is . . ."

"It's lonely there."

"You should learn how to fight, Alex. You are able to take the kind of beating that kills most people. Why did you never learn how to defend yourself more actively?"

"I don't know. I never thought about it . . . I don't like violence, but I have a streak of it that frightens me. It's much less complicated to take the beating and just float away from it."

"Well, think about defending yourself." She smiled as I lit her cigarette. When we went back to our room, I started to pull down the second bed.

"Don't do that, Alex. Sleep with me. I want someone to *hold* me . . . *please*. Just hold me." In the chasm of the night, cradled in my arms, she came alive again. "Alex . . ."

"Hmmn."

"Do you want me?" "Uh huh . . ." I heard myself say before I awoke fully. "Hey, Mari. I thought you weren't ready for that . . ."

"Well, he hurt me, but I asked myself what *you* would do and decided I'd give him no sign of the pain. He twisted my nipple till it was black and blue. I thought my breast was going to explode. When I first screamed is when he . . . he . . ."

"Shh. You don't need to explain."

"But I do . . . when I went quiet and detached for a minute or two, he couldn't keep *it* up. He couldn't consummate the rape. *Gacho* (limp). That's when I first understood your power."

"I've got no power."

"Can you make slow love to me without hurting me? Gentle love."

"Mnn," I nodded as she opened her pajamas, cradling one mis-shapen, yellow-purple breast in her palm. "Kiss it softly, Alex. Do me gently . . . ah, yes, Alex . . . that's power. Love is power. Gentleness is power. Nothingness is power." Hypnotically she repeated her mantras over and over for the best part of an hour, till it came in convulsive gasps. "Power, power, ahh . . . power, ah, ah, ah. Ohhh!"

⁂

Mari's charcoals and sketch pads arrived before breakfast. Our money a bit later. She slept through it all, childlike and serene. Samuel brought a letter from La Sorpresa—rent and two meals daily for two in a rear corner room facing the frescoed pyramid at Mitla—eighty dollars for a month. Cash in advance, beginning December 1 (in two days). I signed for both of us, enclosing two five-hundred-peso notes, then went upstairs to check on Marianna.

She was in the shower, singing to herself, when I entered the room—it sounded like a lullaby again. But it was a good sign, I assumed. We ate a huge brunch then toured Oaxaca City, testing poor Samuel's patience.

The next day we joined a local tour to some of the famous handicrafts villages in the valley: Tlacolula, where we bought polished black clay ashtrays; Teotitlán del Valle, where we bought two colorful wool blankets for use at La Sorpresa; then Teotitlán del Camino, where Mari bought a pretty, flowered *huipil* (Indian blouse).

The following morning we moved into our new home and began our new life in the town of Mitla.

⁂

№ 7 MITLA—TOWN OF SOULS

MITLA, IN THE HEART of Oaxaca and just a few miles south of the Zapotecs' great mountain stronghold, now called Monte Albán, was already more than a thousand years old when Hernán Cortés first saw it in the 1520s.

Like many of the world's long-inhabited places, Mitla's core remained, while time and the effects of the Four Horsemen piled layer after layer of change atop its essence, like layers of icing on a cake.

Even the languages spoken there left it with complex flavors, like cheese crumbles on a salad. In Cortés's time Zapotec was the language spoken. In colonial times Spanish became more common when Mitla's Catholic church, itself built atop an earlier Classic period ruin, began to influence the speech heard in its dusty streets and shaded plazas.

In modern times archaeologists descended on Mitla to excavate its late eleventh-century frescoed pyramid, a hundred yards from the church. Before that the pyramid had been just another angular, over-grown hill with curious rocks peeking out from centuries' worth of nature's detritus. Even the Mixtecs had inhabited it for a while. Then the Aztecs made it a tribute-paying district that collapsed when the Spanish took over in the 1530s.

Years before, some anthropologists had romantically dubbed it the "Town of Souls." That drew ethnologists in the early twentieth century and both American and European missionaries in the mid-twentieth century: Mormons, Seventh-day Adventists, and Bible societies intent on both translating the King James version of the Bible into the native Zapotec tongue and rendering unto Jesus the Indian souls they imagined he craved.

Souls had inadvertently become Mitla's primary commodity, drawing to it the restless, the aristocratically arrogant, the always "right," the soulless, and the spiritually obsessed from afar. Another of the soulless, I was no different. Even Marianna entered the church as we passed it on our way to La Sorpresa. I waited out in the churchyard while she knelt inside, praying for the new life she had dared to imagine.

❧❧

The Hacienda Sorpresa had been reborn from a late colonial hacienda's "great house" that stood about three hundred yards from the church, and within sight of the ornate, flat-topped "pyramid" that jutted up from a dusty plazuela at one side of the village, startling newcomers, who expect "ruins" to be remote and inaccessible.

Samuel didn't accompany us to the hacienda itself. "I'll come to town separately and visit my family. An uncle has a house within sight of the hacienda. I'll stay there. Don't acknowledge me unless I walk up to you."

Mitla's dusty streets, shaded by huge *ahuehuete* trees, were like a step back in time. Laden burros led by huarache-wearing drovers drifted past, carrying net panniers full of firewood, corn, pottery, and items we couldn't identify.

A group of Indian men lounged in front of a small store built into the corner of a huge, thick-walled adobe compound. They stared but made no overt sign of recognition.

As we crossed the street to the hacienda's huge front portal, a local, Spanish-speaking big shot cruised through in his 1957 Chevy Bel Air hardtop, white over turquoise, tooting for us to step aside and let him pass. "*Pinches turistas* (Frigging tourists)," he snarled as we jumped to avoid being run over.

Moments later, mister big shot passed the Indians in front of the store, tooted his horn frantically to scatter them, even though they weren't in the way, and shouted, "*¡Pinches Indios incultos!*" when he didn't get the frightened respect he assumed they owed him.

The hacienda's beautiful forecourt provided a timeless haven from the street. Red tiled roofs jutted out over the shady courtyard. Geraniums, marigolds, and gladiolas in big, brightly painted pots were everywhere, wrapping the dozen iron and glass tables with warmth and color. An ancient carved stone fountain bubbled in the courtyard and lush, blood-red bougainvillea cascaded down one wall.

Beyond the courtyard a *sala*, or public room, was furnished in late nineteenth-century dark wood and formal sofas. The three-foot-thick walls gave it a cool, peaceful hush. The fourteen-foot beamed ceilings contributed to the sense that every room was immense.

Our room was in the rear, just off the shadiest corner of the court-yard. About eighteen feet long by fourteen wide, the room had a tall, iron-barred window facing northeast—cool shade to soften the warm Oaxacan climate.

An age-worn red tiled floor, decorated roof beams, and several leather and wood chairs arranged around an ample table filled one end of the room. Two single beds, an ornate dressing table between them, held down the other end. One immense carved cedar *ropero* (wardrobe) served as the only closet. The adjacent bathroom, shared by two other guest rooms, opened onto the courtyard.

Marianna was enchanted. "Even lovelier than the Hotel Victoria . . . ooh, look—what a view from the window . . . this really is *old* Mexico. It's so peaceful here. Can we bring more flowers into the room?"

"Sure, make it like home. But I get that table for my schoolwork."

We ate lunch, soup first, then rice with tomato, chile, onion, and cilantro, a fried egg perched on top, mashed black beans on the side, and fresh corn tortillas. For dessert, they served flan, a traditional caramel-ized egg custard. Large limeades and a small demitasse of dark, nutty cof-fee went with the meal—at a menu price of U.S.$1.40 each, it would have been cheap even if it hadn't been in the package deal with our room.

Our "Thrift Special" gave us the choice of any breakfast or the set lunch for our first meal, then dinner for the second one, but neither Mari nor I were early morning people, so it was destined to be early lunch and a late-ish dinner for the next several months.

After lunch, I went into the museum and asked how I could contact Dr. John Paddock, one of my professors at the Americas up in El DF. He was temporarily excavating at a site called Maquilxochitl ("Five Flower," in Nahuatl) in a nearby tongue of the valley.

If I could get some dig time, I might be able to keep the next quarter's schoolwork going, unbroken. John's house, it turned out, was in Oaxaca City. They gave me the address.

Meanwhile Mari disappeared, exploring. When she returned several hours later, she looked rather different. She'd bought a big, brightly printed silk scarf, which she'd wrapped around her face, like an East Indian Tamil woman, and had pulled her hair back, covering it with another smaller scarf. A huarache-clad Indian man followed her through the door carrying several large packages.

She'd gotten a cast-off easel somewhere and a narrow pot that stood at least two feet tall. "Oh, Alex. I met a German artist near the market— she loaned me the easel, but I had to buy a pot from her . . . I want flowers everywhere."

"Sure . . . but why the sari-like outfit?"

"Samuel snuck up behind me and asked me to cover up. He said people shouldn't be able to spot me so easily if they were outsiders. But I don't feel at all threatened here. It's lovely . . . and the Indian women are much friendlier than the old men over at the store."

She, the Indian porter, and the easel all disappeared, single-file, into the rear of the cool, shaded courtyard. The patio was alive with bright colors. Shy orange marigolds and bold, erect pink hollyhocks glistened in the flickering sunlight. Long-tailed hummingbirds darted about, hovering above the tables. One hung in mid-air while penetrating a cluster of succulent red bougainvillea blossoms with its long tongue.

Those tongues had once been on the Aztecs' tribute lists. In 1520 the emperor Montezuma had entertained Cortés and his entourage in Tenochtitlán, now Mexico City. During the massive feast, the Spaniards were served an exotic dish made from hummingbird tongues. I was still trying to imagine just how many thousands of those dark, cat-whisker-sized tongues it would take to fill a serving bowl when Mari returned.

"I want a drink, Alex. Sit by the fountain with me." She was in a snuggle mood. "Can we eat late this evening? I am going to the church up the road at Tlacolula with Samuel's niece."

"Is this a spiritual awakening, Mari?"

"I think so. I feel like a girl again." Marianna smiled back at me, pulling my hand to her face. "I'm going to start sketching tomorrow, Alex . . . any suggestions?"

"Yes—set up by the creek where you get a corner view of the stone mosaics. I think it would be a good spot—and the ahuehuete trees by the irrigation ditch are huge—lots of shade to work in."

We sat by the fountain and held hands as the hummingbirds took their late afternoon meal. I leaned back and let my eyes wander upward. The warm brick tones of the old courtyard floor blended into the deep reds of the bougainvillea, to be replaced by the buff tones of the thick *tabique* (rough brick) roof tiles. Above, a turquoise blue sky radiated its warmth and the distinct cypress smell of ahuehuete drifted into our little garden of Eden.

When Mari returned from Tlacolula we went for a walk, pausing to gaze as the late evening sky transformed from the last vestiges of peach, pink, and narrow ribbons of purple into a brilliant, dark azure. We stopped by the ruins' outer walls to hold hands. As if in response, the azure blue morphed into an exquisite indigo.

Most of the Indian houses had gone dark by the time we returned to La Sorpresa. The creatures of the night had taken over—naguales, bats, owls, and the ever-present witches to whom the Zapotec still attributed unexpected misfortune.

We were the last to be served dinner. *Sopa seca de arroz*, spiced with cilantro and savory bits of chicken, then black beans sprinkled with goat cheese, followed by big bowls of corn soup and stacks of fresh corn tortillas. Dessert was a huge platter of sliced pineapple, mango, papaya, banana, and sweet oranges, with limes. "*Lo que queda de la fruta del día—llévelo a su cuarto* (The leftovers of today's fruit—take it to your room)," winked Ramona—the heavy-set waitress who turned out to be one of Samuel's cousins. "Thank you so much," beamed Mari. "I love the fruit."

Ramona chuckled. "Young lovers get hungry in the night." Mari blushed, looking down. Ramona squeezed her shoulder, then unexpectedly planted a matronly kiss on her forehead. Mari's response surprised me. "Hold me, Ramona." Ramona folded Mari into her arms and rocked her. "Thank you, Ramona. Thanks so much," Mari whispered back.

"You belong here, child. Your *tono* is close by . . . Samuel explained you to us. You are safe here. The *güeros* (white guys) cannot get you here. Continue to be brave and all will be well." "Thank you, Ramona," I put in. She looked at me. "Rock her. Hold her often, fierce one. Love is powerful. *No sea nahuat* (Don't be silly—i.e., like an Aztec speaker)."

"*Muy bien* . . . thanks for the advice, Ramona. By the way, how many in your family did Samuel explain us to?"

"We are nearly seventy strong in the immediate family." "Big family," I commented, raising my eyebrows.

"Yes, we have done well . . . and because of Samuel's big salary in Mexico, the rest of us have been able to stay here. Only one cousin lives in Mexico and works as a maid. It is hard being an Indian in the cities. Samuel has spared most of us from all that . . ."

The next morning I helped Mari set up her easel under the great ahuehuete trees next to the creek, then went back to the courtyard to wait for John Paddock. John was late, as usual, but in an upbeat mood. About 5'6", stocky, and balding, he was a dyed-in-the-wool expatriate. Brilliant and eccentric, he had several projects going.

"Well, Professor. Can you use me on a dig?"

"Certainly, Mr. Alexander . . . but for the moment it's got to be some mundane trench and backfill work up at Yagul. I'm awaiting INAH's approval for another trench at Maquilxochitl."

"I'll take anything, as long as I can stay enrolled. I'm not supposed to be 'found' right now and am down here for the next twelve weeks."

"I know. Julia Baker briefed me . . . and I approve, or I wouldn't be here." He continued, "Start day after tomorrow—7 AM sharp at the ticket kiosk. Yagul." I watched him go. Rumor had it that he'd paid a huge price in professional and personal abuse in the States during the late forties and early fifties—the McCarthy era. Those rumors also had it that he was gay and a conscientious objector. All that inconsequential garbage that sets the sexually and socially insecure on edge in the States, where one is supposed to have "rights."

I was still processing the irony that he'd immigrated to a country where he couldn't vote, where the average man on the street hated queers, and where he made one-third the salary that he'd have made in the States—just to get to a world that let him be who he was, whatever that really meant . . . and there I stood, aged twenty . . . fearing the same damn thing he did: "Anything—just don't send me back!" *How many Americans like us are down here?* I wondered.

I waved as John stepped into his little canvas-roofed Fiat wagon, then walked through the small plaza, crossed the creeklike Mitla River and the one-lane paved road out to the Tehuantepec highway, and marched on into the prehistoric part of the town.

Mari was no longer alone on the nearly dry ditch bank. Two Indian women had set up their impromptu craft stands—one on either side of her. Both turned out to be members of Samuel's extended family. We didn't have just one bodyguard in Mitla—we had a small army of Zapotec speakers.

The women nodded as I approached. Mari turned and smiled. "Come see, Alex!" The gray outlines of the scene had already been penciled in. The perspective was superb, but she was still tweaking proportions. The corner of Mexico's most spectacular stone mosaic wall was framed on one side by Mitla's Catholic church, the other by the overhang of an immense ahuehuete's drooping branches.

In the foreground an oversized hummingbird dipped its tongue into a hibiscus. The hummingbirds were to become the signature of her "Mitla" series.

"Damn—you're *good*, Mari . . . better than I imagined." That earned me a surprisingly lustful and lingering French kiss—right there in public. The slender woman selling necklaces made from polished fragments of six-hundred-year-old Mixtec pottery covered her mouth and tittered. "He's *big*, señorita . . . made for love."

"Shhh, Luciana—he speaks very good Spanish," Marianna giggled back. I turned to the lady and took a bow. She hooted; meanwhile her companion, stationed on the other side of Marianna, buried her face in a rebozo, laughing, "You got caught, cousin."

In much of Indian Mexico sex wasn't at the same level of taboo as it was either in Catholic, Hispanic Mexico or in the States . . . and nowhere was sex more in the open than in the area from Oaxaca City south to the town of Juchitán, beyond Tehuantepec. In many regional Indian communities unmarried young men favored slightly older women with babies—widowed, divorced, or never married—on the theory that they already knew the ropes, avoiding the delicacies of "breaking them in."

Mari was absolutely luminous as she clung to me. "Give me an hour,

Alex; I'll meet you in the courtyard. I don't want to stop yet." I went on into the ruins, passing through the first groups of buildings.

Because of the little river and the rich bottom soil, Mitla had been founded by the Zapotecs several centuries after the birth of Christ. It grew in size after their capital at Monte Albán, twenty-five miles away as the crow flies, went into decline in the AD 700s. Mitla flourished uninterrupted until the late 1200s or early 1300s when the expanding Mixtec population from the Mixteca Alta (high Mixteca) near the convent of Yanhuitlán pushed south, displacing the Zapotecs for a century or so. The Zapotecs returned just in time to inherit the "Aztec problem," then came the Spanish conquistadores less than a century later.

Mitla's little tongue of the Oaxaca Valley was encircled by rugged mountains averaging 6,000 to 8,000 feet in elevation. Due east the dormant volcano Zempoaltépetl, at over 11,000 feet, provided a backdrop to the steep hills of the Zapotec Sierra. Just fifteen miles from where I stood lay villages where one still had to walk narrow mountain trails to gain access. Even in the bigger mountain towns, with names like Cajonos, Villa Alta, and Yalalag, Zapotec was the only daily language.

To the south lay the rugged Mixe Indian country, where no roads, no electricity, and little Spanish was spoken. This was Indian Mexico.

Ghosts and spirits were everywhere. Snakes, frogs, birds, ocelot, even *lechu* (rabbits) were candidates for one's animal souls—tonos or naguales, depending on the village and echoes of ancient cultures.

In many ways time had stood still in the rugged canyon country that rose above the three rich valleys, intersecting just south of Oaxaca City. But even in those accessible valleys, influences on daily life ranged from traditional Indian to rich, sophisticated French and German refugee from both Europe's gray winter skies and the more irritating conventions of European class systems.

Just five miles to the north of Mitla, villages were often divided into a Mixtec and a Zapotec "quarter." In others, especially in the eastern valley that snaked down to Zaachila, there were separate, small plazas for the Zapotecs, the Mixtecs, and the mestizos.

In a few of the larger towns north of Oaxaca the stunning colonial period townhouses of rich Spanish-Mexican land barons dominated small plazas—each house the size of a respectable, modern, twenty-room hotel. One of the towns up north was still referred to as "Little

Paris" for the late nineteenth-century Parisian wine, perfumes, and furniture once imported in massive quantities for its ruling elite.

Even as I stood in Mitla in 1961, amid a complex combination of Zapotec people, a few mixed-blood Mixtecs, an assortment of other mestizos, and European expatriates, more than 90 percent of all the farmable land in the state of Oaxaca was in the hands of about 2 percent of the population—rich Mexicans who still squeezed obscenely cheap labor out of "their" regional Mixtec and Zapotec Inditos (little Indians).

The history of this region included indigenous wars, massive epidemics of syphilis and smallpox after the Spanish arrived, political conflict when Mexico declared its independence from Spain . . . and "Indian uprisings" again in the late nineteenth and early twentieth centuries. These agonies and twists of fate had all left a rich harvest of souls floating in the ether, just beyond reach. For more than a thousand years, harvesting souls was Oaxaca's most enduring enterprise.

Oaxaca was a place where one could, on any given day, either find a soul, or lose one. The cosmic excitement of it had brought Mari "into the sunlight," as she said, sitting down to lunch in the courtyard. "It's like someone opened a door for me and I passed into eternal sunlight. I sensed God this morning as I watched butterflies and hummingbirds along the stream." I must have looked unconvinced. "Really, Alex . . . I *did*."

"I'm not skeptical, Mari—just envious." She leaned forward. "Hold me, Alex." While lunch went cold, Mari went hot, dragging me to our room. Starved, I ravished her as if she were the meal. She chanted her "power" mantra again, then dressed quickly and ran out to the table, giggling as she wolfed down the cold food. Ramona hugged her on the way past. "Be happy, daughter—it brings the Virgin joy!" "Daughter?" I asked.

"Yes, Alex, Ramona and the others decided I needed a mom. I love it. I feel like I'm ten again. Bathed in good fortune . . . do you know how old I am, Alex?" I shook my head. "Guess!" *Hmmn, twenty-five or -six,* I told myself. *Better shave a couple off that for goodwill.* "Twenty-three?"

She squealed. "Twenty-eight, Alex. I'm twenty-eight. Sunday is my twenty-ninth birthday . . . and you think I'm much younger. I love it!"

Sometimes women shouldn't tell you everything, I thought. Twenty-nine came as a shock. She was nearly half again older than I was. The idea of it unnerved me even if the reality of it didn't. Twenty minutes later Mari ran off through the courtyard. "I've got to finish my rough sketch . . . tomorrow I want to add some color."

Ramona came by again. "You are fortunate, joven, she is a treasure. So full of life . . . she will bring your soul home . . . and do not worry . . . she is still young enough to bear you many children. They will be strong and happy. You are blessed."

"Don't frighten me like that, Ramona . . . I'd make a terrible father . . . and kids make me nervous. You have to be responsible for them."

"That will change, Juan. With time, all changes. You still have so much to learn about life and love. Let her teach you. Right now her joy is powerful . . . but you must also learn to protect her. She has talked much of you. Shall I send my uncle Mateo to see you?"

"Who is he?"

"He is a warrior. Ask Samuel. He is a fighter . . ."

"I don't use guns or a knife, Ramona."

"Neither does he. Ask Samuel." Later that afternoon I went over to the store across the square. The Indian men parted for me, but were otherwise stoic. I bought smokes, tinned juices for the room, matches, and a large bag of salt-dried prunes for the next day at Yagul. As I paid at the counter, Samuel's voice came from behind. "Ramona suggested we chat. I'll wait for you out here."

Once outside, Samuel took my arm and steered me to a private spot under a nearby ahuehuete. "I agree with Ramona, joven . . . you will need to protect yourself . . . and your woman. The paper will not provide for you when they no longer sell thousands of extras—I've seen all this before."

"So tell me, who is this Mateo?"

"My great uncle . . . *don* Mateo . . . he's a very traditional man. A Zapotec priest and one of the last warriors. As a young man in the 1920s he fought the Mexicans at Huajuapan. He charged their riflemen with nothing more than a machete and his fighting stick."

"And what is it he can teach me?"

"Defense. The stick fighting. With a *bastón* (staff) and slings. He has agreed . . . it would be a great honor for you. Some of us would like to watch. We have lost much knowledge of these things. Besides, you will need an interpreter. Mateo understands Mexican (Spanish) but often refuses to utter even a word of it."

"When, where?"

"Tomorrow, after Yagul—just before dinner—in the ruins here, once they close to the public. The caretaker is another cousin," Samuel laughed.

The next day was a long one in the sun at Yagul. Professor Paddock always took good care of his workers, so lunch arrived in big metal buckets of rice, beans, and tortillas. Mild goat cheese, fruit, and hard-boiled eggs rounded it out. The iced lime water was plentiful, so well fed but knotted from a hard day's work, I stood by the highway waiting for the local bus south to Mitla, rubbing my sore arm muscles.

I met Mari by the creek, gave her a quick hug, and told her I had "things" to do in the ruins before dinner. Her sketch was already alight with color. The ancient walls in front of me had been rendered in subtle umber tones, the mosaic work standing out in her rich three-dimensional shading. The hummingbird's green and ruby feather patterns were stunning. The rest of the sketch was still gray.

"Damn! That's good!" Marianna smiled back at me. "I'll come get you in an hour and a half—at the gate into the ruins."

"Make it two hours."

Samuel and half a dozen other men, mostly young, waited for me at the gate. Handshakes went around, then I was ushered inside—"To the right, *al templo* (to the colonnaded temple)."

In the courtyard a little old guy about five feet tall and one hundred pounds, if that, watched me intently as I walked toward him. The middle-aged Indian man in a black and gray serape standing next to him introduced me.

"Don Mateo Dxubhá. I present joven Juan Alejandro. Norteamericano." He repeated the same in pure Zapotec while the old boy checked me out. Probably mid-sixties, he wore baggy, calf-length white cotton pants, a loose, flowing local cotton shirt, and a head sash adorned with a mosaic design rather like the stone frieze-work thirty yards away. Samuel prompted me, "Thank him for receiving you. I'll address him properly for you. Do not shake his hand unless he extends his . . . he is sacred. It's his right." "Thank you, sir, for being willing to receive me. May I be worthy of your graciousness," I said in my most polite Spanish. "Very good!" said Samuel, slapping me on the back and translating. The old man nodded and said something guttural. Samuel explained. "Take off your outer shirt and extend your arm, palm up."

I did as requested. The old man stepped forward, said something, and handed me a four-foot shaft just a bit thicker than a broom handle. "Protect yourself with it," instructed Samuel. Thirty seconds later, I lay on the ground, panting, a painful knot forming on my left thigh. "You OK?" asked Samuel.

"Yep. But now that he's proven he's faster than a snake, I want to see it in slow motion." When Samuel translated, the old man laughed, grinned, and reached down to help me up. His grip was like iron, his coal-black eyes warm and intelligent. He lifted me easily.

"He's powerful, Samuel—it's deceptive." Samuel passed it on to don Mateo, who grinned in apparent satisfaction. "He responds, 'Always be underestimated . . . but you already know that, young one.'" The old man's shirt came off, courtesy of his attendant, who handled it reverently as if it were a bishop's vestments. Though aged and leather skinned, he was still tightly muscled. He extended his stick slowly toward me. "Do as he does," said Samuel.

An hour later I'd learned two basic movements and was even more in awe of don Mateo's speed. It was almost impossible to focus on his rapid jabs. I commented on it. "Speed is the secret, he says," Samuel translated.

"He says they will make you a longer stick if you become his student, but it will take a few days . . . you are taller than the Mexicans at Huajuapan, he says—that is a compliment. He will accept you as a student, but there are conditions: you are to pray daily, drink no alcohol while training, and his fee will be one hundred pesos per week—five lessons a week. Five weeks. You will meet him here at the same time tomorrow, if you accept. Do you accept?"

"Whew! Expensive. Will it be worth it?" Samuel conveyed the message. Don Mateo shrugged, grunting in Zapotec. "It depends on you, he says," Samuel translated. I paused to think. That unnerved Samuel, who pressed me for an answer. "Don't make him wait . . . just say yes or no—it's your only chance."

"OK. Yes, then." In response, the old man's hand shot out to accept mine. He didn't even wait for a translation. He was two-thirds my size, at most. But half again as strong. I met him the next evening as planned, picking up several more bruises. That night Mari freaked out when she saw the angry welts across my ribs.

"God, Alex, what happened . . . is someone after us again?" I explained. She didn't like it. I argued back, "You are the one who urged me to learn how to fight . . . not just take the beatings." "I was frightened," she protested.

"I'm going to continue a while, Mari. It'll be all right." The next day I mentioned Mari's fright over the bruises. Samuel had a word with don Mateo's assistant and I got fewer lumps from then on.

My own stick was presented me the following week. About five feet long and made of a dark, dense wood, it had a strap on one end and raw-hide bindings in two places—at its center balance point and where I'd hold it as a walking stick. It also had small brass caps on either end.

Three weeks later I took down the old man for the first time. It came as a surprise to both of us. Don Mateo had begun taunting me in what turned out to be very good Spanish. "You daydream like a little girl. Concentrate!" Erlindo, one of the mouthier twelve- or thirteen-year-old Zapotec boys, tittered and called me a mariposa (fairy).

Pissed, I turned to face Erlindo. Don Mateo's stick flicked into the soft pocket at the back of my knee. I sagged into a kneeling position just as Erlindo raised his stick to take a poke at me. The tone of his voice was like Big Jack's, right before he had beat the shit out of Eddy when we were kids. *Goddamn bully!* My stick went out into a low arc, jerking Erlindo's out of his hands, then rose like lightning, coming to rest in the V of his crotch with a dull thump.

The little prick went down like a sack of rocks, gasping, just as don Mateo's stick caught me behind the other knee. Down, I rolled to the left, swinging my stick in a sweeping arc just above ground level. The old man toppled into the dirt.

For a moment everything was quiet. It seemed unreal—I'd lost it, lashing out in anger. But the old man cackled, reaching to me for a hand up. "*Pues, nuestro guerrero namistu tú, se despierta* (Well, our green-eyed warrior awakes)—focus the anger instead of fleeing from it and you shall learn to fight."

Don Mateo was stern, but businesslike. Not an easy man to gauge, but that incident seemed to bring him into focus for me. In five weeks, I could prevent him from bruising me and had learned to concentrate and flip the Zapotec boys nearly as quickly as don Mateo had dropped me on my ass the first day.

By week six, his gift to me without fee, I'd learned how to break both a knife or machete-wielder's grip on their weapon, then immobilize them from front, side, or behind.

By then, the young guys wanted to learn killing blows, so the old man asked me if I wanted to learn. "No. I want to neutralize someone. Smashing a wrist is one thing, but killing or paralyzing is not for me." Samuel translated, Erlindo rolled his eyes and groaned, commenting that I was still a garden-variety pussy.

Don Mateo merely listened to my response, handed his stick to his attendant, and hugged me. "Good. My son! Very good! Then I have nothing more to teach you. Practice often . . . the speed and balance are critical . . ."

Erlindo snickered again. Irritated, don Mateo stopped mid-sentence, turned toward him with a scowl, and shut him up with a lightning-fast hit in the solar plexus. Erlindo on the ground groaning again, the old man shrugged and pulled me aside.

"Your woman is now Ramona's adopted daughter. Ramona baptized her in Tlacolula . . . she loves you and seeks our women's guidance. Ramona asked me about you. Now go, your woman is waiting."

Erlindo, still on the ground, couldn't resist one last taunt as I turned to leave. "*Oye*, gringo—they talk about what kind of lover you are, too." Samuel was instantly pissed. "You shame us, you insolent boy. Besides, your fingers will curl permanently if you don't soon find a woman who will have you."

Don Mateo laughed at Samuel's insult. I turned back. "Thank you for calling me 'son.'" He nodded, still laughing, and gave Erlindo a light, cobralike jab in the nuts, quickly restoring respect among the other teenage Zapotecs, who'd begun snickering at Erlindo's bravado.

It was already dark when I reached the gate to the ruins. Marianna was waiting. "This is a big day for me, Alex. I have five sketches finished. It's too dark to show them tonight, but can we take a break tomorrow and celebrate?"

We walked through the dry December grass toward the great ahuehuete trees, a cool breeze drifting down from the *cerros* above us. Marianna stopped halfway home, cleared her throat, and whispered to me in the dark. "I think I'm pregnant, Alex. Ramona says it will be a girl . . ."

I panicked. "Are you sure?" I asked, the fear in my voice clear. My head spun as she faced me. "Yes—is it OK?" Fireflies rose from the strip of wet grass tucked along the creek bank.

Twinkling, their fluorescent yellow-green jetted me back to a summer night long past. The rushing wind washed across my cheeks and Betty Anne waved to me from below, a ball of fireflies nestled in one outstretched palm. She looked up at me . . .

"Come to me, John. I love you." I floated through the breeze and descended right in front of her.

"I'm going away tomorrow. To a 'school.' Please remember me, John. Promise?"

Mari tugged at my sleeve. "Is it so bad that I'm pregnant?"

"No. Yes. I don't know. I saw the fireflies. I was remembering . . ." She took my face in her palms. "Oh . . . you have tears coming down your cheeks, Alex."

"The fireflies are talking to me. I'm frightened, Mari. Will you disappear like Betty Anne?"

"Don't be afraid, Alex . . . oh, you poor thing . . . I love you so." She wrapped her arms around me. "Let's watch the fireflies." Smothered by her, I wriggled free and turned back toward the creek bed as she stood near me and watched the phosphorescent flickering in the grass.

"Love!" I called out in English as I struck the ground with the butt of my stick. The fireflies brightened. "Betty Anne," I whispered, and a thousand tiny blue-green lights went into instant overload. The hair on the back of my neck bristled and I shivered.

Mari squeezed me. The breeze sharpened and a host of fireflies swirled up into the trees. They blinked rhythmically above us as we passed underneath, crossing the creek.

❦

In the courtyard of La Sorpresa, Mari's face was warm and gentle in the candlelight. The fountain burbled and a breeze rustled through the bougainvillea. I leaned forward and held her face in my hands. "Don't let this ever end," she pleaded, looking as if she might cry. "Explain your feelings to me, please," I asked.

"I am 'happy,' as opposed to 'content' or 'satisfied'—for the very first time since I was a child. I don't want to wake up and find it all gone again . . . do you understand, Alex?" Her face wrinkled like a kid's before it cries.

"Yes. Absolutely. I can't feel what you feel here in Mitla, but I envy you."

"Is Mitla the problem, Alex?"

"I'm not sure, Mari . . . perhaps I'm the problem. Too bottled up. Too wary. I'll get over it one of these days . . . at least, I think so." Mari frowned.

"Sometimes I wish you had Pablo's passion, Alex. At times you seem so . . . oh, I don't know. Let's drop *it*."

It? Well, whatever "it" was didn't hit me right. I couldn't get a handle on her thoughts, so I shrugged.

Ramona served dinner. "Don Mateo sends his regards—he saw the *ca bacuza gui* rise from the acequia as you passed." "Ca bacuza gui?" I asked. "Fireflies," said Marianna. "I've been studying *didxazá*—Zapotec—with my companions at the creek." "They are a good omen," said Ramona, smiling. "Often they announce a pregnancy."

"I've already told him," laughed Marianna. Ramona grinned. "And he hasn't run away . . . that, too, is a good omen." The two women enjoyed themselves while I kept my doubts about the reality of Mari's pregnancy to myself. This revelation, like her recent religious stirrings, struck me as a possible flight of fancy.

Several days earlier she had chattered about her hummingbird sketches. "Sigrid says they are good enough for the Louvre . . . I want to be a famous artist . . . be like Frida Kahlo. Have my own gallery." I had replied with, "Oh, Mari, everyone knows Frida went both ways. She was a classic head case. Besides, who's Sigrid? . . . And how does that fit in with life here? I thought this is what you wanted."

That comment, and question, had set Mari on edge. She hadn't spoken for an entire day. Now, just twenty-four hours later, she was daydreaming about perfect happiness, a pregnancy . . . and me. Was I supposed to instantly become Mr. Sensitive? Or, perhaps I wasn't part of her future plans at all. With women, I'd learned, one could never be certain.

Meanwhile, I quietly grieved again for the missing Betty Anne. *Where is she? Is she still alive? Would she remember me?* My reverie must have been obvious, for Marianna suddenly stopped chattering with Ramona and took my hand. "What are you daydreaming about?"

"Nothing. Why?"

"It's Betty Anne again, isn't it, Alex?" Mari mothered me. She didn't wait for an answer. "She's OK, Alex. No matter where she is, Betty Anne lives in your heart." I wasn't certain which frightened me the most—that I might become a father . . . or that someone was beginning to read my thoughts. I wasn't prepared for either.

Ramona, curious, asked Mari something in Zapotec. I was sure it was a question because of the lilting "*la*" that came at the end of the sentence. Marianna answered Ramona—at least I assumed so since I heard the number *tapa* (four) somewhere in there. I'd guessed right . . . Ramona put her hand on my shoulder.

"A lonely child's first love is precious . . . but those who are fortunate enough to be remembered—live. They live. They know they are remembered." Ramona's ample bosom folded around me. She squeezed, running her work-worn fingers across my forehead. "I never really touched a white boy before—so soft . . . yet Mateo says, so strong." The hair on the back of my neck stood up again, responding to the first genuine motherly caress I'd ever had.

Mexico—in just one year, I'd experienced my first passion, my first "mom," and the first time anyone besides me had ever worried about Betty Anne. And now I might be a father. Might *is the operative word*, cackled the Voice.

When Mari and I went off to bed, I threw open the huge screenless windows, watching the Milky Way drift past. "Waiting for fireflies?" asked Mari, snuggling me.

"They make me happy," I murmured. Her tongue caressed my throat, lingering as if she were absorbing the beat of my heart. "And you make me happy, *baculu naro' ba.*"

"There you go again—showing off—what is 'baculu na . . .'?"

". . . 'Naro' ba'—*baculu naro' ba* means 'big walking stick.' That's what don Mateo calls you."

"You sound amused, Mari."

"I am—I speak much more Zapotec than you and 'big walking stick' is a double entendre. While you ponder that, let me feel *xpaculu naro' ba.*"

"I think I got it, Mari."

"Good . . . now *I'll* get it, no?" She giggled. This time her mantra came as an unexpected experiment, "Fireflies, fireflies, fireflies, ahhh . . . ooh, *Betty Anne*, gasp . . . Betty . . ." As odd as it seems, I deeply resented sharing Betty Anne with her at all. Betty Anne and Eddy were mine. They were me. Without them I had no definition, no boundaries, no permanent referents.

፼

№ 8   *Excélsior Reigns*

When I returned to La Sorpresa from Yagul the next afternoon, I headed straight to our room for a shower. Warm water flowed only when the hacienda's black-painted roof tank was heated up by the sun. So I was in the shower, luxuriating under soapsuds and lukewarm water, when Marianna popped in. "Hurry, Alex! Pablo Virreyes is here and has news for us . . ."

I rushed and found them seated at a shaded corner table in the courtyard. Don Pablo had the usual entourage: Samuel, another bodyguard, his driver, two photographers, and another new, twentyish personal assistant, Mirelle. "*Et vous français* (Are you French)?" I asked her as she pulled a chair out for me.

"*Mais oui. Parlez-vous français?*"

"A little," I smiled. Don Pablo shrugged as Marianna shot him "the look." He begged his pardon in English. "Darling, you *know* how I am . . . it *is* what life is all about." Marianna shook her head. "Oh, Pablo, you will wake up one day . . . and . . . and . . . be so lonely, I fear." A frown flickered across his face, then he waved it off breezily. "I'll face that when it happens . . . *if* it happens." To break the train of thought, he snapped his fingers at Mirelle, who retrieved his flamboyantly tooled leather attaché case. Don Pablo pulled out a sheaf of clipped newspapers.

"Look at these, kids! Your series has sold nearly half a million extras and increased daily circulation by 7 percent across the country." He unfolded the first article and laid it out on the table. A half-page photo of us raising our wine glasses at dinner in the Hotel Victoria graced the upper left of a center foldout. Below were some juicy quotes, the offer of a prize, and a recap of the whole story, including the German mystery woman and wanton sex-capades in Veracruz. Hell, even *I'd* have bought the extras if the general store in Mitla carried *Excélsior.*

But Marianna wasn't amused by this anymore. "Thanks for all you've done, Pablo, but I'd like a private life now. I just want to stay here forever. Do pastels and enjoy life."

Pablo Virreyes, for the first time, was at a loss for words, staring back and forth between Marianna and me. "It's a joke. Right, darling? . . . You are a city girl!"

"No. It's anything but a joke . . . it's wonderful here. I finally have something of a family—and here, look at my artwork!"

Even I hadn't seen Marianna's finished sketches—she'd become secretive about them after I teased her about the hummingbird theme one afternoon.

There were five completed pieces, each a remarkable and different aspect of old Mitla. The ruins, the adjacent church's facade, the Catholic graveyard, the creek and ahuehuetes, and finally, the group of Indian men in front of the store, all the faces cleverly in shadow, so as not to steal their souls by portraying them in recognizable detail.

Urbane, unflappable, oh-so-sophisticated don Pablo Virreyes was speechless for once. He stared slowly at each one, then finally looked up at Marianna. "I'd no idea. None . . . these are stunning. This is *great* art! You should have a gallery of your own . . . some place civilized like Coyoacán."

"Really?"

Virreyes nodded, "I could help someday."

"Oh, thank you, Pablo. I've craved your respect for a long time. It's a joy to have it!"

"You have?"

"Yes, Pablo . . . you are an original. I like originals."

"And young Alex?"

"He, too, is an original . . . and *very* complicated . . . you lost because he found beauty in me when I was maimed." Pablo nodded in understanding.

"Well, then . . . one last piece of business?" Mari's brow wrinkled, so he pleaded, "Please, darling? We'd like to do a big follow-up. The U.S. Embassy remains arrogant, even though Interpol finally identified a vanished East German agent who may have murdered their attaché."

"What kind of story?" I asked.

"Oh, the usual. We'd like to squeeze a last round of extras based on the East German agent and the attaché's blond wife . . . we finally uncovered a photo of her in Veracruz . . . wow! They've both fled now—Brazil, we think. Cuba is also possible . . . then more about you two—recapping how your lives were altered, the two of you trapped like flies as the paranoid Americans lashed out at two innocent students."

"I don't want publicity, don Pablo—some of this might get back to the States."

Marianna looked at me quizzically, then took Pablo's hand and looked him in the eye. "No, Pablo." He leaned back, started to nod in assent, then gave it one more shot. "What if we featured several of your charcoals with your photos—featuring 'the talented artist'?" Marianna wrinkled her face and sighed.

"A final payment of ten thousand pesos (eight hundred U.S. dollars) between you . . . and a few phone calls to DF galleries, even Sanborn's." Marianna didn't move a muscle, not in her body, not in her face. I think she was about to say no when Pablo upped the offer. "Twenty thousand . . . what would that buy here, Samuel?" don Pablo asked over his shoulder.

"A large traditional house with small courtyard, and a garden plot." That hooked Marianna, who nodded, looking at me to see if I objected. "If it's OK with Alex. I'd love a house here." Against all instincts, I caved in, even as the Voice dumped on me. *Sap!*

"OK, Pablo—as long as I'm merely a footnote—nothing beyond the student things . . ." Mari added a couple conditions of her own. "Be discreet about where we are. No photo of the ruin walls sketch. They are like a tourist photo of this place." Pablo grinned.

"*Done.* Cash delivery tomorrow morning in Oaxaca City. Meet me there." He snapped his fingers again . . . "Photos, muchachos." Flashbulbs popped like champagne corks, momentarily erasing the magnificent sunset gathering above La Sorpresa's courtyard.

As Marianna and I walked that evening, I should have known that fate had not blessed our arrangement with *Excélsior* . . . there were no fireflies in the creek bed. I was angry at her response to don Pablo's "gallery" comment and said so. She was defensive. "Don't be a silly boy! I was only daydreaming." I left her there by the creek. She apologized profusely when, hours later, she finally slipped into our room.

⁂

Our money was handed over to us just before noon the next day . . . and by 5 PM that afternoon it had been spent in Mitla . . . on a partly furnished traditional house within sight of La Sorpresa that had once been rented to Bible missionaries.

Built of adobe-plastered stone, the house had twelve-foot-high ceilings, real glass windows, and three rooms: a long, narrow kitchen/dining room, a large bedroom, and a huge front room with five-foot windows facing the creek that flowed past the ruins a few hundred yards away.

A pleasant, partially roofed courtyard nestled in the shallow L formed by the kitchen. Both the courtyard and the front of the house were shaded by huge ahuehuete trees. Hollyhocks, white, pink, and ruby red, grew in the rear. Deep magenta bougainvillea cascaded over the dusty courtyard's one wall. Marianna was in heaven. She set up her easel there even before we moved in a few days later.

I had paying work with John Paddock through the coming spring, earning both the modest wage of twenty-five U.S. dollars a month, free lunch, and fieldwork credits.

John was also interested in the apparent tranquility of the valley's many Zapotec villages, which were in sharp contrast to the frustrating violence that so often stalked communities of Mexico's huge underclass. Marianna, because of her female Zapotec friends and growing command of the language, also got twenty-five dollars a month to keep daily journals in Mitla. John, a pacifist at heart, often invested scarce grant money in "peace studies."

The fifty U.S. dollars we earned a month were plenty for buses, food, bottled water, propane for the two-burner gas stove in our house, Mari's art supplies, and occasional meals out.

In reality we were rather well-off. Mari continued to make a bit of money typing for local artists and was frequently paid in food by the local Zapotecs for whom she both wrote letters and translated correspondence into Spanish.

On one such occasion, when she'd written a series of letters to officials to help one family secure a three-foot-wide stall in Oaxaca's city market, we were paid with a never-ending supply of limes, oranges, mangoes, bananas, or cherimoyas . . . whatever fruit was in season. Another commission of hers brought us four eggs every week. Our biggest food expenses were for sacks of brown rice, beans, coffee, and jugs of cooking oil.

The transition to private life occasionally gave me the jitters and set off the Voice. I'd no experience with any of this ordinary domestic stuff. Had Mari not had a personality I mostly understood, had she been "normal" instead of edgy, sometimes inaccessible, even bitchy when she felt insecure, I would have fled. Instead, she was often like Eddy: wistful, then frightened. Her nightmares comforted me. I could stroke her arms and rock her to sleep . . . all stuff I knew how to do. Then there was also Ramona to mother us both when she was around.

So, in an eccentric way, life was OK, but it—and my relationship to Mari—became more ritualized and less exciting. I walked out to the highway five mornings a week, and Mari devoted three days to her sketches. The other two were devoted to "peace studies." On Sundays Mari went to church in Tlacolula after we ate brunch either at home or at La Sorpresa—our once-in-a-while eat-out.

In the evenings Mari and I often walked over to La Sorpresa for coffee and conversation with visiting scholars and tourists. They nearly always picked up the tab. On Mondays—"our" day—we snuck into Oaxaca City to make purchases in the market and to take in the exotic international scene on the city square. I always wore different clothes and a wide-brimmed panama into town, both to add variety and to soften my outsider's appearance. Mari covered her head and wore sunglasses. The routines soothed me—it was like reform school. Familiar—knowable.

About three weeks after we moved into our own "firefly house" in Mitla, Samuel came to notify us of an unexpected meeting with don Pablo at the Hotel Victoria. That screwed up our schedule and set me on edge, but Samuel had insisted it was critical.

At ten the next morning we met don Pablo's car in Yagul, as per instructions. "Safety concerns," Samuel had told us. Even Mari was nervous; arms folded across her breasts, she took deep breaths and rhythmically shifted her weight from one foot to the other as we stood by the side of the road, waiting for Virreyes's driver. I leaned on my walking stick while Mari made little murmuring noises and rocked back and forth.

When the car arrived, an immaculate light gray 1959 Olds 88, the driver was accompanied by Samuel, don Pablo's driver, *and* another pistolero. He was a burly, dark-skinned cipher the size of an NFL linebacker. As we scooted into the backseat, he turned once to stare at us, snorted, then went back to his duties riding shotgun. He frightened Mari, who leaned to me and whispered in my ear.

"Don't leave me alone with him, Alex. *Please.*"

"Don't worry, baby . . ." But I *was* worried. So was the damned Voice that haunted me when I stressed out. *Watch him. You idiot. There's something wrong here!* I clutched my walking stick, though why, I'm not sure. It barely fit, wedged across the backseat, cramping everyone. I had no way to use it, even if I'd wanted to.

But the trip was uneventful. As the Olds climbed the hill to the Hotel Victoria, Mari began to relax. Her long, slender fingers found the back of my hand, and she caressed my knuckles, her touch as soft as a butterfly's.

Samuel and Fatso ushered us inside, steering us toward the same private room where don Pablo had entertained us before. Pablo was waiting, as smooth and as effusive as ever. "Good day, kids. . . . how is life in mysterious Mexico South?" He was referring to Miguel Covarrubias's 1946 book by the same title that so richly described an Indian Mexico stretching from the Mixteca Alta (north of us) to the south, beyond San Cristóbal de las Casas.

"Life in Mitla is wonderful," blurted Mari. Pablo's reflexive response set off the Voice again . . . "You mean *Yagul*, Mari, darling." I got it and kicked Mari under the table, "Yes, we're renting a lovely house next to the church—part of the *rectoría*." Mari stared at me, biting her lip, but said nothing, her eyes going back and forth between Pablo, me, and Fatso, still standing off to one side and watching *us*, instead of passersby. So unlike a genuine pistolero.

"Ahh, good," oozed the well-oiled Pablo . . . "I've got some newspaper spreads to show you." Judging by their faces, he surprised his entourage by abruptly waving them out of the room. Once the door closed behind his French assistant, Samuel, and Fatso, don Pablo went into an unfamiliar mode. He seemed stressed out, his voice sharp and twangy like a steel guitar string, "OK, I'm sending you, Marianna, to Rome tomorrow. Here, take your tickets—quickly! Plane to El Distrito, then another to Milan. You'll get surgery there."

"I don't want to go anywhere," whined Marianna, sounding like a petulant kid.

"Darling—the fat pistolero works for the States—he's *Chicano*—American. He's a plant." Mari stiffened. I butted in. "Can we get her out safely?"

"Yes. The padre in Tlacolula will arrange it when you go to vespers tonight. Return to Mitla, pack a case, and go to Tlacolula in time for vespers. The padre will take care of the rest." "Why do you trust the padre?" I put in.

"A nephew of my aunt. Family." Pablo spread out the newspapers with an ostentatious wave as I spoke. "I don't *want* to see more newspapers!" stammered Mari, just as the door burst open and Fatso waltzed in with a tray of drinks. "Where's our regular waiter?" asked don Pablo. "*No sé* (I don't know)," grunted Fatso.

"For that matter, where's Samuel?" Fatso shrugged. I stood up, stick in hand, and abruptly stepped out into the main dining area. I found Samuel in the john, a lump on his head, and a gag in his mouth. I cut it loose and jerked him to his feet. "Can you shoot?"

"He got my pistol, señor."

"The Chicano?" He nodded. "OK—can you distract him?" Samuel, rubbing his head, nodded, "I think so."

"Good, let's go." But we were already too late. By the time we reached Virreyes's private dining room, it was vacant, its side door standing open. I sent Samuel out the open door and made a beeline for the hotel's front driveway, trotting through the lobby, stick in hand, as tourists rubbernecked. The gray sedan was still parked outside, but don Pablo's limp driver was twisted bizarrely around the Oldsmobile's steering column, a white hanky covering his mouth.

Samuel and I reached the car just as Fatso and a tall, wiry guy I'd not seen before were pushing Mari, hissing and clawing like a cat, into the backseat where Pablo lay slumped, either dead or cold-cocked.

"Mari—knee his balls!" I yelled. Her knee went up into Skinny's crotch, just as the brass tip of my stick hit him behind the ear. Skinny folded like an accordion, collapsing into Fatso, buying me one critical moment. By the time Fatso swung around to train his pistol on me, I'd already shattered his wrist. It took another second for him to feel the pain.

He looked down, amazed, the pistol still hanging limp in his useless hand, even as his other hand went to his waistband for a second pistol. An imaginary don Mateo flashed in my brain. "It's the *speed*, young one, the speed!"

My stick broke Fatso's other hand just as the small hideaway pistol started to clear his waistband. *Boom!* "Ugggh! Oooh. I shot myself, *vato*," he said in a monotone, as if talking to no one in particular. His blood spread quickly, soaking his pants and dripping into his shoe while he stared down in disbelief.

By then, I'd already thrown Mari into the front seat, right on top of don Pablo's sleeping driver—the odd smell of ether was intense. I shoved the slumped driver toward Mari and got behind the wheel. Samuel jumped in back with don Pablo. As Mari pulled the chemical-soaked rag from the driver's face, I cranked up the car. She rolled down windows and opened the front quarter vent. Outside, Fatso, still leaking like a sieve, clutched the car's roof, trying to stay upright, as I pulled away. He went down hard and didn't move. I gave it more gas . . .

Pablo came to at the bottom of the hill and puked. "Hospital?" I asked.

"No. Terrible headache, though." Since I had little real driving experience, I focused on keeping the car on the highway while Mari focused on the rear seat.

"Me, too," groaned Samuel . . . "Let's go to my aunt's in Yagul—she's a *curandera*—no one will bother us there." When we arrived at her door, Samuel's aunt Noga ushered us into her altar room, lit candles, and sent a grandson out to fan don Pablo's driver, who was still coming out of the ether.

Samuel and don Pablo got herbal tea and poultices. Mari was fine—broken fingernails her only injury—but she shivered and shifted constantly from one foot to the other. Auntie Noga, a white-haired, dark-shawled character right out of an old black-and-white Halloween movie, reached tenderly for Mari and gave her a traditional herbal sedative, which took effect surprisingly quickly.

Regaining some of his cool, don Pablo strategized. "Is there a phone in this settlement?" "*En la rectoría* (In the rectory)," answered Samuel.

"Good. Take me!"

They went off, while I comforted his driver, who was thoroughly confused by his unexpected nap. He asked us several times, "Where am I really?" "Yagul, Oaxaca state," I repeated a number of times. Accepting that, he turned to a new question, "Where's the boss?" "Don Pablo's at the church," I answered, "with Samuel." The driver shook his head in disbelief. "Not possible. Be honest with me—am I a hostage?" I laughed, "No, just disoriented from a *pañuelo* (handkerchief) full of ether."

When Pablo returned, he was in control again. Even his driver had calmed down. "Take Samuel and Marianna to Mitla in my car and get her packed. Off she goes to Rome, late in the night."

"How do you know she'll be safe on the trip?"

"President Lopez Mateos's own bodyguards will meet her at the ladder when her plane arrives in Mexico. She'll be escorted to Milan by one of our best security agents. This whole affair has given the president one of his famous headaches—the nation now has a stake in this."

"What am I supposed to do by myself in Mitla?"

"Be careful. Go to work, as usual. Samuel's family will protect you. You have lost your woman, if anyone asks. You believe she returned to her native Buenos Aires." "Have I nothing to say about this?" put in Mari.

"No, darling. I am responsible for the current fiasco . . . that is, *Excélsior* is responsible. We have provoked rage in the U.S. Embassy. They will stop at nothing to teach us 'greasers' a lesson. Our own president wants them to stew. So you are to 'act impetuously' . . . and seem stupid. Ironically, the gringos may have accommodated us today. I saw flashbulbs pop as they hustled us out of the hotel. I think one of our photographers got photos from the upstairs patio. If so, their agent dragging me and Mari out of the hotel will be on the front page, above the fold, tomorrow."

"It should make for a good caption," I commented, hoping the laconic tone in my voice caught Pablo's attention. It didn't.

"Well, young Alex, we'll make a journalist out of you yet. The headline will read, '*Excélsior*'s Senior Editor Attacked in Oaxaca City by a Chicano Agent in the Employ of the U.S. Embassy.'"

"That'll sell another half a million extras," I laughed. But Mari was pissed.

"None of this is funny. What about our baby, Alex?" Virreyes stared, his mouth slack as he drew in a huge breath, looking angrily from Mari to me.

"It is so, patrón," commented Samuel. "Their union is blessed."

"Well, then," shot Pablo, instantly petulant, "we'll get Marianna an audience with the pope after her surgery." Marianna, her emotional radar switched to "off," answered as credulously as a child. "Oh, Pablo. Could you? I'd be so grateful. It would be so wonderful . . ." Pablo gaped at her, sighed deeply, shook his head, then shrugged . . .

"We'll try, darling. It would make a *great* story." I ushered Mari out the door, pointing her toward Pablo's car, when the latter grabbed my shoulder and had a word with me in English. "Don't walk out on her, Alex. I hope you truly care for her."

"I do, don Pablo—that's why she, you . . . and your driver are alive this evening." As I stepped through the doorway, I heard Pablo query Samuel. "What did *he* do, anyway? I thought *you* saved our hides."

"No—he's a fighter. He used that stick of his on both of the attackers. *Very* fast . . . like a viper. You owe your good fortune to him."

"Well, then, *Excélsior* should thank him . . . can you stay on here for a good while?"

"Yes, patrón . . . whatever *Excélsior* wishes."

"Good—see to it that no one kills him . . . at least until Marianna returns."

❧

№ 9 ALONE

A FEW DAYS LATER Samuel came to the house in Mitla, copies of *Excélsior*'s front page spread—and a bold, headlined extra—in hand. The front-page caption was almost exactly as Pablo Virreyes had phrased it in Yagul. The extra was even more flamboyant, literally stuffing it up the U.S. government's nose.

I laughed at the description of Marianna. "The luminous, Argentine-Mexican artist Marianna Capo di Monte fights for her life, downing an *agente ilícito norteamericano* (an illicit North American agent)." By the miracle of Kodak's Tri-X Marianna's knee was frozen for all time about half an inch south of Skinny's crotch.

I imagined every gringo-hating, upper-class matron in Mexico City rolling around their kitchens in mirth, downing a shot of mid-morning brandy as they gloated over their husbands' discarded morning papers.

Me—I was merely the usual unruly renegade that most norteamericano males are assumed to be. "Officially," we had been staying temporarily in Yagul—"unofficially," I was alone and miserable in Mitla.

Companionship, like sex, had an addictive quality. The house seemed empty and somber without Marianna. I hadn't really expected that, especially since I'd grown increasingly restless in the sticks. Except for Eddy and Betty Anne, I'd never really missed anyone once they were gone. I'd long known that wasn't normal, but no one had ever been curious about what I thought, or felt, till I landed in Mexico.

I thought about María Inés a few times after I left Mexico City—I'd really liked her . . . and she had cared about my soul. But did she actually care about me—the human? Or had I been merely an offbeat cartoon character—an exotic husband-to-be in training? I didn't know . . . and after a few weeks with Mari, I had quit caring.

I thought about Mari even more. Our relationship had been far shorter, but richer than the one I'd had with Inés. It included dancing, sex, souls, and family . . . the baby she claimed to carry, and Samuel and Ramona, who often hugged me . . . for no good reason at all.

Still, at some level I'd accepted Mari's inaccessibility, and now her departure, as inevitable. I never even questioned it, nor really fought against it. Loss was normal . . . the ordained scheme of things. *Move on,* the Voice told me, *Mari is never coming back. Don't hang on around this place—it's time to go.*

I asked Samuel if he knew of someone who might want to buy the place. He didn't react, so it surprised me when Ramona showed up on the doorstep a day later, a hammock slung over one shoulder, a large net bag of possessions dangling from her other arm. "¡*Hola, Alesh!*" she beamed. "I'm moving in. I'm here to take care of you."

"Huh? . . . Look, Ramona, I was thinking of going away for a while."

"You are not going anywhere, Alesh . . . I will watch over you for la Mari."

"But, why?"

"Because I love her . . . and because she will have an image of you here in the house, waiting for her."

"But it's sad here now; I can't bear it." At this, Ramona dropped everything and folded her arms around me again, reaching up to caress the back of my head as if I were a baby. "You will have made la Mari sooo happy . . . I can't wait to tell her," she crooned.

"Tell her what?"

"That you *love* her. What you *feel* is love. Love . . . the healer of all old wounds. That which makes you heavy with sorrow when you are separated from it."

"She's not coming back, Ramona. I'll never hear from her again."

"Oh, child . . . she will return. It is ordained." The Voice laughed in disdain. *Sure she will, you naive idiot. Don't listen to the old cow.* But Ramona was hypnotic . . .

"How do you know such a thing, Ramona?" I asked, sounding a bit hopeful. She released me, took a step back and gazed into my eyes before answering, her voice soft and serious. "*I do not know. But don Mateo knows. The shaman knows . . . she will return, her belly full with your child.*"

In reality, I was painfully aware that all I'd ever had was a natural mother I'd never met, Betty Anne—sent off to God knows where—and a succession of foster moms and institutional matrons who could never be counted on. Women were ephemeral. Bright splashes of illusory warmth and hope that always faded away, leaving me cold and empty inside, like the waning sun on a winter's afternoon. Ramona touched my face again and waited for a response.

I sighed. "I hope that's true."

"It is . . . where shall I hang my hammock?"

"You can have the bedroom . . . I'm not able to sleep in there now."

"Where will you sleep?"

"On the patio. I have a small cot out there." Ramona nodded for me to pick up her net satchel, walked on past me, and began to arrange her things in the bedroom. Twenty minutes later, Samuel showed up with another guy in an old donkey cart.

"We have supplies . . . and a surprise," he shouted cheerily. He and his companion got down and unloaded charcoal, cornmeal, limes, dried corn, chiles, a sack of beans, coffee beans, and, finally, a squirming puppy, which Samuel put in my arms. I laughed, "What a cute little guy." Samuel grinned.

"It's a *she* dog . . . and *you* soon to be a father? I thought they taught such things in your fancy university . . . see, you need us Indians to set you right."

"Perhaps so. Whose dog is this?"

"Yours . . . and la Marianna's."

"So this is my surprise? Many thanks."

"No. This is a gift—the surprise is from Marianna."

"*Sí*, Ramona says she'll be back. Me—I'm worried."

"Here, then, read this." Samuel held an aerogram in his outstretched hand. I took it, shaking a little as I unfolded it. *Alex. Safe in Italy. See Dr. tomorrow. Feel so alone without you. Wait for me!!! Love, M.*

That evening I ate on the patio with Mari's friends. Ramona's rice and beans tasted better than any I'd yet eaten in Mexico. Luciana and her cousin, who watched over Marianna while she sketched, had come over to clean the house and put out fresh flowers. It was touching . . . the women in Mitla really loved Mari. She'd made a huge impact on them; her bright, sunny public disposition and her kindnesses were infectious.

One of Samuel's little nieces, who lived about two hundred yards away, had come with him. Samuel noticed me watching her play with the puppy. "You smile as you watch her . . . you should be a *maestro* (schoolteacher) someday." I chuckled. "What makes you think I'd be a good schoolteacher?"

"Professor Paddock told my cousin that you were the best of his crew—and the only student to ever earn *dieces* (As) in both his archaeology classes."

"¡*Ay!* I didn't know he felt like that. I've been thinking about quitting."

"The professor thought you might, but you are needed. It is important work . . . and la Marianna needs you . . . and this house . . . to be here when she returns."

"I already got that lecture from Ramona."

"Listen to her . . . she knows much of life." Ramona came over and shooed Samuel away. "Alesh . . . don Mateo wishes to see you tomorrow." "About what?" I asked. She grinned. "Things of the spirit. Love . . . and hope . . . and a favor . . . at the ruins about 6 PM."

That night I slept on the patio, watching the stars drift past the portico, wondering how they came to be—wondering if there really was a God who had created the heavens, then earth. A God who could actually hear me, and Eddy.

Young Eddy's face materialized, his sad, lost, little-boy face gazed down at me dreamily. "This is a nice place, John." I nodded. "It is good, Eddy . . . but lonely right now."

"Don't be sad, John—she'll come back—she reminds me of Betty Anne."

"I know. It's the smile, I think . . . or maybe the eyes."

"Yes, John . . . but, like Betty Anne, your friend didn't know her parents, either. That's why she's so happy to have family around."

"How do you know that, Eddy?"

"I know everything now, John."

"Oh, Eddy. I wish you were here."

"But I am, John. I'm right in front of you . . . please think of me the next time Ramona hugs you. I want you to tell me what it feels like." I nodded—not sufficient. "Say it, John."

It had been a long time since my twin's younger self had visited me and I didn't want to lose him. Grown Eddy had finished his training and was soon to be reassigned. I hoped they wouldn't send him off to some place like Vietnam. He was all the living family I had.

"I promise!" With that he smiled and disappeared, just as the sky filled with shooting stars, trailing faint puffs of luminous gas. A shiver of wonder passed through me. It was as if I'd just witnessed a heavenly epiphany.

Startled by the impossibly realistic dream of Eddy, I imagined immense clouds of cosmic gas, swirling across space, masking glowing cinders within. The cinders swirled, grew, then burst forth across the heavens as stars—born of nothing more substantial than luminous waves of cold, pure energy . . . and the hands of God to warm them into life.

I awoke from the dream, an ominous feeling gnawing at me . . . *Why does Eddy know everything* now? I wondered. But the night sky seemed normal enough and all was quiet in the courtyard. I drifted off to sleep again.

❧

Ramona wakened me at dawn, pushing a big mug of steaming milk and chocolate into my hands. "I must go to La Sorpresa now—do not forget don Mateo this evening." She kissed me on the forehead and waddled out the door, her long gray and black hair braided into a thick loop, like a basket handle attached to the nape of her neck.

I fed the puppy, then went to work in the ruins at Yagul, as usual. I directed a crew of Zapotec Indian diggers, opening up an eight-meter square from the west corner of what came to be called the Council Hall. The dig extended into the area called Patio 1. The great tenth-century ball court was just fifty yards to the east.

We'd been removing and screening overburden for weeks. Tough, tedious work, but essential . . . and dicey as the historic period trash layers were removed. The upside was that our area was on the breezy west side of Yagul's cactus-studded hill.

The morning's work was cool, so we made the most of it . . . shoveling by 7:30 AM. John Paddock came to our side of the hill about ten, calling me over. Instructions, I assumed. "Well, JA, how goes it" he asked.

"OK, Professor. Lots of caliche. Tough pick work to break it up, but we're holding up."

"That's not what I meant . . . how are *you* doing?" I must have looked blank. He clarified. ". . . *Alone* in Mitla?" I shrugged. "Will you be staying on here at the site? The academic quarter ends for Christmas break next week."

"Will you close the site for Christmas, Professor?"

"We'll be closing for the season by the twenty-seventh. I'm moving back to my long-term project at Lambityeco in January."

"So you won't need me anymore?"

"Actually, I will—I'd like to have you stay on here from now through the twenty-seventh—I need you. I know it's Christmas, but we have to close up—just a small crew to do some fine troweling and screening before the laborers backfill. I'll give you a raise."

"Really?" He nodded, smiling. "And you'll teach me the troweling and profiling?" He grinned, pulling off his gray Stetson, and rubbed one of the ever-flaking blisters on his bald, sunburned head. We shook on it.

It was my first ever raise. I had money in a bank in Mexico City—nearly one thousand U.S. dollars, some of it foundation money. The rest had been won in late-night one-pocket pool matches in New York and Philly—but walking into that Mexico City bank to make a withdrawal was like asking for an ugly date with the elusive, allegedly banished Semper Fi, or another spook just like him, so I needed Paddock's salary to pay Mari's rent in Mexico City, now that she—and her income—were gone.

That afternoon, Professor Paddock drove me to Mitla, bought me a cold Bohemia at La Sorpresa, and gave me an advance on the new salary. I left him at six, elated . . . and headed toward the ruins to meet don Mateo Dxubhá.

№ 10 DON MATEO DXUBHÁ

DON MATEO WAS WAITING for me inside the ruins, near the ancient colonnades. Alone, except for Samuel, he looked up as I stepped into the plaza. I carried my stick, balanced in one hand, raising it as he waved, then noticed that he carried no stick. Instead, a large pouch and a gourd were slung over one shoulder.

As I approached, he studied me, his eyes expressionless. But when I was about five yards from him he turned without a word and started walking away. Samuel explained, "We are to follow at a respectful distance, until he summons us."

The old man threaded his way through the ruins, the two of us following. In the cool December evening, he'd bundled up in a beautiful jaguar-motifed *gabán* (cloak). His stained felt hat and the gray and black jaguar gave him a mystical quality.

It turned into a long walk and, eventually, a tough climb up a steep, rocky hill about three miles to the northeast of the ruins. Sunset turned to dusk as we crested the hill to find don Mateo already sitting cross-legged on an eight-foot-tall mound of stone rubble, the size of a small house.

"*Lidxibeleguí*," he said when we stepped forward at the wave of his hand. "This place is called House of Stars," Samuel explained. "Very old. A place where those who follow the sun, moon, and stars have always sat to do their work." "Is don Mateo a star watcher?" I asked.

"Yes. Don Mateo is the twenty-third generation of his line to serve the House of Stars."

"Here the stars stand up—*niaza beleguin*," intoned don Mateo, lighting the gourd full of copal-like incense to call the gods. "Oh, *ndayáguba* (holy vapor), summon the evening star," Samuel translated.

Sure enough, ten minutes later Venus peeked at us from the southeastern horizon as the sky transformed into evening's glassy, bottomless blue-black. In reality, copal was ancient tree sap, hardened by time to nearly the density of amber. My brain told me that it should smell like pine, or old leaves. Instead, the cloying musky scent of the incense always reminded me of the salty-sweet smell of blood in the slaughter yard next to our reform school.

I sat cross-legged on don Mateo's left, staring at the horizon as he had indicated. "*Nusiacha ca streya* (The stars stand up)." He pointed with his stick to a spot just above the roof line of the mosaic wall far below at Mitla, where a remarkable line of bright stars rose up toward the zenith. "*Stica yaga ca diuxi* (The stick of the gods)."

"Put your stick up to the stars and make a wish, Alesh. Just one," instructed Samuel. I felt foolish, my stick held in front of me, but wished for the ability to feel emotions, like a normal person. When I was done, don Mateo uttered something in Zapotec, which Samuel repeated. "Your stick is now sacred. Lay it on the great stone in front of you, pointing to the temple at Mitla."

I did as instructed, then gazed out across the starlit valleys as the moon rose, dulling the great standing stick of stars and lighting up the ridgeline of the rugged Sierra Madre, which separated us from the Pacific coast.

Samuel and I withdrew first, feeling our way down the rocky trail. "We are to wait for don Mateo at La Sorpresa—he has to consult the stars," whispered Samuel. "Does the *palo de estrellas* (star stick) in the sky have anything to do with a warrior's stick fighting?" I asked.

"Yes. This is the night of the year when the stars first stand and reveal the old War God's battle stick."

An hour later we crept into the ruins at Mitla, where the trail ended. I guessed that the trail had been there as long as the ruins themselves. In places the narrow path was worn right down into bedrock as it wound through the hills overlooking Mitla's valley.

When we reached La Sorpresa, don Mateo was already sitting cross-legged on the stone steps to the front doorway. "How did he beat us here?" I asked Samuel, amazed. Don Mateo answered, laughing as he spoke, "My tono is a bat. I flew."

"Am I to believe you?"

"I am here, am I not—what more evidence do you require?" "Why not fly now? Right here," I challenged.

"The tonos do not transform in front of others. Turn away from me and race to your front door—I will await you there."

"OK," I laughed. Samuel and I turned, and I took off running as fast as I could, crossing the creek like I was doing a timed hundred yards. As I rounded the wide, dusty plaza fronting the house I got my first view of my huge blue wood and iron front door. There on the threshold sat don Mateo, cross-legged. Relaxed, at ease, no sign of exertion whatsoever. I leaned over just a yard from him, panting, and coughed up a gob of cigarette goo, a thin wisp of residual cigarette smoke billowing out as I gasped for air.

"Well, young one . . . you have your evidence," grinned don Mateo. "Now hear me! You will one day hold your own child and know that you are loved. But the Old God gave me no further clues than that . . . he did not grant me a view of your far future. Meanwhile, you have business among the Nahuat."

"Why do you say that?" I asked, startled. I *had* been thinking about going down to the isolated enclaves of Nahuatl speakers in Tabasco, after Christmas. Just then, I heard someone come up behind me and turned. It was Samuel. "Come on back to La Sorpresa, Alesh—don Mateo is waiting. You owe him a cold beer."

"But you see him—he's on my doorstep."

"I see no one, Alesh. He is still at La Sorpresa." I turned back to my doorway. Empty. Silent. Not even the puppy tethered in the courtyard made a fuss. *You are losing it,* cackled the Voice. *Forget what the old man said. Forget the woman. She'll make you even crazier than you already are.* I shook my head and shut him out as Samuel pulled me away, gently nudging me toward the Sorpresa.

As I walked back toward the inn with Samuel, I lost mental control again and the Voice revisited me. *Don't lose it, idiot! All this over a tramp who claims she carries your child. Hell, she's a freak. Don't fall for this mumbo-jumbo. It's bullshit!* I snarled at the Voice in English. "Go away, dammit!" Samuel winced at the unexpected outburst, but said nothing.

When we got to La Sorpresa, don Mateo was waiting for us, taciturn. "*¿Cerveza nananda?* ("Cold beer?"—Spanish/Zapotec)," he asked. I nodded. He rose, touched my shoulder, and spoke in Zapotec. Samuel translated. "Your mind is fine," he said. "Only some can see a tono. You are able to see mine . . . and one day, will meet your own."

We went inside, irritating the mestizo counterman, who glared at us. The local Indians didn't go into La Sorpresa, except, like Ramona, to work as a kitchen helper or waitress. I glared back. He looked away. So, we were seated without a quarrel.

Don Mateo leaned back in his chair, smiling when the cold Boheemu (Bohemia) arrived. My nerves were jangled from the weird dreams, events of the evening, and the appalling sense of loneliness that pulled at me. I chugged my first beer and ordered another. He took a sip, smacked his lips, and smiled. "*Xpaculula?* (Your walking stick?)"

"Oh, no! I forgot it up on the hill."

"It's on your bed at home—you will need it soon enough." After finishing his beer, don Mateo exited with Samuel. He laughed as he glided through the hacienda's wide wooden doors. I paid up and left. In response to don Mateo's intrusion, a couple of the local mestizos in the restaurant had already started to tell Indian jokes. Me, I wasn't in the mood.

I shuffled back to the house across the creek. Now cheerfully lit up, the puppy yapped in greeting as I went in over the patio wall. Sure enough. My stick had been placed on my courtyard cot. Inside, Ramona was waiting. She sniffed, wrinkling her nose. "*¿Cervezu?*" I nodded and sagged clumsily into one of the big leather chairs. She disappeared and returned with a big bowl of corn and squash stew.

"Here, eat! I'll make coffee."

I needed the food to moderate the beer buzz I'd gotten from three Bohemias. Even more, I needed the backrub she gave me as I slouched in the chair, waiting for the coffee to cool, the puppy wagging her tail at my feet.

※

I worked for Paddock till the end of December, mailed the next month's rent to Mari's landlord in Mexico City, then went into Oaxaca City to check train schedules to Tabasco. I'd started to go emotionally numb again and continued to have odd "Eddy" dreams. The Voice was dumping alarm signals on me hourly. In spite of Ramona's gentle protests, I drank myself to sleep many nights.

The morning of my last day at work for Paddock, I woke with an odd sensation. My heart pounded violently. When I sat up, the puppy barked for her food bowl. That startled me. I panicked. My heart beat faster. My arms tingled and I felt light headed. When I stood up the room swirled. I couldn't breathe. Sweat poured from me and my knees buckled. I grabbed the door jam, steadied myself, and called for Eddy. Someone answered. I stepped into the front room. It spun crazily. I sensed that I was dying. Someone reached out to hold me, but it wasn't Eddy. I staggered back, trying to focus. It was Ramona.

"I'll make you tea, Alesh. Here, sit down."

She made me the herb tea while I shrunk into the chair, took deep breaths, and tried not to scream. She held the cup to my lips. "Take sips."

In a half hour or so, the tea and Ramona had calmed me down. I began to talk normally again. That's when she folded me into her arms, saying, "I think the trip will be good for you." Her touch only made me jumpy again. "Feelings" were as complicated as "no feelings."

"What is troubling you, Alesh?" Ramona asked softly.

"Like an idiot, I asked the stars for feelings."

"Feelings will save you, Alesh." Her tone was matter of fact. "Feelings are what make one human . . . now come, I'll help you pack."

‡‡

№ 11 TABASCO (JAGUAR MOON)

I WAS NEVER CERTAIN that I belonged with anyone, much less with a woman like Mari, who was as complicated as I was. I needed a change.

"You will come back to Mari's house in a few weeks, *la*?" Ramona asked as the train approached the station in Oaxaca City's old rail yard. I nodded, turning toward the platform. "Don't be long, Alesh," she sniffled, kerchief to eyes, as I mounted the platform. "I will miss you." No "mother" figure had ever before bade me farewell. It was a tender, yet unnerving feeling. Flustered and frightened of my growing vulnerability, I smiled and touched her shoulder, then stepped into the coach.

The train to Veracruz was hot and crowded. In Mexico, third class always is. About half the cars' occupants were rebozo- or poncho-clad coastal Indians. Their cottage-made huaraches, fashioned from cast-off truck tires and local, piss-tanned leather, were ubiquitous. So were the men's wide-brimmed straw hats with beaded leather tassels worn down the back.

The men's "bathroom" at one end of the 1920s-era railcar was merely a round, torch-cut hole in the floor's thick steel sheet. It opened right to the tracks below. No water, toilet paper, or soap, of course. I shared the car with about a hundred people who'd likely never earned in a year as much as I had in my pocket for this trip. Screaming babies, a couple of piglets, and two bamboo cages of fighting cocks rounded out the scene.

I took the aisle seat on one of the tattered green baize benches that faced an identical one—my little compartment housed a family of eight, ranging in age from about two to eighty. Only one woman spoke Spanish. The others watched me write in my pocket diary, conversing in an Indian language I'd not heard before. Finally, the Spanish-speaking woman overcame the culture gap and addressed me, "¿A dónde va, joven? (Where are you going, young man?)"

"To Coatzacoalcos, then into the interior jungle nearby. Field studies. Traditional folklore."

"Do they pay you for such work?"

"No, señora, I pay them . . . I'm a university student." She smiled and translated for the older gent seated next to her. He laughed. I offered him a Raleigh 903, a classy cigarette compared to the cheap Delicados he'd smoked earlier. I smoked Delicados only when I was broke—they smelled like sweat and tasted quite like what I imagined dirty socks to be.

". . . And what is 'folklore'?" she asked, translating for the old man.

"Traditional Indian tales and accounts of the supernatural." She translated again. He stared at me for a moment, raised his finger to make a point, and mumbled something to her. She didn't offer to translate, so I asked, "What did he say, señora?" She broke eye contact but answered, "The spirit world is powerful. Best you not pursue it—but if you do, you must first go to confession and wear a cross."

"Please thank him for his advice. I shall accept it." I settled back and relaxed, wishing that the train's grimy, smeared window would open, and that the baby boy nursing a scrawny teenager's exposed breast just three feet away would quit pooping in his nappies. The smell, amplified by the hot, subtropical air, was unbearable.

Veracruz was the last city on earth I wanted to visit again, but that's where the train ended its journey. Fortunately, I didn't even need to leave the chaos of the train station. Forty minutes later, I changed to one of the buses that pulled into the rail yard and headed south toward Coatzacoalcos. We passed through the city center in the middle of the night. Coatzacoalcos was a busy port, petroleum exploration the major buzz. On some maps the city was simply named "Port of Mexico."

I got one glimpse of long, red-tiled colonial buildings and a dusty boulevard lined with dense, closely spaced trees, their trunks whitewashed to about chest height. We stopped in front of its shabby bus station to piss, smoke, and take on new passengers for the trip south.

The next morning we pulled into the provincial port of Villahermosa on the muddy Grijalva River. This entire coastal district had paid tribute to the Aztec empire in the 1400s, and echoes of the overlords still hung in the air, like monkeys in the nearby jungle canopy.

Villahermosa simply wasn't a *villa hermosa* (beautiful town). Rather, it had a hazy, tropical air about it, enhanced by the lead-gray skies, suffocating humidity, and poverty as picturesque as any I'd seen. The bar district, fronting the harbor, was bustling, if not sinister.

In one, the local whores, nearly all teenaged, swarmed me when I first entered. Most were Indian girls with high cheekbones, almond-shaped eyes, and remarkable, aquiline noses. They wanted just twenty-five pesos (two U.S. dollars) for *un ratito* (a little while). But I was put off by the impersonal competition among the hookers.

Mari, as casually bitchy as she could be, especially when don Pablo buzzed around like a bee, intent on pollinating her, offered much more emotional comfort than I imagined these seventeen-year-old hookers could muster. Given their vacant-eyed looks, several of them had already mastered the art of soul flying. I was certain of it. *Mari is too much like me as it is*, I ruminated. *No sense in tangling with one of these exact emotional replicas of me.*

Still, two shots of tequila later, I asked for a dance with a gorgeous teenager named, of course, María. She spoke in monotones, a smile plastered on her face as if it were set in concrete, her eyes a million miles away. I checked. "Señorita . . . could I join you, wherever you really are?" She looked at me for the first time. Startled. Frightened.

This one would never be "there," smiling. Would never *feel* anything beyond primitive fear. It frightened me to see part of myself mirrored in her vacant eyes. Somewhere along the way this Indian girl had been unable to find her way home. Lost. Adrift in the ether. Poor thing. "It's all right," I assured her softly, but she averted her eyes and drifted away.

Uncomfortable, I drifted back to my table and nursed a tepid Yucateco-brand beer, wondering, *Is screwing a girl like "María" for two bucks any different than the fraternity boys in Connecticut getting their dates dead drunk first?* I decided there wasn't really any difference. In both cases the girls were comatose—unable to *feel* anything. Even to say yes or no. And, as Ramona had so clearly put it in Mitla, "*Feeling* is what makes you human."

For me, female companionship was all about "feeling"—warmth, soft eyes, and an air of tenderness that I could inhale. Suddenly, I missed Marianna. Being with her had helped me to feel alive. I simply wasn't going to get that sensation from hookers who were already dead inside.

After an hour at the bar I was done with the scene. I settled into a cheap rooming house for the night. In the morning I took a bus east into the coastal forest.

Our first stop was the town of Teapa. It's Nahuatl name meant "sacred place." Judging from its current decay it had gone downhill since its Aztec days. The ancient gods appeared to have moved on, abandoning it once the Spanish arrived. An elaborate Catholic church sat at one edge of its small, dusty plaza. An incongruous white Victorian bandstand sat in the center of the square, framed by whitewashed trees and four old-fashioned iron benches. Two weathered Indian men played checkers on a homemade board with red and blue bottle caps, oblivious to the world around them.

I decided to get off to see if I could get to one of the interior villages. They don't print tourist brochures for places like this. Perhaps a local bus, or a plantation truck, would pop up. While I tried to get the lay of the land, I grabbed a plate of beans and rice at a small restaurant on the far side of the plaza. The restaurant consisted of just three Carta Blanca–brand folding metal tables set out front in the dusty street—no telling what it was like during the rainy season.

But the food was good. Rice, fried egg, and beans, sliced tomatoes and chiles on the side. Fresh-sliced pineapple for dessert, along with a big mug of steamed milk laced with dark-roast Veracruz coffee. Cost: seven pesos (fifty-six U.S. cents).

As I nursed my coffee, smoked, and stretched my legs, a tall cowboy-booted Anglo guy walked up to me. I must have looked surprised. He reassured me, "Look, I don't want to be a pain, but I heard you speaking Spanish to the waitress and hoped you also spoke English." I couldn't quite place his almost hound dog–like drawl. "Yeah, I'm American," I conceded, "name's JA. Where are *you* from?"

"Port Arthur, Texas." I should have guessed it from the Justin boots and Wranglers. They don't wear Levis in Texas, except in the big cities where folks don't know any better. "Look—my buddies and I drove down here to go hunting—but we don't know the lingo. Hell, we don't even know what the shit is they call food down here . . . can you help us? We'd pay."

"How much?"

He hesitated, taking in my worn boots and frayed, tan field shirt. "Thirty dollars a day." I gave him a sarcastic look, leaned back, ignoring him, and smoked. "OK—fifty," he offered. "We've got a Nissan Patrol wagon and want to go after jaguar in the backcountry." *Well, well, today Fate has a Texas accent*, I chuckled to myself. I nodded yes to the fifty a day . . . "I want two days in advance." He grinned and stuck out his hand. "Here's your hundred. My name's Brody. Come meet Jeff and Jim Bob." *Unfuckin' real*, I thought. I carefully folded and refolded the Ben Franklin, tucked him into my watch pocket, and followed Brody around the corner to their Jeep-like Nissan.

As I predicted, the idiots didn't even have water, supplies, or a good topo map. Thankfully, I'd brought my own National Geographic map. I nagged them till they grudgingly bought bottled water and canned goods at a small old-fashioned bodega just off the plaza. Then we hit a dirt track leading up out of the coastal plain toward the hamlet of Amatlán. Amatlán lay south by southeast along the forested upper Grijalva River.

My map showed the track crossing the Grijalva after passing through Amatlán, then turning into a dotted line. In Mexico, those dotted lines were as in-your-face as casino facades in Las Vegas. They announced official entry to "nowhere." Brody watched my finger tracing the dotted line beyond the Grijalva. "Do you think it's paved, JA?" I cackled, "We'll be lucky if it even looks like a trail, much less paved."

Amatlán was a one-third scale version of Teapa—forty oval-thatched hut houses scattered along the river and a small, unpaved plaza. One twelve-foot-square general store . . . and a friendly Belgian Catholic missionary. "You want Malinalco for jaguar," he told us, "about five kilometers upriver. Cross the river by the old ruins—just above a huge *zapote* tree. Follow the trail across the grassy knoll—about four more kilometers—you can't miss it."

By late afternoon the Nissan Patrol wagon had reached the ancient

Nahuatl-speaking enclave of San Sebastian de Malinalco (Malinalco—
"place of twisted grass"). I don't know what the three Texans expected,
but places like this simply didn't have bars, restaurants, and hotel lob-
bies. Hell, it wasn't even on a standard National Geographic map. As
Jim Bob whined, "There are no cold longnecks anywhere," I gave them
a reality check. "If National Geographic hasn't been here, hell, *no one*
has ever been here."

Instead, San Sebastian had a moldy chapel, an open, grassy market
area (probably how it got its name five hundred years before), a grove
of ancient, thick-branched trees, and a small graveyard. The rest of the
village consisted of oval, mud-plastered, palm-roofed Indian houses and
one much larger "house" that served as the store, restaurant, post office,
and headman's lodge.

The headman and his looks-too-slick-by-half assistant came out as
we parked the Nissan among the trees. Only the headman and his bril-
liantined factotum spoke Spanish. The rest of the gathering crowd spoke
a variant of the Aztecs' Nahuatl language. I introduced myself.

"*Buenas tardes. Soy Juan Alejandro—mis compañeros quieren cazar
jaguar. ¿Es posible?* (Hello, my name is John Alexander. My companions
want to hunt jaguar. Is that possible?)" The assistant replied slowly, "The
cacique of our village, don Magisterio, permits hunting *el tigre* (jaguar)
now and again. What do you propose?" The headman watched us, leaning on his brass-mounted staff of rank. I turned to the three *tejanos* . . .

"What will you pay for hunting?"

"Fifty dollars for the right to look for three days. One hundred for an
animal hanging over the hood of the truck." I turned to the headman's
assistant and conveyed the offer, which was a lot of money in a world
where fifty cents bought a fancy meal. We could have purchased any of
the Indian houses and its adjacent kitchen plot for about sixty bucks.
But the headman wasn't a headman for nothing.

Sinewy, wearing mid-calf-length cotton pants, an elaborate embroi-
dered shirt, and an indigo blue headband, he sported a Rolex Oyster on
his left wrist. His prominent nose and sun-leathered face was offset by
one blind eye—withered and misshapen, a deep scar trailing down his
cheek below it, like a tear.

He fixed his good eye on me and spoke even more slowly than his
assistant. "One hundred fifty *duros* (dollars) to look—two days! Fifty

for me and one hundred for the village. Three hundred duros for a male tigre—all for the school . . . and you must not hunt my nagual—a huge one-eyed male of about fifteen years. His left ear is missing its top half."

I conveyed the counteroffer. The Texans wanted to bargain. The cacique figured it out from the tone of their voices and turned to leave. "Where's the old fart headed?" whined Brody.

"He's rejecting your offer."

"Fuckin' Indian hasn't even heard it." Apparently, don Magisterio's assistant understood Brody's English, as he wheeled back around. "This one is correct!" he sneered, pointing at me but speaking to Brody. "The City People will sell you anything for less. But they do not own what they sell. Our village has little, but its land. The forest wood and the animals are ours. Tigres are few. They have souls. One is the cacique's *cuate* (twin). It and the females are not for sale." I translated again.

The Texans forked over the one-fifty in U.S. bills. "Your time begins at dark," the assistant said. "My name is Gregorio and I will accompany you. Eat and rest until then. It will be a long night and we must prepare."

They slaughtered a dry she-goat and several village men drove a burro laden with the carcass on up the trail to create a bait area. It didn't strike me as a normal kind of sport hunt, but what did I know? I was a city boy and had never even thought about shooting an animal. I'd never even seen a jaguar—reform schools don't take you to the city zoo.

A few minutes later, a woman came out of the cacique's place and asked if we would like to eat. The tejanos nodded. About twenty minutes later several even younger women came out with three large, flat clay dishes of rice, beans, and a fried egg on top. Jim Bob bitched, "I'd love to eat something other than *nigger* food." I blew my stack . . .

"Here, those beans and eggs are worth their weight in gold! Some kid or nursing mom did without tonight to provide for you guys. Eat and shut up . . . and don't even think the 'nigger' word around me again."

Fact was, the only decent foster father Eddy and I had ever had was black. His name was William Willson. Poor bastard had had a heart attack and died when we were about seven. That ended that, again fucking up life for both of us and three other kids of various races, so I didn't want to hear this crap from some East Texas cracker.

106 DAVID E. STUART

I took my plate across the plaza, entered the church with it, and said a prayer to find my soul soon. That done I ate in the graveyard, a stone slab for my table. Then I lay down on it, rolling my serape into a pillow, and waited for dusk.

An hour and a half later one of the young Indian women came to the graveyard's old stone gates, went, "Psst! Psst!" and motioned me toward her. It was time to go hunting. I strolled over to the others, my stick in hand, apparently still seeming irritated.

"Didn't mean to piss you off, man . . . really," shrugged Jim Bob. "Forget it," I said, "it's time to get moving." The Nissan chugged to life. Gregorio rode shotgun in the front seat opposite Brody, who was at the wheel. Me—I was jammed into the steel bed with the two other tejanos. Cramped, we sat on top of their gear. Jim Bob whined again, "I don't like it back here—it's like being in the back of the bus . . ."

"Don't even think about complaining." My tone was as ice-cold as it had been in the Veracruz jail when Chato had pushed his luck. Jim Bob shut up, turned cherry red, and glowered.

We passed more ruins, where piles of ancient stone blocks jutted up into the thick forest. At one bend in the trail we flashed past an elaborate carved stela. It glowed an eerie bone white in the Nissan's headlamps. That reminded me that we were only eighty air miles from the huge ruins at Palenque. Unlike Palenque—already becoming a tourist mecca—the Malinalco district was basically uncharted.

It took about a twenty-minute walk to reach the bait area. We parked just off the trail a half mile short of our destination, followed our guide up a fairly steep hill, then erupted onto a small grassy plateau. The night was in its infancy, still softened by that miraculous interlude of expectant calm that comes just after sundown.

We crossed the thick, twisted grass carefully, moving in single file among the huge gnarled trees that guarded the denser forest behind. The Texans were quiet for once. Apparently, it took the prospect of blood sport to settle them down. We split into two pairs, and Gregorio divided his attentions between the pairs.

I was with Jeff. He was pudgy, about thirty, and wore the biggest damned belt buckle I'd ever seen. It was nearly the diameter of a tea plate and must have hurt like hell where it jammed into his sagging beer gut. We'd tucked ourselves into a shallow depression under an immense zapote tree. Its branches twisted overhead, shadowed by the filtered light of a rising half moon.

Gregorio appeared silently and whispered, pointing toward the moon, "*Luna de tigre . . . Esperamos* (Jaguar moon . . . We wait)." I translated. Jeff pulled out a tin of snuff. Pointing to his nose, Gregorio nixed that. Poor Jeff was getting stressed. "This is hard," he whispered. "Hard is when the animals shoot back," I whispered in response. His belly jiggled.

About an hour later, one huge, twisted branch above us groaned softly and an indistinct shape passed along it. For an instant a streak of moon-light illuminated one dark rosette and the shadow of an animal gliding silently overhead. The jaguar's scent followed it—an unexpected aura of pungent, ammonia-tinged cat piss and dense, foul breath. I may never have truly seen a jaguar in the wild, but I'd just smelled one. Jeff clicked off the safety on his fancy bolt-action rifle.

Ghostlike, a second shape passed above us sometime later. We never even sensed its presence until the branches groaned and the same over-powering cat smell washed over us again.

I was already bored to tears and wondering when I'd be able to light up when we heard someone running clumsily toward us. Then everything went into a crazy fast-forward mode. The night clouds stirred, someone shouted, "No!" A deeper voice to the left yelled, "He's mine!"

Just as the clouds parted to give us a moonlit view of the scene, an immense jaguar tensed to leap from a tree twenty yards away. Simultaneously, a shot rang out. It was followed by a hollow "whump" and an odd hacking cough. For a moment there was no sound. No movement.

Then, without warning, the shot jaguar leapt onto an overhanging branch and glided our direction, closing the distance to ten yards. He coiled to leap into the huge tree above us but missed the next branch and bounced, tail twisting, to the forest floor. He hacked again—deep, wet, and guttural—jerked once, then went still.

Brody, about eighty feet to the left, flipped on a torch and yelled at Jim Bob to be careful. But he wasn't. In his excitement, he straddled the tigre and aimed his rifle to deliver the coup de grâce. The big cat, fighting its death, raked his inner thigh when Jim Bob pumped another round into it. He screamed and fired again. I saw a bright pinpoint of iridescent light rise into the night the very moment that second round thumped into the tigre.

I wondered if what I'd actually seen was a spirit rising as the jaguar died. I wasn't hallucinating—there was a light. It was real. Perhaps souls did exist, separated from their earthly hosts. Perhaps I wasn't alone. And Indian mythology might not be "myth" after all. The hair on my neck stood up and I got the shivers.

Just then, our guide, Gregorio, came up, panting. At the sight of the dead animal, he put his hands to his head and wailed. Then shook. Jim Bob snickered despite the pain in his leg. Brody shut him up.

We gathered under the great tree where the tigre had fallen. As Brody's torch washed over the animal, we saw a massive head, its one good eye still wide open. The top of its left ear was gone, as if sliced off neatly.

"May the saints protect my people," Gregorio moaned, in Spanish. "Hey, what's he whining about?" asked Brody. "You've killed the head-man's spirit animal. Big trouble," I said.

"You don't actually believe that whooo-whooo Indian crap, do you?" cackled Jim Bob, almost peeing himself with pride. "Look at the size of this mother. I'm making me a big-ass rug out of this bad boy . . . he won't fuck with Jim Bob Williams again."

"You're bleeding," I commented. "If those scratches get infected you may wish you could trade places with your kill." "You know," Jim Bob sneered at me, "fact was, I never liked you. You are a pain in the ass . . . I just killed me a real mother of a cat and you want to spoil it. Just like a fuckin' city boy."

Gregorio was still shaking and speechless as Jim Bob congratulated himself. Jeff, standing to one side, started to say something, but Brody, who'd whipped out a camera, began taking photos. The flash illuminated the jaguar, whose good eye blinked when the camera popped. At that, Gregorio declared that he had to go light candles and fled into the night. Brody was worried. "Who'll guide us back?" "I watched the trail pretty carefully," I butted in.

"No fear then!" crowed Jim Bob. "We'll just have to put up with you for a couple of hours. That Injun gave me the creeps, anyway. Let's load this cat onto the wagon, blow past the village . . . and keep our five hundred bucks." He laughed, oblivious to the blood steadily dripping from his thigh, down into his leather lace-up "packer's" boots.

"Here, city boy," he snarled at me, "earn some of that hundred in easy money . . . lift with us!" I lifted.

It was about 4 AM when we neared the village, don Magisterio's animal spirit draped prominently across the Nissan's hood. Amazingly, the settlement was alive with torches. Virtually everyone was out milling about in the night. And Mexico's traditional Indians rarely go out much after dark—too many troubled spirits to contend with.

"Dammit—this isn't normal," I warned. "Don't pull into the crowd." Unlike Jim Bob, Brody had the sense to be concerned and pulled the Nissan into the trees at the edge of the square. "Pssst!" someone hissed as I stepped down from the bed . . . I looked around.

Gregorio had positioned himself a few yards away, motioning me over—I grabbed my stick and the duffel. "Don Magisterio is dead. Tell your friends to go away and leave his nagual. *Quickly!* The people are angry and have machetes!" He pointed over to the crowd.

I shouted back to Brody, but it was already too late. A large cluster of torches throbbed toward the Nissan even as Brody yelled, "Can't hear you!" I yelled again, "Leave the animal and *go*—the cacique is dead." Jim Bob's whining carried over to me. "Fuck you! You city boys are pussies. I can handle these Injuns . . . they aren't getting my cat from me. I'm not giving up my rug."

Me, I turned away in the direction from which we'd come ten hours before. Behind me, two rifle shots echoed through the forest, followed by Jim Bob's angry shouting. Then came screams and the clang of steel blades. I turned one last time to look . . . the Texans had been swallowed by a sea of torches. Moments later the Nissan's headlights flickered and died. I slung the duffel over one shoulder, leaned into its weight, pushed off with my stick, and waded into the forest.

By dawn, I'd spotted the pile of rocks we'd left to make the river crossing. By dumb luck I'd found the ford on the upper Grijalva. Wet, tired, and bruised I fought the rushing current, struggled to the other side, and paused to get my bearings.

I wanted to reach Teapa and get out of the district before the inhabitants of an aggrieved Malinalco sent its men to find me . . . too many points of light had already risen for one night.

An Indian passing on a burro and leading another loaded with firewood offered to let me ride in his place for twenty pesos. It only cost a buck sixty to save a five-mile walk. I accepted, so I rode most of the way to Amatlán. I dismounted within sight of the village and walked the rest of the way. I checked at the general store. There weren't any buses scheduled till evening, so I bought a liter of water and kept walking.

Twenty minutes past Amatlán, a beat-up two-and-a-half-ton plantation truck loaded with pineapples groaned along the rutted lane. I waved another twenty-peso note at the driver as he drew alongside. He leaned out, snatched the note from my hand, and motioned me up as he slowed. I napped atop the load of pineapples.

Around noon we arrived in Teapa, and I stopped in the police station to let them know three Americans might be in trouble over hunting a jaguar near San Sebastian de Malinalco. A burly mestizo cop wearing a tattered, sweat-soaked brown uniform jotted something on a notepad, shrugged, and told me that they would "inquire."

I ate rice, beans, and fruit at the same table where Brody had first approached me the day before. I was one hundred dollars richer, but mighty uneasy about the twenty-four-hours' events. Later I grabbed the one rickety third-class bus parked alongside the plaza and headed back to Villahermosa. Cost—four pesos (thirty-two cents).

Further fieldwork in the district seemed unwise. If those Texans were dead, some pissed-off Indians with new rifles would be wandering the countryside looking for me, hoping to avoid an unpleasant influx of brown-clad mestizo cops from Teapa or, God forbid, Villahermosa.

Once in Villahermosa again, the riverside bars seemed just as sinister as they had before. It should have seemed exotic, forbidden, and excited my twenty-year-old brain, but the scene along the river was quite like the coastal sky at this time of year—merely boring, in a leaden, ominous, subtropical sort of way.

Restless, I took the train back to Coatzacoalcos, then crossed the Isthmus of Tehuantepec on a bus from Acayacan to Salina Cruz on Mexico's other ocean. That name on my map had captured my fancy. I also craved the sun, blue sky, and fresh air tourists in Mexico City talked about as typical of the Pacific coast.

№ 12 MALINALLI PILLI

THE PACIFIC OCEAN JUST north of Salina Cruz was turbulent, not pacific. I'd never seen it before, so marveled at the scene. The sky was a stunning cobalt blue, the water clear. And the air tasted like clear mineral water, sparkling and metallic, seasoned by a hint of salt.

The coast was rocky and high. But there was no beach below—only a sharp, jumbled cliff of volcanic rock and foam-flecked breakers as far as the eye could see. Japan and China were out there somewhere . . . with each new wave, an immense column of water smacked the cliff base with a roar and exploded into the air, like a whale's spout.

Why had they called it the "Pacific" and not the "Restless"? I wondered. All of history involves oddities. It's the eccentric stuff that comes down to us, I decided. Reality gets filtered out because it's either boring or ugly . . . I'd been on a philosophical jag ever since I'd seen the possible proof of a nagual's existence under the surrealistic light of a "jaguar moon"— then those torches closing in on the Texans. I shook off the jaguar incident and walked back to town.

Salina Cruz was one of those port towns that seemed to have been created specifically as part of a B movie set. Of course, no movie would ever be filmed in such a place because the Hollywood crowd likes cold beer, clean toilets, and valet service. Salina Cruz had none of those things, but it oozed atmosphere . . .

It had palm trees, a narrow railway powered by antique, gold-lettered locomotives, and a train station that had already seen better days long before I was born. The whole scene was as if someone had snapped a sepia-toned photograph in 1920 and the photograph had frozen the town in time as it slowly faded under the bright Pacific sky. Long faded, it had already begun to curl at the edges.

The main thoroughfare consisted of a wide, potholed red-dirt lane that dipped down to the Pacific's waters in a tangle of mangoes, oranges, and a low rock seawall, added as an afterthought.

Two or three passers-by gaped at me. The dirty, half-clothed kids in the street didn't even pester me for a shoe shine, or hustle me to buy their shopworn packs of chicle. Rather, they stared, dumbfounded, sucking apprehensively on fingers, pacifiers, or those salty, chilied plum candies that were ubiquitous in downscale Mexico. Apparently, gringos didn't often make it this far.

In short, this was my kind of place. Seedy, far away from any tourists, and just plain beyond the world inhabited by buttholes like Semper Fi.

There were a dozen largish buildings near the water—a restaurant, a general store, a chapel with its gated courtyard, several large warehouses, a small police station, a telegraph office with a visor-wearing *anciano* who still tapped out messages on a brass telegraph key, and a red tile–roofed cantina-cum-whorehouse hopefully named El Farolito (the Little Beacon).

A few yards from the harbor end of the one dusty "avenue" an old concrete slip jutted out into the water, a battered Russian freighter moored to it. I couldn't read its name in Cyrillic script, but one of the kids said it had come from "Arcoangelo." *Could he have meant the Siberian outpost of Archangel?* I wondered. No one in sight to ask.

If one was intent on merely crawling into a hole with no wish to ever come out, Salina Cruz would do nicely. If the CIA boys had ever been here, they'd taken one look, spit on the ground in contempt, and headed off someplace where ice, scotch, American cigarettes, toilet paper, and anorexic white chicks were all available for the right price.

But the environs did have Indians. I heard both isthmus Zapotec and a Nahuatl dialect spoken as I entered the general store to buy smokes, matches, and canned food. John Paddock had told me there still might be one or two small enclaves of Nahuatl speakers scattered along the coast, surrounded by the far more numerous Zapotec- and Tehuantepeca-speaking Indians.

I took my tins of fruit and sardines to the seawall and spread them out, opening the cans with the last birthday gift I'd gotten from Eddy—a battered swiss army knife. I stroked its burgundy handle, thinking of him, worrying, then pulled myself together and dug into the sardines.

The local kids still kept their distance as I ate, but a fellow named Lalo chatted me up while he loaded his fifteen-foot skiff. He was taking supplies to a fishing community called La Ventosa several miles east of town. He asked where I was staying. I pointed to the sand. He laughed. "A friend of mine in La Ventosa will rent you a thatched *palapa* (palm-roofed beach shack) and hammock for eight pesos a day. Very beautiful there!" I told him I'd think about it. He pushed off, poling out into the channel.

I spent the rest of the afternoon napping in the shade of a warehouse, hoping I'd spot a Russian or two. If Semper Fi knew there was a Russki ship down here in nowhereland, he'd have been right here on the quay jabbering about faggots and sniffing out yet another sinister plot to destroy the States.

From what I'd read, President Lopez Mateos had managed to steer a fine line between the States and Kennedy on one hand, and Cuba-Russia on the other. All Mexico wanted was to gain a little breathing room between opposing forces. Mexico needed room in which to expand its economy while the competing behemoths wasted their energy on each other. Nuances like this simply went past street-level spooks . . . and apparently sociopathic brigadier generals as well.

By evening the afternoon heat began to wane and the town came to life with folks strolling its dusty streets. Several taco carts emerged from nowhere and two local cops in tattered brown uniforms began their rounds. Once there were enough spectators to make it worth their while they came over to check on me.

"I study anthropology and folklore in Mexico City. I'm on a research break to visit indigenous communities—tales of spirit beings." The fat older cop nodded. "There are indigenous communities nearby—a small one on the beach near La Ventosa and another to the northwest at a settlement called Ce Xochitl (One Flower). Will you be staying long?"

"A week at most. Do you need to see my student visa?" He hadn't thought of it, but it would make good theater for the crowd of a dozen onlookers who had gathered about a half-dozen yards away.

I pulled out my visa and an ID card from the University of the Americas. Fatso looked them over, not noticing that they were upside down. *Good,* I thought, *he can't read. They won't be able to confirm my name if someone comes asking.* I offered them each a smoke. They went away pleased with themselves.

At dark I wandered into El Farolito and ordered a beer. Corona longneck. "*¿Al tiempo o helada?* (Room temperature or iced?)" asked the barman. "Cost?" I inquired.

"*Cinco al tiempo. Siete helada* (Five pesos room temperature. Seven iced)." Not cheap—the price of a decent meal of rice and beans, with fish or an egg.

"Iced, please." He set the beer in front of me, unopened. I glanced up and stared. He smiled and turned away.

I was about to pursue the lack of service when a slender, perfumed arm snaked over my shoulder. "*¿Destapador, joven?* (Opener, young man?)"

"So that's how they do it here?"

"Yes, joven. I am your hostess." I reached out and took the opener from her hand. She was a light-skinned mestiza, pretty in a blue black, raccoonlike eyeliner sort of way. "I only dance with Indian girls," I smiled.

"Really?"

I nodded in response. She grabbed her bottle opener, shrugged, and disappeared. The cantina was hot and dirty; only one of its three ceiling fans worked. The bar, about fifty feet long, was a huge plank of dark tropical wood. The floor looked like it might be Saltillo tile, but it hadn't been cleaned in so long that one couldn't be sure. An ancient jukebox in one corner sprouted an incongruous string of bare twenty-watt bulbs that had been draped from the rafters.

When a table finally opened up under the spinning fan, I made a dash for it. That gave me a better view of both the dance floor and the door to the street. Half a dozen couples were slow dancing to the jukebox. The men were mostly mestizo, in ordinary street dress. Two were sailors, possibly Asian. No Russians in sight.

There were many more women in the bar than men. That wasn't unusual in these sorts of places. The girls made their living from dance tips and tokens given them by the waiter for every drink their male companions purchased. Typically, some also sold themselves, keeping about half the money they earned from sex.

I ordered a second beer and nursed it while more hopeful girls drifted in. The newcomers were uniformly Indian looking. As with nearly everything else in Mexico the light-skinned women had first pick of the customers. The Indian girls were at the back of the bus.

Being a maid or a hooker was easier and far more lucrative for an Indian girl than being a corn farmer's wife tending six kids, goats, and two acres of hilly milpa (cornfield) ten miles beyond the last dirt road. Adding to the rural burden, running water, electricity, and iced anything were simply unknown in Mexico's vast patches of backcountry.

I was thinking about that, as well as where I'd sleep later, when someone gently touched my shoulder. She was hesitant. "Am I disturbing you, señor?" *Yep, she's Indian. Looks it. Smells it (jasmine in her hair). And calls twenty-year-olds "señor."* In Mexico, deference of that nature only falls on the backs of Indians.

"The *jefa* (boss woman) said you preferred Indians. Would you like me to sit with you . . . ?" She had that scrunched up look women get when they are bracing for rejection. Yet, I couldn't imagine any man rejecting her. She was about five feet tall, slender, and dark skinned, with high cheekbones, almond eyes, and a beautiful mouth, all set off by a cascade of jasmine-scented black hair. I stood and pulled out a chair for her.

"Please, señorita. I'd be honored." She smiled, avoiding full eye contact, and sat down carefully, self-conscious. "I am Juan Alejandro—and your name, miss?"

"I am María."

"Is that your real name . . . ?" She leaned forward, "No. It's Malinalli, but I don't use it here."

"'Twisting grass'—how lovely." What irony, I thought. I'd just left a place called Malinalco and found another. Fate had obviously taken a personal interest in my soul search. "You understand our language!" she exclaimed, appearing both nervous and surprised.

"Only words. But your name was carried by La Malinche long ago. Every scholar of the Spanish period knows it." "Who is La Malinche?" she asked.

"The one they sometimes called Malintzín, wife of Cortés—the white, bearded conquistador depicted in the masks used at *carnaval.*" The girl smiled, "I thought she was called doña Marina."

"She was to the Spanish. But her own name was Malinalli—born a Mexica princess."

"Are you a scholar, then?"

"I study in Mexico City—anthropology and folklore . . ." The waiter interrupted. I bought the obligatory drinks. "Would you like to talk while we dance?" she asked.

"Sure." She was stiff and a bit nervous, but soon relaxed, then snuggled closer as we talked.

"I'm from a settlement on the coast—a few families still speak the *nahua* there. Down here it's mostly Tehuantepeca—their women are very beautiful." Their *women are beautiful? Holy smokes—just what does she think she is?* I wondered, getting a hard-on from the smell and feel of her. But I played it cool, asking casually, "Were you raised traditionally?"

"Yes. My father was a healer. But he's dead now. I provide for the family."

"How old are you?"

"I'm not supposed to say."

"Can I guess?" She nodded and wrinkled her nose.

"Nineteen." She shook her head.

"Fifteen." She shook her head again. *Whew!*

"Seventeen." She wiggled, "Yes, almost."

"Do you spend the night with customers?"

"The *night* . . . ?" Apparently she had to think. *Good sign*, I reassured myself as her exquisite lips parted. "I never have, but La Jefa has been pushing me." She looked toward the boss . . . La Jefa was the same raccoon-eyed mestiza who'd first approached me.

"I'll ask her if you can spend the night with me," I said. She scrunched her face again. "I'm nervous—I am not a *veterana.*"

"No worries. I don't want sex. I want to talk about folklore."

"Really? You would pay just to talk to me?"

"That—and have dinner with you. OK?" She smiled and shrugged.

I arranged it with La Jefa—all night with the teenager and the house's exit fee for one of their girls, called the *salida*, ran just sixteen U.S. dollars.

"María" and I stepped out into the warm, breezy night. Stars winked at us, rather like her stunned girlfriends inside had done when I took her arm to leave. "Where shall we eat?"

"There is a little restaurant near the chapel; La Jefa says the food is good."

"Let's go." We crossed the dusty area that served as the town's plaza. It was the first Mexican town I'd ever been in that didn't have a real square laid out, so I asked her why they had none.

"A bad storm two years ago. The old plaza was very pretty—bandstand. *Bancos* and flowers. My dad took me there for a photograph when we came for my confirmation. I was seven. I still have the photograph . . . is your name really Juan Alejandro?"

"No, in English it's John Alexander." I pronounced it slowly, but she couldn't say it. I laughed. "That's why I gave you the Spanish version." She had a soft laugh. Her Spanish was decent but exotic from the distinctive cadence of her native language. Her words were slow and soft—followed by the air-popping glottal breaks she inserted into many Spanish words.

The restaurant La Bahia was one of those inside/outside eateries that are ubiquitous in Mexico. The kitchen was under an attached tin-roofed lean-to at the rear.

We took a table in the shadows. At her request, I read the eight-item menu to her. I'd met few rural Indians who could read and Malinalli was no exception. We ordered rice, beans, and grilled fish with a relish of chiles, garlic, tomato, and spices I didn't know. The food was good. Malinalli was finally looking relaxed.

"Do you have family in Mexico?"

"No—I'm from the United States. Not much family. One brother in the army. That's it."

"I'm sorry." She sounded like she meant it. "I've heard of your country—'Chon Kannaady' is president." I'd discovered that John Kennedy was the only American name known to many rural Mexicans. I smiled, "Yes."

"Is your country as rich as they say?"

"It's much richer than Mexico . . . and much more expensive."

"Is that why you study in this country? Because it is cheaper?"

"Yes, it is cheaper here. But I came to Mexico to see what it is like. I have only been here nine months, but I like it a lot."

"So what exactly do you study?"

"Anthropology. Folklore—the spirit world and the old cultures."

"What is it that you wish to know?"

"I want to know about the naguales, about *almas* . . . the mirror worlds. I was with some men hunting jaguar recently in Tabasco—a tigre was killed and the local Indian man whose spirit was in the jaguar died at the same time. Perhaps you know of such things?"

"I am a girl, so my father never taught me all of those things, but my grandfather still lives to the north. He might come to town and talk. But I know only a little." She paused for a moment, looking intently at me. "Naguales? Mine is trapped, you know."

"Tell me about it, señorita." "Can we walk?" she asked softly, glancing nervously at a boisterous table of patrons nearby. I pulled out the chair for her and we went down to the shore. Standing on the low seawall, listening to the waves, I lit a smoke, absorbing her scent and the glow of the night sky. She began . . .

"When I was a little girl I dreamed of being a healer like my father. He took spells out of people. Set bones, gave remedies. Knew the old chants. He was strong and people respected him. But I was a girl. That misfortune confined me. As I grew older he fished more and did less healing as the old ways, and the old ones who followed them, began to die or move away to find work. Then he died in the storm two years ago . . ." She paused, tears running down her cheeks.

"On his boat. Two cousins, one brother, and an uncle went with him. They found the bodies of the others, but not father's. I had nobody to say prayers over. But his soul came to me once after his death and he spoke to me: 'I am sorry, little one. I need you to care for your brothers and sisters. I am sorry I did not teach you the old healing ways. Forgive me, Daughter.' Then he floated away. I do not know how to call him back. My nagual became trapped by the sadness when Father died and we could not bury him. It is as if part of me has been separated."

"That's my problem, too."

"Your father's soul?"

"No—my own. It left me when I was eight and I don't know how to call it back."

"I'm sorry . . . and your mother?"

"She died in childbirth . . . and yours?"

"She and her unborn baby died in childbirth when I was twelve. An aunt lived with us for a while. Then she went back to my grandfather."

"So how long have you been at El Farolito?"

"Since I was fifteen . . . but I do not live there. I work three nights a week." I didn't have the nerve to ask more about the club, and she offered no clues, except that she had been "nervous" to leave El Farolito with me.

Several hours later we strolled back to the club. I'd paid both for a place to sleep and someone to sleep with. I didn't know it then, but in so doing I'd joined the legions of pathetically lonely men who paid hookers the world over just to hear someone talk to them. Her girlfriends giggled as we stepped inside. She waved and smiled. Several of the Indian men glared at me . . . it was my first introduction to racial and sexual jealousy in a cathouse. Incongruous but real.

Her "room" was just one corner of the rear hallway, divided from the adjoining one by half of an old sheet. A broken-down double bed in one corner, a small chest of drawers, and a locally made chair left only a two-foot-wide open area. A chipped blue-enameled tin washbasin sat on the chest of drawers, looking like a forlorn Dutch still life. One bare twenty-watt lightbulb dangled from the ceiling; her very own bar of soap and a half roll of toilet paper rounded out the amenities.

She reached up, unscrewed the lightbulb, and asked me for a match. I dug a box of Guerrero-brand matches out of my shirt, slung my duffel under the chest of drawers, and watched her in the half light that bled through the sheet from the other room. She stepped up on the chair and stretched to light a candle on the high blue-wooden wall altar that displayed a cheap print of the Virgin of Guadalupe. "She protects me," Malinalli whispered. "Don't hurt me, please."

I had stripped off my shirt to ease the stifling heat. She took that as a sign of my intentions. Natural, I suppose.

She motioned me toward the bed. I pulled off my Wranglers and Redwings and slipped onto the bed. "Is there a fan, Mal—" She put her fingers to her lips to remind me of her working name . . . "—María," I finished. She smiled.

"Do you like butterflies?" I asked. Her smile broadened. "Why did you ask that about me? I play with them in the garden at La Ventosa. They dry their wings on my hands. But how could you know that?"

"You have a butterfly smile." She looked at me for a moment, deciding something, I guessed, then shrugged. "I'll go get a fan." I lit a smoke, checking her out as she walked away. She stopped at the door, looked back over her shoulder, and paused . . . "And an ashtray." She returned a few minutes later with an ashtray and battered table fan that one screwed into the light socket. "The water in the basin is fresh. You may use my soap." She waited outside while I cleaned up, feeling oddly self-conscious.

I was perched on the bed when she came back, whispering softly. "Souls and butterflies . . . so different than the others who ask about my *chi-chis* (boobs) and beg me to do unusual things that aren't *real* sex."

In the glowing sheet's half light she pulled off her frayed party dress and hung it carefully on the one hanger suspended from a wire strung across the corner. I watched her every move. "The dress . . . it's not mine," she explained. "I must be careful of it." She readied to unhook her equally tattered bra. "Don't, María—I'm just going to sleep here a while." She stopped mid-motion, rehooked the top *gancho* of her bra, and slid onto the one battered chair.

"So, why do you think your soul left you as a child, Juan?" she asked. I smoked and shrugged. She leaned forward. Her lush, jasmine-scented hair, blown by the fan, brushed across my face as she gave me that butterfly smile again.

I was already shaking from testosterone fever when I pulled her to me, my resolve to be faithful to Marianna shot to hell. I wanted to feel again . . . and I'd gone very cold and lonely after Mari left for Rome. "María" cupped my face in her hands so gently that it surprised me. "Is this what it feels like to be a butterfly?" I asked.

"Shh . . ." she answered. Her throat was soft. The pulse in her neck strong and fast. She pressed her lips to mine. I hadn't expected such tenderness. The tips of her fingers moved along my jaw, gently tracing an outline on my face. "What is it?" I asked. She glowed. "I gave you a butterfly—I am glad you could feel it. Your soul is not far."

Wow, this is so different than Mari . . . than anything since Betty Anne. I must be dreaming.

"Your soul is near," she murmured, as if she'd read my mind. My pulse slowed and I became calm. I had the odd sensation that her altar candle brightened in response.

I looked over her shoulder. A dark-skinned Guadalupe smiled down at me. "Your soul is near," Malinalli repeated, "I can sense it."

I thought I could, too. But just then the plywood door to the adjoining room swung open with a bang and La Jefa pulled a client onto the lopsided bed just six feet away. Whatever I sensed of souls, butterflies, and the erotic scent of jasmine vanished as abruptly as it had come.

The pair on the other side of the sheet smelled of sweat, booze, and stale clothes. She said all the things that I imagined whores say. "You are so big. So hot. Let me get on top, *papito*." They rolled around noisily, the bed cracking like snapping kindling. At one point, the privacy sheet pulled to one side when his foot got caught in it.

Malinalli pressed against my chest and hid her face, her hands over her ears, her eyes shut, squeezing out the sounds and the scene. The clattering table fan pushed the scents of their rut to us. They left quickly enough but left their foul, unwashed aura behind.

Globs of custard yellow semen glistened on the adjacent bed, smelling like a musty tidal pool. A dozen huge cockroaches darted out of the shadows to gorge on it, swaying rhythmically. The child in my arms opened her eyes just in time to see them feeding and retched. I held her forehead as she vomited, then helped her dress, gathered her things into a net bag, and took her out into the clean Pacific night.

❧

№ 13 La Ventosa

Dawn broke softly through the grove of palms, so as not to wake her, I imagined. We'd walked the long block down to the water after exiting El Farolito and hitched a twenty-peso boat ride with a local fisherman, who put us ashore in front of the settlement at La Ventosa. She had told me, "I want to go home."

It was the first time I'd ever been someplace where the sea came from one direction and dawn from the other. A local *panga* (small fishing boat) floated in the lagoon fifty yards away. The skinny fellow standing in it poled his way toward us. Beyond the long sand spit and palm groves, breakers crashed over an outlying reef, and a soft breeze rustled through the palms. Somewhere a coconut thudded into the sand with a dull whump, and roosters crowed.

Pelicans dive-bombed the lagoon and the lantern of a fishing boat faded as the sky brightened. Later, the gulls circled a half-dozen returning launches. With them came Lalo, the boatman who had offered me a palapa the day before.

"Thank you for bringing her back to us," he whispered when I walked over to shake his hand.

"Are you related to her, señor?"

"Her uncle. She needed to provide for her family, but it was a sad choice she made." Had she other options?" I asked. "¿'Sabe? (Who knows?)" he shrugged. By then Malinalli had awakened and sat up.

"Lalo, please, make a place for me to work with you, so the children can stay here where they are happy." He stared, arms folded across his chest. But she wouldn't let it go. "*Please*, Uncle! I do not wish to return to Salina Cruz." "You *and* the children?" he asked.

"We are only five. I can help with the fishing." *Who the hell are "the children"?* I wondered.

"Man's work, little one." She looked down. I wondered how many times she'd already heard this, so I butted in.

"Given the circumstances, could you make an exception?"

"If I could use the larger boat, it would work," he shrugged. "But . . ."
"Is the motor still broken?" she asked.

"Yes. I need a crankshaft and pistons."

"I thought you had located them in Puerto Angel, Uncle."

"A thousand pesos, little one!" He shrugged again.

"Did you drink it away, Uncle?" Not a child at the moment, she had a grown woman's edge in her voice. He looked away. I pulled out the money.

"Here. A thousand pesos. A palapa as long as I wish and two meals a day . . . and she gets to work with you." He hesitated, then nodded. I felt weird. Mari gone just three weeks and the old, impetuous JA had taken over again. The Voice scolded me. *Eighty bucks! All 'cause she made you feel good . . . you're a loner, by nature . . . sap!*

She crossed her arms under her adolescent breasts, squeezed herself, and surprised me with her butterfly tone. "I will work hard, Uncle. We will make money. The children will eat." She paused, smiled, and put in her final word. "Rest awhile, Uncle. I will go to Puerto Angel with you later today." She reached out for the money and took it from me. "I'll keep it safe," she smiled. Her voice had a gentle, hypnotic quality to it. Now it was Uncle who had no choice. He took her orders with good grace and shuffled off to nap.

"Why?" she asked softly, staring at the stack of hundred-peso notes in her palm . . . "You could have me any night for but fifty pesos (four U.S. dollars)."

"I want help with the soul part . . . I thought if I helped free your soul, you might help with mine." She shook her head. "You are an odd one." I shrugged in response.

"Let's go and meet my hermanos (siblings). I am their mother now." Mystery resolved. "The children" were her four siblings: Ana, twelve; Alicia, ten; Simón, nine; and Ari, five. They lived in a ramshackle palm-thatched lean-to open on three sides. It faced a dense grove of small palms. A few yards away a tiny kitchen garden nestled under the trees. Four hammocks hung in the shed. Tattered clothes hung from cords suspended through the driftwood rafters. I noticed several large wooden crates, an old kerosene lantern, a tray of dishes and utensils, and a barbecue pit fashioned from discarded orange brick. A large galvanized laundry tub sat just behind the ramada's rear wall. It looked like a Stateside family roughing it by camping on the beach.

Her youngest sister, Ari, played a five-year-old's version of peek-a-boo with me till she worked up the nerve to step up and ask, "Are you our new father? We asked 'Alli to bring us one so she could be here with us."

"No, child. I am your sister's guest. A visitor to the area."

"You talk funny."

"I know. I'm from another country. Spanish is not easy." She nodded but probably didn't understand any of it. Malinalli shooed her away, then turned to me. "Sleep in the big hammock. It's always shady. I'll have food prepared in several hours. I'll wake you." I rolled into the hammock, luxuriated in the fresh, shaded breeze, listened to the surf and the soft butterfly tones of her voice, and drifted off.

It was hot when she wakened me. The midday meal was served on one of the big wooden boxes, the kids all sitting around it expectant and cross-legged in the sand. The one large serving dish held a mound of yellow rice cooked with peas, carrots, and onion. Fresh chunks of pineapple, banana, and papaya circled it. "They won't have beans till evening. Ana, the eldest, knows how to cook them. You supervise, Juan. I won't be back till tomorrow." She hugged each of the kids, gently telling each she loved them. She smiled at me and left, taking her butterfly voice and butterfly hands with her.

I could sense that Betty Anne smiled and watched me eat. So did the four real kids sitting in the sand. I panicked once it sunk in that I'd been left in charge of four kids. The Voice laughed hysterically. *You idiot, hee, hee, snort, you've got to let go of this Betty Anne bullshit.*

The kids were happy and playful. But all except Ari were quite shy around me. Ana and Alicia spoke to each other in hushed Nahuatl. The younger two kids favored Spanish.

I took a walk after eating. An entire community of a hundred or so Indians, and poor mestizos, were sprinkled among the palms along a half mile of wide beach and the dunes. A dozen or so upturned boats had been pulled up onto the beach under the palms' protecting shade. Only two of them had outboard motors. The rest were lagoon-going pangas, the long poles that propelled them stored in the boats.

At the far end of the lagoon, several enclosed houses defined the local elites. All of those families were Spanish speakers but appeared to be of mixed Indian-Mestizo descent. I drifted back to the palapa about four. Ana, the eldest, spoke to me for the first time. She seemed nervous and didn't make eye contact.

"Alli told us you liked rice and beans. Would that suit you for dinner later?" She was a miniature version of Malinalli but looked only seven or eight, not the twelve years I'd been told. Her lanky, jet-black hair billowed in the breeze; her little hands were already bent and scarred from years of work.

"That's perfect . . . and do you know where I can buy fresh water?"

"A truck comes once a week or so from Salina Cruz when the tides are low. We ran out several days ago."

"I'll go buy us some." I offered to pay one of the guys with a motor to take me to Salina Cruz. He waited while I bought four five-gallon jugs of water from the general store. When I went to square up with him, he refused the money. "I am using Lalo's small motor while he is gone. Now I don't have to pay him rent for his motor . . . and we don't go fishing again till nightfall, so you owe me nothing."

He helped me carry the four heavy jugs up the beach. Ana was ecstatic, lining the kids up with their plastic cups as I carefully poured water. Then I napped in the big hammock while Ana chattered in Nahuatl with an old Indian man who had come by, curious about me, I suppose, from his frequent glances in my direction.

Finally, I nodded at him when he looked my way. Ana came over. "Come meet my grandfather." I pulled myself out of the hammock and went over. "Allow me to introduce my grandfather," Ana smiled proudly. "Don Rigoberto Pilli—this is Juan."

"*Mucho gusto* (pleased to meet you), I am, in Spanish, Juan Alejandro." He looked me over for a moment and extended his hand. His Spanish was unpolished, yet his voice was even gentler than Alli's.

"So you are the one who brought my granddaughter back from *that place*." I nodded. "And you wish to know about the spirit world, and naguales."

"Yes. I am anxious to learn."

"We talk after dinner. I have come from Ce Xochitl." Ana had curled up at his feet, stirring the beans with one arm as she gazed at him, her head moving to the cadence of his soothing voice. The old man was gaunt, hints of gray in his thinning hair. His leathery face had an otherwise fragile look to it. Clear brown eyes, a finely chiseled nose, sensitive mouth . . . and a softness to the jaw all made him look rather like an aged philosopher. Not a laborer or farmer.

Later, when little Ari came to shake my hammock for dinner, she giggled, "There is a surprise for you, Papá."

"I'm not your new papá, Ari."

"I know, but Alli promised us! Come . . . it's time to eat." I went over to the smoldering fire. Ana served me and her grandfather simultaneously. On my plate was a small *langosta*—the clawless Pacific lobsters so prized for their taste. Two others simmered in a pot.

"Where did these come from, Ana?"

"From the morning catch."

"You gave me too much, child."

"You are our guest," said don Rigoberto, in poorly enunciated Spanish. I reached into my back pocket for the buck knife I carried and neatly halved the lobster, then tipped one half onto his plate. He grinned, the softness in him radiating pleasure. "I like langosta. First time to eat in many years . . . first time white guy ever call me 'don.' It is a fine meal."

After dinner we put the kids to bed. Ari and her older sister, Alicia, fought to sleep on my spread-out bedroll, leaving me a hammock. But the old man gently pulled me away from the lean-to as they lay down. We walked into the nearby grove of whispering palms, the stars twinkling as the day's heat drifted up into the night sky. Gentle waves caressed the glistening sands facing the lagoon. I turned on my battery-charged recorder. He began, in Nahuatl, which I later had translated in Mexico City:

> *In the days before mortal men were formed, all lived forever. The spirits were one with their hosts. Human in form, but immortal, as remain the gods. Most of the Old Ones lived in caves among the hills and mountains. They ate not of human foods but absorbed their sustenance from the heavens.*
>
> *They were untainted by the experience of mortal sex. They were as seeds, giving life to all else, including the animals. For reasons men no longer know, several among them ate of human food. Their descendants were mortal and had mortal sex. They died and suffered as will you and I. We are descended of these.*
>
> *In this newer age spirits no longer had permanent hosts, but the spirit half was neither tainted by food nor by sex. So the spirits live on in a parallel life—in animals. That is, the world as seen in a mirror. And also they are born again. The spirit that we share with an animal is shared to keep the spirit alive. The animal is untainted by human food but is tainted by sex. So the animal dies and the nagual is freed to be reborn again in another child . . . I think that is all for now, White One.*

"Since I only understood a few words, may I ask a question?" He nodded. "What does the spirit look like . . . and how does one call it back if it goes missing?"

He didn't fully understand my Spanish, so Ana filled in with Nahuatl. "Ah, I see, White One . . . well, then. Some say the spirit is as a breath of air. Others insist it is as a *vela* (candle). A light. I'm not sure which. But I once heard a spirit pass in breath . . . calling a spirit? . . . I need to ask Ana or Alli words. We wait till tomorrow night." I thanked him, but he made no move to go. "I talk to my son now. *Solo* (alone)." I left and went back to the ramada.

When I awoke in the morning, little Ari, who looked three, not five, was tucked into the hammock with me. I started to freak. She was as hot as a radiator . . . and *so* close! Then Eddy materialized. I breathed deeply as he smiled at me. "It's like when we were kids, John. You snuggled me. I'm still grateful." I took deep breaths, relaxed, and turned over to sleep.

The next day seemed timeless. Peaceful. The breeze blew the sand flies away and the sound of kids playing near the ramada calmed me. I was at peace. Don Rigoberto slept late. He had shared a hammock with Simón. This sense of closeness surrounded me with wonder. *Is this what family is like?* As I daydreamed, an imaginary Eddy grinned at me again—such sweet illusions. "Now you know why I have always wanted a family, John!" I smiled back and started to answer, but he disappeared.

At dusk a sky streaked with peach, pink, orange—and layer upon layer of rippling milk-clouds—announced sunset. Two pangas floated in the lagoon, the black silhouettes of their occupants highlighted by the setting sun. Somewhere a sea lion barked and the throb of a far-off motor echoed across the water.

Don Rigoberto took me out to the palm grove again and began to talk of calling spirits, but his Spanish wasn't up to the task. All I grasped was the part about not having sex. We were both frustrated, understanding only cigarettes and a late meal of fish-head soup back at Ana's outdoor stove.

Night came. The palms rustled in the light of an immense orange moon. The waves, as if captured by the mood, sighed in a trancelike rhythm. I leaned against the shack, smoking, little Ari nestled in my lap, and watched the lagoon's surface ripple in the fresh night breeze. The moon dipped lower and, like a puppy, Ari burrowed into me—going for total body contact. Betty Anne smiled down at me from her magical realm and iridescent flashes, like fireflies, swirled in the lagoon, visible as the moon slipped behind a bank of clouds.

I leaned forward to get a better look. Don Rigoberto nodded. "The sea gods. They come with Ehecatl (God of the Winds)." I hung a sleeping Ari over my shoulder, stood, and went down to the water. The old man followed. A glowing wash of pale, opalescent blue-green floated in the lagoon, transforming to iridescent silver, then to green again.

"They speak," said the old man in simple Spanish. "We cannot hear them. They speak to the mirror world."

Sprawled limp over my shoulder, Ari made odd sucking noises. I brushed my cheek against her hair. She sighed, breathed deeply, then stopped. Still as a ghost. Startled, I reached to shake her, but don

Rigoberto intercepted my arm and leaned to me. "Her soul plays with ancient ones. She breathe again soon."

My spine tingled at his words. As the frisson of comprehension traveled up to my skull, I shivered. "Quiet!" said the old man . . . "Her soul, it will return!"

About three minutes later, little Ari took in a deep breath, stirred, and began to make her sucking sounds again. I could feel her essence reenter her, reenergizing her body. A startling wave of emotion washed over me. Emitting their fluorescent blue-green, the sea's fireflies rolled to the surface of the lagoon one final time, then vanished. "Her soul was with her father," said the old man. "It is a good night!"

The soft iridescence gone again, a sudden breeze enveloped us in an unexpected chill. We returned to the shack. I climbed into the big hammock. Ari, awake now, went off to pee. As she climbed back into the hammock to join me, she said, "I saw my papá. He held me. Do you think it was real?"

"I'm sure it was." She was asleep again even before I finished reassuring her.

So trusting . . . and able to sleep in the arms of a near stranger? I envied Ari. Sometime later in the night, I tried to turn over but couldn't. Malinalli lay next to me, breathing softly, little Ari on top of us. The hammock swayed gently and Malinalli's jasmine scent sweetened the night air. Ari made her sucking noises. And I imagined that I felt my soul nearby. I took a breath, just in case . . . and waited, hopeful.

This is the way it's meant to be, I told myself in wonderment, then turned over and slept again, dreaming of Betty Anne, Eddy, and rising fireflies. In my dream, Eddy was still four, his sweet, childlike smile not yet blemished by the horrors that would later haunt us.

This was the first night in my life where man, woman, and child slept together, as had been done since the dawn of our species. I didn't know it then, but it would be the only night I would ever have this experience.

23

Malinalli and her uncle had gotten his big thirty-horsepower Evinrude motor repaired in Puerto Angel. A crew of locals recaulked the ten-meter offshore boat with high gunwales that would allow the family to triple their catch. Malinalli, Ana, and Simón all helped their grandfather repair nets that had been stored in the boat. The local craftsmen were still feverishly working on the boat three days later when the old man decided it was time for Malinalli and me to accompany him home to Ce Xochitl.

We passed through the lagoon north of Salina Cruz, then our small skiff turned and entered a stretch of open water. On a low headland several hours north of Salina Cruz lay Ce Xochitl, a settlement of perhaps a hundred or so. They fished, farmed corn, and made baskets from reeds in a brackish nearby swamp, hidden behind mangroves that went on for miles. Herons, pelicans, sea lions, dolphins, mullet, raccoons, sea turtles, monkeys, and flocks of brightly colored parrots all made their presence known.

As I stepped off the skiff and waded ashore, I walked right into a time warp. "Now and again local fishing boats visit the settlement to sell axes or buckets," Alli explained. But, according to don Rigoberto, the last *blanco* (white) to spend any time in the village had been a padre who had eventually tired of his isolation and gone away some ten or fifteen years before me. They were known in Salina Cruz because the men marketed their fish, woven baskets, and farm produce there. But Ce Xochitl rarely got visitors.

It was heaven on earth—if one didn't care about having electricity, running water, cigarettes, cold beer, and toilet paper. The locals didn't, clinging tenaciously to their language and ancient customs. That included the game in which their teenage boys hip-shot a ball back and forth across the dusty plaza—just as had been done before the conquest. The only obvious accoutrements of the outside world were machetes, several dozen steel axes, plastic buckets, a few kerosene lanterns, and store-made matches. They even grew their own tobacco.

I took photos of the ball game and recorded several songs, but it made folks nervous so I quit and watched. I heard almost no Spanish . . . and the little I did hear was a courtesy to me. They knew nothing of the States, not even John Kennedy, so I was asked many questions. "Are you Spanish?" "Have you a wife?" "Children?" "A mistress?" "Land?" "What work do you do?" "Do others dress as you?" "What foods do you grow?" "Tell us of your family." I was baffling to them.

Don Rigoberto called folks together in the plaza on my second night and explained me to them. "The White One has come from far away to study the old ways and the spirit world. He has been kind to our daughter, Malinalli, and generous to her family. He has little family but knows much about souls—the sea gods spoke to him in La Ventosa. I shall take him to Teapan tonight . . . who will burn incense for us?"

Two old guys volunteered. One of them, named Jerónimo, seemed as gruff and short tempered as Alli's grandfather was gentle. He interrupted don Rigoberto, "And torches?" After a bit of a stare-down, a couple of the teenage ball players reluctantly volunteered. "Good, we go this afternoon and shall return tomorrow," pronounced Jerónimo. Don Rigoberto seemed serene, in spite of the other elder's brusque demeanor.

I was offered a shaded hammock and rested. About 2 PM don Rigoberto led our small column out of the village, but Malinalli wasn't with us. Some gender thing. She had wanted to come with us but was overruled by the old men, Jerónimo leading the "nay" votes. That left her in enough of a funk to extract her grandfather's promise to teach her "things about healing."

The trek to Teapan (Sacred Hill) took about two hours. We skirted the marshes, crossed slash-and-burn jungle clearings converted to milpa, then trudged into an area of low, densely forested hills. The most prominent hill was our destination.

Enshrouded in strangler figs, the hill jutted up into the forest canopy. Carved sandstone blocks littered the ground. I stepped over a large one to avoid a snake, turned to climb further, and came face-to-face with a row of mossy but exquisitely carved faces. It was frieze-work that encircled what had once been a brilliant white pyramid. Faded streaks of green, blue, and red clung tentatively to the stone masks' deepest recesses.

The slope was littered with fragments of large funerary jars. Obsidian blades, once imported from central Mexico and discarded a millennium earlier, glinted in the patchy sunlight of the forest canopy. Somewhere nearby a flock of macaws fluttered and shrieked. Monkeys chattered and insects I could not identify came out as if to challenge our intrusion.

The next hour was spent clearing a space on top of the pyramid. As the teenagers hacked strangler figs from the pyramid's crown, the metallic clang of machetes echoed through the empty forest. There were ancient pottery shards everywhere. I grimaced as large bowl fragments crunched underfoot. About halfway up the pyramid's thirty-odd feet, a narrow, crumbling platform encircled it. Carved faces—quite like Malinalli's—encircled the front and one side. I traced the faces with my fingers, lingering on the beautifully recurved lips and long, arched noses.

The boys set up torches and cleaned out several large stones on top, which, said don Rigoberto, were *incenseros* (incense burners). One of the teenage boys took four balls of dusty-colored amber from his woven shoulder bag. The other set up palm-frond torches soaked in pitch. There were small holes cut into the rock to hold them.

"How long has it been since you came here to clear the pyramid? It looks as if it has been covered by the jungle for centuries." Don Rigoberto struggled with my Spanish, until the sharp-nosed, graying Jerónimo, looking disgusted, translated my question . . . and gentle old don Rigoberto's response.

"We used to clear it every year. The whole village would make the journey. Then the historians from Mexico (City) came looking for our shrines a few years ago and took away two carved stones. After that we let the jungle grow to hide it. Now we come each year and clear only the *techo* (roof)."

"All those figs in one year?"

"Yes, the forest claims everything during the rains." We rested under the trees at the base of the pyramid and waited for nightfall. As dusk enclosed us it became creepy and oppressively silent. I lit a smoke and listened. The match's pungent odor hung in the cloying, humid air.

The old man Jerónimo observed me listening and explained in a hoarse whisper, "All things await the gods of the night as the world is swallowed once again by the Lord of the Dark."

In another thirty minutes it had turned pitch black. Shielded by the great trees, I couldn't even see my hand in front of my face. Don Rigoberto watched the starlit sky from the pyramid's waist, then whistled. The others stirred, ascending in the dark. I moved to follow, but Jerónimo protested, "It's sacred up there. Stay here. Wait!"

Once up on the pyramid's crown, they lit torches and the balls of hard, amber-colored resin—copal—the musty, sweet, smoky incense that called their gods. Jerónimo carried a small deer-skin drum. He palmed a slow beat as the torches flared.

Off in the jungle a jaguar snarled and the world came to life once more. Crickets trilled, animals moved, and a gentle breeze rustled across the dry forest floor. The gods of the night had arrived to claim their domain until dawn stole their power again.

In Mexico City I had studied glyphs that chronicled ancient Mesoamerica's endless cycle of day and night, moon upon moon, dry season upon dry season, rains upon rains, year upon year, century upon century, and millennium upon millennium. This pyramid had likely seen them all. I imagined that the eyes staring out from its stone-masked waist were still actively absorbing the rhythms of the universe.

The Aztecs, and those who came before them, viewed the years as bundles of reeds, carried on the bent back of their god, Old Man Time. They counted in twelves, twenties, and four hundreds. Four hundred was *xiquipilli* (the bundle of four hundred), possibly the origins of don Rigoberto's surname.

I sat perched on the waist of the pyramid, like the village women once had, craning my neck to get a glimpse of the others above me. I made a mental note to ask don Rigoberto about his name. But even from twenty feet above the forest floor, the tilt of the land toward the sea gave a fairly open view to the south. Earlier, I'd watched the sun dip below the horizon, lighting up a glittering sliver of the sea about four miles away.

Torches crackled above me and an Aztec chant floated down, alien and indistinct. Something large rustled through the underbrush to my right. The tom-tom picked up its tempo. The breeze died and stillness reigned. More incense was added; its sick, sweet smell flowed down the pyramid's sides, swallowing all other scents, choking off all other senses . . . it was then that *They* came.

Torches moved below us in the forest, bobbing toward the pyramid. Distant at first, they stopped and clustered about a hundred yards away. Several dozen of them. But nothing corporeal held the torches; they merely floated in the warm night. And though there was no breeze, they flickered.

The hair bristled at the nape of my neck and I got the shivers again. My mind raced to the beat of the drum. I imagined myself crashing through the bottom of my childhood bed, poised to emerge into the night. As I rose through the roof for my evening flight the fireflies rose with me, only to be replaced by brilliant points of light descending from the sky overhead.

A conch shell horn trumpeted above me. The drum's beat slowed to a hypnotic, heartlike thump-THUMP, thump-THUMP. I looked up. High above a dozen stars flared in the inky zenith, then streaked across the sky.

Startled, I shook myself and refocused. I was real and still on the pyramid. The drum went silent. The stars froze for an instant, then their brilliant points of light descended slowly. The drum began again. It reached another crescendo, as if calling the lights. In response, they rocketed toward us, speeding into the top of the pyramid, fifteen feet above me, and bathing it in an eerie light. A pulse of energy shot through the ancient stonework, as if someone had plugged the pyramid into a power company's main feeder.

It passed quickly. The drum stopped, the torches above me guttered, and the remaining incense was wafted upward by a fresh breeze from the sea. Either I'd been hypnotized by the drums or I'd seen the same bright points of light that had marked my own soul when it had gone missing. I wasn't certain of anything, so remained on my perch, transfixed.

A while later, I felt don Rigoberto's hand on my shoulder. He explained. Jerónimo translated, "That is how they are called . . . but we do not command them. It is their choice. Those souls await another child to enter. In the morning we will return to the village and tell the others that the crops and fishing will be good. That we should wish for more children."

"I thought it might have only been my imagination, don Rigoberto."

"Would it matter, White One? They came . . . and showed themselves to you. Had you not believed, you would have seen nothing. If you are real, they are real."

"Do they always come as points of light?"

"No—only the most sacred ones. The others come as naguales. Jaguar, deer, monkey, owl—and rarely so many at once. That is what we heard in the forest. It shall be a fine night. Let us rest now."

"One question, don Rigoberto . . . might I someday be able to call my soul?" Jerónimo translated, more curious than petulant, for a change. The answer surprised me.

"Your soul already came to you at the pyramid, joven . . . it knows you—but it is *you* who do not recognize it. It cannot reenter you as you are. You must not fear yourself." With that, don Rigoberto turned away, smiling . . .

✴

Dawn came stealthily as if it were the dawn of time itself. We gathered our things and made the trek back to the village. Malinalli was waiting for us on the trail, near the settlement. At the sight of her grandfather, she glowed. "Was it a good night?"

"A fine night, little one. Tonight we begin your lessons. At the shrine I asked the old ones if a woman could learn the things you asked. It surprised me that they came in numbers to approve. You must have the spirit of a man in you."

The regal old man smiled at Alli, touched his granddaughter's face tenderly, and turned away to report the night's proceedings to the other elders who had waited behind. They had gathered under the palms at one edge of the plaza, smoking corn-husk cigarettes and drinking coconut milk. Discussing something in animated tones, they looked over at us frequently. Malinalli smiled at me, her huge eyes moist. "It's about me—*us*—they are speculating on our relationship."

"Does it matter?"

"Oh, yes. My grandfather argues to train me as a healer. They want to know if the knowledge will be wasted . . . and whether I might reveal it to an outsider. For a woman to be taught is rare. Their fear is that you will take me away. I'm obligated to care for my hermanos—and you."

"You aren't obligated to me."

"Oh, but I am! You freed me from an ugly existence."

"I never 'freed' anyone from anything! Can't you accept the fact that you are free to do whatever you want?" She gave me the butterfly look again, studying me at length . . .

"I'm not sure what I want. I never had a choice before. I may have to choose between Ce Xochitl and La Ventosa. It frightens me." She touched my face again, running her fingertips down my cheeks, then caressed my lips. Malinalli seemed different than when I'd first met her at El Farolito. More assured. More at peace.

The old men drinking coconut milk noticed. Finally, short, sour Jerónimo came over and inquired.

"Is she your woman, Ojos Verdes (Green Eyes)?" He had been brusque with me since the moment we'd arrived.

"She is no one's *woman*, señor! That is the point. She tells me that her dream of dreams was always to be a healer like her father."

"I want *her* to answer, Green Eyes! A white boy's word means nothing." Malinalli gaped back at him, stunned. Pissed, he leaned down, grabbed her, and shook her violently, demanding, "Why do you act like lovers, then, if you are not his woman?" For a moment I saw Earl's twisted face reflected in old Jerónimo's as he dug his fingers deep into Alli's shoulder and grunted in satisfaction when she shrunk from the pain.

I leaned forward, calmly dug my thumb into the soft tendons of his wrist and pried his hand loose. Trying to sound indifferent, I looked up and said, "We are *not* lovers . . . no disrespect, but what is between us is not your business." Malinalli, now silent, rubbed her shoulder, moving closer to me as we sat on the hard-packed soil.

I turned to her. "If you are to be a curandera, *speak* for yourself." Her eyes moved back and forth between us. Then she looked down at her hands, like a kid. Like Eddy. Defeated. I gave the old man a hard stare. "She respects you too much to tell you what is in her heart." He turned and walked away, his mouth still frozen into a hard, cold line.

He'd no idea of the shit I'd put up with in my life . . . or the fact that this little scene had been acted out countless times by the angry, thin-lipped men I'd known who could never be pleased. For most, I reckoned the art of being continually dissatisfied with those around them was their only talent. Their only source of power . . . and he couldn't have known I was a back-shooter . . .

"I didn't think you would be so frightened by a young woman's dreams, *viejo*," I said suddenly. Malinalli gasped in surprise. Without turning, he stopped dead in his tracks. I drove the harpoon in deeper. "She is more of a man than you are, viejo. In her heart she is a curer. Your heart is merely angry." He turned.

"As angry as yours, Green Eyes?"

"*Tal vez*, viejo."

"If you are not her lover, then why is it that you protect her? Pay for a motor? *Tell* me, Green Eyes."

I moved to get up, but Malinalli pulled me back. "Please, don't! He is mean, but I am obligated to respect him." I mustn't have looked convinced, so she pleaded. "For me? *Please*." Her eyes were moist as her gentle butterfly finger brushed my lips. Her touch sucked the anger right out of me. I shrugged and relaxed. "Thank you," she sighed, then stared off into the distance . . . waiting for the council's verdict on when, and what sacred things, she would be permitted to learn.

☙

№ 14 THE VERDICT

LA VENTOSA WAS AS before. Soft palms swayed and cool breezes blew across the lagoon. Malinalli and I had returned alone. Her grandfather was to join us after the old men made their decision about schooling Malinalli in religious traditions beyond ordinary curing. Unresolved was who would care for her younger siblings if the men agreed.

Her uncle Lalo, wearing a tattered plaid shirt, palm-frond hat, and shorts cut from worn-out Levis, met us on the beach. "How was it, little one? Did your grandfather take you to the pyramid as you'd hoped?"

"No, Uncle, but he will be here in several days. He needs to talk to you."

"I hope he arrives soon. The fishing season has already started . . . and it will be good this year. We need to get the big boat finished and in the water. I have agreed to rent the little one for the whole season—one-third of the catch."

"I don't know whether or not I will be with you in the boat, Uncle—it depends on my grandfather and the other caciques."

"Do you still have those silly dreams of being a healer, little one?"

"Yes, Uncle. It haunts me."

"Let me show you the boat, anyway. You will be surprised at the progress." We crossed the dune to the boat, which was now upright, its hull caulked and painted. Four local men were still working away on the rudder and decks when we walked up. The eldest, a wiry, diminutive middle-aged fellow they called "La Rafa" (Rafael) was wielding his homemade drawknife fashioned from a broken machete. He greeted us breezily.

"This will be the finest *lancha* in La Ventosa. It will hold much fish. Here, Alli—come see your name." He took her by the arm, steering her to the stern. Lettered on it was "Malinalli. La Ventosa. Oaxaca."

She grinned, "Oh, my father's boat named for me!" She was reflective for a moment, then sighed deeply. A tear trickled down her cheek. "Should we not have named it for him?"

"We did, Alli—you are of him. His favorite."

"But what if I leave with my grandfather to learn of the old ways?" Palm out, and expansive, her uncle responded quickly. "You would still be 'in' the boat. The motor will secure your share for the children. Besides, little one, I doubt that the elders will approve you becoming a curer or priest."

We left the men on the beach to their work and went back to Alli's family. The kids were crazy to see her—all competing for her attention and pointing out how well they had done their chores. Ana was stressed out. Alli picked up on it and shooed me off to the hammock for a rest, while she and Ana "took a walk."

I rolled into the hammock, lit a smoke, and sipped water. About twenty minutes later, Alli showed up. "Ana is afraid I'm going to leave with you and abandon them. I didn't really know what to say."

"Try the truth . . . you want to follow in your grandfather's footsteps." Alli sighed in frustration. "They won't understand . . ."

"They might. You won't know if you don't try. Maybe *I* should go away. It's *me* that worries them, Alli."

"*No!* No . . . I'll tell them, somehow."

She didn't have long to wait. Ana had sent the other kids off to do their chores and came over to confront us—well, me, to be precise. Hands on her hips, Ana squeaked, "You can't take our sister!"

Malinalli interrupted. "Ana. It's *not* about him. It's about me . . . I've told you several times that I want to be like grandfather; but you've wanted me to be 'Mother,' so you didn't hear." Ana stared, confused.

Malinalli began again. "*Mira*, Ana, I am waiting for the council at Ce Xochitl to decide if I can become a priestess and curandera. That would take me away from all of you again for a time. If there was money each week, could you look after things?"

Ana looked down at her hands. Barely twelve, she was still a kid but had already been doing a woman's job four days a week while Malinalli was at El Farolito in Salina Cruz. A tear ran down her cheek. "I love you, Alli. Can't you stay with us from now on?"

"I'd try to see you as often as possible, Sister, but if the grandfathers give me this chance, I shall take it. I'll always be able to provide." Ana looked at me again.

"So it's not *him*?"

"No, Ana. I like him. But I want to be a healer."

"OK, Alli—I know that you went to Salina Cruz for us and that it was bad . . ."

Malinalli grabbed her shoulder. "What do you know of Salina Cruz?"

"The men talk. I'm young, but I am not stupid. I see them in their hammocks making babies with their women." Malinalli stared at her little sister, silent tears clouding her beautiful eyes. "I'm sorry. I didn't know people talked of it . . . did they say things to the others?" Ana nodded, "It disturbed Simón." Malinalli gathered her sister into her arms and rocked her.

"We love you, Alli. We didn't believe what they said. Then *he* came." Ana looked over at me. Malinalli started to ask more, but I shushed her. "Ana, your sister is a good person."

"Of course you'd say that—you are lovers." I reached for her chin, smiled, and turned her face to me. "No, we are *not!*" Ana blinked. "*¿Verdad? (Really?)*"

"Yes, verdad—let the men talk. Your sister is beautiful and they have fantasies. Men do that. It's not nice, but there it is." "Alli . . . I'm sorry!" pleaded Ana.

"It's OK. Can you care for the children if I am given the chance?"

"Would I be the 'mother' then?"

"Yes, child."

"I can do it. But don't go away forever, Alli. That's all I ask."

"All right, then." We headed back to the house. Immediately, Ana began to assert herself more than usual. Simón turned to Alli, his senior "mom," checking to see who was really in charge. Malinalli nodded at him. "Your sister is in charge today. I am taking the evening off!"

Ana seemed uncertain, but that worked for the other kids. Oddly, I was the one who understood all this the best. To me, their family situation was normal. I couldn't even remember all the "moms" and "dads" I'd had. Dysfunctional or not Eddy had needed a family, and even I'd been thrilled at my first motherly hug from Ramona, just several months before.

Ana, calmed for the moment, did what her psychological needs dictated. She organized everything, started the fish head soup, adding carrots, jicama, green corn, tomato, chiles, and handfuls of yellow rice. The fish's cloudy eyes stared up at us one last time before they slid into the oblivion of Ana's large iron kettle. Simón went for firewood. I went down to the water, sat under a huge palm, and smoked. Poor Ana—she was destined to become the Protector . . . the Watcher . . . just as I'd been for Eddy. It's a tough role. I felt bad for her, but said nothing.

The lagoon was still. A hushed calm hung over La Ventosa, disturbed only by the sounds of chisels and sanding pads on the refurbished launch. A small motorboat turned into the lagoon and came ashore about twenty yards to my right. Damn! Malinalli's grandfather was accompanied by the angry, thin-lipped Jerónimo.

I liked Alli's grandfather . . . so gentle and unlike any other man I'd ever known. In Mitla don Mateo had brought out the warrior in me. In contrast, Alli's grandfather brought out the family-loving Eddy in me.

Sweet old don Rigoberto approached and greeted me warmly. "Well, joven, have you rejoined your soul yet?"

"No, but I have thought about what you said at the pyramid." Don Rigoberto looked surprised.

"Well, then, I have a question of you . . . Malinalli told us that you were with her when she lit candles for the Virgin."

"I was."

"What happened?"

"She lit candles. They seemed to flare brightly and the Virgin glowed when we spoke of souls."

"Who spoke?"

"Both of us, but it was she who said, 'Your soul is near. I can sense it . . .' and that's when the Virgin in the photograph appeared to smile."

"The photograph smiled?" As he hung on every word, don Rigoberto put his hand on the angry one's shoulder. "See—it is as she told us, don Jerónimo." His thin, angry lips twisted into a sneer. "Let's go see her, then."

"Don't hurt her again," I warned. At this, don Rigoberto stared at Jerónimo—a surprised look on his face. Jerónimo looked away from his companions. Without another word they trudged up the dune and through the palms, their truck-tire huarache soles leaving their distinctive tread marks in the soft white sand.

I stayed where I was and watched a panga float out to intercept the evening tide and its bounty. The lone fisherman poled slowly, gliding ghostlike across the lagoon till he came to the deep pools near the coral. The sun's orange flames lit up the western horizon, framing him and his fishing spear. A fish surfaced in the shallows and a red-tailed hawk cruised above the beach, then disappeared into the sun.

Several hours later the two old men returned with Malinalli. It was she who first spoke. "I am to work this fishing season. When it is done, Ana will be nearly thirteen. She will care for the children. My uncle will help. His wife will look in on them daily, and Uncle will bring water and groceries from Salina Cruz when he sells his catch there. Then I shall be purified by Grandfather and don Jerónimo to receive the lessons . . . but before they can teach me I must first make a pilgrimage."

"That's good, then?" My comment sounded like a question, so she answered it as one. "Yes, it is wonderful . . . thank you for your kindness, *pero* . . . *pero*," she stuttered. "Pero, *what*," I demanded. She broke eye contact as she answered, her voice sounding small and sad, "I don't think we'll see each other again after tomorrow."

Thin-lipped Jerónimo interrupted. "You misunderstood, little one. You are to take Green Eyes *with* you to the Basilica of Guadalupe." I objected, "I have other plans."

"They have changed, Green Eyes. That is our decision." Don Rigoberto, looking uncomfortable, tried to soften it. "You are not ordered. It is a request. Something we ask."

"I'll take her, if *she* asks me," I shot back. Jerónimo gave me another icy look. I didn't need an interpreter. "Don't worry, viejo. I won't return with her. But, just as you feel compelled to dislike me and to hurt her, I shall give you advice in return. Mistreat her, play the angry game with her, or try to reconsider her fate, and I will return."

"You know nothing of me, Green Eyes. You are too young to know anything."

"I am not young, viejo. I simply appear young. I am older than any of you. My eyes see everything that displeased men have ever done. I will take the girl tomorrow if *she* wishes. That is the end of it . . ."

Jerónimo, as if withdrawing from the tension, stepped into the water and waded out toward the boat. This time, it was he who turned. "I have killed men for less than your 'advice,' Green Eyes." I'd heard this kind of crap too many times to care. Besides, such types were usually too selfish to kill. If you are dead, they are automatically deprived of their pleasure. Killing gives them no satisfaction . . . it merely leaves them empty and lonely. I shrugged it off, turned my back to him, and casually lit another smoke . . .

⁂

№ 15 THE VIRGIN SMILES

LATER, AFTER JERÓNIMO LEFT, Malinalli did ask me to take her to the
basilica. The Voice protested, *Don't do it! The embassy guards will catch
you.* But, goaded by Jerónimo into sheer defiance, I stuck to the plan.

We set out two days later. The third-class bus from Salina Cruz to
Tehuantepec was ordinary. It reeked of sweat, cheap cigarettes, and
unwashed bodies. No toilet, no intact windows, no air conditioning, no
empty seats, and no room to stretch. Chickens, piglets, several parrots,
a small monkey, and perhaps a dozen screaming infants were crowded
on board in addition to all the regular seat holders.

Malinalli was excited. Mexico City was her first big trip. She'd only
been as far as Tehuantepec once, but didn't care for it. The Tehuantepeca
language was alien to her and the small city was intimidating in scale
when compared to La Ventosa or Salina Cruz. When we reached Tehuantepec she waited at the bus station while I ventured out to the town
square, taking in the scenery and stocking up on cigarettes, sodas, and
tortas. I took my time, absorbing the local scene.

Finally, I headed back to the bus station where Malinalli was waiting. As I elbowed my way through the lobby toward her, I realized again
just how beautiful she was. Her long oval face was framed by her cascade of glistening black hair. And her mouth was incredible. With full,
recurved lips beyond the skill of any plastic surgeon, she glowed. I could

even imagine how it had come to be that the ancient hand-painted codices left by Mexico's pre-Columbian Indian dynasties always portrayed speech as a cloudlike flow of words encircled by a glyph line. It was as if the speech from such a beautiful mouth was frozen in time, itself a piece of artwork.

Malinalli's nose was another masterpiece. Its high, graceful arch gave her a three-dimensional totality absent among the fair-skinned Nordic and Germanic faces so prized in the States. Her face was deep, shadowed, and still, like the masks on the pyramid at Teapan. Her large almond-shaped eyes slanted downward toward her nose. Echoes of her Mongoloid ancestry, already fifteen to twenty thousand years distant, were coded into the folds of her soft upper eyelids.

She smiled when she saw me, tiny curls opening at the corners of her mouth as if to receive me. Those curls were her most potent sexual feature—millions, perhaps even billions, of women had nice butts and chests. Men notice those because evolution has programmed them into the automatic visual assessment of potential "motherhood," so often interpreted as "prurient," by Stateside puritans.

But only a few women on earth have open curls at the corners of their mouth. Those that do have them drive men wild . . . and the female competition never seems to figure it out. In the States, doctor's daughters I'd known had gotten boob jobs and nose jobs, but none knew enough about male sexuality to request a "corner curl" job. In Malinalli's world those curls weren't rare, but only a very few among the women had lips so recurved and so full that tiny, inviting vulva-shaped ovals actually lay open and exposed at their corners.

Malinalli looked back at me then, just like women do everywhere when they are trying to calibrate their response as a man approaches them. As she watched me move toward her, the corners of her mouth opened a bit wider. I was rock hard from neck to toes.

Odd—when she was in her own world, my testosterone-driven desires had subsided and I had focused on her spiritual side, as well as my own. But out of her element, she seemed much more exotic. I wanted to fuck her right then, right there . . . in a chaotic bus station full of kids, nursing moms, chickens, and baby goats. Her lips beckoned to me as primally as dilated pupils, swollen nipples, or a ripe, dripping vagina . . .

By the time we took our seats on the crowded second-class bus to

Oaxaca, I was suffering from a class A case of testosterone fever. My pulse was at 140, my gut ached, and my balls felt like they were going to explode. The bouncing bus didn't help.

Malinalli sensed my intensity and, looking worried, asked, "Are you irritated because you must take me to Mexico City?" "No," I whispered, "I want you." Her lip curls opened invitingly. "I was beginning to wonder..."

When we reached Oaxaca, we attempted to check in to an inexpensive *pensión* near the magnificent old Santo Domingo church, a long block from the plaza.

Alli asked me to wait in the lobby while she chose a room. But the once-grand colonial mansion that had been transformed into a twenty-room boarding house was family run. They wanted no part of an Indian girl and a gringo, apparently assuming the room was for a call-girl's assignation.

It was much the same story at another converted mansion down the block, except that the fat, burly manager was much more direct. "We don't rent to whores or Indians." "I'm neither, señor," I protested. Apparently, my attempt at dry humor didn't win him over. "Or *gabachos* (white trash) who dress as Indians," he sneered.

I would have punched him but Alli burst into tears. I ushered her out, torn between wrecking the entire hotel and comforting her. In the end I compromised and left her on a bench near the plaza to listen to the marimba music coming from a nearby arcade. I told her I needed to buy cigarettes. Then I dashed back to the pensión where I settled for wrecking just the lobby. In this case, "doing the right thing" gave me a deep sense of satisfaction.

The deskman must have agreed, for he didn't even complain while I broke mirrors and furniture. I assumed he was contrite... or perhaps he just didn't notice. As he first stepped out from the rear office, an angry leer on his face, my stick caught him behind the ear and he collapsed into the tiny cubbyhole behind the desk. Resting, I assumed.

Feeling upbeat, I walked out and crossed to the far side of the plaza, entering a more expensive commercial hotel next to an old convent. As a single white guy with hard cash, I presented no problem. I signed the register "J. A. Blanco" and went back to collect Alli. She was still crying when I got there.

"It's OK, Alli—I have us a nice room. Don't be sad." For a moment she looked incredulous. "I thought you left me after the humiliations . . . it's hard being an Indian in the big towns. That's why don Jerónimo is angry at whites. He came here to Oaxaca many years ago to go to school, but the upper-class whites beat him and drove him away."

Her anguish got to me . . . "I wouldn't just leave you on a bench, Alli." I must not have sounded all that convincing, for she buried her head in her lap and bawled. About then I saw the fat deskman puffing up the street, handkerchief to his bleeding head, two uniformed cops in tow.

"Alli—I've got to go. Trouble. Meet me at the Hotel Commercial in an hour." I took off, heading for the huge city market, where I vanished into the dense crowd. I took time to buy a used shirt and traded my hat for a newer one in a lighter tan, so I was late getting to meet Alli at the Commercial.

Alli was nowhere to be seen at the hotel, so I went to the room I'd rented, changed clothes again, then went looking for her. I found her on the plaza, not far from where I'd left her. She frowned when I walked up. "What did you do? The police watched me for an hour . . ."

"I don't want to talk about it, Alli . . . let's just go enjoy ourselves and forget this afternoon." She sighed. "I'm afraid they'll recognize us together . . . you're dressed differently, but I'm not." I gave her a hundred-peso note to buy "new" clothes and told her to meet me in the hotel's bar in an hour. I settled in at the bar, sipping an elegant, icy Bohemia and enjoying one of my precious British cigarettes.

When Alli did step in, it was a revelation. She wore a backless, knee-length, flower-print dress. It showed off her soft brown neck and the luscious line of her schoolgirl's figure. At about 4'11" she looked like a petite, dark-skinned dream come true. I was all smiles and testosterone as I escorted her to our modest but clean balcony room.

"Do I look OK, Juan?"

"Call me Alex, Alli . . . all my friends do."

"Alesh?" she repeated. "Alesh . . ." Sounded beautiful coming from her lips. She paused a moment and smiled, the corners of her mouth opening just a bit. She asked, hesitant, "May I call you Juan? I met you as 'Juan.' I will always think of you by that name."

"Juan it is, then." She undressed while I lounged on the bed. I assumed she had decided to accommodate me out of a sense of obligation.

"You don't have to, Alli. That is, if you prefer not." She put her finger to my lips, bit my ear, and straddled me, her lithe body taut. I jerked off my clothes, kissed her throat, then tongued a beckoning lip curl. She sighed, groaned softly, and began dripping on my belly. "Make me a baby, Juan," she moaned, digging her fingers into my shoulders . . . I entered her but simply wasn't prepared for the sensation. I pushed into her expecting a physical experience like I'd known with Marianna. Instead, she enveloped me with a softness that stripped away all of my ordinary defenses. I simply vanished inside of her. It was as if all of me entered her and I'd emerged into another dimension—my return to the womb.

Suddenly I was a child again, falling uncontrollably through the bottom of my bed. Only this time there was no basement. Instead I fell into the vast, crystalline realm of her essence. Everything was clear. Fresh. Warm. Generous. Happy. Engaged.

I wanted to stay there, surrounded by her, forever. For the first time in my life I was no longer alone. I had gone to that place I always instinctually sought while soul flying. I had, finally, found home.

Inside her I realized I'd also just experienced the feelings that Eddy had unsuccessfully tried to communicate to me when I'd asked him why he so desperately wanted a family. I had finally discovered the sweet vulnerability of belonging.

I tried to stay inside of her but couldn't. Within moments of falling through the bed, I erupted into flight, soared above her, and looked down to see her on the bed below me. With her head arched back, eyes closed, she was beautiful. Her legs encircled my back, pulling me even deeper into her. I saw myself smiling. *Smiling!*

I didn't look much like I'd imagined I would. I wasn't a child anymore. I'd changed a lot. Fascinated, I wanted another look and tried to pass overhead again. But I somehow lost control, crashed through the ceiling of the hotel room and fell into Alli. That's when I realized I'd wet the bed again.

Panicked, I opened my eyes, bracing for the ridicule and anger that had always followed. Instead she moaned and, opening her eyes, clasped my face between her palms. I tongued the bows of her upper lip and started to apologize, but her hands stilled me. "More!" she groaned. "*¿Más de qué?* (More of what?)" I responded, still embarrassed. "*Moayotl* (More of 'your juice')," she sighed, then closed her eyes again.

Within minutes she had gone to that place where pleasure sometimes takes you. She shuddered. "Don't stop . . ." That was the last Spanish she spoke. Between sobs and moans, eyes closed, she began to whisper in the Nahuatl of her forefathers. It might have been about souls, babies, or nothing at all.

It frightened me when she climaxed. She arched her back and stiffened. Her urgent panting stopped. Her eyes opened suddenly, then rolled up, and the irises simply disappeared. I panicked, certain she'd suffered a seizure. I shook her, getting no response at all.

At last, when she awakened from her stupor, I was already dressed to go to the front desk and call a doctor. "Oooh . . . I fainted when I saw your nagual."

"*My* nagual? Are you OK, Alli?"

"Yes," she smiled, sighing. "But I did not expect to become pregnant." *Huh?* I tried to hide it but went even deeper into panic mode. "When a man's nagual descends to a woman, their blood is mixing. Your nagual entered the child immediately." I took deep breaths and gaped at her. "It is to be a girl," she smiled dreamily. "I shall have a daughter. Her spirit is a great, black mare. Odd. My people say only wild animals can be naguales."

"How do you know it was . . . uh . . . me, Alli . . . that you are pregnant?"

"The mare smelled of you. Your tobacco. Your man scent."

"And the *pregnant* . . . ?"

"Like I said, the nagual enters the instant a child is made . . ."

I was sweating profusely. All the ordinary fears of a twenty-year-old male consumed me. *We're fucked!* screamed the Voice in my head. I shut him out and lit a smoke. Malinalli was still talking—slowly and dreamily. ". . . I like being pregnant . . . and we now know which soul you sense is lost—it's your heavenly one. Your Christian soul."

"So, I have my nagual, but not my heavenly soul?"

"Yes. Everyone has two, you know."

Hmmn, my animal self is intact, but my church-going soul is history. Doesn't sound much like traditional Nahua religion to me, I thought.

I watched her pull on her panties and began to calm down. She touched her nipples gently. They were hard, jet-black buds. "I wonder what it will be like to hold her. To feel her tongue pulling the milk from my breasts. Perhaps she will have light skin and green eyes." "Brown is dominant," I commented off-handedly, thinking to myself, *For her, sex is an affirmation of life. Babies. How different from Marianna, who pursued pleasure just to feel alive for a moment.*

She talked on. "Of course, your nagual is black—perhaps she will be darker, then." I chuckled. Her world didn't give a damn who Mendel was. Spirits ruled. Not chromosomes. My panic gone, I relaxed into an unnatural calm. I felt *good.* I wrapped my arms around her, pulled her hips to me, and caressed her face. She smiled.

"More later. But now, I'm hungry," she grinned. We went downstairs and walked to the plaza. She squeezed my arm. "You will like being a father. I can sense it." I freaked. "I'm not quite ready to, uh, settle down." She laughed, the corners of her mouth opening again.

"I'm not *gachupín* (Spanish), silly. You don't need to marry me! The child is a gift. Besides, I shall not be permitted a man for some time to come. I must first be purified. Then live in the mountains where the old gods dwell."

"Why live in the mountains, Alli?"

"I must first identify my nagual. The naguales come to the old gods for their life force."

"Is your nagual not green eyed?" I teased. She stopped, amazed, and stared at something across the plaza. "Do you think so, Juan? My grandfather hoped it might be a tigre." She didn't get my joke—I was green eyed and of the flesh, but in her world it was the spirit's characteristics that counted.

"Around here that would make you a witch, Alli."

"That's Zapotec. You've spent too much time here among them—my people are Nahuas . . . you know that."

Oaxaca's charming plaza was brightly lit. Its whitewashed bandstand crowded with young, old, Indian, white, mestizo. Brightly colored serapes and rebozos mingled with elegant silk ties and prim dresses.

Old men played dominos. Young men copped feels in the shadows and kids ran everywhere. We grabbed a table under the ancient arcade at one side of the plaza, ordering black beans and rice topped with fried eggs and freshly chopped salsa. Cheap and satisfying food. Malinalli touched my arm often. She was beautiful, her eyes glowing. I reached out to touch the lush mane of glistening dark hair that framed her exquisite face. Even several of the mestizo men couldn't keep their eyes from her.

When she left me for the ladies room a nicely dressed mestizo guy wearing an expensive Rolex watch leaned over and asked in crappy English, "Where did you get her . . . the Bonampak, perhaps?" He was referring to a local club/cathouse famed among the testosterone-driven expatriate archaeology set for the magnificent Indian girls who plied their trade there.

I heard myself answer in Spanish, startling him, "No, señor. *Es la madre de mi bebé* (She is the mother of my child)." I'd never said that of Marianna. In fact, I'd never even quite believed she was pregnant, though she'd had morning sickness. But, with Malinalli, I somehow believed her—or wanted to believe her—even though there was no reason for it. I mean, a woman couldn't just *know* the moment she was impregnated, could she? As I paused to unravel these tangled mental threads the cologned dude with the Rolex apologized elaborately.

"Oh, no offense, señor . . . I assumed you were a tourist."

"None taken, señor . . . a natural mistake." He shrugged, palms up, glancing nervously at my fighting stick. I smiled.

I reassured him. "*¡No hay pedo!* (Cool here!)" He looked away, still tense. It *had* been a natural mistake . . .

After all, even though Semper Fi referred to me as the "little Commie faggot," I weighed 165, went 5'10" with a little to spare, and had fair skin, green eyes, and chestnut brown hair streaked with tan highlights. I sure as hell looked like a tourist, except for my clothing, which was an eclectic mixture of my boyhood idol James Dean, Jack Kerouac, who'd been in Mexico City when I arrived, and local Indian.

When Malinalli returned, she stopped, touched my face gently, and stared at me before sitting. Still embarrassed, the guys at the next table left abruptly. "Take me dancing after dinner?" she asked.

After dinner we walked across the plaza to the hotel called the Marqués del Valle—named after Cortés, the conqueror, who was formally titled "Marquess of the Valley of Oaxaca" before he fell into debt and disfavor and unwisely returned to Spain. There were still "Cortés" last names sprinkled across the region, but none held his lands or a claim to his old title. The hotel was now an upscale local businessman's home away from home.

We walked in and crossed the lobby. She seemed nervous, glancing around her uneasily. "I've never been to a hotel dance before." The bar bustled with activity as folks drifted in from the dining room next door. It was 10 PM, the fashionable set's dinner hour was ending, and the hotel's three-piece combo was about ready to usher in the night.

I pulled out a chair for her at a table near the bar. Her lips parted as she sat, wide eyed. I was so absorbed with her that I didn't notice the hush that had enveloped us; that is, until the white-toweled waiter appeared, a sour, disapproving look on his florid face. Even his tuxedo lapels seemed to curl in displeasure. I ordered. "Two ice-cold Bohemias, *por favor.*"

He raised his eyebrows, his stare unbroken, but made no other sign of acknowledgment. I repeated the order. He was impassive till I asked a third time. "There is no service at this table, señor. Your, *cough*, 'guest' is not welcome here!" He said it loud enough for others to hear. Malinalli started to rise, looking frightened.

I looked around. Well-dressed businessmen and prosperous husbands accompanied by their predictably matronly wives stared back, looking smug and amused. I smiled back at them ostentatiously. Several looked away. It simply wasn't in Mexico's cultural rule book to humiliate someone publicly, but exceptions were obviously made for young gringos and their presumed Indian whores.

Had Malinalli not hung her head and said, pleadingly, "Let us go, then . . ." I would probably have let it go. But compounded by the afternoon's events, the warm, cuddly side of me bubbled up like a shaken soda and I foamed all over the waiter. "*No comprendo* (I don't get it). This is Mexico where respect is important. Am I—and the *mother* of my child—to be humiliated for reasons unexplained?"

At this the waiter was on his own. One of the great differences between Mexico and the States is that nearly everyone actually believes in their social values—it isn't just a bullshit cover for imposing their own idea of a moral code on others. Those who had quite likely suggested that "the gringo and his whore" be ejected turned away, discomfited.

The poor waiter stuttered. I raised my hand, palm out, and stood to full height. "Of course, you had no way to know that we are a family . . .

two Bohemias, please." I was far better at staring than he was. Finally, he nodded. I was gracious. "*Muy amable*, señor." No one looked at us while I gently reseated Malinalli. The Bohemias came promptly, the waiter shrugging in apology to no one in particular as he worked his way back toward the bar.

Several sips of cold beer and a cigarette later, I stood, took Malinalli's hand, and guided her to the dance floor. She was stiff, nervous. "This is hard for me."

"It's easy for me, *chiquita*. I'll hold you close. If you are going to represent your people and keep the old ways, you will have to deal with such things again." She started to say something else in Spanish. I interrupted. "In Nahuatl, please."

"But you won't . . ."

"I'll nod like I do, Alli." She went on in Nahuatl; I nodded from time to time, in agreement, answering her in English. When the power of her own language began to give her a sense of control again, she relaxed her body, said something to me, and laughed. I smiled and answered her in English. "You are adorable!"

Sure enough, the crowd relaxed with us, baffled by our behavior and the strange mix of languages—a gringo who might speak Nahuatl and an Indian girl who seemed to understand his English.

We danced to three tunes before returning to our table. As we threaded our way past, one middle-aged, light-skinned woman accompanied by an impeccably tailored husband leaned out to touch Malinalli on the arm as she passed. "You are so slender; when is your baby due, dear?"

"In some months, señora. I am so happy. I cannot wait to fill out and have the child in my arms." Doña someone or another smiled and patted her, looking at me. "You two make a lovely couple. So romantic . . ."

As we moved on I whispered audibly to Malinalli. "They are a very handsome couple, no? *Digno y culto* (Dignified and cultured)." She nodded in agreement. Back at our table we finished our beers, then left without incident. Walking back across the plaza, Malinalli looked up toward the lights on the hill towering over the city. "What is up there? Do you know?"

"The Hotel Victoria, *chulita* . . . it's very beautiful . . . and quite expensive. Its sala has a ceiling so tall that there are palm and banana plants in huge pots—right on the tiled floor."

"Can we afford to have lunch there tomorrow?"

"Lunch is too expensive. But why are you suddenly asking my permission for things, Alli?"

"Now that you are the father of my child it is custom, Juan."

"You don't need to do it with me, Alli."

"Then, maybe we can have a tea or coffee in their café," Alli suggested.

Back at our modest hotel I awoke later in the night, sweating the possibility that I was to be a father. *She's hallucinating,* I told myself one moment, then repeated, for my own benefit, *No, women* know *such things!* I smoked and paced, waking Malinalli.

"It's the 'father' thing, no?" she asked. "Yes," I nodded. She turned on the light. "Come here. Look me in the eye." I went to her. She reached out for me. "I told you—the child is a gift from you. But I shall be obligated to raise the child alone—it's the path I've taken. Your life will not change . . . unless, of course, you return to hold your child. I will not deny you that. Nor will my grandfather. He respects you in his own way."

Cradling my head in her lap and running her fingers rhythmically through my hair, she sang me a lullaby in Nahuatl. Her voice sounded as if it was somewhere in the distance, far away and magical. Dreaming of babies, the night sky, and Betty Anne, I slept in her arms till morning when she went to the cathedral to pray.

At midday we had a cheap lunch near the plaza, then took the local bus up the steep, winding road that led to the old Hotel Victoria. Alli was enchanted with the grand lobby. A feast of bright flowers hanging in huge, brightly painted pots draped down from the second-story balcony. We picked an alcove under the balcony, ordered café con leche, and took in the scene. Groups of tourists came and went, paying no attention to us.

I had thought it might feel odd to take Malinalli to the same place I'd shared with Marianna, but everything seemed different—calm, gentle, relaxed. Sitting there with her was so serene . . . especially in comparison to the attempted kidnap and tension of don Pablo's endless, shallow river of mistresses that had spoiled the experience for Marianna and me three months earlier.

I gazed at Alli. So dark. So calm. So little need to control me . . . and yet her inner self so centered and under control. Another wave of rare peace washed over me as Alli tasted English tea for the first time. I was mesmerized when she took her first sip and the tip of her tongue moved up to touch the delicate, arched, bow-handle of her upper lip.

That evening, after dinner, Alli surprised me. She wanted to go dancing again—to the same place we'd danced the evening before. "It could be like last night again," I warned.

"No matter. I learned a great lesson at that hotel last night . . . and this may be the last time I ever dance." I blinked several times, trying to contain the unexpected sorrow that overcame me. She ran her fingers through my hair again. "You are so fierce and cold one moment . . . and so gentle the next. I do not think you have lost your alma (Christian soul). I think it is at war with that black horse."

Maybe she's right. I'm not neatly wrapped inside. Hmmn? But I blew it off . . .

"Then let's go. Are you ready?"

"Yes, but do you have a tie?"

"A what?"

"A *corbata*, Juan Alejandro. As a little girl I dreamed of dancing with a handsome man wearing a tie . . . an odd dream for an Indian girl," she laughed.

"Well, I don't have one with me, but I have a dress shirt."

"I'll ask at the desk," she smiled. Alli returned a few minutes later with both a smile and a well-used, deep burgundy tie. I put it on. It made me look older, more serious. When we crossed the plaza again, headed toward the Marqués del Valle, I stopped and got my boots shined by one of the wiry, middle-aged Zapotec men wearing a serape. Moments later we stepped into the hotel bar and took a table.

Two minutes after we seated ourselves, the maître d' came over, a white-toweled waiter in tow. "Dos Bohemias, joven. On the house." I thanked him and relaxed. There would be no repeat of the prior night's tension. Twenty minutes later Malinalli pulled me gently to the dance floor. They were playing "Cuando Calienta el Sol," a beautiful, sweet-sad modern classic in Mexico. She clung to me for a while, then stopped mid-music . . . stood back, framing my face in her palms. "I want to remember the father of my daughter this way . . ."

Her eyes huge and moist, a tear crept down one cheek. Her mouth-curls opened once and she kissed me hard, right there on the dance floor.

A point of light flashed in my brain. Involuntarily, I flinched in response. "Do you see your alma?" she whispered. *How the hell do women sense this stuff?* I wondered. "It is fighting to enter you now that your nagual is in your child . . . close your eyes and accept it."

Brilliant blue-white light flared behind my closed eyelids and yet another wave of profound calm washed over me. Sadly, it didn't last—as I merged into the light the Voice called me back. *She's nuts! You've got to maintain control, idiot.*

The light vanished, leaving me in darkness once again. When I opened my eyes she was still staring at me, looking sad. "Yes, if it returns and makes your body its home, you will feel pain again. But also the joy of love." *Hmmn, well, that's what I asked for when don Mateo blessed my war stick near Mitla. And* some *feelings have returned.*

I pulled her to me, cradling her soft hair, absorbing the scent of jasmine. She was already a shaman . . . a mystic—and even, if imaginary, the mother of my child . . . or perhaps she was really Betty Anne in disguise, radiating the soft essence of a brilliant summer evening long ago, before I'd crashed through a bed and lost part of me to the cosmos. I didn't really know.

We danced slowly, clinging to dreams of things that never were . . . and were destined never to be. But we didn't know that . . . or even notice when the music stopped. When we parted and turned to our table we found ourselves alone on the dance floor, a hundred mortal eyes riveted on us as if we had materialized there from nothingness. It was just as she said it would be, I would discover later: the last dance of her life . . .

※※

№ 16 TO THE BASILICA

THE NEXT DAY WE took a fancy Pullman-class bus to Mexico City. Alli had dressed herself head to toe in a lush off-white native-cotton to prepare for meeting the Virgin. We reclined in the bus's plush seats, still tired from a night where the mysteries of intimacy had trumped rest. She was sound asleep when we passed the great colonial convent at Yanhuitlán.

She was still asleep when the bus stopped and gave me a chance to stock up on Cokes and tortas in the ancient provincial town of Huajuapan de León. The name, Huajuapan, fascinated me—it meant "Place of the Caterpillars." Did that name refer to the silkworm industry introduced by the Spanish after the conquest? Or, perhaps, it referred to caterpillars in the district's ancient fields . . . and just who was "León," anyway? Mexico—sorting the old from the new—constantly baffled me. So many complicated layers.

I stepped off the bus into the bustle of the old highland town. Awninged food stalls lined one side of the unglassed, open-fronted station. The mixed scents of pungent cumin, onion, hot beans, chile, and roasting chickens hung in the warm afternoon air.

The blue shadow of central Mexico's ring of volcanoes rose up to the north—an ancient portal to the Tenochtitlán Basin. For a thousand years or more, before the Aztecs built their capital, Tenochtitlán, the

Valley of Mexico consisted of small, elegant city-states surrounding the shallow, irregular lake called Texcoco. Swamps, floating, man-made agricultural rafts, seas of wild reeds, migratory waterfowl, and canals had all nurtured the rise of principalities with names like Xochimilco (Place Where Flowers Grow), Tacuba, and Xalco (Place of Ponds).

Eventually the Mexica (Aztec) tribes came, specialized in the pursuit of war, and transformed themselves from hired muscle for the minor kings of Colhua, Colhuacan, and Tacuba into the overlords. In something akin to the Roman style, the Mexica enjoyed being at the top of central Mexico's food chain. They made war, traded, extracted tribute, and erected their own cities, often on the ruins of even more ancient ones.

Tenochtitlán (Place next to the Cactus) was their principal city. Built on a smallish island in the middle of Lake Texcoco, it grew, connected to the mainland by long causeways, to become the pearl of their vast empire. By the late 1400s it was considerably larger and more sophisticated than any European city of the time.

When the Spanish came in 1519 they were stunned at the city's riches but myopic when it came to Tenochtitlán's tradition of art, poetry, literature, and astronomy. Within a few years they had destroyed much of what they found. But the name of the Mexica had become *Mexico* (originally pronounced "Méshiko"), then *Méjico* (pronounced "Mehicko").

Eventually it became *México* once again, sans the Indian "sh" sound. Wars, Spanish determination, armor, smallpox, Cortés and his consort/translator/strategist—the high-born Aztec woman Malinalli/Malintzín—and a host of Tlaxcalan Indian allies, weary of paying tribute to the Aztecs, had all combined to bring the Aztec empire to its knees.

In just a century and a half the aftershocks of the Spanish conquest had broken all of Mexico's regional Indian societies, and the pure-blooded Indian population of Mexico had declined from about twenty-five million to about a million.

A Spanish-speaking world soon took over the Mexicas' place in the food chain but not before giving rise to a new race of Mexicans—mestizos, who were the product of mixed unions, mostly between Creole (Spanish) men and Indian women.

Malinalli had awakened by this time and shouted to me from the door of the bus as I stood in line at one of the food stalls. "*Tortas, por favor—jamón y queso con ahuacatl* (ham and cheese with avocado)." Her voice and mixed Spanish and Nahuatl reminded me that I was just one in a long line of men to find peace in the essence of an Indian woman. I was but another footnote in the genetic and cultural upheaval that had absorbed Indian Mexico for half a millennium and given birth to its most recent iteration.

Back on the bus, Cokes and a sack of hard-crusted sandwiches in hand, Alli was playful, reminding me that she was still just a girl. Most of the time she seemed so much older, wiser, and calmer than any woman I'd ever been close to. "*¿Qué piensas?* (What are you thinking?)" she asked.

"I think you are a remarkable woman."

She blushed. "It is equally remarkable that you find me '*más que una India*' (more than just an Indian girl) . . . do you think the Virgin will receive my prayers?"

"I don't know. But I think so." She settled back in the seat. I refocused on the scenery, imagining the scene in the 1500s when a Christian Virgin first appeared to the Indian shepherd Juan Diego—and took on Indian Mexico as her "cause." The bus hit a pothole, jostling me back into the present . . .

Fields of maguey, marigold, and milpa crowded against the road as we rose further into Mexico's central highlands. Burros loaded with firewood trudged along the highway, led by huarache-shod Indian boys in regional dress. Naked kids squatted to pee by the side of the road . . . and occasional autos passed us, headed south to Oaxaca, the heart of Indian Mexico. It was then that I began to dread Mexico City and the dilemmas that might come.

⁂

At nightfall we stopped in Cuernavaca—where Cortés had built his first winter palace in the 1500s—a few years after the conquest. We glided past whitewashed palms, the city's great estates, then rattled along the wide, cobbled main thoroughfare.

"Did La Malinche live here, too?" Alli asked dreamily. "Yes, doña Marina lived here with him for a time and bore him a son." "White guys are good lovers," Alli noted casually. A female somewhere behind us giggled. Alli poked me, smiling. I poked her back.

At about 11 PM we rose up over the last great hill that hid Mexico City's central valley from the south. Stretched before us lay the city, an immense forty-mile-wide sea of lights, nearly five million people tucked into its mountainous bowl at 7,000 feet. "Oooh!" exclaimed Malinalli, "copitli!"

"What?"

"Fireflies—it is an ocean of fireflies."

"Why did you think of fireflies, Alli?"

"Does it matter?" She looked concerned.

"Yes, Alli . . . my soul is tied to fireflies . . . I didn't see any in La Ventosa or Ce Xochitl . . . so why did you think of them?"

"You must be blind to them, then. They were everywhere at Ce Xochitl. When I was a little girl I'd hold out my hands and they would come to me, twinkling. I was always at peace when they came."

"You . . . and fireflies?" I repeated, staring in surprise.

"Yes. Are you all right, Juan?"

"Just surprised."

"We can talk more of fireflies after the basilica, if you like. But the basilica is first . . . I'd like to go tonight."

"I think it's closed after 7 PM. We'll go early tomorrow."

"Then I at least want to sleep where I can see the dome."

"We have two blankets. It will be chilly, though."

"I don't mind—so long as the Virgin will be able to see me." I smiled and touched her face, working one hand down her side, cupping a firm breast. "Don't," she smiled, glancing around us. "I will become wet again—the others will smell my desire—and know."

Even as she protested her mouth opened and the tip of her tongue caressed my lips. She shuddered and stopped suddenly. "Can the Virgin see us from here?" I shrugged and cupped her warm breast again, but the moment had passed. Chaperoned by Guadalupe herself, we took a late-night bus to the basilica from Mexico City's old Central Station. The local bus was already packed.

When we arrived, we watched others on the bus reserve their sleeping places by spreading blankets on the cobbled plaza facing the basilica. We followed suit, using my duffel for a pillow. The detachment of federal police across the street watched intently as poor Indian peasants from Mexico's mountainous waist filled the plaza, as they did every night, hoping for salvation.

Nervous, I watched the troopers watch us, but Alli slept like a child. She awakened about 6:30 AM, disturbed by the morning's never-ending fleet of noxious, honking diesel buses packed with yet more Indian pilgrims. There were only about a hundred people in line ahead of us when the chains roping off the basilica's huge doors were removed at seven. In Mexico, bullfights, nightclub floor shows, basilica doors, and soccer matches were the only events timed to the minute. All else was ad hoc.

It was only twenty minutes until we entered the church, she on her knees the whole way, her hands together in prayer, looking wide eyed like a child. When it came her turn to approach the altar she nodded and in her native tongue asked the Virgin to bless her quest to become a healer and keeper of the old ways. As she spoke, a candle flared below the Indian cloak on which the Virgin's image had miraculously appeared in 1541. It sputtered for a moment, then again flared brilliantly. As Malinalli turned away to be sprinkled with holy water, the candle went out.

The old Indian woman next in line crossed herself and whispered to Alli, "The Virgin smiles on you, child. What is your name?"

"Malinalli, señora." The old woman pulled her head erect, crossed herself again, then turned to stare at me. "Are *you* el Malinche come to life?"

I shook my head and smiled. She crossed herself again. As we exited I heard her tell the next in line, "It is a miracle—el Malinche and la doña Marina are come to life. Look! Right there." She pointed at us, "See them!" Several hundred heads turned. Sniffing like dogs on the hunt, the Federales across the street became animated. A jumble of exclamations in Spanish and Nahuatl rippled through the crowd as we stepped outside. Until that moment, I hadn't fully realized just why our pairing so unsettled the mestizos in Oaxaca—we were an unpleasant reminder of their Indian roots, which most denied.

The troopers stared, trying to get a good look at us through the crowd. I rushed Alli onto a waiting bus, its doors already beginning to close.

☙

I expected the bus to be pursued . . . or for a group of cops, Garands at the ready, to be waiting for us along the route. Edgy, I pushed Alli out in front of me three stops later, next to a big taxi rank. She knew something was wrong, so I explained as we hailed a taxi and climbed in. "There are some Mexican police and agents of my country who want to talk to me . . . and I don't want to be found."

"Did you hurt someone?" she asked. "No . . . the cops beat me up trying to get information about a diplomatic quarrel between Mexico and my country."

"Did you tell them what you know?"

"Yes, but I didn't know enough to suit them."

"You're white, like they are . . . why would they beat you?"

"Oh, Alli—'white' Mexican cops don't think of me as like them—to them I'm a gringo. Something to fear . . . or to despise." She was quiet for a long while, her brow wrinkled. I watched for federal police. Nothing. Alli looked away when I tried to make eye contact. So I concentrated on the taxi. It rattled alarmingly each time we gyrated over the ever-present *topes* (speed bumps). When, at last, she spoke, I was surprised by what she said. "I didn't like us being compared to el Malinche and doña Marina . . . am I betraying my people like she once did . . . by being with you?"

No. Wow! Where did that come from? I wondered. "I'm not a conquistador . . ." She stared, "Perhaps it doesn't matter . . . I have to go back to Ce Xochitl, now that I am purified by the Virgin."

"Can't we spend a few days together?" *Damn. I sound like a ten-year-old begging for a cookie.* She smiled. "No. I must return." We made it back to the bus station without incident. I bought her a return ticket on a night bus, which gave me a few more precious hours with her. Ticket in hand, I returned to the bench where she waited. She actually smiled when I waved the ticket and lied to her, "There weren't any seats until eight this evening. I hope that's OK."

"Good. That gives us more time to be together . . . I'm hungry. Let's go eat." We walked a half block to a large, bustling lunchroom that served a daily *comida corrida* (a multicourse, fixed-price meal). These restaurants catered to Mexico City's huge lunchtime office crowd and were the best deals in town.

Alli was ecstatic. "I've never eaten in a place like this before. It's beautiful, the food is good . . . and no one is staring at us." The

Virgin had clearly blinded her to reality, but I saw no reason to destroy her illusion.

At one point I looked up, only to catch her blotting the corners of her eyes. She tilted her head, looking sad, "I so like being with you, Juan . . ." For once I didn't mind the emotion. I got warm all over, then embarrassed.

Later, we walked to a nearby park, took a bench, and snuggled. I drank in her wondrous face as she napped, her head in my lap. We didn't talk much when she awoke. Walking and looking in store windows made it easier.

It was twilight when we reentered the station. They called her bus . . . and I began to suffer another panic attack. She turned to me unexpectedly, buried her face in my chest. Overcome, I leaked a few tears and tried to hide it.

She was warm, smelled of jasmine, and the curls of her lips parted as she kissed me longingly. She was so full of life that I wanted to go away with her. I was losing control, but the sound of her voice pulled me back with a start. "Thank you for the tears, *teoquichhui* (formal Nahuatl— "husband"). You shall know when the child is born." Her hand brushed my cheek again, then she stepped into the bus.

A kind of pain I'd never felt before shot through me as the bus disappeared. I tried to run out into the street to watch it go, but my legs buckled and the station's lobby went into a nauseating spin. I hyperventilated as the bus disappeared. By instinct—as in reform school—I suddenly wanted to attend classes again. The only domain of life that I'd been able to control. Later that night, after wandering around like a zombie on autopilot, I found myself in front of Campos Eliseos 81.

Looking startled, Chavela answered the bell and disappeared before I could say anything. In Mexico, maids don't ask you questions—they leave you at the door and ask the homeowner. I waited. Chavela reappeared and ushered me into Dr. Baker's private sitting room, motioning me into a chair. I waited some more.

After I'd fidgeted long enough, Julia Baker swooped in, not offering to sit. Her tone was noncommittal. "Well, JA. What can we do for you?"

"I stopped by on the off-chance you'd let me stay a few nights. I need to arrange classes here this term."

"... And the *Excélsior* series, JA?"

"Well, I thought I'd ask. I'm not certain what to do just now."

"Didn't things work out with John Paddock?"

"Yes—it was great, but I need classes here." She stared, appraising me, finally shrugging.

"John Paddock told me you were at loose ends these days . . . and Pablo Virreyes talked to me about you as well—for some reason he didn't seem to want you coming back to Mexico City. Whatever fickle Pablo wants, I'm automatically suspicious of it . . . call me perverse." *Hmmn? Pablo doesn't want me in Mexico City . . . interesting.* "So, you can share the downstairs study room just off the dining room—same arrangements as before. But if there is a new stir at the embassy, we'll have to rethink this."

"Thank you, Dr. Baker. I'll try really hard to stay out of trouble—should this even be my 'official' residence?"

"Probably not, JA . . . I'll tell the staff that you're here—but not here. Keeping a low profile would be quite wise . . . do you have any luggage you need help with?"

"No, just the duffel here. Day after tomorrow I'll go back south and retrieve my books." She nodded—"Pay Chavela for the first month . . ."—and floated out looking regal. Chavela showed me to the downstairs room.

It was large, its walls lined with medical books; it had been outfitted with two single guest beds, two big writing tables, and several nice chairs. The red tile floor and tall south windows overlooking a narrow side patio gave it a cheery air. The bright Mexican blankets helped as well.

A blue-and-white-tiled bath with shower adjoined. Dr. Baker was no fool—the side patio and the room's windows were hidden from any exterior vantage point. The only way into this part of her huge house compound was over the roof facing Chapultepec Park, then down onto the narrow patio where all the maids' rooms were located. Not even a class A spook could have made it undetected, much less an out-of-control Semper Fi.

Exhausted, I slept until about 5 AM when I awoke, desperate to see, touch, hold Malinalli again. I was all knotted up inside, undone by the fact that I'd awakened to the same visceral pain that had overwhelmed me when Alli stepped into the bus to leave me the night before. I simply wasn't used to this . . . I'd always been able to walk away from people, places, events and leave them behind. Not even think of them. They were simply gone. Poof! End of story.

My life's only exceptions had been Eddy and Betty Anne. They haunted me. Now I also had Alli to contend with. As I lay there, my belly churning, I hoped that my anguish would vanish as quickly and as unexpectedly as it had come. It didn't. Clutching my stick I took an early AM walk up Campos Eliseos. Without even thinking, I'd headed to Marianna's apartment. Nonplussed, I turned to head over to the Reforma but stopped and stared up Mari's block again. Marianna remained an enigma and I was curious to find out if seeing her place again would make me feel anything like I felt for Malinalli.

I still had a spare set of Mari's keys. I tightened my grip on the Toluca stick—if Semper Fi caught me, he'd be the one going to the hospital this time. The hidden alley entrance behind her apartment block seemed to be the way to go. I edged into its narrow gap. Seeing no one I proceeded to the small service door that gave trash collectors and repairmen access.

The coast was clear. So was the roof above me. I slipped in quietly just before 6 AM, making it up the cold, poorly lit rear stairs to the second floor without encountering anyone. I inserted the key and opened the door quietly. The moment I entered I knew something was wrong. I slooowly shut the door behind me and froze, motionless, in the foyer till I figured it out . . . fresh cooking smells? Hmmn. I tiptoed into the kitchen.

No wonder. Fresh dishes filled the sink—the remains of omelets. A pot of beans soaked in cold water on the small white-tiled counter. I choked up on the stick, moved stealthily across the sitting/dining room, and used the tip of the stick to gingerly push the bedroom door wider.

Someone snored softly from Mari's bed, hidden partway behind the door. I poked my head around cautiously and craned my neck to get a look.

A lanky, disheveled don Pablo Virreyes lay there alone, tangled in Mari's—hell, *our*—sheets! *Prick*, I thought, momentarily outraged. But within seconds I realized I was relieved. Mari had apparently made a tough decision for me. Maybe she was with him and I was off the hook.

But what about her baby? Not sure what to do, I edged away from the bedroom, grabbed a sheet of notepaper from the telephone stand in the foyer, and jotted a quick note to Pablo:

Why is Poppa Bear sleeping in Mari's bed?—A wayward gringo

I dropped the note onto the floor, closed the door behind me, and had barely made it into the rear stairwell when don Pablo's pistolero, Benjamín, who'd guarded Mari and me in Guanajuato, came up the wide front staircase with a tray of what smelled like hot café con leche and sweet rolls. I kept going.

Downstairs I put my ear to the secluded rear door, listening for any sound outside. All clear . . . I vanished into the alley, turning left at its opening to a side street—away from busy Campos Eliseos. The early bird work crowd was just beginning to float into the street—intent on a leisurely downtown breakfast before hitting the office.

Early risers notice everything. That had been my working assumption since reform school days. Most wouldn't be early risers if they actually had a life. Would they? All the early birds in the next street saw was a güero heading toward a nearby bus stop, then waiting for an uptown bus, instead of one headed down toward the Zócalo.

I ate breakfast at Dr. Baker's, grateful for the light pre–school term fare of hot chocolate and sweet rolls. I know I should have been pissed at finding Pablo bedded down at Marianna's, but she had become just another unintended part of my past. I hadn't meant it to be that way. But I wanted the girl with recurved lips, dark, glistening hair, and jade-brown skin . . . and that want was profound.

Except for Betty Anne I'd never really experienced emotional desire before—wanting to be with someone so desperately that her image tormented me. And, with Alli, it wasn't merely testosterone. The rush of feelings that came with sex excited me, but my obsession with Alli was deeper and more troubling—I wanted to watch her breathe, feel the warm, rhythmic pulse of life in her throat, hear the soft, mysterious cadence of her voice. I even went crazy watching her eat.

What's the matter with me? I wondered. The Voice answered, *You're losing it, lame brain . . . face it, you are out of control.*

"I am not," I snarled back. Chavela gave me a suspicious glance as she cleared the table. There was only one other America's student at Dr. Baker's—a Latino guy named Jaime whose dad was a foreign diplomat serving in the United States. He'd gotten raging drunk in the fall and rampaged through Dr. Baker's private upstairs theater, cutting up the curtains and savaging Dr. Baker's vintage French theater posters.

He got away with it because his dad had both money and political juice. Jaime was in his perennial brood. Staring petulantly, he opened fire. "Where you been, JA . . . down in Indian country valiantly trying to get a case of the clap?" He almost never made eye contact when he dumped on folks. Apparently the little prick felt unusually brave, since I was his only victim. Jaime liked it when the odds were clearly in his favor. He was usually sullen and quiet when they weren't.

Jaime tried to rile me again. "What happened to the blonde Argentinean slut they wrote those cheesy newspaper pieces about?" I foamed inside but didn't bite. Jaime pressed, "You know, the one who's fucked every newspaperman in town . . . bet she even takes it in . . ."

Poor Jaime. So moody. So pissed off at being brown in a world he perceived as unfairly dominated by the fair skinned. He looked surprised as I stood to leave the table, still unable to comprehend why he was suddenly rendered speechless. A moment later, I think he made the connection between the stick in my hand and his sudden muteness. For a brief moment his startled eyes fixed on my stick before the first wave of pain left him flattened on the table.

"*Borracho, otra vez* (Drunk again)," I told Chavela, who'd returned for the empty chocolate mugs and had shot me another inquiring glance after spotting Jaime sprawled on the table. I might have been more considerate of Jaime had he not always been screwing the younger maids for fifty pesos (four U.S. dollars) a pop, then bad-mouthing them cruelly, and often, when "Dr. Baker's boys" assembled for dinner.

Professor Paddock was in town, so I went to see him later that day. He was going back to the Lambityeco dig, but not till spring quarter, which began in late March. That worked well—I had time to take lecture classes before fieldwork began again.

"There has been a last minute permit hitch," John explained. That usually meant, "The grant from your U.S. foundation is, *cough*, larger than we realized, Señor Professor Paddock—that will require us to re-review your permit." I could picture Paddock walking away with a shrug—stating his bargaining position without uttering a word.

In contrast the greenhorn Stateside archaeologists almost always expressed outrage, only to eventually wind up paying some official a "processing fee" large enough to pay for an excellent used car. With John Paddock, the officialdom would panic within a month and settle for the price of a long Semana Santa weekend in Acapulco. I said nothing about the "unexpected" delay in my job, but I admired Paddock. He was not only a good archaeologist; he was a tough little guy in his own quietly unyielding way.

I left Paddock feeling upbeat—I'd have a job at Lambityeco . . . and could be near Alli . . . or could I? Would I be trapped—kept from Betty Anne again by the hand of fate in the form of Marianna or old, angry Jerónimo?

The next day I took the bus out to the University of the Americas, nestled on the edge of a steep, picturesque barranca west of Mexico City. One reached campus from the Toluca highway. I registered for classes, then went for a beer with Peter Mennen, who'd been hiding out from both his dynastic responsibilities and the most irritatingly curious lawyer on his family's retainer team, which is why he had missed out on the fun on our trip to Veracruz. We were in a small bar about a block off the Reforma, near the National Lottery building.

"I 'screwed' someone in the States and now there is unpleasant litigation," he explained to me. I was never certain whether the screwing was of the biblical or of the more ordinary, everyday, material kind but imagined them equally possible.

Peter updated me on Semper Fi's activities, divulging material gleaned from family sources. Semper Fi hadn't exited Mexico without a fight and, as I'd feared, was thought to have returned. According to rumor, he was still hanging out in alleys near the Academy San Marcos. Mennen explained, "When the Federal Judicial Police came for him, Semper Fi had failed to display good grace." "Mexico has more kinds of cops than the Galapagos have species of finches," I laughed. Mennen grinned.

According to Peter, Semper Fi had taken a swing at one of the troopers while screaming at the detachment's young but upper-class captain, "Keep your oily greaser hands off of me, you socialist faggots!"

"Unfortunately the captain's English was quite good," said Peter. "They took him to precinct *número nueve* (number nine), the same hole they took us to after that party on Calle Río Tiber last September. Remember?"

"Yep," I nodded.

"Well, they say that the fag-hater got the cattle prod, up-the-ass treatment till he got on his knees and apologized to the captain's entire squad. Humility didn't suit Semper Fi—he said the Argentine model is a dead woman and that you, JA, were going to be gutted alive and fed to the local dogs." If Peter expected me to be nervous, he was disappointed.

"Yeah, he used the same 'gut and dump' line on me the first day we met in Veracruz. Hasn't happened yet."

"Still cold, eh, JA? Well, I'd be careful if I were you—he's crazy."

"What's new? Besides, he's out of the country . . . right?" Mennen rolled his eyes. "*Right* . . . my source is pretty reliable, so don't take any bets on it. Official or unofficial, he wants his pound of flesh from you." Actually, I wasn't taking bets, but I shrugged as if I coulda' cared less and pumped him for more . . . "Anything on General Birdsong?"

"Nope. He was handled more quietly. Given the photograph of him in *Excélsior* with the pistol butt showing, unlike Semper Fi, he couldn't get out fast enough . . . that's all I know."

"Did lots of people see the *Excélsior* stuff?" Peter nodded, grinning. "Hell, yes, JA—every female on campus was hot for your program after seeing your photo with that former Milan model . . . nice head there. Hell, nice everything!"

"Really?"

"Oh, yeah. Really . . . Suzy Q pouted, 'What's *she* got that I haven't got?'"

Suzy Q was our nickname for Susan McQueen, one of the flashier American coeds at the Americas. "I couldn't resist answering that one for her, JA . . . so if she's not speaking to you, you're warned."

"OK—but don't leave me in suspense. Today started out shitty . . ."

Mennen cackled. "Shitty" has no real impact on rich guys. To them, shitty means, "My lawyer got served papers today." In my world it meant something more basic had gone wrong. Like in the words of a friend named Greg, who'd once commented when his wife walked out, "If things get any worse, I'm going to strap on a big wooden beak, head for the barnyard, and go peck shit with the chickens." That kind of shitty—wooden beaks, Marianna, Semper Fi, and don Pablo shitty— simply didn't compute with Mennen. He quit laughing once he noticed me scowling.

"OK, I told her there were two things she didn't have: experience and the heart of a slut. She let the experience thing go but made the mistake of asking, 'Just what kind of heart do you think I have?' I told her—'The heart of a bitch.'"

"So why's she pissed at me?"

"Because I said I was quoting you."

"Nice! I assume you're paying for the beer." Looking a touch sheepish, but still pleased with himself, Mennen pulled out his roll and paid the barkeep.

Once outside Peter headed back toward the Americas, while I headed to the National Lottery building to take in one of their free late afternoon variety shows. The Lottery sold tickets everywhere—mostly to folks who could neither afford them, nor afford to pass up the possible miracle of winning five million pesos—no matter how long the odds.

In return the National put on a number of free-to-the-public variety shows each week. You lined up for a ticket till the hall was filled and got to see big time talent. Even the cold sodas—at two pesos—were subsidized.

That was the evening I first heard Compay Segundo—the Cuban musician who played "Chan Chan" as his closing song. The deep bass beat and Afro-Cuban tonalities vibrated right through me. I was hooked . . . no wonder they didn't want us to see, hear, read about, or, God forbid, actually visit Cuba. Given the music it couldn't be just one big cane field full of scrawny chickens and addled Commies, starving . . . the dirty secret they were apparently keeping from us in the States was that the place had both culture and a soul.

For a few hours I even forgot about Alli, Mari, and Semper Fi and simply enjoyed myself. Still too wary to go back to my favorite haunt, the Punto Blanco, I drifted into the big, plush Sanborn's a few blocks from the huge bronze statue of Diana, the huntress. Tourists usually crowded Sanborn's, so I reckoned I'd go unnoticed.

✳✳

№ 17 THE PLEASURE OF BLOOD

THE SUN HAD ALREADY set when I slipped into a plush chair near the rear of the main coffee room of Sanborn's—adjacent to a huge plate glass window facing the side street. Said to be the largest single piece of glass in the republic, it gave a lovely view of the huge nearby angular glass-block-and-stucco houses and four-story apartment buildings that lined every side street in the city's famous and sophisticated Zona Rosa (Pink Zone).

Embassies, top-end coffee houses, pricey hotels, Arpège perfume, Van Cleef & Arpels diamonds, the latest women's fashion from Milan and Paris, not to mention one of the original three Delmonico's steak houses all graced the Pink Zone. Other than coffee or a sandwich the Zona offered virtually nothing that an ordinary Mexican, or I, could afford.

Its women were beautiful, its men well suited, and Mexico City's huge flock of decorative downtown female "office assistants" invaded it every weekday from about noon till 2 PM and again about 6 PM just before they grabbed buses back to the grubby, overcrowded, inner-city neighborhoods where most of them lived.

When I first arrived in Mexico I quickly caught on to the rhythm of the flock, following it as obsessively as any other birdwatcher. You don't get to see many examples of the opposite sex while in custody. Perhaps that's why women fascinated me. Ruminating about women while feeling sorry for myself may also have been the reason I didn't notice the two thick-necked pistoleros working their way toward me through the crowd . . .

Had an impatient driver outside on the corner not honked, I might still have been daydreaming about Alli and staring out the big side window at Sanborn's as a .45 auto's round slammed into my skull. Instead, I jerked involuntarily when the horn startled me. It was just enough that the bullet grazed the tip of my lower jaw, burning my chin like a searing poker.

Nearby, a woman screamed. I jumped out of my chair and twisted to see what was going on. Two guys in cheap, poorly cut suits stood about ten feet away. One held the standard nickel-plated automatic. The other merely looked surprised, his black-gloved hands as empty as his coal-black eyes. He acted like the type who goes in for the "delicate" knife work. Some of these guys got intense pleasure from cutting on their victims. I'd already met my share in reform school.

The woman who screamed was with a large group seated at the table underneath the shooter's extended arm. One of the men in the group, a coat and tie and "where's my driver?" type, stood to protest. Black Gloves cut him across the face in response. It was fast, efficient . . . and ugly.

Both of the killers looked down for an instant to enjoy the sight of blood, which sprayed across the table, and onto expensively jeweled bosoms. I tightened my hold on the Toluca stick . . . "It's the speed," I heard don Mateo chant as he materialized in my head.

As don Mateo looked on, my fighting stick arced out and collapsed the knife-man's windpipe. I wheeled around, looking for the quickest exit. None. So I turned toward the plate glass window and threw a massive wooden chair through it, then jumped out into the street. The big .45 exploded behind me—twice.

An intense jet of gunpowder and hot air blew past me, but I felt nothing. I made it a block and a half before a new pain in my leg reached around the adrenalin and overpowered the burning sensation in my jaw. I stopped to check it out. No bullet hole, but there was a deep cut in my shin from a fragment of shattered window as I'd jumped through. A two-year-old could have followed my blood trail. I started to go light headed, but the boom of another .45 round stimulated me back up to operating speed.

There was a commotion up the block as I reached into my back pocket for a bandana to use as a tourniquet. The big pistolero was headed for me on a fast trot, his nickel-plated .45 gleaming in the artificial light of the evening streetscape.

A half block farther on, I began to get woozy again from the blood loss. The hit man had gained on me. To my right rose a high stone wall topped with wrought iron—not the broken Coke bottles embedded in mortar so favored by the local elites.

Panting and dizzy, I tossed my stick over, then followed. I fell clumsily into a bunch of bushes. I lay there—how long I don't know—until a reassuring voice said, in a British accent, "There now! Stay calm." "Huh? Where am I?" I heard myself ask. It sounded as if I was somewhere off in the distance, my voice muffled by a dense fog.

"You're at the UK Embassy residence, young man. The gunman who tried to follow you over the wall was stopped by our security staff but got away. A doctor is on the way." I looked down to check out my leg and found it had been properly bandaged.

"I'm Howard Jenkins-Smith . . . the United Kingdom's consul general in Mexico. The gent in uniform is Lieutenant Williams, chief of our security detail . . . you are American, we assume?"

Still groggy and disconnected I answered, "British Embassy residence . . . ?"

"Right-o."

"Am I under arrest?"

"Why would we arrest you?"

"I broke the big window at Sanborn's to get away."

"My, my . . . you Americans certainly are impetuous. Have you a name, young man?"

"My name is John Al—" Lieutenant Somebody, the security chief, I think, butted in. "—A word, sir . . . *now*."

I thought they might be discussing me, but I was unable to maintain focus and went to sleep again. When I awoke I found myself in a real bed, wearing only a bathrobe. My leg burned. I looked down to inspect it. Sutured. Neat job. It was already light outside, and the constant hum of early morning traffic drifted in through a barred side window.

I sat upright, trying to spot my clothes and marveling at the fact that I wasn't tied down by restraints. The door opened.

In walked the prior night's bubbly voice, reintroducing himself. A security guard was with him. "You had a close call, Mr. Alexander." *He knows my name?* I winced. "Oh, yes . . . we checked the ID in your pocket. Seems like the newspapers here find you rather intriguing, just as your own embassy finds you tedious."

"Yeah, it's complicated. But I'm not the one generating trouble, sir . . . I just want to stay in Mexico, finish a master's degree and be left alone . . . are you turning me over to the cops . . . or to the U.S. Embassy?"

"We've not decided. Have you a preference, young man?"

"A preference?" I grinned. "That sounds so civilized. Since you're asking, I'd prefer to take my chances with the Mexico City cops."

"Really? How interesting . . . an American who isn't demanding that his government step in and save him from assault charges?"

"Assault charges?"

"Yes, according to Pablo Virreyes, one of the editors at some tabloid that they insist on calling a 'newspaper,' you attacked one of his personal bodyguards after breaking into his uptown apartment . . . this according to a contact at the American Embassy." "*What?*" I groaned. He chuckled in response. "Our security people thought you might find this odd. They tell me you were recently living with Mr. Virreyes's current mistress."

"*Current mistress!*" I heard myself say, even as my brain tried valiantly to process what Jenkins-Smith had just told me. "She can't be his current mistress . . . she's, uh, 'overseas.'"

"We need to talk privately, Mr. . . . . Alexander."

"It's JA," I offered. He nodded, "Perhaps we can meet a bit later. I've got a tight schedule till lunch." With that he left, to be replaced by a young woman carrying a breakfast tray. She was pleasant and unaffected, with an even thicker accent.

"Hi, I'm Annie, the ambassador's maid. You must be a pretty special guest to have me serve you breakfast. Security ordered the local staff to stay away from you . . . is there anything you need?" "A bathroom . . . and my clothes?" I asked casually, hoping she'd take me seriously. Annie smiled.

"Bathroom is behind you—the shutterlike doors. It's a half bath, but it will do for the moment . . . your clothes are locked up—no luck for you there. Here, drink this juice. Lots of it! You are still dehydrated from the bleeding. They didn't want to IV you, though. Thought it might attract too much attention from the local staff."

"Like, what am I . . . some exotic trophy?"

"Ooh. That's a lovely way to put it . . . *everyone* is looking for you—the Mexican press, Sanborn's, the U.S. government, the Russians. I've read some of the newspaper accounts . . ."

"In Spanish?"

"Yes, I'm not stupid. I finished my baccalaureate."

"So, why—" She cut me off, "Because this is a *very* good job. I'm saving money and will go to university one day. Spanish literature . . . so there."

Annie was OK. Real. Right up front. I leaned back with the juice and drank it down. She made no move to go, acting as if she wanted to say something else. I started the conversation again. "Your accent's a bit different. What part of England are you from?" She smiled again, not coy at all.

"I'm Scots. Born near Glasgow." She pronounced it "Glazzgo," her throat catching on the second *g*.

"I wonder if you sound like my mother might have."

"Oooh. Why do you say 'might have'? Don't you remember your mum's voice?"

"No. I never heard it. She died from complications of childbirth— after having me and my twin brother . . . she was from the Glasgow area . . . her birth certificate said 'Greenock.'"

"I'm sorry. So you never knew your mum. Well, I didn't mean to be rude by asking."

"You weren't. No one has ever asked. I wish I'd known her." Annie looked puzzled for a moment. "*Born* in Greenock, you say?"

"Yeah, why?"

"Does Mr. Jenkins-Smith know that?"

"Don't know—but why would he . . . and what does it matter?"

"Perhaps it doesn't," she smiled, "but I'll tell him anyway." With that Annie breezed out. "Till lunch. 12:30!" "Clothes!" I shouted. "Yes . . . do *close* the robe," she laughed as she pulled the door behind her. I went to the bathroom, looked around for my clothes and stick. No luck. Then, tired, I went back to sleep.

Just before 1 PM the bedroom door reopened. Howard Jenkins-Smith, looking very spiffy, came in, followed by Annie, who was carrying my Wranglers, shirt, and underwear, all freshly laundered. "Well, sport, we're going to dress you for lunch with the ambassador, me, and a recording secretary . . . 'casually official' is the drill. Can you handle it? The tie is a loaner." Annie butted in, "He means, 'Be civilized and not try to break out on us?'"

"Sure, Mr. Jenkins-Smith, but don't do the fancy tableware bit. I never know which fork to use."

Jenkins-Smith warmed up even more. "In private I'm just Howard . . . and Annie has made it very clear what we need. Decisions about what to do with you must be made . . . and the ambassador is *very* old-fashioned—to you he is simply 'Mr. Ambassador.' Got it?"

I nodded. Annie handed me my duds, pockets empty, and smiled. "You'll be wearing slippers. Two minutes to dress. If you don't come out the door then, we shoot you." "I've already been wounded," I put in. "Best not mess with Annie," Howard piped in. "She's rather tough when she's riled." "OK," I shrugged.

ӟӟ

Lunch with an ambassador wasn't quite what I imagined. The food was great—soup, grilled fish, curried rice, and vegetables, and Mr. Ambassador was more than just old-fashioned; he was a throwback to another age. The first words out of his mouth got my attention—fully.

"I knew your father, young man. A brilliant scholar. My government helped him get out of Germany—'36 I think it was. He wasn't a Jew, but he was one of the world's leading authorities on criminal behavior. The Reich was closing in on him—his subject probably upset the führer, sordid little criminal that he was, through and through."

"You *knew* my father? Tell me about him!"

"I just *told* you about your father."

Howard gave me The Look. So I shut up and nodded.

"Your mother met your father when he lectured briefly at the University of Glasgow. Lovely young woman—a great-grandniece of Dr. David Livingston."

"*The* David Livingston . . . Tanganyika?"

"Of course . . . who else could that be, young man? Well, to the point. The American government believes that we have you and wants us to turn you over to them. Same with the Mexicans. Ordinarily I'd be inclined . . . but, given your family background, I'm feeling balky on the matter. You see—Churchill pushed for your father's British citizenship and your mother, the uh, Scot, was, technically, also a citizen." Annie arched an eyebrow and rolled her eyes.

Oblivious, Mr. Ambassador didn't miss a beat. "If you were to apply for asylum and petition for British citizenship, it would tie things up for six months to a year. Such a petition might—or might not—be granted. But I could tell both the Mexicans and the Yanks to, er . . . stuff it." He looked sheepish for a moment and turned a bit red . . . "But no trouble out of you, mind you. No heroics, mister! Understand?"

I nodded. "Good, then, young Alexander, do you wish to petition for asylum?"

"I do. I DO! I can't believe it; I'm catching a break from parents I've dreamed about but never knew," I stammered. For one moment, Mr. Ambassador's face lit up with what might have been empathy; then the ambassador role overtook him again.

"Jenkins-Smith here will see to the details . . . well—that's that. I'm off to see the French ambassador. Good afternoon, all." He rose and withdrew, leaving me to stare at the others . . . Annie smiled and pointed at my plate, "Eat."

Jenkins-Smith said, "I'd no idea how he'd react. We only got info back on your parents about an hour ago. Sealed files in Pennsylvania had to be opened. They were reluctant, till our embassy suggested their custody of you might have been illegal all these years. After all, your parents would still have had the right to petition your citizenship and automatically obtain passports when you were infants. Nothing moves a bureaucracy like raw fear."

I ate, dazed by just having talked to someone who'd actually seen— and remembered—both of my parents. Till that moment both had been but dream images in my head—not quite real. In the realm of myths.

Later, Howard came to the room where I was again sequestered. I filled out and signed reams of papers emblazoned with Britain's royal seal. Afterward, Annie brought me several newspapers and a book to read, borrowed from the residence's library.

I was on my way to a new passport, merely because some goon had taken a shot at me in Sanborn's. But why did the Brits think that goon was linked to don Pablo . . . and just why was Pablo staying at Mari's? I suffered another panic attack while trying to figure it out. Finally, the Voice and I decided I'd been way too trusting since Mexico had softened me up. I chain-smoked to calm down.

When Annie returned I told her I needed more smokes. She laughed, "That's the least of your worries—the U.S. Embassy went ballistic when the ambassador told them we wouldn't release you . . . imagine the stroke of luck that he actually knew your father!"

"Yes, it nearly undid me. I can't wait to tell my twin brother." She broke eye contact and changed the subject by asking what kind of smokes I wanted.

"Raleigh 903s, if they are available."

"That should be easy enough, Mr. Alexander. Meanwhile I can bring you a pack of Dunhills from the residence's guest supply—will that work?"

"*Sure*. Dunhills are fabulous. Here's a twenty-peso note for the Raleighs. Should buy five packs with a tiny tip left over." She took the note and turned to leave, stopped short, and looked back over her shoulder. "I think you need to talk to Mr. Jenkins-Smith again. Gossip has it they got a rather extensive report on you."

"Something I don't know, you mean?"

"Perhaps—can I call you JA?"

"Sure. But why? Am I going to be here for a while?"

"A few days, I think, JA . . . and you're interesting. Most guests here are very stuffy. They don't talk to 'the help.'"

☙

When evening came, I was ensconced at the guest room's writing table, penning a long letter to Eddy. It took me forever. I'd never imagined writing him about our parents . . . and struggled with the oddity of it.

Dear Eddy—I don't know where this letter will find you. I can only hope it's not Vietnam. I've thought of you often lately. I miss you . . . and will always admire you for your ability to see the good side of things. That, and your kindness, have always meant a lot to me. Those are things I respect.

I'm not a very good communicator, but today something really remarkable happened—I met a diplomat here in Mexico City who actually knew our father. Father had to flee Germany in the mid-thirties as the Nazis rose to power and began to round up intellectuals. He was big time in psychology. So the Brits gave him citizenship—and the guy I ran into today was involved in getting him settled in England, then Scotland, where he met our mother.

The Brit here met her, too, but didn't really "know her." He called her "a lovely young woman" and told me—get this!—that she was a great-grandniece of Dr. David Livingston . . . The "Dr. Livingston, I presume," Livingston. Amazing, huh! No wonder you've got this doctor "thing." Turns out it's in the genes! I'm going to find out more, if I can.

I can't wait to see you and tell you all about it . . . I miss you, bro!

JA

p.s. Hey! I love you!

When Annie returned with my smokes I asked if it would be possible for me to go out and mail the letter. There was a mail slot up on the corner at a branch of the Banco Nacional.

"JA, for a chap who's caught in deep diplomatic cross-currents, you certainly are in denial. You are under a gentle version of 'house arrest.' Officially, it's 'diplomatic asylum,' but if you walk out into that street you won't make it ten meters. There are both Mex and Yank agents just aching to get their hands on you. Here, give me the letter . . . I'll get it out."

As I unwrapped the Raleighs she produced the latest issue of *Excélsior*. "See page three, JA." As the door closed behind her, I found it. Below the fold was a cropped picture of me and a caption that read, "Have you seen this fugitive? Call *Excélsior* with information: Tel. 1-09642. Story below."

The story began, "'Johann Straus Alexander,' also known as 'John Alexander' is wanted by Mexican federal authorities in the ongoing murder investigation of Dieter Gerhardt, an East German diplomat, assassinated last fall in Veracruz." As I finished reading, Howard knocked and entered, *Excélsior* in hand. "JA—you've got to read this. Virreyes is upping the pressure."

"I just read it, courtesy of Annie, here. But I don't get it. What do you guys know that I don't?"

"That Virreyes is not actually your friend . . . his lifestyle has been supported by payments that our people believe originated from American intelligence activities. I'm waiting to brief the ambassador. I think he may also have received other security files to which I'm not yet privy. But the number of Mexican Federal Police now outside is remarkable. We are bringing over reinforcements from our embassy detachment."

A few minutes later the phone started ringing downstairs and seemed never to stop. Annie came and went, keeping me posted: "AP," "UPI," "Reuters," "*Time* magazine," ad infinitum. I stewed and paced about this new information on Virreyes until Annie returned, plunked down in the chair, and asked me for a smoke. Perhaps it was her tone. Perhaps it was the six inches of mid-thigh, lavishly exposed, but more likely it was her announcement that Eddy's letter had already gone out in a diplomatic pouch. I smiled.

My compulsion to write Eddy and tell him I loved him had been digging at me. I felt much more in control knowing the letter had gone out, breathed deeply, and relaxed. "You owe me," she grinned. She continued to stare at me, smiling. To lay off the discomfort I made eye contact, "So, just what do I owe you?"

"Anything I ask of you?" Coy, she tilted her head to one side and stretched her legs, exposing an even more luscious patch of soft inner thigh. She watched me, a sardonic smile on her face. "It's as good as you think it is," she grinned. "And what I want as payback is for you to tell me what you are thinking this very moment."

"I'm not 'thinking'—just reacting. Testosterone. Mexico is a mystery to me. I arrive here a virgin . . . then all hell breaks loose. Suddenly I find myself lost in the 'Testosterone Zone' . . . and I've already got *two* girlfriends."

"No you don't—that is, if you are counting this Marianna, the Argentine model . . . so who's the other one?"

"Well, I *am* counting the Argentine—*we* have a house in southern Mexico. And the other one is nobody's business."

"OK, OK. Just womanly curiosity. But trust me, the model is now with this Virreyes bloke at the *Excélsior* . . . I thought you should know this before Jenkins-Smith or the ambassador tells you in the middle of another dinner conversation. Blokes like you don't like to be caught off guard."

"Like you know me."

"Don't be cranky . . . you are just like my older brother. He's a hush-hush military agent. All bottled up. He raised my sister and me when our parents were killed in the blitz. You are *quite* like him, just more interesting. Handsomer for that matter. Look, I'll leave you alone for a while. Dinner is at eight. I'll check in on you later tonight."

With that she left. The Voice and I had an ugly quarrel about "love," toughness, and betrayal. I won, telling him to fuck off when he dumped on me for writing Eddy that I loved him. *Well*, I told myself, *I've won.*

But Mari and don Pablo? In one way I was relieved . . . since, emotionally, I'd already started to let go of Mari. Still—the Pablo part didn't make any sense at all. *Why does he want a woman with a face that freaks him out . . . who's pregnant by another guy?* I wondered . . . *and why the hell have his pistoleros and* Excélsior *turned on me?* There was a big piece of the puzzle missing somewhere. Plus, I must have gone completely brain-dead since meeting Alli. I wanted desperately to hold her. Smell her hair. Watch her lips curl as she readied to smile. The pain of her leaving washed over me again, so I refocused by staring out the window at the sizeable detachment of blue-uniformed federal police and wondered how many plainclothes Mexican agents were lurking out there in the evening crowd.

Someone knocked at the door; Annie popped her head in, "Mr. Jenkins-Smith will be in momentarily, JA." She disappeared again. Moments later Howard knocked and stepped in . . .

"Some background before dinner, JA—our equivalent to your CIA tells us that this 'newspaperman' Virreyes *was* recruited by the States as some kind of agent, while still a young man at Harvard. I think the ambassador has more details. A friend at the Russian Embassy hinted that he may also be on the KGB payroll."

"*What?*"

"Look—as hard as this is for you to believe right now, an ordinary newspaperman he's not. We're still getting details. The ambassador is talking to the president of Mexico as we speak. When that's over, he's going to pay a call on the U.S. ambassador. Dinner has been set back to 9 PM."

I interrupted, "You're certain don Pablo isn't just a newspaperman?"

". . . don Pablo?"

"Virreyes."

"Absolutely. But just who he reports to . . . and how many 'interests' he represents may be information that we can't tie down. Or that the ambassador will decline to divulge."

"And Marianna?"

"We're drawing a total blank on her right now. May mean nothing, but she's a cipher for the time being." When he stepped out, Annie stepped back in with tea and cucumber sandwiches. "You OK, JA?" She set the tray down and poured tea. "Here, the tea will do you good."

"So would some thigh."

"*Really?* Well, the mood has passed."

"Why would you have ever been in the mood in the first place?"

"Ah, yes . . . we never quite finished the 'I was a virgin, then *every* woman in Mexico was after me' conversation, did we?"

"*Two* women—big difference."

"OK, two women . . . and it is a big difference. Do you have any idea how boring this life usually is? Diplomats—furtive, crisp, predictable, oh so well dressed, oh so well schooled. Sexually repressed. Terrible, distant relationships with their wives. They aren't *men*. They are well-dressed automatons." I shrugged. "Well, JA . . . I *do* care . . ."

"Hey, OK . . . and any woman who shows me some thigh gets to drop the 'JA' and call me 'Alex.'"

"See. Right there . . . another nickname and another whole layer to you. You are like a bomb with three fuses—handsome, dangerous, earthy . . . and emotionally tough."

"Tough?"

"Jesus and Mary . . . they sutured you up—no anesthetic—and you looked relaxed . . . off in a world where you were in total control. No gritting teeth . . . no brave groans. The doctor about soiled himself. Jenkins-Smith whistled when we went out the door and commented, 'Never saw anything like that before . . . forty sutures and that bullet groove on his chin and as peaceful as a baby.'"

"Were you there, Annie?"

"Hell, yes . . . and there I was—staring right at the first real, two-balled man I've ever met. You're even tougher than my brother. Damn right, I'll show you thigh! First time I ever craved a damn good rogering on the spot."

"Don't fantasize like that—I'll disappoint you. I'm not a two-balled kind of guy—I'm your basic lost kid . . ." "Even better," she sighed. "'Sensitive' doesn't do a thing for me. Breed me. Make me laugh. Mystify me and give me some space—that's my A-list."

"Well, I'm taken, I think. Besides, I'm a bad bet right now. The whole world is out there, watching. I'm going to wind up in prison again, dammit."

"Actually, I don't think so, JA . . . Alex . . . whatever your name is. Jenkins-Smith is never impressed with anyone, and last night was an epiphany for him. He's a wonderful judge of character . . . and he says you're straight." I liked Annie. "Your straight-talk is pretty intoxicating, too," I commented.

"Really?"

"I wish I'd met you six months ago."

"Don't torture me . . . what I'd really like now is to—"

An abrupt knock at the door shut her off. "The ambassador wishes to see you in his study," a uniformed member of the security detail announced. I turned back to Annie. "*Now!*" he insisted. I turned away from her and walked out with the young officer.

⁂

№ 18 She Had Mystical Eyes, You Know

THE AMBASSADOR'S STUDY WAS one of those ornate book-lined rooms, rich with the smells of leather, aged brandy, and expensive cigars, which ordinary folks never see except in old movies.

The ambassador looked tired. "Well, young man, you certainly are at the core of a fine mess."

"Sorry, sir."

"Oh, don't be sorry. I am tired. But I haven't had so much fun in years. Both the Yanks and Mexico's finest are apoplectic. That's worth a lot. Usually it's lost passports, angry businessmen, and tourists who think they were cheated by their tour agents. Being an ambassador is too often a combination of party host and tour guide."

Jenkins-Smith chuckled and weighed in, "Well, it's anything but boring right now . . . we're waiting for a call from Los Piños."

The ambassador swirled a half inch of brandy and refocused. "Let me, Howard . . ." He paused, sipping. "We're not certain just whom this Virreyes is loyal to, but he's on several different governments' secret payrolls." Jenkins-Smith winked at me. I nodded. Obviously my prior briefing about don Pablo had been unauthorized. The ambassador, not noticing our little signals, went on, "The men who attacked you definitely worked for him."

"Why do you say 'worked,' past tense, Mr. Ambassador?" I asked.

He paused and looked toward Howard. "Go on, Howard . . . your turn." Howard nodded, "They have both been found dead. In a shallow remnant of the old lake—near Texcoco."

A nearby phone rang and the ambassador jumped up to get it. He was animated when he returned. "President Lopez Mateos has weighed in on this by sending members of his own elite security detail to invite Virreyes to meet him in the president's office tomorrow at 8 AM—let's eat. I'm starved."

I took a quick detour to put on a tie after Jenkins-Smith made odd choking hand signals to me. When I ran to my room the borrowed tie and a well-used gray tweed jacket were laid out on the bed. A note lay on the jacket.

JA. Borrowed this from one of the security guys—he said it was bulletproof. Just what you need. A.

The ambassador's table was set for eight, but there were only six present when I entered the room. I was nervous. Watching everyone carefully spoon their soup away from them, I followed suit. They made small talk I didn't quite understand.

I had no idea what "Arsenal" and the "Manchester United" were, until Jenkins-Smith noticed my blank look. "Football, JA, football. World Cup." When the conversation lapsed back into that British cultural code, I switched to off mode. Americans don't like cultural mysteries. In contrast, Brits apparently love them.

Dinner was over when the ambassador stood to excuse us. I moved to exit with the others, but the ambassador motioned me into his study again. "Sit, young man. You smoke, I hear." Passing a wooden box to me, he motioned me to open it. "Try one of these. Cuban."

I took one of the slender cigars and lit up. The ambassador smoked, silent, till Annie came in with his hot toddy. "Here, sir—just what Annie ordered after a long day." He grinned as she withdrew with a wink. The ambassador's eyes followed her as she went out. "I'm crazy about that girl, young man. Reminds me of your mother." *Well, you've got my attention again*, I thought to myself.

"I only met your mother once—sat across from her at a formal dinner. She was a stunner. A natural beauty. Mystical eyes—soft emerald green, like yours—yes, mystical . . . the Celtic thing, you know. After dinner she sang . . . Old Winston Churchill, you know, insisted. The old letch.

"I never heard anything like it before—or since. She had the clearest vibrato tenor I've ever heard. Sang in Gaelic. Again, the mystery. Mournful. She reached right in and pulled the soul right out of every man who heard her. Only the good Lord knows where she was. Those eyes. A million miles away in another world. Like the rest of them, I fell in love with her. Right there." He paused to sip at his toddy, staring at me over the top of his glasses . . .

"But she was spoken for. I never saw her again . . . and I never married. It's not on account of your father that I've given you refuge here . . . pulled a few strings. Your father was brilliant, but cold. It's your mother. Her eyes . . . they had pale flecks of luminous blue green in them when she sang . . . rather like those little twinkling insects . . . you know . . ."

I heard myself say, "Fireflies?" in a voice I'd never used before. Every nerve ending in my body was on fire. Every hair erect. Head to toe.

"Yes. Yes . . . like fireflies!" He sighed, slumped back in his leather chair, brushed back his thin, graying hair, and smiled at me. "Don't let me down, son. You're in the middle of dodgy stuff. Stay calm. Don't bolt on us . . . it's a waiting game now." He sipped again and sighed, then waved me off, an embarrassed, kidlike smirk lingering on his aging lips. If he noticed the tears running down my cheeks he gave no overt sign of it.

That night I had finally met my mother—the radiance of her soul still shining in an old man's eyes.

✸✸

That was also the night don Pablo Virreyes fled to the airport. "Both Mexican and Russian agents covered the Sala Internacional," Jenkins-Smith confided the next day. "But they didn't count on Virreyes exiting the country aboard a U.S. military flight from a private runway."

"Well, I guess we know the identity of his primary employer," I commented.

"Oh, it gets better, sport," Howard whispered, eyebrows raised. "He had a woman with him—tall, slender, face and hair covered by a scarf."

"*Slender*—Marianna? Pregnant?" Howard shrugged in response. "An enigma as to identity, but not obviously pregnant. When the plane landed in Tampa, there was *no* woman aboard. *None!*"

"You're kidding."

"Not kidding, sport. She went poof. Gone. '¿*Sabe?*' as they say here."
I gaped. "Virreyes changed planes in Tampa. Learjet to a private airport near Langley, Virginia," Howard said.

"What's that mean?"

"CIA. Maybe DIA. He left 'attached' and arrived one witness short—your ex, his wife, another girlfriend? No one seems to be sure at the moment." A breeze of unfamiliar emotion rippled through me—sorrow? Wistfulness? Guilt? I wasn't sure. It's one thing to "feel"—and quite another for a new learner to sort one basic emotion from another. "How do you get on a plane and 'lose' someone?" I asked.

"I love your combination of tough and naive, JA—but losing someone from a plane in the Gulf of Mexico is a high-level Mexican specialty. It's as much a signature item as the Russian's cyanide capsules, or your Mafia's tommy guns in violin cases." I shook my head, resisting yet another wave of unidentifiable emotion. Jenkins-Smith noticed, "Sorry, sport . . . thought you should know. By the way, is the key to her flat among the items we're looking after?"

"'Looking after?' Nice way to put it . . . sounds civilized . . . yes, it's the biggest modern key on my chain. The big skeleton key is to the house in Mitla."

"Good. We'll borrow it and have one of our specialists sniff around." I turned to go.

I was already working on another letter to Eddy back in my room—about our mother—when Jenkins-Smith came in and dropped his final bombshell. "Guess who the pilot of the Learjet was?" *This is going to be good*, I thought.

"Uh, don't know. Amaze me, Howard."

"Glad to—none other than your General Birdsong!" A weird chill shot through me. "Not possible," I suggested, "they hated one another." Howard grinned, "Not so deeply that they weren't on the same payroll. Well, on that note, I'll let you piece it together." Apparently pleased with himself, he strolled off, whistling a tune I didn't know.

☙

I stared out the side window, daydreaming about Eddy. *Where is he right now?*

I refocused on the scene across the street when something bright flashed and jerked me back into the present . . . odd, there weren't any federal police out there. Gone. *Hmmn? All peaceful for a change*, I told myself. Another brief flash made me blink again.

I scanned carefully, moving only my eyes. Body movement always attracts attention. Finally I spotted the source. A young man across the street inside a shop was scanning me, or my window, with a lens of some sort. Every time he moved it, the overhead sun flashed from its polished surface. Moments later I casually pulled away from the window, sat down at the writing table in front of it, and went back to Eddy's letter. I finished it, folded it, and stood, letter in hand.

I found Jenkins-Smith in his little office, just off the study. "I need another letter posted . . . by the way, it might interest you that someone has been using a camera or binoculars to check out my window from across the street. The perfume shop." He smiled.

"We spotted him several hours ago. The remote camera on our roof has already been reloaded twice. The first packet of film is on its way to the boys across the pond in London. They'll get an ID, if anyone can. Just go about your business. Oh, here's an envelope." I thanked him, wandered into the kitchen to bum a piece of fruit, and ran smack into Annie. "Where have *you* been?" I asked.

"Depressed, if you must know . . . I was ordered away from you today. Don't know what's up. Do you?"

"Only bits and pieces. Why?"

"Just thought I'd ask . . . and just when our conversations were getting interesting. Well, get out of here! Officially, I've not seen you. Got it?"

"Got it," I murmured and wandered back to my room. I took another look out the window, feeling edgy. I needed fresh air. Being cooped up in the residence was nearly as bad as reform school. I'd become accustomed to walking all over Mexico City late at night, simply to enjoy the exhilaration of freedom. Going where I pleased. On my own schedule. In fact, I'd begun the walking tradition the moment I got out of the halfway house in Connecticut, just a week before I came to Mexico.

I stood at the window, elbows on the sill, gazing out into Mexico City's bright afternoon sunlight and bustle. I was daydreaming again, this time about the ambassador's description of my mother's eyes when another flash from across the street startled me. My elbows suddenly slipped and my head smacked the windowsill. At least that's what I thought. Then, surprised, I found myself on the floor, sprawled on my back. The ceiling surprised me, too. Lavish swirls of dark ink stained it. *Hmmn?* Agitated, the Voice shouted something in my ear, but I couldn't quite hear it. My head buzzed, the ceiling receded into a fragmented blur, then everything went dark.

Why is someone shouting at me? I wondered. *For that matter, why are they trying to wake me up? It's not time for morning assembly yet, is it?* The shouting turned into an angry scream. I laughed, *Our housemother must have caught my roommate jacking off again. That always wound her clock. She'd wave the Bible at him and scream in his face about being an abomination in the eyes of our Lord and Savior, then tell him he was going to burn in hell. Fat cow!*

"Mooo!" I cackled. Uh-oh—the shouting went ballistic. "*Mooo?* You bastard—don't you goddamn dare die on me! Jesus and Mary. Somebody get the medic in here. *Now, GODDAMMIT!*" Whoever it was shook the shit out of me. Someone else scolded, "Easy, Annie. Breaking his neck won't help. There now, that's a good lass. Easy does it. Easy, girl. Let's have a look."

I tried to focus my attention but couldn't. My head hurt too badly. Someone kept talking. ". . . Over the eyebrow. Nasty exit wound at the back of . . . too much blood to tell . . . I'll get an IV going. Pulse is . . . and he's breathing on his own. We need to get him to . . . STAT!"

Someone sobbed. *Who are they talking about?* I wondered. Then a dignified voice I recognized penetrated the fog. "Son . . . it's Ambassador Seymour. If you can hear me, I want you to think of your mother. She was full of love. Can you see her eyes?" "Oh, you are even prettier than they told me," I heard myself say. "Are you real?"

The eyes answered, a bottomless iridescent green the color of rare peridot bathed me in its sublime light. A mouth pressed down and soft lips caressed my forehead. An ancient pool of anger bubbled up from somewhere deep inside me, then merely floated up and away, leaving me in a state of total contentment.

My mother's soft Scottish accent was like the taste of honey on a warm biscuit, "I love you. Oh, my darlin'. I'm here for you. Aye, I am. Rest now . . ." *Why is it that something I've wished for my whole life finally happens and I can't quite wake up?* I wondered. She kissed my forehead again and I let go. "Sleep with the angels," she said.

Two or three days later I finally awakened. Hospital bed. Tubes. Odd whooshing sounds and mechanical beeps. "Christ! I have the freaking headache to beat all headaches," I muttered to no one in particular. Annie answered, "Oh, my God. Can you hear me?"

"Sure, why not . . . and what am I doing in a hospital?"

"You've been in a coma. You got shot in the head. At first, I thought you were dead."

"Yeah, right!"

"Yes! And you were wandering on about 'green eyes' before you went into the coma. Can't you go a week without being shot or something?"

"Where did the shot come from, JA?" asked Howard from a chair in the corner of the room.

"I don't remember. I was writing a letter, I think. Then daydreaming about something the ambassador told me, I think."

"Well, you are the luckiest guy in town this week," announced a third voice behind me. "The bullet was a full metal jacket from a small custom American caliber .217—likely from a short-barreled rifle or long parlor pistol. You got it on the right eyebrow. It didn't break up but entered your skull, following the dura mater and the skull right around and out the back."

"Am I brain damaged?"

"Don't think so, beyond an unusually nasty concussion. We packed the right side of your head in ice and sedated you. We'll know if it worked in a few days."

"Who are you?" I asked. A tall, slender lab-coated man stepped forward to the side of my bed. "Dr. Simmons, your neurologist—you are currently a resident in the American-British Cowdray hospital. Our records indicate that you're a return guest here. Apparently the student life here in Mexico is considerably more interesting than in the United Kingdom. Our own students occasionally get falling-down drunk. Not very original, I'm afraid," he chuckled.

"How did I get here?" Annie, sounding flat, answered, "In a casket."

"Huh?" Jenkins-Smith explained, "Annie here suggested we take you out in a casket. We weren't sure if you'd ever be getting out of the damn thing, but we got a hearse and brought you in through the morgue at the rear of the hospital. You've been reported as deceased in the States."

"No shit?" Annie tittered, "We put you in a casket and all you can say is 'No shit?'" I tried to turn and look at her, but the pain was overwhelming. "Damn!" "We'll fix that," said Dr. Simmons. "Meanwhile, we've made out a death certificate and released it to both your embassy and the press."

"So, I'm dead." "Yes," said Howard, "and now you need a name . . . you know, for the you who's still alive. Oh, and your government has requested that we deliver your personal effects—including all documents. They've already pawed through your stuff at Julia Baker's—not much there, from what we hear."

"What about my books? Did they take those, too? I want my books!"

"Depends on the ambassador and the foreign office. We might be able to claim you—your body, that is—and your books."

"What about school?"

"Does it matter that much?"

"Yes."

"I don't know the answer yet. The ambassador will sort out the end game."

I tried to say more . . . explain why I wanted to get my master's in Mexico . . . but the painkillers and sedatives suddenly took effect.

☙☙

№ 19 THE END GAME

ON THE DAY OF my funeral, I was still indisposed at the ABC hospital and couldn't attend.

My funeral, I'm told, was a quiet affair. The ambassador, Howard, Annie, and an ordinary security detail saw me off in a nondescript funeral parlor near the residence.

"Afterward, your casket was carried out, put into the back of a lorry, and taken to the airport—unceremonious, but there you have it," said Annie later, when they'd all returned.

"At least I got a casket."

Annie sighed, "The American 'cultural attaché' (read CIA) showed up and asked lots of questions. Wanted us to open the casket. I thought the ambassador's answers were appropriately petulant: 'He was shot in the face. I am *not* opening the casket. He is to be buried with his mother near Glasgow—the church at Rothesay. If you want a postmortem report you'll need to go through channels—once Scotland Yard's forensic unit is done. After all, he was murdered on a small but rather sacrosanct plot of British soil . . .'

"Then the ambassador reminded the Americans that the residence was a diplomatic refuge and let them know that the prime minister wanted to know why you were murdered . . . 'And just why are you Yanks so interested, anyway?' Then he told them, 'The queen herself is furious.' That sent the oily little rat scurrying back to his embassy."

"Really, Annie . . . the Queen of England is worried about *me*?"

"Don't flatter yourself, JA—in her view it's her precious sovereignty that took the bullet. You, I fear, are merely incidental."

"That's not very warm, is it?"

"The queen is the queen . . . and, officially, you are dead!" She flashed more thigh, perhaps to soften the finality of it.

Then it hit me. "What if my brother, Eddy, thinks I'm dead? He'll freak out."

"No he won't . . . he isn't likely to hear about it where he is . . ."

"What do you mean?" Annie looked guilty for blurting it out. A frown wrinkled her forehead. "I overheard that his unit is somewhere in Vietnam. But I don't know more." I stared her down. "Really, I don't."

"Can you get me pen and paper, Annie? I've got to write him."

"Sure, but can you focus well enough to write?"

"I think so . . . can you help me if I need it?"

"Sure—I'll be back in five." As her footfalls echoed in the gray-green tiled hall that led away from the ward, the Voice returned, derisive and tense. *So, you're dead—and you think you are going to stay in Mexico? You are a riot. I hear it's cold and gray in England this time of year. That is, if they actually get you out alive.* "Why are you dumping on me?" I asked it suddenly. *You're supposed to take care of* Eddy—*not get wrapped up in this stuff.* "Shut the hell up!" I snarled back. "Oh, stuff it! I haven't even said anything," Annie retorted, tossing the paper and ballpoint at me before stomping off.

As a kid I'd tried to explain to a pissed-off house mother at my first orphanage why I'd been yelling at the air for "no reason." All that had got me was a long separation from Eddy for a psychiatric workup.

I'd decided then and there that the Voice was my problem—not something to be shared. So, I took a few deep breaths and focused on the paper Annie had tossed onto the bed. It went pretty well, at first, then my eyes started involuntary loop-de-loos. Apparently, getting shot in the head was more than a minor irritant. My hands began to shake.

Worse yet, the jagged script looked like a six-year-old had written it. I'd taken pride in my penmanship once I'd discovered that teachers equated a gentle-flowing hand with good grades and perks such as on-request hall passes. I gave up on the letter and napped.

I awoke with a start when the metal chair next to my bed scraped across the floor—the sound yielding a damn good facsimile of the black-board effect. It was Howard. "JA, you owe Annie an apology. She came back to the residence in tears. Not nice, sport."

"Sorry—but I didn't even know she was there—I think it's the concussion . . . I can't even focus to write . . . and my hands shake." He softened a little.

"Well, it *is* a wonder that your funeral had to be staged. Perhaps I should update you."

"Yes—please! Um, what happens to me now? Get to stay in school?"

"Easy, sport . . . let's start with the basics. You are dead—your body is being shipped to Glasgow. You'll be buried at the high church above the village of Rothesay on the Isle of Bute—it's out beyond the mouth of the Clyde River. Your mother is there. So are other kin of hers. News reports have been released. Now, as to the future . . . the ambassador has a lot of thinking to do."

"About what?"

"As in, what are we to do with you? You can't return to the United States under your old name. If you stay here under a new name, we may flush out who shot you and what it is that the United States doesn't currently want us to know, or we may not. Simplest would be if you go to the United Kingdom under a new passport. But that won't help us find out anything."

"Do I get a vote in this?"

"No, sport—the ambassador may ask your preference, but you are officially our problem now that you are 'dead.'"

"Sounds complicated."

"It is, sport."

"What about my things? The books. My footlocker, etc."

"U.S. agents took a few items and left the rest—your books included—rather a mess. Dr. Baker wasn't amused."

"Can I get what's left? I want to stay in school."

"You're nuts, sport. But you already know that, I suppose." I shrugged. "Well, is that your preference?"

"Yes. I want to finish this master's. I need the education to get a job . . . here, hopefully. Anywhere but the States . . ." Perhaps the desperation I felt came through in the tone of my voice.

"We'll talk about it again tomorrow. Do you still want someone to help you with that letter?"

"Yes, I need to write it. Do you know more about my twin brother . . . where he is?"

"Apparently assigned to a Ranger unit in Vietnam. A hush-hush assignment of some sort." I sighed. Howard reacted again. "We got lots of background on you and your brother. It hasn't been an easy go, has it?" I shook my head. He stared at me for a moment, as if he were deciding something, then turned, waved once over his shoulder, and disappeared into the hospital's green-gray tileway.

I panicked. The Voice took advantage and visited me again when Howard left. *These people will screw you! Don't trust them.* When you've never had more than a fragile identity, losing some of it, even "a few items," gets to you. My soul had once so effortlessly compressed into its little point of light, then vanished. I was afraid that the rest of me would suddenly follow suit if I wasn't careful. By the time Annie arrived again, still foggy, I'd forgotten about the letter to Eddy.

Annie sat, a blank look on her face, and said nothing for a while. The rhythmic sound of her breathing calmed me. In control again, the Voice vanished.

"Annie—I'm sorry! I didn't even know you were there when I was throwing a fit." Still silent and looking resigned, she continued to stare. Nonplussed, I started to repeat the very same phrase, but she threw up her hand. "Stop . . . look at *me* when you say it, JA!"

"Does that make it different?"

"Oh, JA, you sound so childlike. You really don't get it, do you?"

"Uh, I don't think so, but I didn't mean to yell at you. Really."

"OK. Apology accepted. Let's work on the letter to your brother— you dictate."

"Uh, *dictate*—the personal stuff, too?"

"Sure, why not—just think of me as 'the maid.' Nothing personal . . . just 'the help.'" She was angry, her eyelids fluttering rapidly, but I ignored it and dictated.

Dear Eddy—uh, make that "Ed."
You may hear that I'm dead, but I'm not. I am in a hospital in Mexico but doing great. School starts again in a couple of days and I'll be in classes. My third quarter is coming up. I'm working on a master's in anthropology. Great stuff.

I'm worried to death to hear, secondhand, that you are in Vietnam. Be careful, brother. You are my only family. We'll be twenty-one next month—I'll put candles on Tasty Cakes for us like when we were kids.

Love, John
p.s. Alive in Mexico—honest!

Annie handed me the letter to sign, her hand lingering gently on mine for a moment.

"Thank you, Annie." She smiled.

"Do you think he'll notice it's not in your handwriting?"

"Yeah, good thinking. Let me write another postscript."

p.p.s. Ed—my friend Annie . . .

I looked up. "I don't know your last name."

"It's McIlvaney. Mary Anne McIlvaney."

Annie (actually Mary Anne McIlvaney) is writing most of this for me since I got wonked on the head and am temporarily fuzzy on the eye focus. I got a decent concussion out of this mess. See you soon. JA.

I didn't think of the letter as particularly touching, but a tear trickled down Annie's cheek as she watched me struggle to pen the spidery postscript.

⁂

The next day they transferred me to a private clinic in Cuernavaca. A week of rehab. By then I had new British residency papers in the name of Jonathan Antón Blanco. My birthday was listed as January 21, 1941, so I had already turned twenty-one, three months before Eddy. I found that amusing, but the clinic was an odd place, full of secretive transformations and closed wards. It sported multitudes of unusually gorgeous light-skinned female aides, a magnificent palm-studded garden, and several putting greens, not to mention an Olympic-sized outdoor swimming pool, complete with lounge chairs and poolside waiters.

When Annie and Howard came to check on me several days into my stay, I commented, "Jeez—this place is like a country club. But weird—I never saw so many folks wandering around with bandaged faces in one place before . . . so where am I, really?" Howard was serious.

"Courtesy of the queen . . . and don't ask too many questions. You are here for rehabilitation and some cranial reconstruction. Other minor changes may be made . . . go with the flow, sport!"

"Changes? What changes?"

"Annie—brief him while I see to the details. Be back in two." Annie smiled as Howard disappeared down the hall.

"Rehab and subtle changes of identity are specialties here. As Howard instructed when we dropped you off, don't chatter with folks. Anthropology and class work is OK, but, officially, you have a case of short-term amnesia from an accident."

"I *do*?"

"Yes, idiot—you do." At that Annie handed me a large folder. "Here is your new residence card and some 'family documents.' Memorize everything. It contains school records from Glasgow. Your father was a Portuguese importer of spirits. Your mom, Scots . . . it's all in here. Written in third person as a set of school and university applications. The seals are authentic, courtesy of M16."

"What's M16?"

"Our version of your Defense Intelligence Agency."

"What does all this mean?"

"You will continue at the Americas—but as a new student. For gosh sake, be discreet." She brushed my arm with her hand, lingering for a moment. That felt good.

"What happened to Marianna?" She broke eye contact, looking over my shoulder as if waiting for something. That "something" was Howard.

"Hey, sport, listen; she simply disappeared on the plane trip to Tampa. Interpol is now certain she returned to Mexico City from Rome about five days before you snuck into her apartment. Word among the culture vultures has it that Pablo had promised to set up a new ingenue with her own gallery. I don't think you'd have recognized her. By all accounts she was a slender brunette, with a still-healing, but very different face. If anyone knows more, our best boys haven't been able to pry it out."

"What about Marianna's pregnancy? She would be showing by this point. Did she miscarry?"

"We still have nothing on that, sport, but I wouldn't rule out an abortion, along with the face job—that is, if she was ever pregnant." I shook my head. "And the house in Mitla?"

"Don't go near it, sport. A sudden, suspicious influx of new 'missionaries' hit the town about ten days after you went over to the Gulf Coast in early January."

"How'd you know where I went?"

"Give us *some* credit, JA—how damn many 5'10" twenty-year-old Americans with dark brown and gold hair who also speak Spanish and several Indian languages are floating around down there?" "Could be dozens," I suggested, "and the streaks are *tan*, or *khaki*, not 'gold.'" Annie cackled, "Tan-streaked chestnut-brown hair and carrying a walking stick like yours? You might as well have taken out a notice in the *Times*."

"So where's that bastard Pablo?" "Officially," said Howard, "it's privy information. Unofficially, the States no longer has any idea who he was or where he might be . . . leave it at that, sport." I took a deep breath, "I'd like to get my hands on him. I liked Mari. I wanted her to be happy."

"Well, get in line. He is unlikely to be enjoying an idyllic future . . . and Annie's right about your stick. The ambassador is going to hold on to it for the time being." Annie butted in, "And you won't be doing any handwriting anytime soon, either—it's far too distinctive. When you get out of here and back into classes, you'll be turning in typewritten reports . . . and no letters on the sly." I shrugged.

"You must promise me, sport," Howard insisted. "The ambassador hung his tights on the line for you. Don't go jerk them off."

"OK, I promise." Howard stared me down. "OK! I *promise*."

"Good! You owe the old man that . . ." With that Howard turned to Annie. "You've got two minutes to make a permanent impression on him. Then we're off . . ." Howard left the room and Annie leaned to me, "Breed me, make me laugh, mystify me, then give me some space— don't forget my A-list, JA. I shan't see you again unless you come looking. Here . . ."

She pressed her lips to the unblemished side of my forehead, and dropped a small, flat package into my hand, then left quickly. I leaned back. *Well, it's just another transition. I've become someone new before . . . I can do it again. But, dammit, I was finally beginning to like who I was.*

Sap! Idiot! screamed the Voice. *Why do you let them control you? Fuck them! They don't care about you.*

I was starting to lose the inner argument to the Voice as I opened Annie's package. Inside was a note: *Your mother at age twenty-one. Love, Annie.* I stared at the old, framed, sepia-toned photograph of my mother. My eyes filled as I studied her face. High cheekbones. Large, riveting eyes, and a cascade of wavy hair streaked with lighter highlights. Her mouth and smile were classic Eddy. But her arched nose and haunting eyes were me, too. *She lives in us,* I told myself.

⁂

I emerged from the clinic ten days later and, as instructed by phone, took a bus back to Mexico City. I had a small tantalum plate in the back of my skull, a mustache, close-cropped, dark-brown hair, new clothes, and ordinary shoes—all genuine UK labels. I took up residence again at Dr. Baker's—back in the same downstairs room I'd been the sole occupant of before jumping through the window at Sanborn's.

Dr. Baker met me at the door and escorted me to dinner. "Well, it's nice to meet a new student . . . Jonathan Antón Blanco . . . what an unusual name . . . you remind me of a student who left us last month." Had she not commented, "You come to us with a special reference from the British ambassador," then winked at me, I'd never have guessed that she had any clue. Then she added, "I don't like my guests spending time talking to the maids—it disturbs their routine, you know. Besides, I'm told you *don't speak Spanish.*"

OK, I told myself, *I've got to let go of talking to the maids.*

⁂

As Jonathan Antón Blanco, learning to control my reactions required constant vigilance. The process reminded me of childhood days when I'd watched over Eddy.

It was hard to resist my signature penchant for being a cynical wise-ass in the course of casual conversation. But hardest was not talking to the maids at Julia Baker's. True, I was practiced at ignoring pricks, cops, and the all-too-common thin-lipped women who folded arms under breasts and looked pious before they proceeded to ruin someone's life. But distancing myself from a bunch of maids who reminded me so much of Malinalli seemed nasty. They hadn't done anything to deserve that.

I consoled myself by daydreaming about Alli. It was an odd experience. True, I *thought* about Marianna from time to time. But I didn't *dream* about her. In contrast, Malinalli's eyes, smiling and full of warmth, filled my dreams. Her lip curls would open to receive me, even as her belly bulged—full with our child. She visited me one dream-night at Dr. Baker's. It had been a day full of odd tensions out on the campus of the Americas. I was sitting alone, eating my midday plate of beans and rice, when a group of students at the next table began to talk about the incident in Veracruz.

"*They* got a sniper and had the tall one called JA shot in the head at a house in Colonia Anzures," said one pimply guy wearing an Ohio State sweatshirt. "How do you know that?" asked a petite blond sorority type.

"I got connections at the embassy, baby."

"Yeah, right! So, if you know so much, who is '*they*'?"

"The Russians, of course. The German woman they were sharing was married to some *East* German diplomat. This has 'Cold War' written all over it."

"*Sharing* her? . . . like, *all* of them?"

"Yeah, man—they were a happening bunch—all did her at once."

"Cool!" crooned another acne-blemished idiot, who was drooling.

"But there were *four* of them, right? . . . so, how did they all . . . ?"

That's when I grabbed my plate and moved out to the patio overlooking the steep barranca below the student union. Not jumping in and correcting their bullshit had left me rattled. The one thing you never get as either a foster kid or an inmate is the chance to explain your side of anything. Since the halfway house, my newfound right to speak up had meant a lot.

Frustrated, I had taken the Americas' bus back to the big stone lions at an entrance to Chapultepec Park, then walked the four blocks to Dr. Baker's. Chavela had met me in the kitchen, staring through me as I nodded to her on the way past. The maids undoubtedly knew who I was, but in pretending otherwise, I was "desconociendo" them—the very denial of Indian existence that had typified Spanish and upper-caste mestizo Mexico for more than four centuries.

After dinner that evening, I retired to the double room, still its sole occupant, and lay on the bed, half dressed, waiting for the house to quiet down, so I could go out walking. I hadn't intended to drift off but glided, unsuspecting, into that half-awake, half-asleep state where one has little control over the thoughts that drift through.

That's when Malinalli came to me. Her warmth surrounded me even before she visually materialized. Disrobed from the waist up, she smiled at me, her huge eyes full of light and life. She was rubbing a pungent salve into her swollen breasts and her lip curls opened for me each time she pronounced the distinctive popping "tl" sound in her native tongue. "*Ah, mi teoquichhui, me duelen mis chichihualyacatli* ([Nahuatl/ Spanish] Oh, my husband, my nipples are sore)." "I'm sorry, Alli," I heard myself say.

"Don't be sorry, Juan. The gods are readying me to give our child *chichihualayotl* (milk)." Her look was serene. Gentle. I smiled back. "Thanks for visiting me, Alli. I miss you. I'm lonely."

"How can you be alone, Husband? I love you. Love is all around you . . . I will come to you again soon. Rest now. Enjoy Mexico. You are an *altepehuah* (city boy) at heart."

It was true. I was more comfortable in Mexico—or any city, for that matter—than the countryside. Mitla may have been Mari's heaven, but it hadn't been mine. Raised in crowded foster homes, then jammed like a rat into an eight by ten double-bunked room in the orphanage, later a six by ten in reform school, I was accustomed to the kind of packing that sardines experience just before they become part of the food chain again.

I complimented Alli on her perceptions, but she had vanished. It occurred to me that in my whole life, only three people had ever visited me in daydreams—Eddy, Betty Anne, and now Malinalli. *Is this what love is?* I wondered. *If someone is "alive" inside you . . . is that love?*

I slept with Malinalli that night. She was warm. Her luscious mouth curls opened to receive my tongue. "You must stop now, Juan," she said later. "I will have twins if you don't . . ." At that she giggled. The giggle had a glittering, erotic tone to it. Still giggling, she drifted away . . .

The January quarter's class work went smoothly. At the Americas I'd made it a practice to eat alone, walk alone, and never speak out in class. John Paddock and Charles Wicke—the two professors who knew me the best—were, thankfully, on leave that quarter. Wicke was in the States and Paddock was back in Oaxaca, awaiting Mexican officialdom's hoped-for cave-in for his next stage of work at Lambityeco. I'd carefully chosen new lecturers who hadn't known me when "JA" was alive. One was an Italian woman who taught Mesoamerican art and religion. Another was a young archaeologist the students knew only as Miss Rattray.

My only problems on campus were the occasional leftover grad students who had known the old me in Paddock's Mesoamerica classes or who got a momentary glimpse of my green eyes when I let down my guard or I took off my *gafas* (sunglasses) to wipe them down.

The thick-framed black gafas and a pompadour I'd affected gave me a distinct Roy Orbison look—those outlandish frames also hid the puckered, round scar over my left eye. To any pro the scar was both the obvious result of a bullet wound and "probable cause" proof of my identity. Both Howard and Annie had argued that I needed to see a plastic surgeon and excise the evidence. I'd decided to do that at Easter break, just a few weeks away. That meant a return to the clinic in Cuernavaca, courtesy of the British government.

One evening I risked a visit to the Punto Blanco; I'd been craving a cappuccino. My pocket calendar open in front of me, I was making plans for the clinic trip when the cappuccino arrived. Hypnotized by its smell, I sipped, leaned back, and relaxed. When I looked up a moment later, I realized that I'd automatically taken off my gafas, as I always did before I leaned back, cup between my palms, to inhale the scent and absorb the warmth of my coffee.

I leaned forward to retrieve the glasses, rubbed the puckered scar over my left eye, and casually put them on again. It was then that they spotted me . . . and my Roy Orbisons. Green eyes and a small-caliber head wound. Bingo! The CIA boys made me. I could feel their cold, unblinking shark eyes zeroing in even before I spotted them.

Two thirtyish Anglo guys were sitting at a front table where they could watch both the street and the Punto Blanco's clientele, which regularly included prominent Mexican Commies. I caught them out of the corner of my left eye. They had frozen like Irish setters pointing a pheasant. Normally, young guys never sit still voluntarily—they rubberneck, fiddle with their spoons, jiggle their knees . . . and *always* check out the tits and ass floating by. When males don't move, it's trouble.

The giveaway on these guys was their predator-like stillness, even as a stunning young brunette wearing an eye-popping lavender mini-falda nearly left butt-cheek prints on their gringo faces. They never even noticed her. Trouble. *Don't react. Keep working the calendar*, ordered the Voice.

I took a deep breath, another sip, and continued to fiddle with the calendar, trying to think of a solution. Hmmn . . . When the waiter returned, I took a long shot to an out—"Señor, do you see those two men at the front table?" His head turned instantly toward the front window. "Yes . . . the jacket-and-tie ones . . ." I continued, "One of them is the American man whose picture appeared in *Excélsior* several weeks ago—wanted for a murder in Veracruz. There is a huge reward, but I am afraid to get up and call the police. Can you help?"

Two milliseconds of processing was all that the waiter needed to go still, lock them in again on his visual screen, then turn casually toward the kitchen. I went back to my calendar and continued to sip.

About five minutes later three big Mexican agents wearing their badly tailored signature suits stepped through the front door and circled the CIA boys' table. The gringos looked up at virtually the same moment the three cheap, gray-striped suits closed in. There was a commotion of some sort, but I was already halfway out the side door by the time it got ugly. I turned the corner quickly, then headed away from the Reforma at a trot.

At the next bus stop I jammed my way into a packed bus headed northeast on the six-lane Anillo Periférico, the bypass that circled part of Mexico City, and which led to the tin roof and cinderblock outer barrios of the working poor.

I got off with a big crowd at Ciudad Satélite's central bus stop, then caught a third-class local that crossed the Reforma again forty minutes later. I went down as far as the National University and rented a room in a cheap (three U.S. dollars) pensión in one of the nearby student ghettos.

The next day I worked my way up to the city's huge La Lagunilla Market, the lake and lagoon that had first lent their name long gone, and bought another set of secondhand clothes. The pickings were slim, given the fact that I was about six inches taller than the average local who'd need to sell used clothes in order to buy newer ones. Finally I found a striped gray suit jacket sans pants for twenty pesos (U.S.$1.60) and a really decent pair of size ten black shoes that had been made in Paris. Perfect—and less than one U.S. dollar.

The pants were the hard part, so I had to take a pair of black gabardines to a local while-you-wait tailoring stall where they turned the cuffs all the way down and took in the butt and waist, then ironed them out. The well-worn pants cost eighty cents. The tailoring, another buck sixty. I bought a tatty black French beret for a pack of smokes and traded my Roy Orbisons for a wide, wraparound pair of used aviator glasses, like the Colombians always wore. Satisfied with the makeover, I worked my way back to Dr. Baker's via a combo of third-class buses and peseros.

❧

The next twenty days were among the hardest I'd ever endured. I was determined to finish the quarter's classes but found that hiding was hard work. I asked Dr. Baker if I might come and go through the alley entrance hidden behind the maid's quarters. She grinned, expansive, "Well, Jonathan. I have a better idea. Why not come and go from the roof of the house next door? That's what my late husband always did when he snuck out to see his mistress—there is a narrow passageway to the end of the block between the three end houses—it was once used by servants and vendors. There is an iron gate at the end . . . would you like a key?" I paused . . .

She went on, "The owner of the house next door is in Europe till May. The caretaker used to work for my husband . . . here, take a key." I took it . . . "By the way, the Mexican-European look is a good one for you." Pointing to my hair she laughed, "But I need to send you to my hairdresser tomorrow—your roots are showing." I started to say something, but she put her palm up to stop me.

"Bill Seymour is a dear friend," she chuckled. I shook my head and shrugged. "People often refer to him as *Mr.* Ambassador." I nodded. Conversation over, we never again spoke. That night the maids and gardener moved my gear and books to a small, unheated servant's room at the rear of the upstairs gallery.

Each evening I ate alone from a tray set in the room and stayed out of sight—coming and going at odd hours. The trips out to the Americas were a pain. Riding their school bus was too risky, so I took peseros to the end of the Reforma each morning, then grabbed third-class buses that carried factory workers to the city of Toluca every ten minutes. I'd get out about a mile past the Americas and walk back downhill toward the campus. No "most wanted" Americans would be coming from Toluca, I reasoned. That worked for a while.

A week before finals, I found a note tucked under the napkin on my lonely dinner tray. Carefully penned in Dr. Baker's lavish, Spencerian hand, it took me a moment to process: *Toluca is lovely this time of year!* I folded the scented, flowered notepaper, put it in my shirt pocket, and decided she was right.

It took me more than half a dozen trips to get all my books and gear up and across the next-door roof terrace and down to the iron gate. About 3 AM I walked to the taxi stand eighty meters away and woke the lead driver, who had been asleep on the hood of his old Chevy.

By dawn the third-class bus was descending into Toluca, having crossed the high, scenic mountain pass near the Desierto de los Leones national park. Toluca was a medium-sized district capital city with a split personality. Its mestizo upper classes spoke Spanish. Its Indian-dominated working class spoke mostly Nahuatl. Farming and traditional handicrafts competed with a Ford factory, a tire plant (Euzkadi brand), and a monstrous nearby facility where most of the United States' birth control pills originated.

I found a decent pensión adjacent to the colorful, old-fashioned city market. A clean upstairs rear room with its own exterior stairway, community bathroom at the foot of the stairs, cost twelve U.S. dollars for the week. I settled in.

An hour's bus ride each mid-morning and afternoon got me to the Americas through the rest of the academic quarter and allowed me to finish my final exams. Each afternoon, after class and the return bus trip, I'd wander in the market, checking out the colorful, hand-loomed wool jackets, called *orongos*, chess sets, and exotic foods: cactus candy, moldy blue corn cobs roasted on sticks, even *itzquintli* (dog meat) tacos slathered with rich and mysterious chile sauces already in their third millennium as standard cuisine.

One afternoon I noticed a number of walking sticks displayed at one of the market woodworker's stalls. One of them was made of a dark, dense wood I couldn't identify. It was the right thickness, but too short to replace the one that the ambassador had sequestered. The stall's owner watched me heft and twirl it. He asked, "Do you wish one made for you, joven?"

"Could you? This would be perfect if it had a half meter added to it."

"One piece or two, like a billiard stick, joven?"

"Two would be perfect. Can it be made with a long steel screw-pin?"

"Of course. The same wood and circumference as this one?"

"Yes, how much?"

"One hundred pesos—half in advance." Four days later and I was the owner of an amazing two-piece stick that wouldn't draw much attention. When taken apart it had a brass walking stick handle and steel spike tip, which I disguised with a rubber cup from an ordinary crutch. Screwed together it was a pound and a half of protection. The extension fit easily into either my duffel or the field trunk.

On Saturday, the fourteenth of April, I repacked my gear, caught a bus at the edge of Toluca's market, and headed east toward Mexico City again. I had decided to take the long way around to the clinic in Cuernavaca. Of all days, the fourteenth was not the one to be caught by the cops—it was my twenty-first birthday.

The birthday should have been joyous, but I had always imagined I'd share it with Eddy. I wondered where he was and how he was doing. Somber memories of his wistful, boyish smile kept me company. Oddly, it wasn't till I reached the bus station in Mexico City that it dawned on me—the Commonwealth of Pennsylvania no longer had formal custody of me. For the first time in my twenty-one years, I was legally free . . . just "on the run." *A temporary situation*, I assured myself.

❊❊

№ 20 CUERNAVACA

I HAD BEEN IN Mexico City for exactly twenty-two minutes when I stepped onto another bus, this one eastbound to Puebla, where spooks had few ways to hide among hordes of locals. I changed buses again in Puebla and stepped up into a big Isthmus Lines double-decker for the run south to Izúcar de Matamoros. It was a through bus to Oaxaca City, but I got off in Izúcar anyway and checked the big "departures" board for my final bus, northwest to the clinic in Cuernavaca.

I trimmed my month-old beard and changed clothes in one of the bathroom stalls. When I emerged I was wearing baggy, cotton, Indian-style pants, a native cotton pullover shirt, and an orongo from the market in Toluca. A tattered green-khaki army jacket and a pair of battered Clark's Chukka boots finished off the "He's a Euro gone native" effect. I didn't have on a single piece of clothing tagged with an American label. Not even the socks or underwear. Only the wraparound wire-rimmed gafas were the same.

The bus station in Izúcar, like all regional stations south of Guanajuato, was crowded. Mostly Indians and mestizos, a sprinkling of French college kids on trek, several black-tied Mormon boys on a mission assignment, and a couple of rejects from the last gasp of the Beat generation rounded out the scene.

There wasn't a pair of penny loafers, knit cotton ties, nor American

PX–purchased cigarettes sans state tax stamps in sight. I took a deep breath, relaxed with a strawberry pop at a stand-up torta cart, and casually surveyed the scene. Yep. Spook free . . . not even a hint of that dead giveaway, the hideous Stateside de rigueur men's cologne called Canoe. Clean air, spiced only by the usual scent of the unwashed. I relaxed and smoked.

A half hour later I stepped onto a beat-up northbound local bus to Cuernavaca, my footlocker stowed up on the roof rack. I took a seat deep in the bowels of the bus and within range of its rear emergency door. The drive north to Cuernavaca put me less than one hundred miles south of Toluca. I'd traveled a long way just to go to a fancy clinic and get tissue work.

The clinic looked much more imposing than I remembered it. Perhaps that was because I had only been semiconscious when I arrived the first time. Or perhaps it seemed that way because my rattling, late '40s taxi passed a private airstrip adjacent to the clinic's golf course. Its parking area sported more than a dozen private planes, most of them twin engined. In a world where owning one's own telephone was a mark of singular prosperity, and owning a private car a mark of near royalty, the sight of those airplanes made me nervous. *What if don Pablo made it back from the States and is right here being remade into an Anthony Quinn (Quintana, originally) when I walk in?* I asked myself.

As the taxi pulled up to the estate's circular drive, two attendants stepped out and asked my name. I gaped for a second, wondering which to give them, but was spared a miscalculation by an attractive, light-skinned woman who stepped out from the lobby, hand extended. "Jonathan Blanco, I presume." Her accent was very British. Her legs, nice.

By the time I'd furtively worked my way up to her face, she was already grinning. "Annie told me what to expect from you." "And what would that be?" I asked, feeling safe at the British accent, the only accent shared by those who had protected me; I hoped this was a welcoming committee of sorts.

"Annie said, 'You can expect anything that is tall, dressed exotically, has a fresh scar on his chin, is left handed, and checks you out systematically, toe to head, out of the corner of one eye while he pretends not to notice.'" "Well, that was fairly complete," I smiled.

"Actually, that was just an abstract. She went on about you forever."

"Really? Anything interesting?"

"Well, her conversation was spiced by words like *testosterone, mysterious, angry, over-the-top* . . . and a few more insights just between girls. Well, that's that. Let's get you registered—you are late. You were supposed to be here at 6 AM. We sent instructions to Dr. Baker's."

"I never got them. So who are you?"

"I work for the British. I'm to be your guardian angel for a week—you can call me Natalie."

"Is that your real name?"

"Is 'Blanco' yours?" I shrugged. "Well, then. Come on, Mr. Untamed."

At the desk they asked me several medical questions and wanted to see my ID. I had a temporary photo card identifying me. The bold queen's coat of arms emblazoned on it made an instant impression. The tall, light-skinned Mexican deskman must have been born to a mother who hoped that he would grow up one day and become a maître d'. His voice was as unctuous and as precise as his expensive, perfectly fitted navy blue suit.

"Ah, well, señor—you are a returning patient. Yes, all is as expected. You will be in Clinic C. Enjoy your stay, señor." He waved us away, turning to a white-coated attendant standing at attention nearby. "José, show the gentleman and his 'secretary' to his room."

Natalie grinned, waiting for me to react to the description by the maître d' of her as my secretary. But I had returned to my usual "underreact" mode and was checking out the lobby for thick-necks, oversized cheap suits, American cigarette packs with no tax stamps, or hints of Canoe. *Hmmn. All clear. So just who the hell are these people?* I wondered.

Natalie murmured and nudged me forward. "The checking things over, Mr. Blanco, is *my* job. Understood?" There was an edge to her voice.

"Habit," I explained. "It pays to be attentive to one's surroundings."

"So why didn't you ask me for ID or something when I came out to meet you?"

"The guys looking for me wouldn't know me as Jonathan Blanco. Besides, you said . . . 'Blanco, I presume.' An American would have said, 'I assume'—fake accent or no. You conveyed Annie's description of me, and when we got to the desk you asked about the room *booked* for 'Mr. Blanco.'"

"And you consider those details as proof of some sort?" I nodded but didn't answer, wary of the elevator door in front of us. José smiled as he, pressed the button. The bellhop pushing the cart piled with my foot-locker and luggage watched us carefully. I fidgeted while we waited. As we headed upstairs in the elevator I tensed.

"Something wrong?"

"Don't like elevators." José was listening, so I left it at that.

When the doors opened we followed José down a bright, care-fully decorated corridor that looked much more like a luxury hotel than a clinic. I was silent till José and the bellhop piled my stuff in a closet, showed us the room, and departed. As soon as they were into the hall, I closed the door and started to check out the room. Natalie stared at me, arms folded under her boobs. "I already checked it out. *My* job, remember?"

"José was listening too carefully . . . and he didn't wait for a tip. I'm checking again. How long were you downstairs waiting for me?"

"OK, damn you. Here. Out of the way. Let *me* do it." I threw up my hands, then lit a smoke and sat in the room's one large chair. Natalie began in one corner, quickly and thoroughly examining every surface and crack—top, bottom, and sideways. It was impressive. Finished, I thought, she headed for me and the chair, an "I told you so" look frozen on her face. "Up, big boy." I rose and stepped away from the chair, com-posing a softening response.

"Natalie, I'm sorry. But that José—" She hissed, "Shush!" her head under the chair. I waited. When she came up for air she turned and motioned me down onto the floor—pointing to the underside of the chair where she'd found a small, black-cased device. She made like a telephone with her hand and motioned me to the other side of the room. Then she spoke in a normal tone.

"Well, that's done! You owe me a cigarette and an apology. I should have simply remained your secretary and never gotten involved in an affair with you. Your paranoia drives me nuts." Hmmn . . . bullshit time. Reform school prepares one for this. I got into the role.

"Sorry, old girl—the elevator set me off . . . and I haven't been taking my medicine as regularly as I ought. Here, let me light it for you." She arched an eyebrow, cocked her head appraisingly, and nod-ded in approval. Then she shrugged an apology of sorts at me and set the agenda.

"Well, Jonathan. My room adjoins and I'm already settled in. I'm going downtown to get some girl stuff and smokes for you. Do you want me to refill a prescription while I'm gone?"

"Yes, I'd guess you'd better."

"The Librium?"

"'Fraid so. Look for Dunhills, too, won't you?"

"In *Cuernavaca* . . . ? Oh, God. You are so spoiled. I don't know why I put up with you, Jonathan!" She sounded authentically petulant but actually smiled at me as she said it. Three puffs later, she was out the door. I checked it—no inside lock, so I fished around in my gear till I found the compact wooden wedge Roadmap had once given me and kicked it under the jamb. *See you later, José . . . as in* much *later*, I chuckled to myself.

I laid out some fresh clothes, checked out the small French-style balcony overlooking the palm-studded gardens, and looked for stairways. None nearby. That was an oversight—Natalie hadn't been quite cautious enough, so I started a list on the notepad I kept in my shirt pocket: "Rope, two pairs of work gloves, bottle of Clorox, can of scouring powder. More smokes." I stuck it in my pocket and checked out the bathroom between Natalie's room and mine. It looked OK, so I put my heavy footlocker in front of her door, screwed my stick together, tucked it next to the shower, and stripped off the traveling clothes. Hot water was a luxury in Mexico, so I made the most of it, adjusting the shower flow low enough to hear above the water.

Sure enough, someone turned the knob on my door but left quickly when they couldn't figure out why it wouldn't open. Several minutes later Natalie's door opened a crack, smacking loudly against the back of my textbook-laden footlocker two inches away. "That you, Natalie?" I called out of the shower, stick in hand. No answer. The door shut again and someone scuttled away. Whoever it was would have to guess for a while. Not sure if we'd figured them out; they'd either come in shooting when we were together again or wait till I underwent the coming surgery.

I had just finished dressing when Natalie returned, knocking gently at the door. "Jonathan, got your smokes and medicine." I kicked the wedge loose and let her in. She looked up at me and stopped in her tracks, staring at my eyes. That was the first time she'd seen me without the sunglasses. She shook her head and sighed, "Old Annie has very good taste."

I handed her the list and wrote her another note: *Furtive, would-be guests while I was in shower. Suggestions?*

"Well, Jonathan, I'm going to freshen up. Here. Take your medicine and relax for a few minutes—then I'd like to walk out by the pool. They serve drinks there, and I could use one. Ta . . . darling." She disappeared into her room and did whatever Brit secretaries expert at casing rooms do. When she returned a few minutes later she was wearing a tourist's tennis outfit, right down to the short-shorts and cute white tenny pumps. It was a good thing that I already had on the sunglasses or she'd have seen me lose my cool.

She talked fast as we headed outside toward the pool at a normal pace. "OK. We thought this place was totally secure. Reinforcements will be arriving in about an hour and a half. We'll pay no attention to them. They've been briefed. José and whomever he goes near will have instant new friends. No telling where the others will turn up . . . by the way, I liked the footlocker and the wood wedge bit . . . but what's with the stick?"

"My security blanket."

"Rather primitive, don't you think?"

"Nope. Underestimated. Just the way I like it. What happens next?"

"Day surgery for you tomorrow at 6 AM. We moved it up from noon—orders from you. Nothing unusual with the clientele here. We'll have you out of here by Friday . . . you'll have to strike out on your own then, unless you want us to ship you to London."

"No thanks. And the surgery tomorrow—will I be out?"

"Yes, a general anesthetic—but fairly short acting . . . and I'll be your loyal, if indiscreet, secretary while you are anesthetized."

"I like the indiscreet part . . . should we be indiscreet tonight?"

"You don't give a damn about 'indiscreet'—you like my legs. Besides, Annie told me she'd gouge my eyes out with a teaspoon if I gave you a tumble . . . still . . ."

"So, you'll fuck me?"

"Jesus. What a line! That approach *never* works."

"It never worked till Mexico City."

"Oh, God. Not the one who . . . disappeared on the way to Tampa?"

"Yep. That one. You remind me of her. Smart. Beautiful . . . edgy."
Natalie glanced at me, then said softly, "Well, I have no intention of
disappearing . . . but Annie's tops . . . she's the only true female friend
I've ever had . . . and she's crazy about you. You're out of luck."

We'd arrived at the pool, possibly the only place in central Mexico
where my height, light skin, and obscuring sunglasses didn't stand out
in a crowd. Every female lounging around the pool was more decorative than any ordinary group of spouses. And every sunglass-wearing
male was incognito.

I ordered us two Bohemia beers, caps on—no way to doctor
them—leaned back in my chaise lounge, and, from behind my gafas,
checked out every inch of Natalie stretched out next to me. She had
black hair, cut short. Penetrating pale amber eyes, a squarish jaw, and
a very pretty mouth. At about 5'6" she was muscled, trim, and had a
dancer's legs.

She sensed me checking her out, glanced my way once, looked disgusted, and pulled the sorority girl sunglasses down from her forehead.
Her head never moved, but the muscles at the corner of her eye nearest
me flickered ever so subtly about every twenty seconds. She was scanning constantly—an alpha wolf underneath the female outer layer, her
nostrils flared each time the visuals picked up new information.

I knew when reinforcements began to arrive because her nostrils
flared on cue, and she took a deep breath, relaxed, and quit scanning.
Apparently some of the other predators around the pool sensed the
new outsiders' presence as well, for several drifted away casually, leaving half-finished tropical drinks to melt in the sun, their miniature
parasols slowly sinking into the pineapple and shaved ice slush.

⁂

Dinner came to the room about 8 PM—much later than would have
been medically appropriate for one getting a general anesthetic in the
morning. It looked good—steak of some kind—but we'd already gotten
our food. A bag of tortas had been placed in Natalie's room while we
were down at the pool, "Courtesy of the queen," according to Natalie.
While she dug into the bag, I took the long part of my stick out of the
duffel and wedged it lengthwise between the edges of the mattress and
the box springs. Natalie looked disgusted again, shaking her head like

I was a kid preparing for monsters under the bed. So I stopped fiddling with the stick and reached for the torta she shoved at me.

While I ate, Natalie went over to the fancy dinner cart, sniffed it, then abruptly pushed it out onto the balcony. I followed and watched her bag several small samples of the food. I drooled over the steak. "Hey—they wouldn't dope me with all of you guys hanging around, would they?"

"Who knows. But this whole setup is giving our people the creeps. I'm worried about tomorrow morning."

"You'll be with me, right?"

"Yes."

"Well, then. Nothing to fear . . . I'm going to have a beer and watch the sunset . . . join me?" She glared back, took the samples, and disappeared out into the hallway, acting mighty weird. *Hmmn, guess not.* I opened a lukewarm bottle of dark Modelo and lounged on the miniature balcony.

The palms below rustled in the soft twilight breeze. Someone splashed in the swimming pool beyond the trees. To the northeast, behind the Valley of Mexico's stunning palisade of snow-covered volcanoes, the city itself emitted a fifty-mile-wide glow that mushroomed outward like a nuclear explosion as Mexico's lights bounced off a dense, unyielding sea of clouds hanging at 15,000 feet. The trapped light escaped wherever it could. *Just like me*, I thought, *anywhere that is free will do.*

Enough of Mexico's wasted streetlights had drifted the eighty miles to Cuernavaca that I could make out white-jacketed José watching me from a dense cluster of palms about thirty yards away. *You won't catch me napping, you little prick*, I chuckled to myself. The Voice agreed with me for once. *Good thinking! Don't trust anyone. This "gentle" phase you've been in is bad for us.* "So who the hell is *us*?" I asked out loud.

The Voice vanished, and my mind cleared. I stood up, took another sip of the beer, and took two steps back into my room. *Well, it's time to fake drunk, take a fall . . . and see what happens next*, I decided. Backlit by the French doors I suddenly collapsed, bounced off one side of the bed, and rolled, lying face up. I had a great view of the ceiling. The Voice was jubilant. *Hee, hee, oh . . . cool move. But be careful. He'll come for you . . . and not alone.* I waited.

From my position on the floor, I could see the balcony in one direction out of the corner of my right eye. With the left I could see both

Natalie's door and the hallway door to my own room. The fingers of my left hand were curled around the Toluca stick, still mostly hidden in the edge of the mattress.

I slowed my breathing, cleared my brain of all human thoughts, and went instinctual. Those primitive senses had saved Eddy and me a number of times. As my instincts took over, the world took on a peaceful air. This was no different than hiding behind a heater in a dark basement. Waiting was something I was good at—and there were no hot trains to slow me down.

It was restful in the room until a faint, pungent scent intruded—overconfidence. It was a smell quite like the subtle musk an aroused bully gives off after a successful, chest-pushing contest when the weaker kid blinks and runs. It's the same smell a poker player radiates when a mentally weak opponent with a stronger hand folds to a reraise.

In this case José made the mistake of emitting it *before* he'd won. I smelled it. Then saw the pale strip of light brighten under Natalie's door. I closed my eyes and quit breathing. There were two of them; the Voice had been right. José's wispy footsteps were echoed by a second, deeper thud on the hard floor. Someone's shoe squeaked on the tile as a rear foot braced to open Natalie's door.

It swung open slowly, making a gentle swish as it arced toward the bed. Baby Bear and a big poppa bear poked their heads in to check me out. Me—I was in oxygen conservation mode, eyelids almost shut, when José stepped forward and started to lean over me, gleaming knife-tip at the ready. NOW!

My arm swung out in a circle, the stick making an ominous whoosh. I couldn't even feel the movement. Odd. The ugly popping sound José's kneecap made as it detached also seemed surreal. I circled overhead, looking down from the ceiling above, and watched as my brass-mounted stick swung through, completing its arc against José's other leg. He fell on me, obscuring my view.

Someone gasped as bright red arterial blood sprayed around the two of us. I could see my legs jerk spasmodically. *Jesus!* the Voice screamed, *we're fucked!* I crashed into José from above and emerged just in time to hear an odd "Fsaap!" a hollow thump, then a wet cough, rather like the tigre's in Tabasco.

I looked up from the floor, José still sprawled over me, gasping, to see Natalie crouched in her doorway, a pistol gripped in both hands. She was shaking. José's big companion coughed again and fell—making it a bloody three-way pileup, me on the bottom.

In the next thirty seconds a lot happened. Natalie and another guy I couldn't see, except for his black and white tennis shoes, pulled both attackers off of me. A third light-skinned guy wearing a ridiculous Hawaiian-print shirt burst through my hallway door, gun drawn, and helped Natalie and his other colleague drag the big guy out to the balcony. Big boy hit the ground below with a heart-stopping thud.

José was the next to go over the rail. Still alive, he whimpered and jerked spasmodically as he sailed out into the warm background glow of Mexico City's lights. Something metallic thumped the ground below a second later. Poppa Bear's pistol, I assumed. Hawaiian Shirt complimented Natalie. "Quick thinking, Major. That should buy us a few minutes to get our principal out of here." *Principal? Who the hell are they talking about?* I wondered, as I snaked my head around to get a look. "Who else is here?" I asked him.

Three people stopped in their tracks and stared at me in disbelief. Natalie moved first, jerking the transmitter from under the chair. She stomped it and tossed it over the balcony. "God of our fathers," she commented as she leaned over me. "Look at all this blood. Where did he cut you?"

"Don't know. I don't feel anything." She and Hawaiian Shirt checked me out while the only properly dressed guy in the room leaned against Natalie's now-shut door, training a big pistol on my hallway one. I had a small but copiously bleeding pie-shaped flap dangling from the side of my neck where the tip of José's knife had penetrated.

Natalie had already bandaged the small cut, stripped me, and shoved me into the shower when the first urgent knocks at our hallway door began. I started to panic, but Natalie had it under control. From the bathroom I got a glimpse of her at the door wearing nothing but a towel, pistol behind it. No telling where her "colleagues" were hidden.

"We were, uh, in the shower together. Do you *mind* . . . and by the way, what is all the commotion about? Go do something about it!" Whoever was at the door took just long enough that Natalie let the towel slip. I wish I'd been in the hallway. But the view of her from behind was a nice consolation prize.

When I stepped out of the shower about five minutes later, the room was spotless and Natalie was alone—dressed. I went into wise-ass mode. "Well, *Major*, I'm impressed."

"Really?"

"Yes! The view from behind was spectacular." She rolled her eyes, "*Thanks*, you jerk . . . and here I was, sure you were . . ."

"Could *dead* be the word you had in mind?"

"Don't be smug . . . this is a mess."

"No it's not. You did a spectacular job . . . how are the guys who, uh, fell, doing?"

"Carlin says they're history."

"Carlin?"

"Yes—my lieutenant—Hawaiian shirt."

"So what do we do now, Natalie?"

"Actually, I used up all my reserves. I'm rattled . . . but you seem calm."

"Tired is more like it . . . want to get some rest?"

"No! I'll sit in the chair while you sleep." There was an understandable ruckus going on below in the garden, so I went out onto the balcony in PJ bottoms. "I have surgery in the morning. Why the yard work so late?" Someone shouted back. I ignored it and bellowed, "*¡Silencio, por favor!* (Silence, please!)" slammed the patio door, and went to bed. Natalie stared at me with an intensity that seemed to require a response. But I was too exhausted to care. She let me get about four hours before we changed places.

The clinic staff came for me about 5:45 AM. Natalie was tired and on edge, the operating suite surprisingly small, and the number of attendants surprisingly overdone. It was an easy decision for me when the anesthesiologist finally pulled the face mask toward me. "No . . . no anesthetic." It got quiet for a moment till the surgeon reacted. "But I can't operate with someone who isn't sedated."

"Then find me a surgeon who can—I won't move." Natalie bristled, "You *can't* be serious. You can't do this without anesthesia."

"I'm serious. Watch me . . . and I do mean *watch* me. Doctor—are your hands steady enough? It's a small scar . . . nothing, really. I won't move. But, if you aren't capable . . ."

"Of course I'm capable. Are *you*?"

"If I move you can stop and let someone else close up . . . but, unless you need them, I'd like some of these assistants out of here. The men especially. It's too crowded."

As he waved three of the men out, Natalie relaxed a little. "Are you ready, señor?"

"Just give me two or three minutes . . . then start. Don't talk. Don't ask questions. Just work." The doctor rolled his eyes.

. . . I breathed deeply, following Betty Anne across the empty corner lot to her backyard. It was dusk on a warm summer evening. Lightning bugs, as she called them, rose by the hundreds. The scent of moist air blended with the sharp tang of freshly mowed clover. The sensuous flavor of maple icing filled my mouth. Betty Anne's eyes were alive with the pale blue-green light of the fireflies who adored her . . . "I love you, John," she smiled, her slender fingers reaching out to touch me.

I ascended into the night sky, free and at peace again. I got one glimpse of myself reclining on a gurney, a tallish masked guy hovering over me . . .

A woman's insistent voice brought me crashing to earth. "Betty Anne?" I asked.

"It's Natalie . . . we're done and in a small recovery room. Are you OK?" I nodded. "Upstairs," she ordered someone. "Now!" One of the cart's wheels drug irritatingly, like a beat-up grocery cart at an inner-city A&P. Upstairs we were met at the door by Hawaiian Shirt.

"Glad you made it back, Major . . . Williams got a radiophone in the van from the ambassador. He's nervous. One of the guys who went over the balcony worked for the Yanks. Not sure which one . . . and a 'telephone repairman' has been up here twice."

"Lord!" said Natalie. "You mean the Yanks don't claim both of them?" The lieutenant shook his head. Natalie tensed again. "Well. So which one was the Yank agent . . . and who was the other? Christ! We'll never figure it out." I was groggy and my forehead felt like it had been through a meat slicer, but I had an answer, so I interrupted, "The big one smelled of Kool Menthols and his shoes were steel capped—not a Mexican thing— Chicano, from LA or the Southwest. Walked like a maniac—not sneaky like a spook."

Natalie's voice rose. "*What?* Oh, save me! I'm babysitting *you* and now you're doing *my* job again. 'Spook' my arse." I shrugged with one shoulder, turned over on my uncut side, and slept. The exertions of soul flying always left me wasted.

⁂

The next morning I awoke when breakfast arrived. The third and still only properly dressed Brit from the balcony incident was sitting guard in the armchair next to me. I checked him over. "Natalie?" I asked him. He jerked his head toward the next room and made the sleeping sign with both palms together. He looked silly doing that with a huge-assed, silenced, big-bore revolver balanced on his lap. Hawaiian Shirt startled me, snoring on the floor from the far side of the bed.

"You'd be Williams?" I commented. He grunted, I think. I wasn't sure. In any case it was the only sound he made over the next three days. He was big and dark haired like a Welshman. Quiet and tranquil on the surface, the vision of him tossing the burly Chicano over the railing like a rag doll after Natalie shot him hinted at dangerous levels of inner turmoil.

We ate cold poached eggs in the shell and equally cold toast when Natalie and Carlin woke up an hour later. Natalie seemed much calmer. I was still learning about life after institutions and had a long way to go, but conventional wisdom had it that women were the species' stoics. The few I'd known, however, sure got cranky if they were hungry or deprived of a little sleep.

An uncheerful Natalie yawned, consumed three turgid eggs, and went through the cold toast like a track athlete carbing up. "Well, two dead. Our cover blown, one smashed transmitter . . . and Annie's fantasy here cut on without anesthetics. Not bad for just thirty-six hours!" She slapped Carlin's hand when he indiscreetly tried to get some toast away from her. Williams reached out, pulled the toast from her, and handed it to Carlin. Natalie pouted, "Welshmen. You can't mess with them."

"Yeah! Big pistol!" Carlin smiled as he buttered the confiscated toast. "The Welsh never got over Rorke's Drift—a .455 Webley. Slow, but hits like a cricket bat." Natalie pounced, perhaps still a bit peckish, "Lieutenant, he won't know . . ." Feeling smug, I butted in, "What? The four Williamses who were at the Drift? And one of them won the Victoria Cross during the Zulu Wars? Major, you underestimate me." Natalie stared at me, astonished.

"A Yank who knows some history . . . amazing . . . and just where the hell were you when they did the surgery? That was scary. Your face was as relaxed as a baby's. But your eyes were wide open. You even told the doctor you were fine when he checked for a pulse. And for the second time . . . who the bloody hell is Betty Anne?"

Carlin, staring at Natalie, was firm. "Let it go, Major . . . he's earned his privacy." Something in Carlin's tone subdued Natalie, who muttered, "Men. Nothing but trouble . . ." as she rummaged through the remains of the meal, hunting scraps like a she-bear emerging from hibernation. I turned to Williams.

"Any of those at the river your grandfather or great-grandfather?" He nodded, one corner of his mouth turning up. Probably the closest he'd gotten to a smile in ages. Natalie's eyes went back and forth between us like a country-club girl's watching a tennis match. That sent her over to the shower. She slammed the door behind her. "May I join you?" I shouted.

"Get stuffed, Yank!" I turned to the two guys. "She didn't really mean that. We'll work it out later." Carlin snickered. I think they had gotten to like me by Thursday, the day of my eighth major dressing change. It looked like I'd have nothing more than a shallow, U-shaped dimple where the tumorlike mass of scar tissue had previously bulged out like the insides of a large squeezed grape.

That same night we checked out of the clinic on very short notice. I was dressed in Kerouac style again: Chukka boots, black dungarees, baggy tweed jacket, Indian shirt, and a fresh pair of silver wraparound gafas, courtesy of Williams.

The British government had insisted I either "return" to the United Kingdom or disappear southbound on my own. I was too expensive to babysit forever . . . and too politically radioactive to go back to Mexico City. I opted for southbound, taking a late-evening third-class bus from Cuernavaca south to Oaxaca City.

My books were to be shipped to Scotland in my footlocker. I hadn't wanted to part with them but the extensive marginal notes in my own hand were a prosecutor's dream come true. Annie's aunt in Glasgow would keep them, according to the note Natalie handed me before I departed. Written in Annie's distinctive script, it ended: *Remember, breed me, make me laugh, mystify me, and give me some space. The offer is still open. I go to university in Glasgow next fall. See you there.*

Natalie smiled. "Annie said you were an original. Frankly, until this week, I thought she'd lost her senses. Don't go get killed on us . . . officially, the ambassador never wants to see you again. Unofficially, if you ever need to climb over a wall . . . make it his." I nodded, slung my duffel over one shoulder, balanced the brass-mounted Toluca stick in the off hand, and, forehead throbbing, waded into the crowded bus station.

※

№ 21 HEGIRA

IN SOME WAYS MY reentry into Indian Mexico was every bit as exotic as my flying episodes. Stripped of the illusions of closeness created by shoulder-to-shoulder city crowds and the familiar hum of languages I understood—especially the Mexico City body language I'd long since mastered—the isthmus cultures were like flying with my arms severed. My body missing. I was free and there were moments of extraordinary joy—but I could neither avoid the loneliness nor steer the course I chose. Free—but not in control.

Somewhere along the road between Izúcar de Matamoros and Huajuapan—where don Mateo had once fought the Mexicans—I came to terms with my obsessive quest for freedom . . . It wasn't so much that my soul had abandoned me. The reality was that I was the one who had walked away from it in order to insulate myself from a world I feared.

I had always been free to face that world and rejoin my soul whenever I grew enough balls to face the fear. *I'm not sure why I'm having this conversation with myself*, I ruminated while I smoked my last Dunhill—a gift from the queen. I laughed out loud. Apparently, the Indian-looking guy next to me took that as a sign that I was human after all.

"*Nimexicatl, uh, soy mexicano e azteca. ¿Y usted?* (I'm Mexica—a mix of Mexican and Aztec. And you?)"

"*Escocés soy* (I'm Scotch)."

"Ah, that is far away, *¿qué no?*"

"Yes, far away . . . six thousand kilometers. Perhaps more." His handspun cloak was brown and creased from years of wear, just like his face.

"*Huetzquiztli es bueno . . . sí* ([Nahuatl/Spanish] Laughter is good . . . yes)."

"Very good . . . here, have a smoke." His eyes lit up as I extended a fresh pack of Raleigh 903s.

"Gracias! So, you speak a little of the Nahuatl."

"*Palabras, no más, señor. Unas palabras* (Some words . . . a few)." He smoked in silence for a while, then announced, "I am an old man— I have no family now . . . and you?"

"*Tampoco* (Me either)," I heard myself say, inexplicably. Of course, I had Eddy. *So where did that come from?* I asked myself. The Voice butted in as I stressed out. *Hell, yes! You are on your own now. No more baggage!* The old man must have sensed my mood change at his question. He smiled and disengaged, leaving me to retreat into myself, undisturbed.

At Huajuapan he grabbed his tattered bag, nodded in my direction, and stepped off the bus. I watched him disappear into the crowd, bag over his shoulder, just as I'd done the evening before at the bus station when Natalie walked away. *That will be you thirty years from now if you don't figure it out*, I told myself. A wave of sorrow engulfed me . . . and *I'd* been the one who had wished to feel again.

By the time we passed the cactus fields and rugged, semiarid hills surrounding the large Mixtec town of Nochixtlán (Place of Prickly Pears), I'd gotten over my self-indulgent funk and begun to think about how to reapproach John Paddock about excavating for him at Lambityeco— without attracting unwanted attention, of course.

Oaxaca City felt weird—too close to Mitla, and too far from the mystery of what might have befallen Marianna . . . and just why did I care? Ordinarily I didn't reflect on things like that—Betty Anne excepted. When women disappeared, they disappeared . . .

Making sense of reality—which rarely makes sense—is a waste of time, I reminded myself. Still, Oaxaca City disturbed me profoundly. In spite of its beauty, everything now seemed off-center. *It looks the same. Is it me who has changed?* I wondered.

I arrived at mid-morning on a warm Good Friday. The sky was blue and unblemished, horizon to horizon. Bright splashes of pink, orange, and rich blood-red bougainvillea hung in clusters everywhere, cascading from high street-side walls, peeking out from shaded courtyards, brushing against me as I crossed the well-kept medians of the city's wide boulevards.

It took me nearly an hour to walk from the bus station to Professor Paddock's lovely gated house compound in one of the city's more prosperous *colonias*. Gringos don't walk, but Europeans do. Since I was now Jonathan Antón Blanco, I walked.

John wasn't home when I arrived and I must have looked too unlike my former self to be admitted by the gardener/gateman—*not a bad thing. I'll just wait it out. Paddock and his little Renault canvas-roofed station wagon will show sooner or later.*

It turned out to be sooner—right on schedule for a one o'clock lunch. I approached the gate but John paid no attention to me, waved me off when I hollered, and, after whispering something to the gardener, disappeared inside. Pissed off, I turned to leave but the gardener hissed at me—that uniquely Mexican "pssst! pssst!" that means, "Stop dead in your tracks and listen up, fella!" I turned back toward the gate. "*El patrón dice que esté en Lambityeco a las siete de la mañana* (The boss says to be at Lambityeco at seven in the morning)."

I got to ask no questions. Message delivered, the wiry little gardener and his floppy straw hat disappeared, slamming the door behind him. So much for Good Friday . . .

¤¤

№ 22 EASTER

I REACHED LAMBITYECO'S RUINS about 6 AM on an early third-class bus. Being a Saturday during Semana Santa (Holy Week), it was deserted. Wearing my beret and gafas, I spoke to no one on the bus.

I didn't even respond to probing comments in Spanish made by a curious Indian-looking male seatmate. He appeared to be in his late teens. Dark skin, prominent nose, and black ponytail, he exuded persistence. I ignored him.

As the bus drew nearer to the small settlement at Lambityeco, it also drew nearer to the house I'd shared with Marianna in Mitla, and I became even warier. Convinced there was someone following me, incognito, I viewed everyone on the bus, babies, chickens, and three bleating gray lambs, as a potential adversary.

The more I ignored my seatmate, the more curious he seemed. Finally, I pulled out a black-jacketed pocket Bible and pretended to read. *That and my beret are all I want you to remember*, I reminded myself. The Voice approved, cackling, *Nice touch!* At least the Voice was lightening up a bit.

Otherwise, the trip was a total pain in the ass. It required more effort than I imagined to avoid smoking. And to carefully reach for everything with my right hand, instead of the left. And to ignore people I'd have ordinarily found comforting. I didn't like it at all—as a kid, simply being heard, or noticed, had been a major challenge. And when I was noticed, it nearly always turned ugly. Reliving that feeling sucked.

As the bus pulled off to the side of the narrow two-lane road that passed through modern Lambityeco before winding its way south to Mitla and beyond, I shouldered my duffel, stepped out quickly, and vanished behind the bus. Its doors closed again. I stood, rooted to the same spot, till it disappeared around the bend. Before moving on I did a 360, checking out the surroundings.

It was an ordinary, early AM in rural Indian Mexico. The scent of charcoal fires heating the morning coffee and tortillas was pungent. A thin haze of smoke hung close to the valley's earthy floor. A donkey cart passed, as did a parade of six- to ten-year-old girls, water cans and jars balanced on their heads. Best of all, other than mine, there wasn't a single pair of European-style shoes—or a private car—in sight.

I walked directly through the small field of agave cactus behind me, blending into the close-spaced rows of huge gray-green plants that looked like pineapple tops on serious doses of steroids. Beyond the fields, the valley floor was bisected by a shallow creek, then rose to a gentle, rocky slope: the original Lambityeco rested there, screened behind a huge patch of bushes, most of its treasures still hidden in the rich soil beneath it.

Crouching to appear shorter from below, I worked my way into the area that John Paddock's crews were working and dropped my duffel. Then my trousers. Everyone has to poop somewhere. If seen from below, I'd be written off as merely another itinerant looking for a toilet.

I was desperate for a smoke but didn't dare light up. I'd run out of Delicados in Oaxaca City and had only a pack of the upscale Raleigh 903s with me. If I lit one, it wouldn't necessarily identify me as a foreigner— rather, the smell of money would drift down to mix with the valley's charcoal haze. In rural Mexico, it doesn't matter how thin the scent of that money is . . . it will quickly be detected by someone, drawing in those desperate for it, like a pack of hyenas to a wounded wildebeest.

I pushed my duffel under the shade of a tilted archaeological screen, set up expectantly at the fresh edge of a new test trench, and used it as a pillow. Rocks don't make it through the screen, so the piles of soil behind them are soft and cushy—at least till the cycles of rain and dry season sun bake them into something with the consistency of low-grade concrete.

I drifted off, only to be awakened by Professor Paddock's soft, even voice. "Well. I've missed you. But rumor has it that it's been an interesting sojourn for you. For a young man who is dead, you seem to be doing rather well. Do you want to work?"

"Yes. I need five more field credits . . . and I can't be in Mexico City, uh, just now."

Paddock chuckled. "I imagine not. Julia Baker had a word with me—she thought you might show up down here. I can give you four weeks' work—in the laboratory, while others are digging. Pottery sorting and bagging. Not exciting . . . and you'll have to disappear when the crews come in for lunch about one. We'll get you a meal in the tent before they come." "No digging?" I asked, disappointed.

"Best I can do. Don't even know how we'll record the credits. I'll figure that out later . . . and I recommend that you avoid Mitla. I've been asked questions about you by agents from at least four different countries."

"And what did you tell them?"

"Good student. Calm. Pleasant. Sense of humor. Reliable and a hard worker—a family man who has a Latina wife in Mitla. All the usual."

"Doesn't sound much like me."

"Well, it *is* you on the outside. Like most of us, it's the inner self that makes life complicated. By the way—how do I record your name on my local payroll? INAH is always looking it over . . ."

"Jonathan Antón Blanco. Citizen of the United Kingdom. Do you need the ID number?"

"UK? I didn't know that . . . I thought you were American. By the way, do you expect anyone to buy the 'Blanco' last name?" he grinned.

"Anyone who speaks English . . . well, Americans, perhaps . . ." John guffawed. "And where do I stay?" I asked.

"Don't know. Don't want to know . . . and can't afford to know. Be here Monday at seven." I nodded as he disappeared, hidden by the lip of the hill and thick patch of brush that separated the ancient site from the road.

✿

I put my duffel in one of the work sheds, changed hats to a roll-up straw, which hid my hair, and emerged by the side of the road. Another third-class bus floated by. It was still early, so I took the bus to the village of Yagul and ate a breakfast of fried eggs, rice, beans, and tortillas at the town's one open-air café.

The smell of dark-roast coffee blended with cilantro, chocolate-laced chile sauce, and fresh corn tortillas. Zapotec, Spanish, and several fragments of French all swirled around me. A group of masked locals worked their way toward the church, carrying a small statue of the Virgin of Guadalupe. She looked regal perched on an elaborate blue, deep red, and gilt wooden platform. They scattered rose petals and the scent of copal in her wake. There were no Easter egg hunts in this part of Mexico. Indeed, no one had ever even heard of the Easter Bunny.

Mexico's traditional version of Easter included masked worshippers, saints receiving their annual street-side adoration, copal . . . and, somewhere nearby, at least one willing male penitent hanging from a real cross—both tied to it and hands nailed. The sword thrust to Christ's vitals had been redefined over the centuries as merely a shallow machete cut.

The books I'd read about Mexico before leaving the States had made a big deal of the country's penchant for "magical-realism": "It is a dominant cultural and literary theme," the scholars asserted. Obviously, none of those writers had ever spent Easter in rural Mexico, where reality was rendered in gritty, blood-soaked Technicolor each Holy Week.

I ought to know. I spent the afternoon on a hillside near Yagul, talking to Jesus . . . and a group of German tourists who came in their own tour bus. They seemed to be enjoying the spectacle a bit more than I'd have imagined. Me, I gave Jesus water and, later, handed up a cup of *atole*. He reminded me of Eddy.

Later, after they'd run out of film, the Germans offered me a ride back to Oaxaca City on their tour bus. Had any of them been curious enough to have asked personal questions, I'd have declined and vanished. But I really had no place to go, so disappearing among the diverse tourists who flocked to Oaxaca each spring from virtually everywhere in western Europe seemed like a plan.

It went pretty well. I even managed to get some sleep in a European-style youth hostel I hadn't known existed. Packed onto a cot in a large, twelve-bed dormitory room fashioned from a nineteenth-century town house parlor on a quiet side street, I rested among a chatty bunch of young men who spoke French, peninsular Spanish, Dutch, Swedish, German, and heavily accented English—sometimes all at once. And, at other times, in no particular order. "I'm Jonathan," I commented. "UK citizenship, but my dad was an American . . . I'm passing through. Headed toward Tehuantepec." That seemed to work.

The guys spent the rest of the evening talking about what males talk about nearly everywhere—beer, chicks, food, and cops. In Mexico, all of those were exotic. The next day, Easter Sunday, I did what all the other tourists did. I took in a church spectacle at the old cathedral. Sightseeing with tourist map in hand, I sampled food-stall fare. At one stall I stocked up on Delicados, since all the regular stores were closed, then drifted back to the hostel at dusk.

No one paid any attention to me at all. That was an epiphany. Act like a tourist and you are one. Act like an Indian and you get treated like one. Act like a cautious loner . . . and suddenly your local interest value skyrockets.

So I spent nights for the next four weeks at the cheap (eight U.S. dollars per week) hostel among the most obvious pilgrims "doing" the waist of Mexico . . . perfectly visible . . . still in beret and baggy jacket . . . and yet, not! *This is magical realism in its most useful form*, I told myself one night after a long, boring day sorting pottery shards.

True, it was odd out at the dig. That required a different there-but-not-there routine. The occasional inquiring glance from the local Indian laborers curious about the "tall" one made me jumpy, but the other American students I bumped into occasionally alternated between diffident and contemptuous. Someone had decided I was French or Belgian. I didn't correct anyone.

In fact, I generally didn't speak, settling for a flash of a smile or a quick nod of the head. Paddock paid no attention to me when the others were around. So, like most Americans, they didn't think I was worth paying attention to, either.

I learned a lot about pottery. And had a routine again. Routines had always grounded me in the various institutions Eddy and I had been consigned to. Paddock told me privately that he was very happy with my work. "I'll make an Anna Shepard out of you yet," he grinned one morning while the others were out, digging down the hill. That was a huge compliment. He was referring to the brilliant female scholar from

Boulder, Colorado, who had written *Ceramics for the Archaeologist* some years before. Her work had transformed the practice of archaeology in Mexico, though she, like Paddock himself, was generally ignored in the States.

Hmmn. Ignored in the States? No wonder I'm drawn to these people. Now, if only I could find something I was really good at—something that would make life less boring . . .

⚡⚡

№ 23 THE EIGHTH DEADLY SIN

My gig at Lambityeco might have continued beyond the academic quarter had I not decided to visit the house in Mitla. I am not certain why the mysteries about Marianna and the house began to work at me. Perhaps it was the loneliness of sorting shards in the tent for hours each day. Perhaps it was the long, boring nights in the youth hostel. Perhaps I'd cared for Marianna more deeply than I realized. Whatever the cause, I'd broken the rule that said, "Once they are gone, they're gone!" and I began to have recurring dreams where Marianna chased me . . . nude and demanding. But I never knew what it was she wanted. Later the dreams transformed into ones where Marianna chased Malinalli, me watching helplessly from the door of a train. Ramona was there, too— hugging me. It was wonderful until she squeezed and wouldn't let go. Then I'd wake up, gasping for air.

I was losing Eddy and Betty Anne to the others. Hell, I was just plain losing it. For the first time in my life curiosity about events not right in front of me had jammed a wedge into the psychic door I had always closed at will to hide stuff I didn't want to deal with. So, I just had to see that damned house in Mitla one more time.

The Voice was hysterical the night I went. Had the son of a bitch shut up, I might have pulled it off and not lost focus. The whole venture was risky and out of character for me—and those kinds of ideas always made the Voice crazy.

It was about 10 PM when I slipped out of the hostel in Oaxaca City, the Toluca stick broken down into two pieces and stuffed into a soft, woven sling bag, like the Indian boys carried while tending their goat herds.

The third-class bus station was only a ten-minute walk away. I didn't even go inside to buy a ticket. Instead I waited out by the platform with a large group of locals returning home from Oaxaca's bustling Saturday market. When a bus that went as far as Mitla pulled up, I let it pass for fear of running into someone I knew.

About ten minutes later another pulled up, "Yagul" marked on hand-lettered cardboard over the front window. Three pesos and fifty cents in small change covered the fare. I took the front seat opposite the driver and wrapped myself into my striped orongo, my floppy straw hat pulled down.

A few of the locals checked me out, then forgot about me as I huddled against the window glass, my face turned away from everyone. I never even turned or looked up when I felt someone's weight bounce into the seat next to me. When the bus reached Yagul it was already half empty. It slowed in preparation to pull off the highway and enter the village.

I pulled the stop cord and ducked quickly into the door well under the steel pipe in front of me. By the time most folks had registered my move I was out the door, headed toward the hill on the right. Once the village's tangle of adobe houses across the road swallowed the bus I turned south, walking the last few miles to Mitla.

It was a beautiful night. Stars glittered blue white, like diamonds suspended from a velvety indigo ceiling so vast it was unfathomable. A fresh breeze blew down the valley from the mountains to the north. Catching my outlander's scent, the skinny, ever-present farmstead dogs barked and growled. The roadside houses were already dark and shuttered against the dreaded forces of the night.

In most of Indian Mexico the night is left to spirits: errant naguales, witches, owls, tigres . . . and the few who didn't fear them. Halfway to Mitla, a donkey cart full of locals passed, silent, their rebozos pulled up over their mouths to filter out the infectious night air. I touched the brim of my hat to be courteous, and lowered my chin further into the cloak that covered the bottom half of my face. No one turned to look as the cart passed.

Perhaps he is one of the brujos, *a nagual stalking an enemy to seek revenge*, I imagined them wondering. So, I made an on odd grunting noise for effect. A whip snapped, urging the donkey forward, and they were gone.

By the time I reached the turnoff to Mitla, a brilliant quarter moon hung low over the trees. Ripples of heat rose into the northern sky from the dark strip of asphalt underfoot. The quarter moon shimmered in response. Stars danced, their glittering colors momentarily transformed from white and blue to pale pink and yellow.

The sound of my footfalls softened when I stepped off the hot macadam and into the cool, dusty lane that angled northeast into Mitla. Five minutes later I passed the open door and bright lights of La Sorpresa— its bar emitting the sharp sounds of clinking glasses and the harsh, guttural tones of English and German.

I moved into the shadows on the far side of the lane, turning right to cross the creek. Except for several dogs, it was quiet. Kerosene lanterns cast a glow from a nearby courtyard, hidden behind the house's walls, which still radiated the day's heat out into the fresh night.

Studying our darkened house, I stood under one of the immense ahuehuete trees where Mari had first sketched her hummingbird series. Nothing moved. Ramona was nearly always up at this hour—putting beans to soak or putting her feet up and sipping a mug of exotic tea to relieve the pain of waitressing at La Sorpresa.

Carefully, I moved to the next tree about ten minutes later and leaned against its immense, twisting trunk to hide my profile. Still. Silent. No dog. Nothing. As I stood there taking in the night, deciding whether or not to take a closer look, the Voice erupted into overload. *Get out of here! She's not your problem. This place is bad news. Run, run,* RUN!

The Voice was so penetrating that I went into autopilot, trying to shut it out. I didn't even realize that I'd subconsciously screwed the Toluca stick together and sprinted to the low rear courtyard wall until I was already leaning against its rough stucco, my pulse hammering away. I took deep breaths to slow my motor, wiped the adrenaline-induced sweat from my eyes, then concentrated on shutting out the Voice. That was unsuccessful, so I shut down my hearing and swung over the wall. My feet crunched on the patio's fine gravel when I landed. I waited. Nothing. I waited more. Still nothing, so I moved stealthily to the rear door and opened it carefully. Nothing . . .

Finally, I stepped across the threshold, entering our old kitchen. It took another few minutes for my eyes to adjust to the dark. I didn't rush it. When I could see again, I surveyed the interior around me. Our pots and pans were gone. So was the kitchen table. There was nothing but empty space around me. Even the tiny propane gas stove had been removed.

Puzzled, I rounded the corner, my back to the wall, and stepped into the big front room. Empty. No furniture. No artwork. No books. Nothing. Back still to the wall, I turned my head toward our bedroom, but its thick, wooden door was shut. Odd. The Voice weighed in again. *Run . . . now!* I shut him out and moved toward the bedroom, reached out, and eased the door's antique *manija* (lever) down to release the old-fashioned latch . . .

The door opened a crack. I tilted my head to get a look inside. Empty—like the other rooms. For one moment I had the odd flashback that Mari was there with me, waiting to show me her latest sketch . . . The sensation faded as I backed out carefully, still trying to shut out the Voice's hysteria.

Three backward steps later, I felt something hard and unexpected poking against my backbone. *Uh, oh.*

"Well, well, *boy*. You are one infuriating son of a bitch! Waiting for you has been *very* . . . and I do mean *very* . . . irritating. So I'm going to blow a big hole right through your fucking Yankee spine. If you live, you'll be a pathetic, limp-dicked quadriplegic . . ." Birdsong cackled and continued, "So, what do you think, Barry . . . do I update this damn Yankee before I pull the trigger?"

"Good idea, General . . . if he weren't compulsively curious about his woman, he wouldn't be here." Birdsong emitted another ominous chuckle.

"Well, *boy* . . . it seems as if your woman preferred the chance to open up a gallery of her own artwork to this rustic pigsty you bought her here in the sticks. You just didn't count for much in the big scheme of things.

Worse . . . you don't understand her *needs*. You've got to work on that—"
Barry interrupted.

"Yes. You've got about five minutes to make up for all the screw-ups
in your pathetic, wasted life . . . and you thought you were smarter than
the general. Typical Yankee trash." While Birdsong cackled I tried to
think. Something. Anything.

"Don't!" Birdsong snarled as my shoulder blades tensed to swing. I
felt the barrel of his pistol wiggle as he noisily pulled back the hammer.
In the empty house the moving metal sounded like a truck hitting a light
post. I twitched, involuntarily.

"The smart-ass Yankee's frightened," crooned Birdsong. "Well, to finish my little story, your slut screamed like a piglet as I kicked her skinny
ass through the airplane's door. She screamed all the way down . . . and
she thought going down on me for slapping me in the Embers would
smooth things over. Stupid bitch."

"Yeah," laughed Barry, "Virreyes gave her to us as the price of saving
his own ass, at least for a little while. He actually shrugged as she went
out the door . . . and do you know . . . she never even mentioned your
name while the general was . . ." The rage welled up inside me, expanded,
then foamed over like a shaken cola.

I had already started to spin when I heard a separate whoosh, followed by a sharp whack. Birdsong groaned and collapsed behind me.
My own stick broke Barry's jaw, his face cracking like a pecan shell, and
I heard one word in Zapotec-accented Spanish, "*¡Huajuapan!*" I got a
fleeting glimpse of don Mateo's backside as he vanished into the night.

I stood there, paralyzed for a second or two before my feet got the
message. Stick in hand, I ran headlong out the kitchen door, leaped over
the garden wall, and rocketed out into the night. I angled into the ruin
on a trot, jumped its metal gate, and headed toward the Star House trail
we'd first used when don Mateo consecrated my stick.

As I entered Mitla's ancient temple, I saw don Mateo, arms crossed,
standing in virtually the same spot where I'd first been introduced to
him. "How did you know I was here?" I asked.

"After you left they tortured Ramona to find out where the blond one
had gone. Ramona loved her, so she told them nothing. Then they killed
Samuel a few weeks ago and took all the things from the house."

"How can I thank you?"

"You can't—do not go to the sacred hill—turn south toward the land of the Mixe. You will pass the town of Matatlan to the right. Do not take the highway there. Go on to the village of San Baltazar Guelavila. There is a dirt road there—less than half a day. Turn south. Descend to the highway. Go to the girl-child who awaits you."

I stepped forward, unstrapped my watch, and held it out to him. He shook his head and started to speak, just as what sounded like a door slammed a few hundred yards away. "¡Lárgate! (Clear out!)" barked the old man as he bounced into a trot and disappeared.

By dawn I'd made it to the narrow dirt track that served as the primary mule trail into the settlement of San Baltazar Guelavila, a Zapotec village of about forty low-roofed, adobe-walled houses; latticed, open-air kitchen ramadas; and the ever-present down-and-out haze of charcoal. The pungent scent of roasting agave was pervasive. This was mescal-producing country and the local handmade copper *palenques* (stills) burned through the night.

The locals stared at me as I walked through the center of their settlement but said nothing. Outsiders were rare. Tall ones wearing Indian garb even rarer. But rarest was the local people's inclination to involve themselves with the outside world. The trail I walked led out of their homeland and down to the Tehuantepec highway. As long as I was leaving, no one apparently saw any compelling reason to slow me down.

The dirt track, deeply rutted from generations of passing mules and burros, was rocky and uneven. It made for hard walking. The dry morning heat sucked moisture from me until I was too dehydrated to sweat. Two hours later, I stopped at a small general store within sight of the highway. I bought cheap Delicados cigarettes and drank several large tepid cans of mango fruit juice.

I rested. Sitting under the shade of a ramada, and staring at a rutted dirt track to nowhere, I had a waking nightmare. Marianna screamed, then fell out into nothingness. I didn't know how to handle it. Couldn't sort the feelings, so I squeezed it out.

I knew, intellectually, that in the normal world I should grieve, reliving losses till they eroded away, leaving me free to move on. But guys like me don't have the time for that. If I didn't bury this stuff on the spot, my whole life would have consisted of overlapping grief cycles. I only had room for Betty Anne, Eddy, and, for the moment, Alli. Truth be told, it was the best I could do. I said "Good-bye" to Marianna, out loud, so she'd know I'd cared. Then I shut the door to her memory, slung the net bag over my shoulder, and moved farther down the trail to the highway.

☙❧

Just before noon I spotted a bus descending the hill and headed toward Tehuantepec—my destination. I trotted out to the highway to intercept it, waving a twenty-peso note. In southern Mexico, waving banknotes fairly reliably added "unscheduled" stops to the long-haul routes. Protocol dictated that you pass the money to the attendant's arm extended out a partially open bus door and head for the roof. If, as happened rarely, the doors opened wide, you got to move inside and ride in luxury.

The doors opened all the way for me, but I headed up the ladder to the roof anyway. Fewer people to ID me later. It was cool and breezy aloft. The midday sun was penetrating, but the sky was a clear, light azure, enhanced by compact puffs of egret-white clouds. Oaxaca's rugged, cactus-studded mountains rose up from the valley in every direction, ending in distant blue-green vistas softened by the dissipating heat and haze from the region's breakfast fires.

I had to turn my back to the wind in order to smoke, so I watched the highlands recede behind the bus as the highway plunged into Mexico's narrow waist. The salty, barnyard scent of my Delicados cigarettes screamed poverty. The other rooftop passenger, a twenty-something Indian fellow, wrinkled his nose at the streaming smoke from the Delicado and left me to my own reverie.

I settled into a cavity between the large sacks of rice and beans stowed around me and relaxed. The gafas obscured my green eyes. I pulled down the straw hat's leather chin strap both to cheat the wind as the bus picked up speed and to further obscure my hair, the lighter roots having grown out an inch since going to work for Paddock.

About three hours and several more unscheduled stops later, the aging converted school bus pulled into the station at Tehuantepec. But I was no longer on it. When the bus stopped for another waving bill about two miles before town, I'd grabbed my big woven bag and scrabbled down the rear ladder, stepping off just as it pulled away.

Once down I changed hats, stuffed my cloak into the sack, and hailed a diesel truck carrying lumber. The truck took me to a big Pemex station past Tehuantepec. I got off when they stopped to refuel and walked back to the central bus station. By evening I'd reached the Russian freighter, still moored at the terminus of Salina Cruz's dusty main street.

As I crossed the dune to the palms and big ramada where Alli's siblings made their home, the sun's swollen orange disc hung low, giving the Pacific's foamy gray-green waters their first tentative caress of the evening.

The one to spot me was little Ari, who came running. "Papí—you came back!" "Stop, Ariana!" shouted Ana. "We don't know him! Stop! Don't go running off to strangers. ¡*Vénte acá!* (Come here!)" Little Ari ignored her big sister, running headlong into me. "You've come back to Alli!" I pulled her up into my arms and carried her. She'd grown, her legs dangling.

"Ooh. You do look different, Papí. Why is your hair so dark? I don't like the *barba* (beard), either. It scratches!" Ana, in a panic, lunged at us, machete in hand.

"Put my sister down! Go away!"

"Aay, Ana! I'm not going to hurt her!" Ana stopped and stared, still clutching the machete, menacingly. Finally, she loosened her grip on it, "Is it you . . . Juan! You look so different." "No he doesn't," butted in Ari, "he *walks* the same!"

"I guess so . . ."

"Sorry, Ana. I came to see Alli."

"You can't see her . . . besides, she isn't here. If it weren't for you she wouldn't have gone to be a curer . . ." Ari interrupted, a scolding tone in her high-pitched child's voice. "Is that true? Are *you* why Alli went away?"

"No, Ari . . . your sister had that dream before she met me. Remember, she left me, too. I want to see her. I miss her. Where is she?"

"Salina Cruz or Ce Xochitl. I'm not sure." Ana looked away. She was confused, not remarkable, given the adult responsibility she'd been asked to take on at just twelve. I was pissed off at her but let it go, remembering how I'd once overprotected Eddy—even when he didn't want to be protected.

Fortunately Alli's uncle Lalo walked up behind me as the conversation came to an impasse. "Hello, Uncle," Ana greeted him, sullen. Lalo surprised me by admonishing Ana, "Why have you not greeted your *huepulli* (brother-in-law) and offered him shade, water?" "I didn't know him, Uncle . . . truly!" she defended herself, still bewildered and angry. I turned to him, "Thanks, Lalo. It's good to see you . . . how's the boat?"

"It's wonderful, Juan. We have money . . . a little . . . in the bank in Salina Cruz." He turned abruptly to Ana. "Well, little mother, may your brother-in-law stay with you, or do I have to shame you by taking him in?"

Ana's brow furrowed deeply while she struggled with her emotions. When she answered it was tenuous and plaintive. "He's not really my brother-in-law . . . *is* he?"

"Yes, child. You will be an aunt in some months." Ana knitted her brow even more deeply, "Alli told me, but I didn't believe her . . . will I have to take care of their baby, too? If I do, how will I give it milk . . . if I'm not a woman yet?" "It won't be your problem, Ana," I said. "Alli and I will care for our own child . . . and, as for you, you ought to be in school."

"I don't want school, Juan . . . I want to be a fisherman."

Lalo rolled his eyes at me but conceded, "Well, it is Alli's motor on the big boat . . . we'll see when you are a bit older." Ana finally unfurrowed her brow and relaxed. *It's just not good for a kid to be a parent too soon*, I sighed to myself. *Jesus . . . look what it's done to me.*

⁂

I lounged in a hammock under the shaded ramada, drank jugged water, and watched the sun's disc kiss the watery horizon a final farewell before the ghosts of the night clocked in.

A soft breeze rose soon after sunset. The palms overhead whispered, as if answering the gentle rhythm of the lagoon. Ana added a palmful of *sal de gusano* to a big pot of boiling rice. A combination of local sea salt, finely ground red chilies, and pulverized cactus worms, it had originally been concocted to drink with mescal. Subsequently it became a poor man's condiment and protein enhancer.

Dinner consisted of limed corn tortillas and bowls of spiced rice, each topped with a spoonful of fish bits simmered in cilantro. After dinner Lalo took his leave and returned to his own family camp about three quarters of a mile away.

I lit a cigarette and leaned against a palm, listening to the soft, repetitive whoosh, whump, shhhoooo as gentle twenty-inch waves hit the beach, sucking seaweed and small fish onto the sand spit in front of me.

Every third wave rose a bit higher and crashed a little harder, setting up the backbeat of the night's melody. I stubbed out my smoke, peed one last time, and headed for the big hammock that had been mine when I first came here with Alli.

I settled in, little Ari my bed partner, and listened to the night's rhythm while she wriggled into a comfortable spot against me—she still sucked her thumb, I noticed, before drifting off to sleep, lulled by the surf.

Later, lost in the middle of an erotic dream about Alli, I stirred to find the real Malinalli next to me in the hammock and little Ari gone. As in the dream, it really was Alli's tongue caressing my lips . . . and my own fingers teasing her swollen nipple into erection. She put her lips to my ear and whispered, "Slowly, *teoquichhui*, I don't want the children to hear." Jasmine swirled from her hair, then floated into the night, mixing with the soft breeze. We swayed to its rhythm, the hammock ropes creaking, till they reached a soft crescendo.

Nearby one of the kids giggled. Alli pressed her face into my chest so that I absorbed the muffled aftershocks of her orgasm. I kissed her warm, swollen belly, then drifted off to sleep again.

When the morning sun and heat awakened me, Alli had already disappeared, to be replaced again by little Ari. "She said to tell you good-bye," giggled Ari.

"Will she be back?"

"She went to Salina Cruz to sell Lalo's catch," the child giggled again . . . "Oh . . . and she said to tell you she misses you."

"Is that everything, Ari?" She nodded rapidly like kids do, then rolled out of the hammock and made a dash for the lean-to toilet behind the dunes. I rolled out after her, stretched, and dipped warm water from a pail next to the fire.

I took my standard issue "resident's" tin cup to the low table where we ate and carefully shaved my beard in the reflection of the army surplus polished steel mirror I'd also been issued at the halfway house in Connecticut. Miscreants weren't allowed to have glass, or big blades of any kind, till they'd been there six months without incident.

Ariana watched intently while I sculpted the three-month-old beard.

Dark brown and black with only one lighter streak in the shallow notch of my lower lip, the beard had done wonders, both aging me and making me harder to identify.

"Shave it all!" pleaded Ari as I worked. I heard Lalo's laugh from behind us. The big launch had already been beached after the dawn's catch was unloaded, and Lalo had come over to lounge and avoid going home to do chores.

"Can't. Need it . . ." "It *scratches!*" she whined.

"Alli loves it. It's for her!" Having lost, Ari disappeared. I smoked, nervously watching a low-slung speedboat approach from the direction of Salina Cruz. As it neared I emptied my shaving mug, shoved it and the razor into my duffel, grabbed my bag and stick, and headed casually for the tangle of stunted palms and dense brush behind Alli's camp.

Ten yards into the riot of shrubbery I turned toward the water and sat down, cross-legged, focusing on the beach. As I'd feared, the polished teak boat came ashore right at the foot of the low dune where Lalo's big launch perched atop its palm-log rollers. Two men walked up the beach toward a small group of local fishermen still repairing nets a hundred yards away. A third stayed with the boat.

I didn't smoke, didn't move, and didn't even breathe noticeably until the two men reentered their fancy boat and pushed away nearly twenty minutes later. I waited another ten minutes for the smooth sound of their expensive motor to fade before standing up again. They headed east, skirting the great sandbar that separated the inner lagoon from the Pacific.

Lalo waved me forward and started toward me. "Señor Juan—it was a 'customs official' from Salina Cruz—but not one we've ever seen before . . . and a gringo *grandote* (huge) who doesn't speak Spanish. Expensive black shoes. Fresh haircut. They are looking for a tall Americano with streaks of light hair and emerald eyes."

"What did you tell them?"

"That such a young man passed through here some months ago but spent at most three days sleeping in a palapa a mile from here before going back to Salina Cruz."

"Nothing else?" He shook his head. "No reaction at all?"

He started to say no, then stopped himself. "The Mexican official said something to the gabacho . . . part of it was in *inglés*; it sounded like something 'kote'—but he repeated it in Spanish, 'cold trail.'"

"Good. Thanks, Lalo . . . perhaps I should move on."

"Not in daylight, Juan. Stay up here in camp and wait till Malinalli returns. I'd better go now. I told the children they hadn't seen you. They are afraid of being taken away to an orphanage, so they will say nothing. I told the strangers that they were my kids so no one would take them . . . I hope you understand." I nodded. Stressed out for once, Lalo rushed off.

I understand all too well, Lalo! I thought as he trotted down the dune toward his own homestead at water's edge.

⁂

Alli returned at sunset, a fat roll of cash in hand. She'd already sold the catch and seen Lalo, so she pulled the children into the ramada, motioning me away. After her talk with them, she came to me in the underbrush.

I hugged her. "I wasn't sure you were real last night."

"I met Lalo in Salina Cruz and stayed to sell the catch. I come from the village and meet him there every ten days."

"Are you at Ce Xochitl the rest of the time?"

"Yes, *teoquichhui*, I am learning marvelous things."

"I miss you, Alli."

"I am glad, but we can't stay here. These men came for you—a Mexican and a gringo. We will leave in the night after I visit El Farolito again. That must be where they asked about you. La Jefa was angry when you took me away from there."

"Where are we going tonight, Alli?"

"Ce Xochitl, *teoquichhui* . . . I must see Grandfather. I owe him a share of the catch. I left money with Lalo . . . for the children."

"I don't want to go back to Ce Xochitl, Alli. I don't even speak the language!"

"But you *must*. It is not safe here. I have been seen in Salina Cruz. The *güera* (La Jefa) at El Farolito will have described me to them. She is mean. Angry." She frowned, then smiled, her mouth curls opening, her swelling breasts rising as she sighed. She looked up at me again, turning her head as if studying a portrait.

"I love you, Juan! I long for you when you are not here. Ce Xochitl is safe. You *must* come with me tonight . . . I have to go now and talk to Ana. Then see La Jefa at El Farolito. Wait here for me." I watched her walk away, her long flowing hair bouncing. The rich curve of her hips, widening from the life growing inside of her.

We left at midnight, after the children were asleep. Lalo met us a mile up the beach with the family's small launch, its smoky single-piston outboard engine strained against the prevailing coastal current as we edged our way west, passing the lights of Salina Cruz about a mile off to our right.

We reached the small lagoon at Ce Xochitl about 3 AM. Lalo cut the motor and we drifted in, using only an oar at the stern. Don Rigoberto and two younger men were waiting for us at water's edge. I was puzzled that they knew we were arriving. Alli explained, "I sent word from Salina Cruz . . . a cousin who sells parrots was returning here from market."

Surprising me again, don Rigoberto gave me a gentle hug after he embraced Alli. Raised in America, I still couldn't understand why Alli's pregnancy wasn't a scandal. "Welcome, my son-in-law . . . we must go quickly now. Come." He motioned Lalo to stay with the boat.

The three of them led us toward the right, skirting the village on the same trail that led to the pyramid called Teapan, but several hundred yards later turned abruptly to the right again, following a shallow weed-grown creek into a small field. Almost invisible in the fringe of forest trees, an old thatched roof farmstead was our destination. "We grow corn here when the rains come. Enter."

He showed us in; Alli, beaming, turned to me. "This was their rainy season farm when my grandmother was alive . . . thank you, Grandfather."

"We have brought food . . . it is not much, but it is cooked . . . no fires. Just a candle . . ." He hugged Alli gently, kissed her forehead, nodded to me, and disappeared into the night. The three made no sound at all as they retreated toward the village.

Alli lit a candle and we ate several mangoes. The hut was a twenty-foot oval, its arched ceiling supported by hand-cut poles, overlaid by thick thatch. The hut sat on a slight cobble-walled artificial rise, about two feet higher than the surrounding terrain. An old-fashioned scooped-out clay hearth dominated the far end of the structure. Hammocks, the other. Several small hand-carved palm-wood stools and a crude table were arranged in the center.

The smoothed clay floor was exactly like those currently being excavated in lower Yucatán by a team of archaeologists from Tulane who were studying ancient farming villages. At Ce Xochitl nothing had changed in nearly a thousand years, apart from a worn machete, the flickering candle, and a large plastic bucket full of fresh water. Every other object in sight was handmade of local materials: coconut-shell drinking cups, wooden bowls and spoons, and large orange and gray pottery storage jars lined up along the wall nearest the hearth.

I stepped out to pee while Alli folded her clothes over a trapeze-like pole suspended from the rafters. The night was warm, and the merest hint of a breeze brought salt-tinged air from the lagoon. Stars twinkled brilliantly in the cloudless dry-season night sky. Unspoiled by electric light.

To the southeast, an ephemeral glow on the horizon radiated from the harbor beacons and the twenty or thirty electric lights still on in Salina Cruz. The shadow of Oaxaca's rugged coastal range loomed up behind the trees, hiding the distant electric glows of Oaxaca City and Tehuantepec. I heard Lalo's stuttering motor come to life as I zipped my pants.

Alli came up from behind, so silently that she startled me when her arm slipped across my back. I turned. Her bowed lips parted as she embraced me, driving her tongue into the deepest recesses of my mouth.

The next three days were idyllic. We made love, walked in the forest, watched the parrots watering in the muddy streambed, and laughingly pitched mango seeds at a low-flying turkey buzzard that circled over the hut to check us out.

I chased Alli around the hut. Played *barajas* (a medieval card game) with her on the hard-packed clay of the hut's wide doorway. She showed me how to make yucca twine, rolling the long fibers between my palm and thigh. She even caught a huge blue-green iguana and leashed it inside. It ate cockroaches and darted after scorpions hiding in the jacal poles that formed the house's adobe-plastered walls.

Nervous, her grandfather came alone on the second night. “They say in Salina Cruz that there are white men looking for you, my son. Is there trouble?” Alli translated, staring at me as she awaited an answer.

“Perhaps. I saw a murder in Veracruz last fall. Secret agent things, they say. They tried to kill me in Mexico City—that’s why I left school and came south again.” “Is that a new scar?” he asked, pointing to the fading circle of pink on my forehead.

“Yes, don Rigoberto. They shot me in the head.” Alli gasped before translating. Don Rigoberto shook his head slowly from side to side after Alli had explained. “It is a troubled world out there beyond the mountain . . . if only we had enough women here. We lose our young men, seeking women and money,” he reflected, a sad tone in his soft voice. An hour later, he left with the fat iguana, our gift to him, a worried look still etched on his face.

№ 24 THE TRAIL TO
SAN BARTOLO YAUTEPEC

LATE ON OUR THIRD night at the ancient farmstead, Alli and I were "playing" in the hammock, undressed, when a burro brayed nearby. The forest had gone silent, but we hadn't noticed till then. Alli grabbed her cloak and I pulled on my underpants. Someone stepped up onto the house platform. I grabbed the Toluca stick and braced for a confrontation. Alli, hoarse with fright, shouted "Don't!" as a head popped into view . . . don Rigoberto's. "A government launch is coming. I have two burros . . . the old trail to the sierra—do you remember it, Granddaughter?"

"Of course, Grandfather. Which direction do we go when it branches on the mountain?"

"Right. North . . . across the Río Otate country, then northwest toward the road at San Bartolo Yautepec. Take everything! Go quickly."

Outside, I recognized one of don Rigoberto's male teenaged assistants, who held the burros. He helped me strap our bags onto the rear burro, while Alli mounted the first. I was far too big to ride, so we headed up the trail at a slow trot. Rigoberto and the teenager disappeared. "Can the other boy be trusted?" I asked Alli, nervous.

"Yes. He's a cousin."

"He sure doesn't say much."

"He's *sordo-mudo* (deaf and dumb) since birth. Very patient. Very gentle with animals . . . can you see where you are going, Juan?"

"Not really."

"Here, let me bring the burro to the front. You follow. The animals know this trail . . . be careful as I pass. Don't let Chachi—the burro—step on you . . ."

An hour later we topped the first huge hill where the trail forked, giving us a fair view of the small moonlit lagoon and village below. A large naval boat, its lights penetrating the sanctity of the night, was moored just beyond the lagoon, a huge searchlight beam exploring the shore in sweeping arcs.

I panted from the heat and exhaustion. Alli handed me a large gourd full of fresh water. I sipped as we watched the eerie light probing for us like a serpent's tongue. We moved on. The next hour was even tougher. The hills were rocky, the trail narrow, and the switchbacks overlooked breathtaking drops down into black nothingness. Sharp-spiked, narrow-leafed yucca and thorny, spadelike cactus blades covered the hillsides and seemed to reach out to torment us at each narrow spot along the trail.

Once the sun rose we made much better time on a long downhill stretch, but by 10 AM we were both sun scorched and looking for shade in rugged terrain that had probably been stripped of its big timber by the end of the rapacious Porfirio Díaz regime in the late nineteenth century.

Finally we found a large rock overhang sheltering a shallow pool of scummy, algae-polluted water. The thirsty burros seemed not to mind, so we spent most of the afternoon there, hiding from view . . . and from a relentless sun.

Facing southwest, only one corner of the overhang offered shade. It was hard for me to process cardinal directions in the isthmus—raised on the East Coast in the States, my instincts insisted that west lay straight out across the Pacific, but the reality was otherwise. Facing the beach at Ce Xochitl, the sun set over my right shoulder, behind the great headlands near what later came to be called Huatulco.

So we huddled into the narrow strip of shade among the rocks. For the first time since I'd met her, Alli was frightened. Her people's enclave at Ce Xochitl numbered about one hundred. Including those in La Ventosa district, there were about 130 in all—the very last pocket of Nahuatl speakers south of Oaxaca City. Her people had most likely arrived from the central valley surrounding Mexico sometime in the AD 1400s during the Aztec empire-building period.

The people of Ce Xochitl had never mixed with the region's Mixtec and Zapotec speakers. Now, just like Alli, their young people drifted away to other worlds. Ce Xochitl had become a fragile piece of history, a living diorama. A world fading away.

And, like most of her people, Alli was deathly afraid of the surrounding Zapotec world. She understood only a few words of Zapotec, and the modern Zapotecs did not ordinarily lower themselves to speak to the last of the invading Nahuatli. At El Farolito, La Jefa was a mestizo manager for two good reasons—she enjoyed a higher social caste and lighter skin than the local Inditas, and she acted as intermediary so that the different Indian women in the club didn't have to communicate instructions to one another. That interaction would have reignited tribal feuds, some already two thousand years in the making.

At El Farolito, the Zapotec girls had looked down on Alli, while the Mixe and Chinantecas merely ignored her. Her only "friend" had been another Aztec speaker from the town of Cupilco in northern Tabasco, over on the other side of the isthmus. Even the two of them had a hard time communicating, she had confided, since their long-separated dialects were so different.

We talked about her fears while snuggled against the shady east face of the overhang. "The reason I wanted to learn the old ways is because I feared my father's and grandfather's worlds would soon be gone. You see—only three of my siblings speak the language . . . and among them only Ana and I will retain it . . . the others are becoming Mexicans."

"But there will be other children, won't there? I mean in Ce Xochitl itself."

"Perhaps, Juan, but even now only four women young enough to bear children remain there and speak the language. Ana and I are the fifth and sixth . . . when I met Magdalena from Cupilco and discovered that we are so few, and our language so different, it made me think of father . . . and his death. When he died, we lost not just a father but his dream to teach Simón the ways of a holy man . . . to make of him a teacher to others. I wanted to do something . . ."

"And your child is only half-Indian. A mestiza."

"*Our* child! *Nuestra* . . . she will be very powerful. Beautiful and light skinned. I shall pass on the language and the old ways to her."

Her head on my lap, I caressed her cheeks and gazed at her mouth. "Say something in Nahuatl to me . . . I like its sound." She giggled and sang me a child's melody. I watched her lip curls rhythmically open and close as those little Aztec puffs of air punctuated her words.

When she stopped singing, she smiled and giggled. "Are you eighteen yet?" I asked. "I don't even know your birthday."

"Last month . . . in the Spanish calendar it is April 14 . . . in my language, you would not understand." A wave of emotion rippled through me . . . exiting my body as my hair stood up at the nape of my neck. "Why are you staring at me like that, Juan?"

"It's my birthday, too, Alli."

"Oh, you say that. Men will say anything to make a woman want them."

"But it's true, Alli . . . we share the same birthday!" Her huge brown eyes widened, and a small crease on either side of her nose wrinkled. As her brows rose, her recurved lips parted. "It is fate . . ." she whispered, then closed her eyes, looking serene.

As the shadows lengthened I filtered water through my bandana from the algae-laden pool and filled a large gourd for the burros. Alli's grandfather had told us to head north toward the valley of the Río Otate once we crossed the first great range of mountains.

"The valley runs northeast toward the Zapotec highway (the Oaxaca highway)," he had explained. "But there are no villages left in the upper valley . . . and no roads until you near Ecatepec . . . it is now a Zapotec settlement . . . from the dirt road there you will see the peak the Mexicans call Catalina . . . keep it between your left jaw and shoulder as you cross into the Mixe country near the highway."

It was time to move on, so I watered the burros again and hoisted Alli—now increased to over one hundred pounds of her—onto Chachi, the lead burro, and started up the hill.

Our second night on the trail was miserable. The country was hopelessly rugged and the trail so faint and little used that we lost our way several times. My legs were cut from the sharp-bladed yucca and cacti

I couldn't even see. Alli's calves had also taken a beating. Dehydrated, my lips cracked and bled.

The sky turned overcast about 3 AM, as a huge layer of clouds carrying the faint, tantalizing scent of water drifted overhead, without yielding even a single, stingy drop of it. About 6 AM I found a shallow *tinaja* (natural pool) near a smoke-stained cleft in a tangle of rocks above the trail. The tinaja yielded about three gallons of putrid water. Alli and I sipped some that I'd squeezed out of my pañuelo before the burros got to it. The poor things were as desperate as we were.

By noon we had crossed the first sierra and started to descend into the tilted basin that gave birth to the Otate River—below us we could see its muddy shallows overgrown with the coarse reeds after which the creek had been named.

Four hundred yards from flowing water and already savoring its taste in our overheated minds, we startled two Zapotec *tobala* (wild agave) cutters resting in the underbrush, their burros tethered to a stunted tree above the trace.

I almost stepped on the first guy, who was snoozing under a large bush with his walking staff across his knees. Wiry and about forty years old, he wore a wide-brimmed straw hat with a leather strap and tassels hanging down behind. The other fellow with him appeared to be just a boy, a machete slung across his chest.

Alli panicked at the same moment that the older fellow jumped up, banging into me as he dropped his stick and rushed to get away. I picked it up and called after him, "*Xpacululula?* (Your walking stick?)" He stopped in his tracks, amazed. I extended the stick to him, turning to Alli. "*Vámanos, señorita* (Let's go, miss)," as if I didn't really know her well.

"*¿Gringu?*" asked the teenager, who'd also frozen at the unexpected sound of Zapotec from a tall white guy. "No," I answered in isthmus Zapotec and Spanish, "*Castellanu* (Mexican). *Mi tío es patrón de una finca acerca de Teotitlán del Valle* (My uncle is the owner of a farm near Teotitlán)."

We moved on, catching one last glimpse of them moving their burros along the ridge . . . back toward the more heavily settled Zapotec hill country about fifteen miles to the west of our route. When they were gone, Alli began to cry. "It is a bad omen. We have been seen. They will tell someone."

"Who will they tell? There are no paved roads in their direction."

"Perhaps so, but I am frightened." I pulled her off the burro when we reached the narrow creek bed a few minutes later. She looked so different on this trip. I'd never before seen her wearing an Indian man's cotton pants, huaraches, and a sombrero. For the first time she looked like what she really was . . . an Indian peasant girl.

As she sipped warm water from the muddy creek bed, I massaged her shoulders. Her muscles were as hard and rubbery as the truck-tire soles of her sandals. I lifted the knot of flowing hair she'd ribboned into a thick ponytail and nuzzled the hot nape of her neck. She sighed, "Can't we find a cave and just stay here forever?"

"Do you really want to?" She leaned back, pulling my arms around her. "Why are my people so few in the world now?"

"I don't know, but our baby will make one more." She smiled and pulled my head to her belly, pulled up her shirt, and pressed my ear to her navel.

"Talk to her, Juan. Talk to her. She can hear you now."

I felt stupid at first, then it all came out in a rush, "I love you, Betiana. I've always loved you. I always will. I won't disappear . . . or die. You'll have parents. I promise . . ." When I finished, I imagined Alli's belly answering. I caressed her stomach, stroking the soft fuzz that trailed down from her navel. And, for a moment, I did want to stay there forever with Alli. "Was the garden of Eden dry like this?" I asked Alli. She ran her fingers through my hair. "Oh, Juan . . . Edén is where all souls are at peace . . . perhaps we'd better go after all."

The next night we reached the rutted dirt road at the Zapotec outpost of Ecatepec. We slept in the brush on a hill above the village—just far enough away to avoid the local dogs and goat herders. We'd run out of food but dipped water from an abandoned farm's big clay cistern next to its well. It had probably been filled by hand for a local herd of goats. The water was musty but filtered out fairly well. I filled the gourd and tossed in my last half tablet of halozone.

That water got us through the night and gave the burros time to forage along the banks of the dry arroyo. By the time the sun began to glow on the eastern horizon, we followed the arroyo at an unmarked fork in the road, reasoning that other settlements would straddle it in the country below. Our destination was the Tehuantepec highway— Mexico Route 190. The plan was for Alli and I to separate at the highway. She was to turn south to Tehuantepec. I was to head north again . . . and disappear.

At mid-morning we stopped at an isolated rancho just off the road, drawn by the smell of cooking beans. Gourd in hand, Alli walked to the house, leaving me with the burros several hundred yards away. She returned twenty minutes later, the gourd filled with spiced beans poured over rice. "Three pesos was all they wanted . . . the girl was Zapoteca but nice—my age . . . she wanted to practice her Spanish with me . . . or I'd have returned sooner." She shook as she held out the gourd to share the food. This trip was taking a toll on her.

We ate our meal together, huddled in the stingy shade of the lead burro's belly. "The food is good. I feel stronger," smiled Alli. I wiped out the gourd and lifted Alli to the burro. She leaned over and kissed me gently on the forehead . . .

Several miles later the track widened and we passed a settlement of about a dozen farmsteads huddled together on the east flank of the mountains we were traversing. We passed a short, scrawny tortilla peddler inching along on an old bicycle, its tall tail-rack stacked with tortillas. He had no front teeth and was missing two fingers on his left hand but smiled at us, pointing to his merchandise. We bought a dozen and asked him how far it was to the village of Animas on the Tehuantepec highway. His Spanish was minimal, but an "ocho" embedded in his Zapotec/Spanish seemed clear enough.

"*A la derecha*," he pointed . . . "*La, uh, es neza nabata* (Go right on the wide road)." He waved to the right again as his bicycle clacked past us. "If we reach the highway, can I stay with you?" Alli asked.

"That's a bad idea. I believe they will keep on hunting me, Alli . . . and what about your people?"

"I want to be with *you* . . ." No one had ever simply wanted to be with me before. Even Eddy wanted a family. María Inés had wanted to play out her stylized Madonna role, Marianna had wanted Mitla, her art, and fame . . . and Annie wanted her space . . .

It took me a few more paces before it dawned on me that what Alli had really said was that she loved me. *Can it be so simple?* I asked myself.

Well, why not . . . it's the same as me wanting Betty Anne . . . and that was love.

I slowed down until Alli and her burro were alongside. I rested my hand gently on her thigh. "I like the idea."

"What idea, Juan?"

"That you want to be with me."

Her mouth curls opened and she smiled. I grinned up at her, "Is love so simple, Alli?"

"Yes, Husband . . . it is a wonder how simple . . . your daughter moved just now when you asked. Tell her again that you love her." We stopped. I leaned to Alli, my face pressed against her belly. Her fingers caressed my neck. "Listen . . . you can hear her . . ." I pressed my ear closer, closed my eyes, and listened.

Perhaps that's why I didn't hear the approaching truck. Or perhaps I'd slipped into one of my private reveries again . . . a dreamy, almost flying mode . . . preparing to visit Betty Anne . . . anticipating the fireflies glowing in her palms.

I heard another vehicle blow past us and jerked my head away from her belly to check it out. A battered white truck sailed past us, disappearing around the bend. I didn't want to be found. Nervous, I lifted Alli onto Chachi and insisted that we move on. A half hour later, I heard a vehicle coming up from behind us. "Perhaps they have water," smiled Alli. "I'll ask," I said, blowing her a kiss. While I positioned myself in the road, she continued to smile at me tenderly, still lost in the mystery of love.

She was still smiling when the truck came into view and roared toward us, its engine screaming. I jumped out of its path as two well-dressed young men hooted at me from the cabin, "*¡Muévate, peon!* (Out of the way, peasant!)" A well-aimed beer bottle hit Chachi on the jaw. He bolted into the underbrush. Everything went into a weird slow motion.

Twenty yards away the burro lost his footing on the rim of the nearby arroyo. Alli floated into the air and fell down into the rocky arroyo bed. The truck disappeared in a haze of dust.

I ran to Alli, slid down the arroyo bank, and cradled her. She groaned, "*Don't squeeze!* My shoulder is broken, I think." I laid her down gently. She grimaced, "Is Chachi all right? He's my grandfather's own burro." I shrugged, "Are *you* OK, *tecihuan* (wife)?" She smiled.

"That is the first time you've called me that. I will be fine now, but don't let the animal suffer. Find Chachi, Juan. *Please.*" I left her and walked up the arroyo. Poor Chachi was dead, his neck horribly twisted; his head looked as if it had been put on backward. I checked to be sure, then went back to Alli. She cried when I told her.

The commotion must have caught a local farmer's attention, for we heard a donkey cart plodding up the road. Minutes later, a wizened huarache-clad farmer peered down at me from the edge of the arroyo. "Can you help?" I asked. He nodded, motioning to someone behind him. The two men descended and helped me carry Alli up to the cart. We tied the other burro to the back of the cart and took off. The trip out to Yautepec's miniature plaza took about thirty minutes. So, I sold the remaining burro for two hundred pesos and a truck ride south to Tehuantepec.

On the way, Alli groaned and perspired, slipping in and out of consciousness. Every time the battered pickup truck hit a pothole, Alli stirred, whimpered, then fell asleep again. When at last we reached the public hospital in Tehuantepec, we found it small, crowded, and old-fashioned. Checking in, for a foreigner, was agonizingly slow. Forms. Questions. Show ID. I didn't like it, but Alli came first. After sitting in a hallway by her cot for what seemed like an eternity, they took us to an examining room.

A young, dark-skinned mestizo doctor, a Zapotec interpreter by his side, came, then shooed me away. A few minutes later, the same doctor came back to find me in the hallway.

"Señor . . . she seems not to understand us . . . can you help?"

"Certainly . . . but she speaks excellent Spanish . . ."

"Really . . . I assumed it would be Zapotec."

"No, she speaks Spanish and Nahuatl. How serious is it?"

"Ah, she is not from here in Tehuantepec, then." "No. She's my wife . . . we are from Puebla," I lied. "Well, Tehuacán, a town south of there. My family is European. We have land there."

"Ah . . . well, she is in serious condition . . . but will live . . . fortunately it is primarily her upper body that seems to have suffered the trauma. Let us hope her child has not suffered . . . so you are the father?"

"Yes. Please do everything possible, Doctor." He shrugged, "Of course, of course."

That evening, on a cot in a hot, crowded ward, an IV dripping, shoulder set and in a cast, Alli reentered the world around her. "Oh, Juan. It's so dangerous for you—there may be police here," she whispered, groaning at the pain from her mangled shoulder and one collapsed lung. "You must leave me here."

"I can't do that, Alli. Who will care for you?"

"Take the last bus to Salina Cruz and find Lalo . . . he'll know what to do . . . *please*?"

Twenty hours later, exhausted, I was napping on a northbound bus headed to Oaxaca City. A lot had happened. I'd reached La Ventosa late the night before and woke Lalo, who put his small launch in the water and steered toward Ce Xochitl.

Ana, hysterical over the fate of her sister, sent ten-year-old Simón with me when I returned to the clinic in Tehuantepec. We arrived at Alli's side about 6 AM. Simón turned out to be more of a trooper than I'd imagined. In twelve hours he transformed from the semispoiled, doted-on eldest son to a little man-in-training. He insisted on referring to me as "don Juan" . . . but had no clue why I grinned each time.

Around noon, don Rigoberto arrived with the mute burro handler, whose name turned out to be Tércio (the third one born) Pilli. Alli's grandfather thanked me . . . and asked for an account. I explained, Simón providing a rough translation.

"Don Rigoberto, I told the doctors here that you all are from a village south of Puebla." He nodded, "It shall be Ixtapalapa . . . I know a holy man from there . . . one of our people . . . that is where you should go. You must hide from the Mexicans. Here, take my amulet and show it to don Natalio Xico there . . . he speaks Spanish. We will take care of Alli."

I handed don Rigoberto a lean roll of hundred-peso notes, apologized for the loss of his burros, and was pocketing the pendant when little Simón went, "¡Psst! ¡Vienen! (They are coming!)" I jumped up and dashed out through the gallery's rear door, don Rigoberto on my heels, just as several silver-sunglassed, pistol-toting Federales entered the ward.

Rigoberto pressed his carved shell amulet into my palm. "Go quickly! We will send Malinalli to you when she is able to travel."

"How will she find me?" He answered in broken Spanish, "Don Natalio . . . at the Mexican church in Ixtapalapa. If he find you. She find you."

№ 25 El Cerro de la Estrella (The Hill of the Star)

CE XOCHITL'S ISOLATION HAD left don Rigoberto with a rather eccentric grasp of geography. Ixtapalapa wasn't near Puebla at all—it was actually a suburb of Mexico City. I arrived there about six slow buses later. It was already 3 am when I stepped out of the last bus and sat down on my duffel to wait until the crowd dispersed.

The reflected lights of Mexico City swirled up into the night, bouncing off the parapet of the nearby chapel, and bathing Ixtapalapa in the equivalent of full moonlight. A tightly packed row of windowless houses faced the ancient village's plaza, adorned with wrought iron benches and a small bandstand. Dogs slept in the cool potholes, which pockmarked the wide dirt street like acne scars. A row of tightly trimmed trees, their trunks whitewashed to mid-chest height, marched down the lane until they vanished into the dark.

The outline of the imposing Cerro de la Estrella to my left marked the spot where the Aztecs had once come at each calendric cycle to break their household pottery after first extinguishing every torch and cooking fire in their realm. That's how they initiated their "new fire" ceremony and prayed for an uncertain dawn—a dawn that, if it came, would ensure the world of the living another year's cycle before the gods threatened eternal darkness again. I wondered what effects Mexico City's glowing lights might have had on that traditional cycle during modern times . . . then realized that except for the dogs, I was alone . . .

Still atop the duffel, I checked out the empty street one more time to be certain, then headed directly to the one-towered chapel's huge front door. I tried the lock . . . it clicked. I opened the door a crack and entered. The church was lit only by an elaborate black iron stand glowing in the soft light of a dozen votive candles.

I saw no one, so slid into a rear pew and waited. I dozed . . . in Mexico, churches and graveyards were safe places. About 5 AM a skinny, older version of don Rigoberto entered, carrying a box of candles. Had I not known otherwise, I'd have assumed them to be brothers: high foreheads, silvering hair, erect, aquiline noses, and the fleshy, dangling earlobes that seemed to be an Indian trait.

My presence must have surprised him, for he spilled several yellow beeswax candles onto the floor. I helped him to retrieve them. Finished, he put the box down and asked, "Might I assist you?"

"Yes, señor. I am looking for don Natalio Xico." He stepped back, as if stunned.

"Who are you? Why do you want him?" Stepping forward, I held out the talisman and answered him, "I was sent by a native priest." He glanced down, keeping one eye on me, then asked to see the carving. He studied it, and looked up.

"It is the place glyph of a village now gone. They were once keepers of a holy place, just as I am. How did you get it?"

"From the native priest who asked me to find Señor Xico here at the church . . . and the village is not gone." He paused, his brow wrinkled in thought. "Natalio was my eldest brother. He died some years ago . . . so some of our people still live in Oaxaca?" I nodded, "Very much alive." He blinked, as if contemplating. I took the talisman from him, hung it around my neck, and tried for a favor: "May I sleep here in the church?"

"The early Mass will begin in another hour. *Siga, no más* (Just follow me)." We stepped out of a door exiting the transept, crossed the church-yard, and walked into another century.

His house had a long, high-ceilinged front room—fully thirty feet long by about twelve feet wide. The room's double rear door opened onto a sprawling patio, thick with shade trees, the scent of peaches, and pots that radiated the pungent odors of local herbs. Water trickled some-where nearby. Up on the roof a rooster on the roof began to crow, and dawn's first gray-tinged light began to mix with the fading electric glow of the vast city already awakening to the northwest of us. A half-dozen wooden doors opened onto the shaded patio. He pointed to one in the far corner, "Rest there. I will awaken you after Mass. We can talk then." "Facilities?" I asked. He pointed to a wooden stall-like structure a few yards behind the house.

"Have you paper?" he asked. I nodded. He pulled the door open, ush-ered me into the empty room, and left quickly. A few minutes later two voices in Nahuatl drifted to me on the dawn's moist air. A door slammed, unnerving me, then came the sounds of someone drawing water from a well or tap. By then I'd settled down onto the straw-and-blanket cot in one corner of the sparsely furnished room and fallen asleep, the duffel as my pillow.

A rapping on the door awakened me several hours later. "*¡Hola, joven!* May I enter?" "Yes," I answered, groggy and disoriented. The sac-ristan stepped in, "Come meet my wife and eldest daughter . . . we don't even know your name."

"It's Juan, señor."

"Oh, that is my name, too." We did the handshake thing. I combed my hair and followed him into the courtyard. It was shaded, breezy, and beautiful—a row of tall, pale-barked eucalyptus trees rose above the lane out front. Pansies and marigolds filled the big clay pots that were grouped in the patio's sunny spots. Cilantro, sage, and basil peeked out of lush pots.

Both his wife, Juana, and her daughter María were warm, pleasant, and ample, reminding me of Ramona. They all spoke Spanish to me. "You will be staying with us, joven," smiled Juana . . . "And how did you know my brother-in-law, Natalio?"

"I didn't. I was not a *socio* (acquaintance) of his . . . my wife's grand-father sent me to him."

"And who is your wife . . . do we know her?"

"Her name is Malinalli Pilli. Her grandfather is don Rigoberto Pilli. They are from a small village of Nahua on the coast of Oaxaca. It is called Ce Xochitl." It became very quiet for a moment. They looked at one another, then back to me. Then Señora Juana spoke.

"We did not know that village still existed. It is said that they left our people here long ago. The clan of the Pillis were of my own father's people . . . they were Star Catchers in the old days before the *gachupines* (Spanish) came—keepers of pyramids, like the one under the cerro above us. The Mexicans celebrate Holy Week there now, and the pyramid is long covered by the broken pottery from our ceremonies. But, in the time before the gachupines, the stars came to the holy men there."

"They are still Star Catchers at Ce Xochitl, señora . . . there is a pyramid near the village where don Rigoberto calls the stars. I saw it done there some months ago. The temple is called Teapan." "And why would he let *you* see it?" asked the sacristan, Juan, his voice hinting at doubt.

"Perhaps because I am the father of his granddaughter's child-to-be . . . and the granddaughter has begun to learn the old ways." Juana took over the conversation again. "Why is she not with you, then?"

"Because she is in a hospital in Oaxaca. She was thrown from her burro on a country road in Oaxaca. Don Rigoberto will send her here when she is able to travel again." The sacristan grinned, "Do you eat our food? Rice, beans, fruit, tortillas."

"Oh, yes, and I shall pay my share for meals, if I can stay." ". . . And cigarettes?" beamed the sacristan.

"Yes, cigarettes, occasionally a liter of Coca-Cola or *fresa* . . . if you like such things." He laughed, "Well, my brother-in-law has given us a gift. Of course you shall stay here . . . if there are things you need, let my daughter know . . . she can buy them for you. I must go again—there is another Mass in thirty minutes."

The sacristan's wife tossed me a scolding look as he hustled away. "You don't have to buy *too* many Cocas and *cigarros*—not good for him . . . can you tell me more of Ce Xochitl?"

It seemed odd to be confirming the existence of one enclave of Aztec speakers to another, but they hung on every scrap of description: the houses, the food, fragments of the Nahuatl language as I'd heard it spoken there. We talked for nearly two hours while I sat on a small wooden bench near the charcoal cookstove under a ramada at one corner of the courtyard, convinced that I was boring them until María commented to her mom, "Isn't it wonderful that the Star Catcher still lives . . . do you suppose he would come here one day and teach our people the ceremony?" Her mother turned to me. "Could you ask that of him . . .

a Pilli has not called the stars here in at least one bundle of the years (four centuries)."

"I will find a way to request it, señora." At that, María asked me for a list of things I needed, then left with a hundred-peso note (eight U.S. dollars) to get supplies. She returned about an hour later, carrying several woven plastic market bags. She held one of the bags out to me. It held my cigarettes, matches, soap, TP, candles, several blue-jacketed local student notebooks, a small vial of ink for my old Pilot fountain pen, a liter of Coca-Cola, and twenty pesos in change.

"Thanks," I grinned. She confided slyly, "I bought a *dulce* (candy) for myself from your money. Also rice, beans, and oil for the house. Is there anything else you need?"

"Water jug for my room. Perhaps some more straw for the mattress." She nodded and smiled, "I like shopping . . . and such an impressive banknote to hand the manager."

I went to my temporary quarters, set out candles and matches on the one heavy-planked, old-fashioned table, and retrieved the two halves of the Toluca stick from my duffel. But when I stepped out onto the patio with the stick, María stopped me. "Father said you mustn't go walking about—you are to be our family secret for now . . . some coffee, perhaps?"

"I don't see how anyone could know I am here."

"You are tall and fair skinned. No one else like that lives here in Ixtapalapa."

When the sacristan returned later, the family discussed the situation at length, mostly in a patois of Nahuatl and Spanish. I got about half of it: they were fascinated by the charge to harbor me for a while, worried about the ever-curious village gossips, and excited by Ce Xochitl—throwbacks of their own kind—and don Rigoberto: living proof that their sacred Star Catchers had survived.

During the next eight days I wrote in my journals to pass the time and keep from worrying about Alli. I recorded everything I could remember about Ce Xochitl. If the local Nahuatl speakers were blown away by the details I told them, then Alli and her few remaining people must have been an even greater rarity than I realized. This had potential "master's thesis" written all over it.

A week into my "house arrest," I snuck out one night and climbed the Cerro de la Estrella that shaded the immediate neighborhood from above each afternoon. The huge cone-shaped hill's apex was littered with pottery fragments, broken figurine heads, orange-ware clay incense burners, and intricate ceramic spindle whorls once used to hand-weave native cotton.

Mexico—a spread-out city of about four million people—eclipsed New York in extent. It pulsed with electric energy in the night, part of its glow hidden by the distant outline of a cluster of hills to the north-west—the Lomas de Tecamachalco, they called them. The lights from several new trophy homes dotted the northeast slope of one of the hills, but the rest were dark, in stark contrast to the city crowding up against their bases.

In the Spanish colonial world, the elites traditionally lived on low ground near a city's central plaza. The peons lived in dirt huts on the hillsides. That pattern still prevailed in much of Mexico, but by the early sixties the capital and Guadalajara had began to morph into residential patterns more familiar to Boston or Manhattan. The elites were rap-idly moving to the high ground, leaving the desperate poor to the old city centers.

I sat on the sloping crown of the hill and smoked, longing for down-town Mexico. The Voice interrupted me—*This country stuff is terrible. Besides, it will be the Federales who come for you—not her!* The Voice sounded jealous, even petulant. I ignored it. *Look—don't shut me out— I've stuck with you, haven't I?* "Jesus!" I asked it out loud, "Who the hell are you, anyway?" I never got a direct answer. But the Voice softened up on me after that.

While I snuck back into the farmstead, the sharp barking of scrawny dogs echoed in the night . . . the Indian dogs didn't care for mestizos, who often kicked them, or gringos, who must have smelled ominously different.

María caught me coming in, chuckled, and extracted a cigarette as the price of her silence.

"I didn't know you smoked, María." "Neither does my father," she whispered. "Hey, you're a grown woman—you don't have to hide a ciga-rette now and again," I teased. "Perhaps not," she whispered, "but I'm saving that knowledge in case he ever catches me up at night." She patted me on the shoulder and disappeared. Two nights later, we bumped into one another on the patio. "Father?" she asked, panicky.

"No—Juan. Are you OK?"

"Oh, *por Dios*, you frightened me . . . I thought it was my father . . . I have a lover, and Father thinks I'm still a virgin. *¡Fíjase!* (Imagine that!) . . . I'm thirty-three."

"Your secret is safe, María . . . good night."

She'd been the one chosen from all her siblings to stay and care for her parents. She was like me with Eddy and Ana with Alli's kids. Obligated to be the Watcher.

⁂

On the ninth night of my stay, there was a commotion at the front of the house. I could hear María wakening her father to go to the main door, which opened onto the dirt lane. Straining to listen, I held my breath and waited. More commotion followed.

I screwed the stick together and grabbed the duffel, ready to run, just as three people entered the courtyard, the sacristan calling to me. "Your wife, joven . . . and her grandfather . . . María . . . a lantern please! We have guests . . . the *teohuah* (priest) of Ce Xochitl and his granddaughter. Praise the Virgin!"

The sacristan was still babbling as Alli slipped into my arms. "*Oh, teoquichhui. Mi corazón.*" She melted against me, the bow of her lips quivered, her face wet. A wave of emotion coursed through me. My pulse quickened. Then a profound sense of tranquility replaced my normal angst. For a few minutes I was not alone.

They showed us to a bench at the ramada. Alli wept. Even don Rigoberto hugged me, then stroked Alli's palms as she sobbed, "*Todo bien, cihuaixhuiuhtli* (Everything's fine, granddaughter)—*todo bien.*" He calmed Alli in a way that surprised me. Firm . . . yet tender.

"And the Federales in Tehuantepec? I was afraid they would take you!" I asked her. "No, *teoquichhui*," murmured Alli. "They told us they had captured *you*. Simón refused to answer where you lived, so they kicked him, but he didn't really know. Simón cried that he didn't know, since you always come unexpectedly . . . then vanish the same way. You aren't quite real to the children, except Ari. They let him go, finally."

The riddle of their survival explained, the sacristan asked many questions of don Rigoberto in his mixed Spanish/Nahuatl; most of them were about Ce Xochitl. Finally, Señora Juana broke in. "They need rest, Husband. We can talk tomorrow."

They vacated a room for don Rigoberto; I took Alli with me. She fell asleep instantly, my fingertips caressing her swelling belly. I listened for her breath, touched the tip of my nose to the warm pulse in her neck, and drifted into a cloud of euphoric bliss.

※※

We arose about ten the next day. The morning sun had already insinuated itself through the spying row of eucalyptus above the big streetside room's roofline, where about a dozen of the local Indian men had gathered. Don Rigoberto was the center of attention. The younger ones called him *tahtli* (father), the older ones *teohuapilli*—noble priest—one meaning of Alli's surname was "noble," I'd been told.

Arriving after the others, an old man with a cane came through the door; the rest of them bowed to him. The eldest among them, he addressed don Rigoberto formally. His Nahuatl was smooth, polished.

"We, the *pipiltin* (nobles) of our lines welcome you—the keepers of our ways in the land of the Zapotec." I lost the drift of the rest of the speech . . . and Alli couldn't translate much of it, either. The old man from Ixtapalapa spoke Nahuatl very differently than the people of Ce Xochitl, separated from one another, at that moment, by four or five centuries.

Part of it, Alli assured me, was the count of each elder's Nahuatl-speaking community on the outskirts of Mexico City. Don Rigoberto answered at some length . . . his voice, crisp and rhythmic, had none of the smooth, Spanish-influenced cadence of the Ixtapalapa delegation. Don Rigoberto was overwhelmed. "I had no idea there were still so many of us in the world," Alli translated in a whisper to me, "and here I thought my granddaughter's coming child might be among the last half-dozen of our people's young ones . . ."

At a break in the conversation, Alli told her grandfather that the sacristan had inquired about performing the Star Catching Ceremony. Don Rigoberto asked the crowd if this was so. They were animated, a chorus of "*¡Quemahcatzin!* (Yes!)" greeted his inquiry.

When the conversation turned to these matters of traditional religion, the women and I drifted away. Local Indian dignitaries came and went constantly. There were at least fifty or sixty thousand Indians and Indianized mestizos in the Ixtapalapa district, sandwiched between the Cerro de la Estrella at the northwest terminus of their lands and a rapidly expanding, modern Mexico City "working class" graveyard on the east. To the south lay the pure agricultural districts—little changed from ancient times.

The next evening a great throng came to the front of the sacristan's house to accompany us to the Hill of the Star. There, atop the hill, where all could see the plumes of smoke drift from the ancient volcanoes of Popocatépetl and Iztaccíhuatl to the south, one could also watch modern jetliners land below at the huge Benito Juárez airport some ten miles due north.

On the same spot where a scourged, Spanish-inspired stand-in for Jesus Christ had been crucified only a few weeks before, don Rigoberto and his borrowed drummers performed the Star Catching Ceremony for the first time since Cortés had skirted the base of this very hill on his way to an inaugural meeting with the Aztec nation's ambassadors in 1519.

There were, perhaps, two or three thousand local Indians on the hill listening to the drums. The sacristan had borrowed a tape deck from a rich mestizo churchgoer to record the ceremony. The stars did not come because it was not their appointed time in the ancient calendar. But that did not diminish the crowd's enthusiasm one iota.

By 1 AM the crowd had doubled in size. Small bonfires had been lit, encircling the top of the hill. Obviously, the chanting could be heard easily at the old trolley track that skirted one side of the hill below. And a federal police station was but a hundred yards from the terminus of the abandoned Ixtapalapa trolley line.

Nothing unnerved both mestizo and Spanish Mexico more profoundly than Indians acting out genuine elements of their preconquest culture. Stylized tourist performances were OK. Even the eccentricities and socially inappropriate antics of the gringo tourists crowding the tony Zona Rosa left Mexico unperturbed. But more than five thousand Indians on a hill that the mestizos called "Calvary" because of their Easter reenactments? This was ominous. This demanded investigation.

Undoubtedly a few of Mexico's ubiquitous plainclothes "agents" had already penetrated the fringes of the crowd, but gone unnoticed, before the Garand-toting line of federal troopers rose out of the night at about 2 AM, demanding, "Disperse, or be shot on the spot. This gathering is a threat to the nation!"

The local Indian men, long familiar with the Federales, locked arms, perhaps two thousand of them, and formed an immovable phalanx, while don Rigoberto, the Star Catcher, his family (including me), and the women and children were ordered by the local Aztec clan leaders to retreat down the southeast trail into the part of Ixtapalapa abutting the Mexicans' new graveyard.

Exhausted, we reached the sacristan's courtyard by 3 AM. He came in quietly about 3:45 AM, and by five the district's dirt lanes had been secured by platoon trucks loaded with regular army troopers. That's when don Rigoberto, Alli, and I were "evacuated" in a donkey cart to a more isolated farming town to the south called Milpa Alta, where another of the sacristan's brothers oversaw their traditional family farms.

⁂

№ 26 MILPA ALTA

IF IXTAPALAPA WAS A cultural surprise, tucked up against a sophisticated city of more than four million people, Milpa Alta was as exotic as the Tyrannosaurus Rex on display at the natural history museum in Manhattan.

In spite of my city-boy roots, I found it exhilarating: beautiful pine forests on the nearby slopes provided contrast to the dense stands of corn, beans, squash, and tomatoes planted in the winding, narrow valley tongues and on terraced hillsides. I studied Nahuatl daily. Wrote in my journals. Took long walks with Alli. I also learned how to plant, hoe, and make yucca fiber sandals . . . for the first time, I felt content.

But the real reason I remained exhilarated was that our daughter, Betiana Xochitli Pilli, was born there on August 28. An early-term baby, she was small and coughed a lot. But the smell of her, her hot skin and tiny fingers, her bowed lips and dark hazel eyes all intoxicated . . . and transformed . . . me. The Voice faded away and left me in peace.

The night Alli groaned, then broke water all over me, was a night alight with miracles. The miracle of life. The miracles of intimacy. The miracle of family. The crown of a baby's fuzzy skull appearing to the native midwife, Alli rhythmically chanting, "*Véte a tu papito, mi yolita* ([Spanish/Nahuatl] Go to your father, my newborn girl), it is time to leave my *xillantli* (womb)."

And, as commanded, the child did come to me. Wet and warm like a puppy. I dipped her in tepid water, Alli laughing at the sound of her first cries . . . and I wept like the child I still was deep under the layers of anger and cynicism that had contained my inner malaise since the time when I first crashed through a slate roof in Philadelphia, and lost myself.

Don Rigoberto was no longer in Milpa Alta when Xochitli was born. Unnerved by the bustle of central Mexico . . . and even more bewildered by the constant attention from local Nahuatl elders, who romanticized him as a real Indian priest, he left Milpa Alta about a week after he arrived.

Alli and I decided to stay for a while in Milpa Alta, where she could begin to receive instruction in *curanderismo* from the local Nahua healers. We settled into a large one-room house, once a manger, on the sacristan and Señora Juana's ancestral farm. We commissioned construction of an outhouse and extension of the trickling acequia that bubbled nearby. Labor and food were cheap, but I was down to about fifty dollars and began to calculate the risks of sneaking into Mexico City to make a withdrawal.

About a week before Xochitli was born I left at dawn, taking a local bus to the plaza in Ixtapalapa, then another local due west into the university city area, where I attracted no attention. But standing in line at the Bank of Mexico seemed surreal. Surrounded by the sounds of English, French, and high-class Spanish, a once familiar world had become deeply unsettling.

The smells were different, too. No rich scents of warm pine boughs or the pungent odor of rotting apples. I missed the exotic scent of chile plants, gently bruised as pickers carefully worked their way through the rows, filling their woven baskets for the Friday market. In contrast the bank's patrons radiated the scents of soap, shaving lotion, expensive tobacco, outrageous perfumes, and factory-tanned leather.

Even the sounds were different. In Milpa Alta the soft crunching of passing huarache-shod feet, the clank and clop of burro carts, the clatter of worn-out bicycles . . . and the occasional belching diesel bus's sharp *braaap* were the sounds answered by bleating goats, braying donkeys, an occasional cow, and the ubiquitous yellow-brown Indian dogs.

But Mexico City was a world of honks, screeches, grating metallic noises, and the constant clatter of expensive high-heeled shoes clicking on the tile and concrete. If Milpa Alta was nature's melody, Mexico City was a polyphonic hard-rock concert . . . and it got to me.

The Voice put in an appearance just before I handed over my numbered ticket and stepped up to the teller line. *Don't do this!* They *will find you.* I snarled back, "Shut up . . . the baby will be here soon and I need money now!" The Voice vanished. I collected the equivalent of U.S.$275, leaving just $8 (100 pesos) in that account.

I ate a torta at a coffee shop from which I could see a distant piece of the muraled library at the National University. I ordered a café cappuccino but was too edgy to relax and linger over it, so I grabbed a bus that went to the end of the Calzada Ixtapalapa route, then took a broken-down rural bus back to Milpa Alta. As the bus bounced and jolted along the curving, unpaved mountain stretch near the village of Tlaltengo, I imagined myself a father—one determined not to disappear on the child. Panicked by the potential responsibilities, I let those images go and lit a smoke.

                        ❧

Waiting for the other shoe to drop, I was uneasy for days after the trip into the city. But the night Xochitli was born erased the fear . . . it was as if life was good to us. One of the sacristan's nieces was a young mother, and the local midwife came by often, showing Alli how to nurse and clean the baby.

Alli was a bundle of bliss. "I like it here, *teoquichhui*. It is cooler than Oaxaca, but I miss the sea. Take me for a walk . . ." So, we walked the lanes most evenings, holding hands, the child wrapped in a traditional rebozo slung over Alli's shoulder. Alli pestered me about bringing the child to bed with us, so that the three of us could sleep together.

When I demurred in panic, "It is too soon, Alli. Too soon. She is still so little," she would smile. One night she touched my face and whispered, "Then hold her to *mi chichihualli* (my breast) while I nurse her. Your fear will soon pass, *teoquichhui*. She will be part of you soon."

She was right. The fear did subside. Several times I became hypnotized by Xochitli's baby smells and sounds, until the loss of emotional safety would pull me out of my momentary sense of peace. Alli insisted that I hold her more. I did and finally slept with the child. One night, while cradled in my arms, Xochitli stopped breathing for a moment . . .

I shook her gently. She reached out and touched my face. A great wave of warmth washed over me.

But about three weeks after she was born, the baby began suffering fevers. None of the traditional remedies seemed to work. In a panic, Alli insisted that we take her to the public clinic in Ixtapalapa. We made the trek on a hot Tuesday afternoon in September. Everything seemed dusty and exhaust-choked. The child coughed and wheezed even more than usual on the bus to Ixtapalapa. Alli's fears grew. "She is so frail. I am frightened for her, Juan." "It will be all right. We'll be at the clinic soon," I insisted.

The clinic, a long block uphill from the church, was run by the government's Seguro Social health ministry. I hadn't realized we'd need to sign in and show ID. Alli, of course, had none. Like nearly any rural Indian girl, a government ID was an alien concept. "Let's go," I urged. "We can find a private clinic over in Coyoacán." Coyoacán was an upscale district, or colonia, in Mexico City's southwest quadrant.

But Alli insisted we stay and get the child to a doctor, so I showed my British ID as Jonathan Antón Blanco and signed the wait list. The clerk looked at my ID and shrugged—sooner or later everyone and everything happens in Mexico City . . . Compay Segundo plays "Chan Chan," Fidel Castro and Che Guevara play revolutionary, Gina Lollobrigida goes to Bellas Artes on the arms of a Russian diplomat, Jack Kerouac pops up . . . and Leon Trotsky gets himself butchered . . . so what's some young "Brit" with a good-looking Indian woman?

"Nothing" is the correct answer, I assured myself as the clerk walked away and we found a seat in the waiting room. So powerful is motherhood in Mexico that even an Indian girl, babe in arms, will get a seat from nearly any male. I stood, watching casually in all directions for any sign of trouble. *Nada*, I told myself. *Just the ordinary public clinic chaos.*

Two hours later Alli and Xochitli got ten minutes with a tired-looking young doctor and a diffident, light-skinned nurse. After the obligatory skin test, they gave the baby a shot of penicillin. "Probably the water," decided the doctor. "Come back in a week if she still has a fever . . . and boil all her water. Let it cool in the pan you use to heat it . . ."

Relieved, we stepped into the street and hailed a pesero down to Ixtapalapa's plaza. The one available bus from Ixtapalapa went only as far as Tlaltengo, halfway to Milpa Alta. But anxious to leave, I pushed Alli into it anyway. At Tlaltengo we waited by the side of the road for the next local to Milpa Alta.

An hour later, and no bus, we decided to walk down the hill and hail a ride with a waving twenty-peso note. Alli was upbeat, "Our daughter is breathing better." She smiled and pulled the rebozo around, pressing the child's lips to her nipple. She never even broke her stride to do it.

We'd rounded a bend with a steep drop-off when we heard a vehicle behind us . . . I pulled out a banknote and turned to see a big black Ford LTD head toward us, slowing as I waved. Alli smiled and handed me a ripe, freshly soiled baby, then dug into her woven bag to find a clean pañuelo.

Caught by surprise, I stood there as the car pulled alongside and a door opened . . . Semper Fi shouted in English, "Well, now . . . the Commie and his *squaw*. How touching . . . and here I thought you were a faggot." Birdsong crooned from inside, "I told you not to piss me off, *boy* . . ."

Like a peacock, he preened, "And you thought you could take the woman to a clinic and no one would notice, hey *boy*?" Like a cobra staring a mongoose in the face, I froze. Birdsong went nuts, "I asked you a question, you little Yankee bastard!" It came through as a wolf-like snarl.

I called to Alli, "Here, take the baby!" She reached out, still smiling, "Friends of yours, *teoquichhui*?" I never got to answer her, or give her the child. Birdsong slammed the big Ford into reverse, changed gears, and floored it, aiming for us.

Semper Fi, standing in the road by himself, stared at the Ford. "This isn't the plan!" he shouted. But Birdsong was on his own track. I pushed Alli away, the baby tucked under my right arm, and jumped backward toward the edge of the precipice.

Birdsong corrected course, steering right for me. Dirt sprayed up in a huge rooster tail as he swerved. Semper Fi shouted, "Stop! He's got a baby!" He waved his arms helplessly, eyes wide. Blinded by the spray of dirt and the huge dust cloud, I couldn't decide which way to jump, so I leaped forward, hoping Birdsong would still be aiming for the place behind where he'd last seen me . . .

The car's brakes locked and the Ford slid, spraying me and Xochi with gravel as it barreled past and sailed out into empty space. Lost somewhere in the dust cloud, Alli screamed. About three seconds later the car connected with the ground below. More dust billowed up, clouding the entire road.

At the same moment, the bus Alli and I had been waiting for topped the hill, its worn-out breaks squealing when the driver saw us. The dust from Birdsong's car cleared just as Semper Fi shrieked, wide-eyed with horror. Arms still waving, he went through the bus's huge grill like a crushed bug, leaving a gaping hole in its radiator. The bus shuddered and yawed on the loose gravel, hit something else, and thumped to a stop somewhere on the road below me. I panicked, thinking Alli had been hit as well. Another dust cloud cut off the scene.

When it cleared, Alli lay by the side of the road. One rib grotesquely poking through her side like the shaft of a pork chop, she gasped once, shivered, then slumped back into the ditch.

I ran to her, cradled her head in the crook of my free arm, trying to rouse her. Finally, her lids fluttered and her eyes met mine. She smiled. . . .

I took a deep breath, certain she'd be ok. Butterflies flickered in her deep brown eyes. She was still smiling at Xochi when they took her from me, covered her with a blanket and carried her body away.

Afraid others would come to avenge the death of the rogue Americans, I asked the Sacristan and his daughter María to take the baby to her grandfather in Ce Xochitl after we buried Alli at Milpa Alta. I wanted to bury her in Ce Xochitl, but I was hotter than a pile of atomic waste, so vanished into the bowels of Ixtapalapa, hidden, and moved frequently by local clan leaders.

As an act of defiance, I went to the Civil Registry in Ixtapalapa one day and, with one of the Sacristan's nieces standing in for Alli, signed the registry. Alli and I were legally married exactly thirty days after her death. But I didn't feel much of anything until weeks later when don Rigoberto came with Simón to find me in Ixtapalapa—our little daughter had succumbed to the fevers.

My baby. The child I'd sworn to protect . . . the only being I'd ever met who made me feel something every time I touched her or listened to her breathe. Even her crying had filled me with unreasonable joy.

Four days later, don Rigoberto stood next to me in Milpa Alta, speaking in Nahuatl as the local nobility and holy men opened Malinalli's grave and lowered little Xochitli's white-swathed body into Alli's casket.

The inevitable reality of Alli's decomposition shocked me. I stood there, silent, as they place the child on what remained of her mother's bosom, closed the coffin and lit copal to erase the scent of death and urge their souls to rejoin.

As the musty scent of the incense hit my nostrils, the warmth and vulnerability that Alli and our child had so profoundly kindled in me guttered—my ability to feel again snuffed out like a candle. Nothing left of it. Gone like the two of them.

I gave don Rigoberto money to rebury the two in Ce Xochitl some-day, then turned away . . . I had a wall to climb in Mexico City.

⚡

Epilogue

THE STREETS OF MEXICO City's Zona Rosa seemed strange and dream-like as I worked my way past the still-boarded-up window at Sanborn's that I'd jumped through a few months earlier. It was late and even the city's famously lively theater crowd had evaporated into the night.

The residence's street-side wall was inviting . . . but I was numb—no adrenalin left in me to help me over. It took three tries. When I finally toppled over and had finished bouncing around among the shrubs, a familiar voice greeted me. "Well, sport, half of Mexico has been looking for you . . . I'd say it was about time to send you to the United Kingdom."

"Hi, Howard, how's everyone here?"

"We're doing fine. Annie's gone off to university—left several weeks ago . . . she got a flat with a spare room, just in case . . . and the ambassador is heading home in three days . . . Parliament opens . . . want a ride with him to London?"

"Please . . . and my stick, if you don't mind."

"Why not . . . Williams here will make certain you don't get into any trouble with it." Williams loomed out of the shadows and pulled me to my feet.

There was a letter there waiting for me from Eddy, dated some two months earlier. It read:

Dear John,

Thank you so much for the letter. I'm amazed that someone there knew our parents. It's hard to think of them as real. It's scary here, but I'm learning to be brave. You'd be proud of me. The men in my unit are great. The work is tough, but I've helped save a few. I dreamed of this—I'm almost like a doctor, John! When I'm out I'm going to try for med school again. Be happy for me!

I love you, Eddy

At dinner, the ambassador was kind. "Since you didn't get to finish the master's here, I've wired the provost at Edinburgh. You can work out a course of study there . . . and by the way, the U.S. government compensated us for the furniture that they seized in Mitla . . . there will be a little money for you in the Bank of England in several weeks . . . and do visit your mother's grave. I'll see that you get directions."

I enrolled in the University of Edinburgh for a master's in folklore, using my Ce Xochitl notebooks for graduate paper material, then moved in with Annie in Glasgow, taking the bus to Edinburgh twice a week to meet with Professor Dalrymple, my proctor.

Like my spirits, winter in Glasgow was cold and gray. My mother's grave behind the high church's stone wall above the picturesque village of Rothesay on the Island of Bute was as lonely as I'd feared. Standing on top of the wall, I watched the sea for a while to gather courage, then jumped down and stepped up to the grave, but left without saying anything.

The Caledonian ferry ride back to the mainland was somber, the firth of Clyde a swirl of turbulent gray nothingness flecked with foam. Eddy had reenlisted for another tour in Vietnam . . . and I still couldn't fly.

For the first few months I lived in Annie's spare room. She never asked me anything about Oaxaca . . . though the ambassador had known enough to console me in his own way when we'd parted company at Heathrow Airport.

"Yes, well, I know it's been a tough year . . . er, uh, *cough*, well, let's hope old Annie can cheer you up. Reminds me of your mother, you know." The problem was that I didn't want to be reminded of anything at that point.

By Christmas I'd moved into Annie's bedroom, working my way down her A-list. The "make me laugh" part didn't come easily at first, but by spring, I'd settled back into a less frustrated mode. Within a month I'd composed my game face, even cracking half-hearted jokes. Annie and I began to have fun, but my birthday—also Alii's—put me on another downer.

That summer, I wrote a couple of articles about fading indigenous communities in southern Oaxaca. That got me a small research assignment from a fellow in New York with the unlikely name of Dr. Thorogood Penrod. He was into "human rights" research.

Annie and I were still together when two events changed things. In

May, the U.S. government, still being prodded by Mr. Ambassador over Birdsong's transgressions, formally cleared me of any possible charges— "posthumously," the letter said—and finally replaced my passport. Mr. Ambassador laughed when he handed it to me. "Just think, young Alexander—now we'll have to declare the mysterious Master "Blanco" deceased and reissue residency papers in your own name. The paperwork never ends." "Oh, you needn't bother," I chuckled. Finally, things were looking up.

That proved to be only temporary. In July, a telegram came from the department of the army informing me that Eddy had been killed in action. Numb, I returned to the States for his service at Arlington.

When it was over, I collected his things and flew back to Glasgow. I worked up the nerve to visit our mother's grave again. "I was going to bring Eddy with me . . . you had twins. I don't know whether you lived long enough to find out—take care of him for me . . . I tried to look after him, but . . . it didn't work out. Please be his family now."

Annie was with me, and gentle. Afterward, I delivered on part three of her list, mystifying her. In retrospect, I may have overdone the mystery when, during a late summer "vacation" to Belgium, I enrolled in a martial arts school, leaving her to the museums. By the following Christmas she wanted her space and, in a way, so did I.

Unable to get over Eddy, I drifted back to Manhattan and accepted another human rights assignment—destination Mississippi.

"It's temporary," I'd assured Annie, even though we both knew it was a lie. Eddy came to me in frequent visions, and the Voice hammered away at my failures.

Still unable to fly, I also daydreamed of Alli, imagining her rocking Xochi at the ancient farm in Ce Xochitl. I didn't want to let go. Finally, I tired of remembering them.

On my twenty-third birthday, while hanging over a pool table in Jackson, Mississippi, I said good-bye to Xochi, out loud, so she'd know I had cared, then whispered, "Good-bye . . . and happy nineteenth birthday, Alli . . . I loved you."

∗∗